I0831770

OUT AND ABOUT

ALSO BY

STACI TROILO

THE CATHEDRAL LAKE SERIES

TYPE AND CROSS

OUT AND ABOUT

PRIDE AND FALL

THE MEDICI PROTECTORATE SERIES

BLEEDING HEART

MIND CONTROL

BODY ARMOR

TORTURED SOUL

OTHER WORKS

MYSTERY, INK: MYSTERY HEIR

OUT AND ABOUT

CATHEDRAL LAKE
BOOK TWO

STACI TROILO

an imprint of
THE OGHMA PRESS

Bentonville, Arkansas • Los Angeles, California
www.oghmacreative.com

Library of Congress Cataloging-in-Publication Data

Names: Troilo, Staci author.
Title: Out and About/Staci Troilo | Cathedral Lake #2
Description: Second Edition | Bentonville: Foyle, 2022
Identifiers: LCCN: 2020935335 | ISBN: 978-1-63373-570-5 (hardcover) |
ISBN: 978-1-63373-571-2 (trade paperback) | ISBN: 978-1-63373-117-2 (eBook)
BISAC: FICTION/ Family Life/Marriage & Divorce | FICTION/Medical |
FICTION/Romance/Medical
LC record available at: https://lccn.loc.gov/2020935335

Foyle Press hardcover edition June, 2022

Cover & Interior Design by Casey W. Cowan
Editing by Gordon Bonnet

Published by Foyle Press, an imprint of The Oghma Press, a subsidiary of The Oghma Book Group.

For Seth—My favorite son.

With all my love.

ACKNOWLEDGEMENTS

I AM GRATEFUL TO SO many people—those who supported me through the process of writing this novel and those who support me every day through love and friendship.

Casey—for editing, designing, and publishing the book you now hold in your hands. Aaron—for your patience and medical expertise. Mom and Dad—for your unwavering support and love. All my family and friends—for putting up with a temperamental writer.

And, most importantly of all, Seth and Sammi—for being the best kids a mother could ask for.

OUT AND ABOUT

CHAPTER 1

JENSEN SLAMMED ON THE BRAKES and fishtailed out of his lane. He regained control, jerked the wheel, and skidded to a stop on the berm, barely avoiding the accident in the middle of the road.

He recognized one of the vehicles involved as the classic black Impala that had flown past him—on a blind curve, no less—only a few miles back, probably skidded on the wet road, left his lane, and plowed head-first into the Dodge Ram.

Idiot.

Another accident on Dappled Oak Lane.

He swallowed the lump in his throat, pushed the negative thoughts away. Didn't matter that it was almost Hope's anniversary. No time to dwell on that now.

Jensen jumped out of his truck and raced over to the car. A quick glance in the car's window made his decision easier. Damaged windshield. No seatbelt. Bloody, still body. Unlikely he'd survived. He yanked open the door, checked for a pulse. Nothing.

A few cars drove past. One stopped on his way around the wreckage and rolled down the window. "Need help, kid?"

"Can you call 9-1-1? I'm going to check on the other driver. This guy—"

"I'll call now."

He heard him talking to a dispatcher through the car speaker. Satisfied that help was on the way, he dodged another passing car and rushed over to the silver truck to check on the driver. The door was locked, so he banged on the window. "Hey, man! Hey!"

Jensen cupped his hands to block the glare of daylight, pressed his face to the tinted glass, and peered inside. The driver turned his head slowly and squinted at him, then raised a hand to his head. Through the lingering dust particles from the airbag deployment, he saw the man had a laceration on his face and minor burns on his hands. His gaze seemed unfocused.

"Unlock the door!" Jensen pointed toward the lock. The man didn't look like he understood, didn't seem to move, but then the lock clicked.

Thank God for lock releases on the door, and for the man to have been lucid enough to hit the button.

Jensen flung open the door, and the driver listed to the side. Other than the cut and burns, no other injuries were visible.

"Are you okay? Can you move?"

The driver's eyes watered, and he coughed. Jensen waved his hand in front of the man's face, trying to clear the air.

"Wha… What happened?"

"You were in an accident. We need to get you out of the car." A faint smell of gasoline lingered in the air, and Jensen feared the car would catch fire or explode.

More coughing accompanied by wincing and clutching his side. That could be bad. Possible trauma to his internal organs.

Jensen repeated himself. "Can you move?"

He fumbled with his seatbelt. "Can't…."

"I'll help you." Jensen stepped onto the running board and leaned over the guy. He felt for the seatbelt release and soon had the driver free.

The guy slipped his arm out of the restraint and started to fall out the door.

Jensen caught him, at least two hundred fifty pounds of dead weight, and assisted him out of the truck and over to the side of the road.

He lowered the man to the ground and looked for visible injuries. Seeing none, he ran back to the Impala and again placed two fingers on the man's neck.

Nothing. Not that he'd expected anything to have changed.

Fear tingled his spine as the smell of gas grew stronger. How long did he have? Minutes? Seconds?

Fighting the urge to run, he reached into the car for the man, pulled him out, and dragged him to the side of the road, too. Even though he doubted it would make a difference, he began chest compressions.

He glanced at the guy from the truck. "Hey! Doing okay?"

The man didn't answer.

Jensen looked around. The guy who called 9-1-1 had driven away. A few other vehicles drove past, most of them slowly while the passengers rubbernecked, but no one else stopped.

He continued with CPR on the unresponsive Impala driver while he searched the truck driver's face for notable signs of impending medical distress. His eyes remained glassy and unfocused. Might be concussed, might have other issues. Bleeding from his cut seemed slower. Good. Still would need stitches, though. Coughing had stopped. Held his arm close to his side, but breathing didn't appear labored.

Thank God his lung hadn't been punctured. Couldn't deal with a tension pneumothorax on the same road Hope had suffered one. Still, what was wrong with the guy? Shock?

His father would know.

Jensen didn't have his father's experience. Just some knowledge, and nowhere near that of his father. Nowhere near his confidence, either. So, he did nothing for the truck driver. Just kept pushing on the other guy's lifeless chest.

Another car rolled past. Then the distant sounds of sirens snapped Jensen to attention. He looked down the road to see if he could see the lights. Wonder if Hope had heard the sirens?

The pain of losing her rushed back, the memories he'd already quashed re-emerged in a flood of despair, drowned him in wave after crushing wave of agony… Another reason to hate coming home—the grief was harder to suppress.

The guilt was harder to suppress.

Lost in his misery, everything else faded as he revisited that day eight years ago.

He jumped when a firm hand squeezed his shoulder.

"You can stop now. We've got it."

Jensen looked around, blinked, recognized where he was and what was currently going on. He looked at the lifeless body below him and stopped the compressions. An EMT started checking the body as he backed away.

Stretching his fingers, stiff from being interlaced for so long, and shaking his hands out, he took in the scene. Two ambulances, a firetruck, and a police cruiser blocked the lane, their flashing lights bathing everything in a surreal red haze. Someone worked on the Impala, probably making sure it didn't catch fire. An officer set up traffic cones even as another patrol car arrived.

Present day. Really here. Not eight years ago. Not Dappled Oak and Sycamore, but Dappled Oak and Elm.

Not his sister's accident.

"Hey, buddy. Can you tell me your name?"

Jensen stared up at an EMT and furrowed his brow.

"My name is Dan. Nod if you understand me."

Jensen sighed. "I understand you. I'm not injured. I wasn't in the accident. The guy in the car—"

"Were you in one of the vehicles?"

"No. I just told you I wasn't." He resigned himself to Dan going through his protocol regardless of what he said. "I came on them right after it happened."

Dan shone his flashlight into Jensen's eyes. He blinked and turned away. Then the EMT grabbed his wrist and looked at his wristwatch.

Jensen yanked his hand away. "I wasn't in the collision."

"You might be in shock."

Irritated, Jensen scrambled to his feet. "I'm fine. It's been about fifteen minutes, maybe twenty, since the accident."

Dan stood, too. "How do you know?"

"The guy in the Impala passed me a few minutes before I came on them. Between the time I got here and the time you arrived, it can't have been more than twenty minutes."

Dan scanned Jensen from head to toe. "Are you sure?"

"Yeah. I'm sure."

"The closest passing lane is at least fifteen miles back. Should have taken you twenty minutes from there. If he was speeding, he could have been here ten minutes before you got here."

Following that logic hurt Jensen's head. Instead of dwelling on it, he said, "I didn't say he legally passed me. He was in a no passing zone. Somewhere near Birch Street."

Dan put the stethoscope on Jensen's chest. Jensen batted his hand away and stepped back. "Anyway, the guy in the car was unresponsive when I got here. No pulse. The guy from the truck looked dazed. Disoriented. Given the cut and bump on his head, I'm guessing he has a concussion. He kept coughing, probably from the airbag particles. But I don't think his ribs are broken. Breath sounds are okay. Maybe bruised from the seatbelt and airbag. First degree burns on his hands and face, but they don't seem to be bothering him. After I got him away from his truck, I got the car guy over here and started CPR."

Dan took the stethoscope off and studied Jensen. "Doctor?"

If the guy only knew. He shook his head, snorted in derision.

"EMT?"

Jensen sighed, opted for half the truth. "Doctor's son."

He checked on the truck driver, who was being loaded into the back of an ambulance. Then he walked over to one of the officers who'd responded to the call. He just wanted to give his statement and get the hell out of there.

After fifteen minutes, four retellings of his story, and more questions than he could count, Jensen was back on the road. Traffic would be backed up for at least an hour, but because he stopped on the side of the road past most of the debris, they let him drive on.

HE BEAT HIS FIST ON the steering wheel once, twice, a third time. He didn't want to be back home. Had avoided it for as long as he could. His house, his family, hell… the very town itself, reminded him of Hope.

His sister.

His dead sister.

His murdered sister.

But his father had summoned him home, and with nothing keeping him in Philadelphia and time running short, he had packed up his belongings and loaded them into his Chevy Avalanche. Five hours and countless potholes later, he'd traversed the turnpike and arrived in Cathedral Lake. The last place he wanted to be.

The very last thing he had wanted to do when he got to town was deal with a wreck. On Dappled Oak, of all places.

Well, maybe it was a toss-up between that and dealing with his father.

He tried to look at the situation rationally. Deferring for a year was just a time-suck, and there was no guarantee he'd get a different outcome if he reapplied. Besides, holding down a low-paying job until the following year rolled around did nothing for him long-term, particularly when he had a perfectly good opportunity just waiting for him.

Okay, so it wasn't perfect. It was in Cathedral Lake. It was still a prestigious opportunity.

It would be good to see his friends again. It had been a while, and they were all back, having graduated, and returned home to work in the city. It would be nice to catch up with his mom and Faith, even if he had to suffer painful reminders of Hope in the process.

In four years of undergraduate classes and four years of graduate school, he'd managed to avoid returning more than twice a year—Christmases and a week every summer. Jensen had used summer classes and jobs to justify staying away, but those excuses had run out.

Partly because he had graduated and had to move on.

Partly because his father didn't give him a choice.

When "Home" by Daughtry blared through the speakers, he smacked the power button of the radio and drove on in palpable silence. Soon he bypassed the turn to his house and stayed on Dappled Oak. Instead of immediately getting mired in more drama, he headed to the lake. When he passed the site of Hope's accident, a tear rolled down his cheek, guilt and grief churned in his stomach. He swiped it away with the back of his hand, clenched his teeth, and kept driving.

The lake always gave him solace, and it beckoned him like a siren's song.

It was early in the summer, and he expected a crowd at the beach. As soon as warm weather hit, people flocked to the northern side of the lake, where ample parking and a large expanse of flat land welcomed them to sunbathe, swim, picnic, or play. The southern side of the lake always appealed more to him, though, and that's where he headed. Few people ever ventured there, no matter the weather, and he preferred privacy. He liked the wild, uncultivated foliage, the rolling hills and rocky outcroppings, the copse of pines and oaks bordering the land. If he had to be back in town at all, that wasn't a bad place to be.

Jensen parked near the road and looked down the hill and across the lake. Not a soul in sight. Stepping out of the truck brought him into a crisp breeze. He took a deep breath, letting the wind fill his lungs and clear his head. Picking his way down the steepest part of the slope, the part no one would bother climbing down when the land was smoother further left, he reached a large rock and clambered over it. When he swung his leg down, his foot struck something. Hard.

"Hey!" A young woman sat there, rubbing her head.

He jumped clear of her and squatted down so he could talk to her, face-to-face. "I'm sorry. I thought I was alone and didn't see you. Are you okay?"

She put her hand down. "Don't worry about it. I'm okay. My dad would tell you I have a very hard head."

"Are you sure?" For the second time that afternoon, his medical knowledge kicked him into action. He searched her eyes for any sign of concussion.

When she smiled, the corners of her eyes crinkled. "I'm sure."

Jensen relaxed, and he, too, smiled. He stuck out his hand. "I'm Jensen."

She shook it. "Bella."

"So, Bella." He looked around. "My truck's the only vehicle parked on the road. How'd you get here?"

"I walked."

The only houses he knew of in walking distance belonged to rich people. R-I-C-H people. His family had money, but the people near the lake? They had more money than Midas. She looked to be about his age, give or take a year or two. He searched his memory but didn't remember her from school, and there was no way she lived there and went to public school. Curiosity got the best of him.

"I don't remember ever seeing you around here. Are you new to town?"

She turned her head and looked away. A quiet sigh escaped her—so soft he almost didn't hear it.

"No. I've lived here—well, my family has lived here—all my life. You probably don't recognize me because I went to private school."

"So, did I, and I don't remember you."

Another smile crossed her lips, but this one didn't reach her eyes. "Not Cathedral Lake Prep. I went away. To boarding school."

He let out a low whistle. Definitely, the upper rung of the economic ladder. "That must have been tough. Being away from your family, I mean."

The crease in her forehead and the shrug of her shoulders told him more than her answer. "It wasn't so bad. Got a great education. Made a few friends."

"Sometimes I think it might have been nice to be away from here growing up." He looked out across the lake, scanning the dark still water, watching the reflections of clouds drifting by in the mirror-like surface.

"Was CLP so bad?" she asked.

"Not until near the end."

"What happened?"

He lay back against the sun-warmed rock, cradled his head in his hands, and stared at the clouds in the sky. The sun shone through one, backlighting it with a golden halo. The crepuscular rays—Grandma Rose called them the Fingers of God—stretched toward him, beckoning him. For a moment, a fleeting fraction of a second, he thought he saw Hope, her hand reaching toward him. He blinked back the image and took a deep breath. Maybe he wasn't okay.

"It was a long time ago."

"It still bothers you."

He sat up and fidgeted with a blade of grass. "Some things stay with you."

She put her hand over his, stilling his fingers. "Well, whatever it was, I'm sorry."

"Thanks." He swallowed past the growing lump in his throat. "So, what about you? What's your story?"

"Mine? There's not much to tell."

"What's it like, going away to school?"

"I'd imagine it's a lot like what you felt when you went away to college. I was just a lot younger."

"Co-ed school?"

She snorted, then covered her mouth with her hand. She giggled, which made him laugh with her.

"Co-ed? If you knew my father, you wouldn't have to ask that question."

"That must have sucked in junior high and high school."

Another shrug. "You get used to it."

"I hope you at least got to go to a co-ed college."

"Oh, yes. I'm sure it killed my dad that Harvard was co-ed, but he always insisted I follow in his footsteps. That's where he went, so that's where I would go. Couldn't join the family firm if I hadn't met all his rigid expectations."

"Sounds like your dad had some definite ideas about your life. Didn't you get to make any of your own decisions?"

It was her turn to look across that water. "I'm afraid you don't understand how domineering and opinionated he can be."

"I understand. My dad's the same way. But after… there was an incident. It changed him. Well, it changed him a little bit."

"An incident?" She turned toward him, but he looked away.

"My dad's a doctor. As I grew up, it was a foregone conclusion for him that I'd be a doctor, too. He had dreams for both me and my sister, Faith. All centered around his vocation and interests. He foresaw her working in hospital administration. For me, it was medicine. He always talked about med school, my residency, my specialty. He taught me first aid almost before he taught me to ride a bike. Things got bad in my family around the time I graduated, and he became… more flexible. For a while, at least. With certain things, anyway. My sister and I were able to talk to him, explain how his vision for our futures was far different from our own desires. He relented and let us pursue our own paths."

"So, what path did you take?"

"If I had listened to my father, you and I might have met sooner. He wanted me to go to Harvard, but I chose the University of Pennsylvania. Penn has an excellent three-two program for engineering and business, and that's what I was interested in."

"Three-two program?" she asked.

"Three years to a BS in engineering, two more for an MBA."

"You must be really smart."

"Funny, coming from a Harvard girl."

She smiled. "Penn's a great school, and an MBA that fast is impressive."

Smart? Impressive? Hardly. If he was, he'd have figured out a way to avoid being sucked back into his family's drama.

"I said I was accepted into the three-two program. I didn't say I finished it."

"Oh. I'm sorry. I didn't mean to…" Her voice trailed off.

Now he really felt like a loser. Why it mattered to him, he couldn't fathom, but it was imperative that he let her know he wasn't a dropout, even if he didn't tell her everything. He chose his words carefully. "I changed my major. Eight years later, I've got my graduate degree."

"Did you just graduate?"

"Yeah. I didn't walk the ceremony, but I've got my papers."

"And now?"

He thought about how his plans had taken an unexpected turn, how he had no idea what to do next. How his only option was Cathedral Lake or nothing at all.

"I'll figure out something."

"Here for a summer vacation before the grunt work starts?"

His turn to snort in derision. "No. My father called me home. I had no excuse not to come."

"Sorry. It sounds like your dad and my dad should meet."

"I shudder at the thought. They'd either become an unstoppable force or start World War III."

She laughed, and he did, too. When they'd sobered, she said, "So, why'd your dad want you home now?"

He glanced at his watch and dodged her question. "Now is right. They were expecting me an hour ago. I just came here to clear my head before entering the lion's den." He scrambled to his feet and brushed off the seat of his pants. "Do you want a lift home?"

She also rose. "That's okay. It's not far. Sorry about ruining your pre-family meditation."

"Don't worry about it. You were much better company than my thoughts."

He extended his hand to help her up the hill, but she was already making her way well enough without his assistance. She had probably done this many times over the years. He couldn't believe he'd never run into her before.

Oh, well. If she didn't need his help, he could at least enjoy the view. He watched her bend over as she climbed the hill and grinned. Definitely, an appealing sight.

When they reached his truck, she turned to face him. "It was nice meeting you, Jensen. I hope we bump into each other again while you're home."

"You know, if you give me your number, that would put the odds solidly in favor of another meeting."

She grinned. "Give me your phone. I'll put my number in your contacts. That way, if you don't call, I won't have to wonder if you mis-entered my digits. I'll know you chose not to get in touch."

"Oh, you don't have to worry about that." He handed his phone over, watched her add her name to his contact list. When she passed the phone back to him, both let their hands linger a little longer than necessary. Her fingers were warm.

"I know three days is the typical waiting period, but I won't think less of you if you call earlier than that." She winked and walked toward a path in the woods.

He climbed into his truck and glanced at his phone. Bella. Beautiful name for a beautiful woman. He shook his head. He didn't know how long he'd be in town, but he knew he'd be there long enough to enjoy her company again before he left.

JENSEN'S MOMENTARY EUPHORIA WAS SHORT-lived. The closer he got to his house, the more he dreaded being back. Why hadn't he had the balls to just tell them no this time? Every time he returned, his mother tried to force him to the cemetery to visit his sister. She brought out old videos, mementos and photo albums. She tried to keep Hope—or at least the memory of her—alive for him, but all she really did was make him want to leave.

He carried Hope in his heart every day. Carried guilt for not being a better brother like a millstone around his soul.

He didn't need a constant reminder of her from his mother.

Despite his father's acquiescence years earlier about med school, he didn't sense pride when they visited. He felt resignation. Maybe even a little resentment and hostility. They could discuss very little without an argument. Even things they agreed on devolved into heated disagreements. They both loved football, but if Jensen commented about one controversial call, his dad took the other side. They both enjoyed skiing, but if Jensen mentioned a resort, his father listed three other better ones. They didn't discuss Hope at all.

He wasn't sure which was worse—his mother's constant reminders of his sister or his father's refusal to acknowledge her.

Returning home sucked.

He assumed Faith would be home for the summer. He hadn't seen her in about two months. When she had spring break, he'd driven to her campus for a visit. She made things easy. No grieving, no complications… conversation between the two of them unforced and natural. If Hope's name came up, she understood his reaction because she had the same one. They both could have been better siblings, more involved. More aware of what Hope had gotten herself into. In fact, it might have been more difficult for Faith, because she and Hope had been twins.

Who was he kidding? He was the big brother. He should have protected her better.

God, he hoped Faith would be there, because an extended stay with his parents—alone with his parents—would be more than he could bear.

He gritted his teeth when he made the turn onto Dappled Oak Lane and again passed by the site of Hope's wreck. It made him sick to think anyone could intentionally tamper with a motorcycle to try and scare someone, let alone cause the deaths of three people in the process.

Over money.

That it had been one of his father's best friends made it almost inconceivable.

When he pulled into the driveway, he realized he had driven there by muscle memory and the grace of God. Try as he might, he couldn't recall any part of the trip from Dappled Oak on. But there would be no more time for drifting thoughts and emotion-overload. He had to go inside and find out what the emergency summons was all about.

Leaving his bags in the truck, he let himself in the front door and looked around. Same table and mirror in the foyer on his right. Same bench and coat rack to the left. Same gleaming hardwood and lemon wax scent.

But it all felt different. Less vibrant. Had since Hope died.

Out of habit, he tossed his keys on the table, hung his jacket on the hook, and sat on the bench for a moment. Someone really should remind his parents of the adage about not being able to go home again.

"Jensen! You're here!" His mother rushed down the hall from the kitchen and wrapped him in a jasmine-scented hug before he could even stand up. "I was just starting to worry."

"You're late." His father followed along behind her, mug of coffee in one hand and newspaper in the other.

"Royce." She stood and faced him. "He just got here. Don't start already."

"I'm not starting, Vanessa. I'm just observing a fact."

"Sorry, Dad," Jensen pushed to his feet and lifted his arm, intended to shake his father's hand.

Instead, his father tucked the newspaper under his arm and wrapped Jensen in a single-arm embrace. Surprised, Jensen started to back away, but his dad just gripped him tighter. Meeting his mother's gaze, he raised an eyebrow, asking her a silent question.

What was going on?

She shook her head and looked away.

His father broke away and held him at arm's length, looking him over.

"Do I pass inspection?"

"I'm not inspecting you, Jensen. I'm just making sure you're okay."

"We heard sirens," Mom's voice quivered, and tears pooled in her eyes.

"There was an accident on Dappled Oak." Her hand covered her mouth, her eyes widened in horror. He continued before she broke down completely, fudging the details a bit. "I got stuck in traffic. I'm fine."

Well, he wasn't really fine, but not because of the accident.

She threw her arms around him again, squeezed him tight. When she finally pulled away, she held him at arms' length and looked him over. His father stood, stoic, silent, assessing.

Jensen pulled away. "Why was it so important for me to be here? What's going on?"

"Let's go to the kitchen. Sylvia just made a fresh pot of coffee."

Sylvia. Their tenth housekeeper since Hope died. He hardly remembered the names of the other ones, they'd come and gone so fast, and he had barely been there. In fact, there were at least two he never met at all. Maybe three. His parents had trouble trusting any of them after how badly things had ended with their first housekeeper, Lydia. She always had a thing for his dad, and when he didn't reciprocate her feelings, she tried to ruin him.

Because things weren't difficult enough after Hope had died.

None of the housekeepers after Lydia lasted more than four months, though, not until Sylvia. She answered their mistrust with competence, their distance with kindness, their pain with compassion. She'd been with them for more than four years, and she'd become a member of the family.

His parents could say whatever they wanted. He was convinced Sylvia won them over because she brewed a tastier cup of coffee than Lydia did, which said a mouthful right there. Lydia's coffee had been good. Damn good.

He followed his parents to the kitchen, where Sylvia had just poured a cup of coffee. She set it at his usual place at the table and offered him a big smile. "Jensen. So good to see you. How are you?"

"Fine, Syl. Thanks for asking. How've you been? Are you having trouble keeping these two in line?"

She giggled like a schoolgirl fifty years her junior and patted his cheek. Then she scooted around the table and bustled over to the oven. "Those two aren't the ones I'm worried over. Why don't you visit more often?"

"I've been busy." He sat at the table and held the mug in both hands, letting the heat of the ceramic warm his fingers and palms. Then he took a sip. Liquid heaven. "Mmm. Delicious. This hits the spot."

"Does it, now?" She bent into the oven and came up with something steaming. "I guess I'll have to give this to someone who isn't so satisfied, then."

He put the mug down with a thud. The scent of cherries wafted to him from across the room. "I won't be satisfied until I eat all that pie."

She smiled and put it on the table, along with plates, forks, and a pile of napkins. "Dig in, honey. I know it's your favorite." Then she headed down the hall. He heard her heavy footsteps on the stairs before they faded away.

"Do you want ice cream with this?" his mom asked. "I think we have vanilla and strawberry swirl."

"Nope," Jensen said. "It's best warm and plain."

"Vanilla?" his dad asked.

"Vanilla bean." She smiled and went to the freezer, returning with a half-gallon container and a scoop. Once the pie had been cut and distributed, she put a scoop of ice cream on everyone's but Jensen's.

"How can you possibly turn down vanilla bean ice cream on warm cherry pie?" Dad asked.

"Because I don't want to cover the taste of the cherries."

"It doesn't cover it. It enhances it."

Jensen jabbed his fork into the pie a little more forcefully than he intended. The fork made a loud clink before sliding off the dish and taking most of the pie with it.

"What was that all about?"

"My fork slid, Dad."

"It slid because you stabbed the pie like you were trying to kill it."

"Sorry!" He plucked the pie off the table and flung it into his dish. His fingers burned, the nearly boiling syrup sticking to his hands. But instead of giving his father the satisfaction of knowing he'd hurt himself, he moved slowly, deliberately, to wipe the scalding juice away. His hands were red from more than the cherries, he'd sustained a first- degree burn. Be lucky if his middle finger didn't blister.

God, how he'd love to show that one to his father.

"Jensen," his mom said. "Don't get so upset over nothing."

He sighed and pushed his dish away. He no longer had an appetite for anything at all. "Will you just tell me why I had to come home?"

"Maybe after we've had something to eat," She fidgeted with her fork.

"Just tell me now." He crossed his arms and sat back. If he decided to, he could be just as stubborn as his father.

"It's Wade," his dad said.

"Wade? What about him? And why should I care?" Wade had grown up with his dad. They'd been the best of friends. Until he tried to steal his father's promotion, frame him for stealing drugs, and, oh yeah, been responsible for Hope's death. After all that, Jensen didn't give one good god damn about Wade. He couldn't believe his father still did.

"You should care," his dad said, "because he's up for parole."

CHAPTER 2

BELLA SLIPPED INTO THE MUDROOM, toed off her shoes, and hung her keys on a hook. She couldn't resist a quick peek at her phone. Maybe he'd called, but her phone volume was off. No missed calls, and the volume was on.

She shook her head and pocketed the device. Completely unreasonable to have expected a call or text so soon. They'd just met, and he had been heading home to deal with something. It would have been so flattering, though, if he had reached out.

"Isabella!" Her father's bellow could probably be heard down at the lake. She hurried out of the room and down the hall to his study, paused, and took a deep breath before entering.

Victor Perish could only be described as formidable. He sat behind his colossal desk, suit jacket draped over the back of his tufted leather chair, crisp white shirtsleeves rolled up revealing thick forearms, vibrant red tie loosened, shirt collar open at his throat. The expression on his face was darker than his midnight pinstripe Armani.

"Dad?" Her voice sounded stronger than she felt. "You called?"

He stood, resting his fists on the blotter and looming over the folders he'd been reviewing, leaning in her direction.

Despite the urgent desire to cower, she stood her ground, not wilting at his heated glare.

"Damn right, I called. Where the hell have you been?"

"I went for a walk. I needed to clear my head."

"Clear your head! How could it possibly be convoluted? You haven't done any work yet. This hearing is in four days. When do you plan on preparing?" His eyes narrowed, his voice dropped low. "What have you really been doing? And with whom?"

Did she walk around with her thoughts tattooed on her forehead? How could he possibly know she had been with someone?

"Isabella?" The veins in his neck pulsed.

"I told you. I took a walk. To the lake. To think. I'm just not…"

"Not what?" He returned to his seat and leaned back in the chair, elbows on the arms and fingers steepled in front of him.

She sighed. "Dad, I… I just don't feel comfortable working for him. He's not a nice man."

He leaned forward and rested his arms on his desk. "So, being nice is now a prerequisite for having a strong and competent defense?" His steely gaze penetrated her, chilling her to her core. " How would you feel if no one would defend you because you weren't nice?"

"I'd like to think I'll never be in a position to need a defense attorney."

"And I'm sure our client didn't set out to become a convict, either. Sometimes things happen we don't like, things beyond our control."

Did he just compare accidental circumstances to their guilty client? He'd confessed, for God's sake.

She closed her eyes and took a deep breath. When her tumultuous thoughts cleared, she realized her father still spoke.

"—our duty as defense attorneys to make sure the courts are fair, and the defendants have good representation. Everyone deserves a defense. Everyone. Now, get to work." He started perusing a file, his lack of attention a silent dismissal.

She snatched a file off his desk and stormed out of his study.

Up in her room, she sat at her desk, staring at the papers without comprehending their contents.

Why couldn't her father understand? She didn't want to defend criminals. She wanted to put them away.

A better question was why she couldn't stand up to him. Had never been able to.

Maybe she learned blind obedience from her mother.

When Bella turned five, she wanted to go to kindergarten like the maid's son. Her father insisted on homeschooling. She didn't argue. Her mother told her she understood, but she didn't argue, either.

When Bella turned thirteen, she wanted to continue homeschooling. Her father insisted on boarding school. She didn't argue. Her mother told her she'd miss her, but she wouldn't talk to Victor for her.

When Bella graduated, she wanted to tour Europe before beginning college. Her father insisted she enroll for the summer semester, just to get a jump on things. She didn't argue. Her mother didn't even discuss it.

When Bella received her BS in poli-sci after just three years of schooling, she wanted to go to DC and work on a campaign. Her father wouldn't hear of it, demanding she attend law school. She didn't argue. Her mother had been on a cruise when her father's decree had been issued and never weighed in on the subject.

When Bella passed the bar, her father took her into his firm. She never had a chance to even apply to work at the DA's office. Her mother threw a big party.

She sighed, tucked her hair behind her ear, and stared at her computer screen. No matter how much she wanted to let her client rot in jail, she had a job to do, and she refused to do a job half-assed. That was her reputation on the line and that of her father's firm. No, regardless of her personal feelings, she'd make certain she'd put together an unshakable case.

Four hours and three supporting statements later, she had the beginnings of a solid argument.

And a raging headache.

She put everything aside and lay on her bed. She'd already missed dinner, and no one had called to her or brought anything up. Her stomach growled, voicing its complaint at the injustice. Instead of going downstairs and foraging in the kitchen, she closed her eyes, vaguely aware of her phone ringing but far too weary to answer it. Rolling onto her side, she fell asleep.

A SOFT TAPPING ON HER bedroom door awakened her from a troubled dream of handcuffs and jail bars.

Bella tumbled out of bed and stumbled to the door. She rubbed the sleep out of her eyes and reached for the doorknob.

The door flung open, barely missing her face but slamming off her elbow. Wide awake after the jolt to her arm, she massaged what was sure to be a bruise and turned to face the whirlwind that was her mother.

Olivia Perish marched into Bella's room leaving a subtle scent of Chanel No. 5 in her wake. She headed straight for the desk, leafed through the papers sitting near the computer, then rounded on her daughter.

"Where were you last night?"

"Good morning to you, too, Mom."

Her mother smoothed her sable hair, already pulled into a neat twist, and leaned against the desk. "Isabella, I asked you a question."

Bella wondered how her mother could stand complying with her father's rigid standards. She hadn't seen the woman in sleepwear since nightmares sent her running to her mother in the middle of the night.

She had been four years old. It was right after—

No. Must not think about that.

Olivia Perish took her role as Mrs. Victor Perish seriously. Whether she wanted to or was expected to, it didn't matter. At any moment on any day, she might have to receive someone of great importance that meant always being impeccably dressed, coiffed, and made up. Christmas mornings. Birthdays. Illness. Didn't matter.

This day was no exception. From the tips of her high-heeled Manolo Blahnik's to the collar of her latest Chanel acquisition, not a wrinkle could be found. Up-do smooth and pins tucked, invisible, into her dark brown hair. Cosmetics applied with a professional finish—brown eyes accentuated with subtle champagne shadow, complexion dewy and fresh, lips lined and glossed. Barely the crack of dawn, and her mother had dressed, styled her hair, applied makeup, and accessorized. Like she always did. Every. Single. Day.

She twisted her strand of ever-present pearls and stared at her daughter.

Bella would look just like her. If she primped. She glanced down at her rumpled clothes, ran her hands through her hair until her fingers got stuck in the tangles. A quick glance in the mirror revealed raccoon eyes from not removing her makeup before falling asleep.

Not that she cared. At that moment her arm hurt like hell, and she was still sleep-disoriented, despite having been jolted awake.

"What did you ask me?"

"I want to know why you missed dinner last night. Where were you? Your father was… displeased."

"I was here. Yesterday afternoon, he demanded I work on this case, so I came up here and worked on it."

"So why didn't you come to dinner?"

"Why didn't anyone call me and tell me it was dinnertime?"

Her mother sighed, crossed her arms. "You know dinner is served promptly at seven. Your father expects you to keep your appointments without a reminder."

Bella plopped down on her bed and cradled her sore elbow in her hand. "See? That's the problem. A family dinner is not an appointment. It shouldn't be a scheduled event I have to put on my calendar. If he wanted me at the table, he shouldn't have let me work so long. He should have called me."

"You know he doesn't like it when there's yelling in the house."

"Oh, yeah? Then why was he roaring my name yesterday when I came home?"

"Bella…."

"For that matter, he didn't have to 'call' me to dinner. He could have come up and knocked on my door or sent someone. That's far more his style anyway, isn't it? Making others do the things he considers beneath him."

"Isabella." Her mother approached the bed. "You shouldn't talk about your father that way. He's a good man, a good father. A good provider. He works too hard to see to every tedious detail. That's why he has help."

"A good man? A good father? That's why he kicked—"

"Not another word on the subject, young lady."

Bella sighed, changed tactics. Downgraded the hostility about ninety percent. "That's why he made me become a lawyer. So, I could handle the 'tedious details' he faces at work."

"Oh, honey, no." She sat beside her daughter. "He loves working with you, and he didn't force you into becoming an attorney. You chose that path yourself. You always looked up to your father. It's only natural that you'd emulate him."

"Wow. You really believe that, don't you?"

Her mother's eyebrows lifted, her eyes widened. "What on earth do you mean by that?"

"I may have recognized, from a very early age, that Dad was a powerful and important man. But I never emulated him. I hated all his decisions. Keeping me out of public school, sending me away." Always sending her away. Sending anyone and everyone away if they didn't measure up to his standards. "Forcing me to take summer college classes. Law school." Not to mention the worst decision he ever made, the one she was forbidden to speak of.

"He made all those decisions because he wanted what was best for you."

"If he wanted what was best for me, he should have asked what I wanted. What I needed, and you knew how I felt, but you never came to my defense."

"Well, your father—"

"Don't. I don't want to hear more excuses, and I certainly don't want to hear more praise for him. I'm doing what he expects. That should be enough."

Her mother reached for her hand and squeezed it. "I just want you to be happy."

"It's a bit late for that." She pulled her hand away. "Why'd you really come in here this morning?"

"I heard you moaning, and I wanted to be sure you didn't miss breakfast because you were sick."

Moaning? Oh, right. That weird nightmare.

"I'm fine. But that's not why you really came in."

Her mother rose and walked to the door.

"He sent you to find out if I did any work on the case, didn't he?"

Somehow Olivia's already rigid back snapped straighter. She didn't answer, but her hand paused on the doorknob.

"Let him know I'm almost done. I'll finish this morning."

Her mother gave a curt nod and slipped out the door, pulling it closed behind her with a soft click. Bella heard the rapid clack of heels on hardwood as her mother retreated.

It wasn't bad enough that her mom didn't stand up for her. Did she have to spy for her father, too?

Her stomach growled again, and she decided to forgo work in favor of eating. And, damn it, she wasn't changing her clothes before breakfast. She would go downstairs in her rumpled clothes from the day before. Her own empowered version of a walk of shame.

Not taking the time to even brush her hair or scrub her face, she left her room. After a quick glance down the hall at the closed door of the room she was never to enter, she blinked back tears. Then she turned around, squared her shoulders, and headed downstairs, her father's standards and expectations for appropriate table attire be damned.

CHAPTER 3

JENSEN AND FAITH SAT AT the kitchen table, breakfast dishes pushed aside. His sister munched on apple slices. He had a plate of cherry pie in front of him. Heated, non-à la mode.

His father came in from the back yard, frowned at Jensen's dish, placed a kiss on top of Faith's head, and walked out of the room.

Jensen swallowed a smart remark along with his bite of pie. Then he looked at his sister. "So, what do you think?"

She toyed with the edge of her napkin. "I don't know. I mean, I feel like we should testify at the hearing. You know, for Hope. But I really have no interest in ever laying eyes on Wade again."

"They said we could write a letter to the board."

"It doesn't feel like enough. She'd be there for us." She sighed. "I never was as strong as her."

Jensen took another bite of pie, the sweetness now sour in his mouth. He swallowed it past the lump in his throat and pushed the dish away.

"That's bullshit, Faith."

She shook her head. "I don't know. She stood up to Jimmy Salvo. It's because of her that the police arrested that Sturgis guy, stopped the dog-fighting ring and the pharmaceutical thefts. I never would have been brave enough to get involved like that."

"Yeah, she was something." Guilt gnawed at him, and he looked down at his dish. He should have seen what had been going on. Protected her, but he'd failed as a big brother. She'd given her life for her convictions. He'd barely given her any attention at all, let alone his help.

He lifted his head and looked at Faith. "But you're strong, too. Strong enough to face Wade and testify against his release."

"You think so?"

He nodded.

"And what about you? Are you really going to look him in the eye—the guy we grew up calling Uncle Wade—and say why you want him to rot in jail? Can you do that?"

He leaned his elbows on the table and stared at her. "I don't even want to be here, let alone there. But now that I am? Yeah. I'm ready to stare that SOB right in the face and tell him he doesn't deserve freedom. He tried to ruin Dad. He killed Hope. It doesn't matter that he didn't mean to hurt her. It was his greed that did it. Nearly destroyed our whole family. Why the hell not? We didn't get to speak at his trial. We deserve to be heard now."

Faith dropped her napkin. "But what do we say? Do we read from a prepared statement? Speak from the heart? Will they ask us questions?"

"I don't know. I guess that's why Mom and Dad scheduled a meeting with a lawyer."

"Good. That's good." She picked up her fork, twirled it through her fingers. "Mom said Wade hired a top-notch firm."

"A different lawyer than his defense attorney?"

She nodded. "I guess he must have felt he got screwed over, so he fired that guy and hired some shark. Perish, or something. He's a named partner at a firm in the city."

"If he's that good, you'd think we'd have heard of him."

"People that good don't advertise, Jensen. He's not an ambulance-chaser.

Dad said it's really unusual for a guy with his name on the door to take a small-potatoes case like this."

"Hope's murder isn't small-potatoes."

"Not to us, but it is to the world at large." She held up her hand to stop his argument. "It doesn't really matter what we think. This isn't the type of case the guy usually takes, so it has Dad worried. I guess this lawyer was unstoppable before, and now he's brought his kid on board. They've gotten a reputation as quite a formidable team. People used to make comments about his name being Perish and him being a killer in court. Now with the two of them, they're being called vipers."

"I don't get it," Jensen said. "How is that worse?"

"Oh. Sorry. The guy's first name begins with a V, and his kid's name begins with an I. V-I plus the P-E-R from their last name. Viper."

"That's ridiculous. Who comes up with this stuff?"

"Probably just an intimidation tactic. Anyway, they're supposedly impossible to beat."

"When'd Mom tell you all this?"

"A couple of weeks ago."

"I thought we were brought home to discuss this in person."

She shrugged. "I've known for a while. Mom's been keeping me in the loop."

"But no one bothered to tell me."

"I thought Dad was telling you."

As if. His father told him nothing.

"Do you think that new lawyer is going to get him out?"

He sighed. "We'll find out, I guess."

They sat in silence for a moment. Then she cleared her throat. "Mom and I talked last night. She doesn't want to speak at the hearing. Honestly, I got the sense that she didn't even want to go. Maybe she'll feel better after the meeting today."

"I don't think Dad's giving her a choice about attending the hearing. I'm surprised he's giving us one."

"He made it perfectly clear. He wants us to do whatever we feel comfortable doing."

Jensen smirked. "Get real, Faith. Maybe he isn't going to force you, but he made sure I came back to hear about this rather than just telling me on the phone. He expects me to be there."

"He made me come home, too."

"Apparently, they told you on the phone. Besides, you were coming home anyway, weren't you?"

"And weren't you? It's summer."

"I haven't spent a whole summer here since high school." No point in saying any more than that.

"Maybe it's time you did. Besides, you're done with school now, right? You need to find a job, settle down."

He scowled at her. "I'll deal with my life and my decisions on my own time."

She shook her head and sighed. "We need to talk about this."

"No, we don't."

"Yes, we do. Maybe after the trial. In any event," she rushed on before he could argue, "Dad isn't forcing me to go."

"Your relationship with Dad isn't quite the same as mine."

"What are you talking about?

"Remember how he had my life planned for me? Be a surgeon, follow in his footsteps?"

"So what? He had my life mapped out, too. We stood our ground. Made our own choices. It's all behind us now."

He shook his head. Dad may be okay with your choice to become a vet, but he never got over me choosing to study engineering. Things between us have gone downhill ever since the day we had that talk."

"That's in the past. You've finished school. Have another talk and put this to rest."

"If I bring it up, I give him the moral high ground. I won't let him think he's won."

"Won what? It's not a competition, Jensen. You're making way too much of this, and now you're sucking me down with you."

"I'm not, Faith. Why do you think I avoid coming home when I can? He's mad at me. Has been since I left for college."

"Jensen—"

He ignored her. "All we do now is fight. He picks an argument every time I open my mouth."

"That's not true."

"That is true. Ask Mom. She'll tell you. Unless she's afraid to. I wasn't even out of the foyer yesterday, and he already started."

"Well, none of that matters now. You can resolve that at any time. What matters now is what we're doing about Wade's hearing."

"I don't know. I know I'm ready to face him, to stand up for Hope. But I don't know if I can sit there with Dad."

"You act like he's insufferable."

"For me, he is."

Faith looked up, eyes wide, mouth agape.

Jensen closed his eyes and dropped his head.

"Well, isn't that what every father wants to hear." Royce walked over to the table and pulled out a chair. "May I sit, or can't you suffer through my presence?"

"Dad, I…." But he had no words to follow that up.

"You what, Jensen? You didn't mean it? You meant something else? I know you aren't sorry, so tell me. What?"

Faith cleared her throat. "How'd the meeting go, Dad?"

"Your mother's upstairs. She's not feeling well. Maybe you should go talk to her."

Faith stood, looked back and forth between her father and Jensen. "Okay. Before I go, would you like some pie and ice cream? There are only a couple of pieces left. Better get some before it's all gone."

When Royce answered, he kept his gaze pinned on Jensen. "No, thank you, Faith. Jensen and I need to talk, however. Please go and check on your mother."

Faith started walking without saying another word. Her eyes pleaded with Jensen before she left the room, but he didn't even nod as she scurried out.

What did she want from him? He could only sit through so much of his father's attitude before he answered back in kind. He steeled himself for battle and sat back in his seat. "What do we need to talk about?"

"You're joking, right? After what I just overheard?"

"I don't know, Dad. How long were you there?"

"Why? Was there more Dad-bashing than what I heard?"

Jensen sighed. "I wasn't 'Dad-bashing.' Faith and I were just talking."

"About me."

"No, not about you. The few minutes we discussed you just happened as an aside to the main conversation. She and I can't decide if we want to go to the hearing."

"But you're going?"

"Is that a question or a command?"

Royce rested an elbow on the table, stared at his son.

"What did the attorney say?" Jensen asked.

"Why can't you ever answer a question?"

Jensen snorted. "Me?"

"Why does everything have to be a battle with you?"

"With me? That's a laugh."

"And we're back to me being insufferable, I suppose."

Jensen ran his hand through his hair. "Dad, I'm sorry if what I said hurt your feelings. I really am. But ever since I left for college, you've been different."

"After everything that happened when Hope died, I thought different was good. Was what you wanted. I accepted you not going to med school. I paid for your tuition, your books, your housing. Hell, I sent you money every couple of weeks for food in addition to your meal plan. I'm sure I've even funded your social life, which apparently was a long and sordid one, given how long you took to get your degrees. So, tell me, how have I not been a help to you? I've been here all along, whatever you needed."

He gritted his teeth, counted to ten. Still couldn't bank the rage coursing through his veins. "No, Dad. You may have given me everything Mom told you I needed, but what I really needed isn't something you can fix with a check."

"And what is it you really need?"

Jensen jumped to his feet, his chair toppling over behind him. "You, damn it! I needed *you!* I needed your support, your understanding. But that's been in short supply for a while now. If you can't throw money at it, it doesn't get fixed, and all the money in the world isn't going to fix this."

He spun and dashed down the hall, passing his mother on the way. "Jensen? What happened? What was that noise?"

But he kept going, toward the door.

"Jensen, wait!" Royce called.

He didn't stop, though. He didn't want to hear anything his dad had to say. He headed for his truck and didn't look back.

HE DIDN'T HAVE A DESTINATION in mind when he stormed off. More like an anti-destination—anywhere his father wasn't. But he somehow ended up driving past the scene of Hope's accident again, another anti-destination, only to wind up back at the lake.

The short scramble down the craggy hill only took a little effort, not nearly enough to burn off all his anger and frustration. He sat with his back against the rock he and Bella had shared, playing with the crunchy blades of dormant grass and thinking.

When he was young, like any boy, he suffered through nine-months of school just waiting for summer vacations. But, boy, when those vacations hit, he made the most of them. Swimming, biking, playing outside, hanging out with his friends… sure, all that kept him busy.

But what really made the summers fun? The time with his dad. Hiking trails, camping trips, sailing at the lake. Picnics and starlight movies. Canoe rides and bonfires. Those excursions made all the tedium of the school year worth it. That's how he and his dad bonded.

They went over sports strategies while biking. Talked about his friends while roasting marshmallows. He got 'the talk' while fishing off the edge of the dock. Wasn't even as mortifying as he thought it would be. They had a lengthy discussion about Simone—and a rehashing of 'the talk' which was more embarrassing than the first one—while floating on rafts in the lake. They'd discussed Jensen's future. Well, his dad's plans for his future.

These precious moments of connection grew fewer and farther between with each passing year. They stopped altogether when Hope died. By the time he started college—as an engineering major, not a pre-med student—any conversation with his father pretty much dwindled away. Except for utilitarian necessities and arguments, of course. His father always had time to argue.

When he changed his mind about his major, he never told his family. His father never asked about school, so, clearly, he didn't care, which made Jensen's decision to keep quiet about it easier to make.

As far as dear old Dad was concerned, once Jensen disobeyed him, there was no point in discussing his education. No point doing anything more than tolerating his son, either.

If only his dad knew how ridiculous the whole thing was. Wonder if he'd even care?

A smattering of pebbles landed on his shoulders and startled him, knocked him out of Memory Lane. He stood up and looked around to see Bella scrambling over the rock.

Despite his efforts to get out of her way, she bumped his head with her foot and yelped, surprised. She looked down and, upon seeing him, giggled and jumped to the ground.

On a reflex, he grabbed her around the waist to help steady her. She grasped his shoulders, her mirth abruptly gone.

It would be so easy to dip his head, press his lips to hers. Easy, but wrong. Not with his current frame of mind. He let her go and stepped back, the mood charged, awkward. He fumbled for something to break the tension and came up with the world's lamest line. "We've really got to stop meeting like this."

Bella smiled, and just like that, the uncomfortable silence dissipated. She had a brilliant smile. "Either that, or you will have to go to medical school."

He leaned against the rock and frowned, his amusement gone.

"So, am I interrupting?" she asked. "You look like you're thinking through some things. I can go, if you want."

It boggled his mind. How could his father be so obtuse when Bella—a girl he'd just met—was so attuned to his moods? She recognized his sadness, appreciated his poor attempts at humor. Her smile lit up the gloomiest of days, lifting his mood with it.

And she smelled like cherries.

What was he thinking? No way would he pass up his next opportunity to kiss her. Hell, he'd make an opportunity if one didn't happen naturally. In the next minute.

"You have as much right to this spot as I do." Despite the brisk breeze, he felt warm.

"Maybe we should name this rock Our Spot. Put up a sign to keep trespassers away."

Time to make an opportunity. "I know just how to christen it."

He leaned in and touched his lips to hers. It was only supposed to be a soft kiss, a tease at what more there was to come, if she was interested, and he supposed she was. Before he could pull away, though, she grabbed his shirt, tugged him toward her, and deepened the kiss.

In high school, he had lost his virginity at the lake, probably not forty yards from where he sat. At the time, he couldn't imagine feeling any better than he did at that moment. But that night didn't come close to comparing to what he felt while kissing Bella. Kissing her made him understand the clichés about fireworks and time standing still.

The realization shook him to his core.

He broke the kiss. Not ready to back away, though, he wrapped his arms around her and buried his face in her hair.

Cherries. Man, he was in serious trouble.

She rubbed his back, seemingly content to snuggle against the whipping wind. A storm was rolling in. He could smell it in the air. They didn't have much time.

Thinking about fleeting time, about how his father had changed, about Hope and her last weeks, he nearly lost it. He fought back tears—seriously, what kind of pussy cried at all, let alone in front of a girl he just met—but he grieved in her arms. Grieved for his sister, for the father of his childhood, for the innocence taken from him when Hope died. He marveled at Bella's capacity for compassion, especially for a man she hardly knew. If only he could find that closer to home.

He took in a deep breath and unraveled himself from her.

"Are you all right?" she asked. The tears swimming in her eyes told him she'd clung to him as much for herself as for his benefit.

"Better than you, I bet." He saw her shoulders stiffen. "Don't do that. Tell me what's wrong."

She sighed and ran her hands through her hair, pushing it out of her face until the wind caught it and whipped it back into her eyes. "My family. Nothing new."

"Maybe not. But you have a new, captive audience who's happy to listen."

She chewed on her lip and looked at the lake. "Did you ever wonder what it would be like to just say no?"

He laughed and leaned back against their rock, pulled her to rest against him. Her body fit perfectly against his, and he took a deep breath before continuing. "I don't wonder at all. I did it."

"And?" She didn't turn around, but she shifted a little, her body searching for an answer her eyes wouldn't see.

"It was when I told my dad no to med school. Things haven't been the same since."

"Because you're free of his control?"

He snorted. "No. Because he hasn't accepted my answer yet."

She sighed and shifted position again, back to the comfortable cuddle they'd started at. "At least you had the courage to stand up for your convictions. But I'm sorry to hear it didn't work out the way you'd hoped."

"Nothing ever does." He felt her shift in his arms, so he cleared his throat and changed the subject. "But I'm more worried about you. What happened?"

"It doesn't matter. I'd rather sit here with you than dwell on all that."

So, they sat there, snuggled together against the wind, against their respective problems. The billowing clouds churned, roiled, threatened to open and drown them in a deluge. Jensen knew their time together ran short, but he hadn't felt that good since his arrival in town. Given that Bella didn't rush to leave, he could only assume she felt the same.

The first drops of rain fell, and they hadn't even broken their embrace when the expected torrential downpour hit. She leapt to her feet, planted a quick kiss on his cheek, and darted up the hill to the wooded path before he could offer her a ride or even say goodbye.

He climbed into the cab of the truck and cranked on the a/c, anxious to dry off. With nowhere else to go and nothing else to do, he headed home, the faint scent of cherries distracting him from his troubles.

This time, he'd call her. Definitely.

After he got home, he entered the house without his father—or anyone—noticing. He raced up the stairs, took a hot shower, and headed to his room.

CHAPTER 4

BELLA SAT IN THE TUB, bubbles enveloping her in a frothy cloud, soft jazz playing from the speakers in the ceiling. Her phone sat on the tile platform surrounding the tub, the only reminder of a pressing life outside the warmth and serenity of her bath. A glass of pinot would have made it perfect, but eleven a.m. was a bit early to break into the wine cellar, and she couldn't have managed to sneak upstairs if she'd stopped for a bottle and glass first.

She missed the days when her father went to the office at the crack of dawn and didn't return until after dinner. Now he often worked from home, and she spent as much time avoiding him as she did working.

Maybe she should have gone to the office instead of working from home.

Maybe she wouldn't have to avoid her father if she worked instead of running away to the lake.

Maybe Jensen would call and take her away from her troubles.

Maybe. Maybe. Maybe.

She sighed and slid deeper into the bubbles. She needed to relax, soak her problems away. Drown the damn things.

When her phone rang, her first impulse was to ignore it, but it might be about work—hell, it might be her father—so she glanced at the caller ID. She didn't recognize the number, so she couldn't summarily ignore it. Could be a client. Or opposing counsel.

Damn it. She'd have to take it.

Cursing both technology and people, she swiped her thumb across the screen and answered, hoping it was a telemarketer or wrong number so she could just hang up and go back to her warm, relaxing soak.

"Hello, Bella?"

She sighed. Tension tightened her neck and shoulders. Not a friend, and the man using only her first name meant it probably wasn't a telemarketer. Which meant work. "Yes. Who's this?"

"It's Jensen. From the lake."

She smiled, put the phone on speaker, and slipped deeper into the bubbles. The stress drained from her body, melted right into the hot water. "Hi, Jensen-from-the-lake. What's up?"

"You said I didn't have to wait the obligatory three days to call."

"That's right, I did."

He cleared his throat. *"So, I'm calling."*

"I'm glad. I kind of felt interrupted by the rain. I'd been enjoying myself."

"Me, too. I didn't even really have a chance to say a proper goodbye."

"I yelled it over my shoulder."

"I didn't hear you over the downpour. Besides, I meant a little more than a verbal farewell."

She ran her hand through the bubbles, watching them part beneath her fingers. "Really?" She grinned. "Were you going to wave, too? Maybe salute?"

"Nothing as formal as all that. I was thinking something more… personal."

His voice sluiced over her, warmer than the water, softer than the soap, seeping into her and heating her blood. "Oh, yeah?"

Jensen replied, but she never heard his words.

Her bathroom door flung open with a bang, startling her. Had she been holding the phone, she'd have dropped it in the tub, ruining it. Maybe that would have been better than letting Jensen hear her father ranting like a lunatic.

"What the hell do you think you're doing?"

She scrambled for the phone, said a hasty goodbye, and ended the call. Scooping the bubbles into strategic areas, she yelled right back. "Me? What are you doing? Barging in here? Not even knocking. I'm in the tub! I don't think a little privacy in my own rooms is out of the question."

"*Your* rooms?" He grabbed a towel and flung it toward her. "Last I looked, it was *my* name on the deed. I let you live here. I'll go anywhere I damn well please in my own house."

"Then maybe I shouldn't live here anymore."

"And where are you going to go?"

"I have a job. I'll get my own place."

"Try it. Good luck getting a place when I'm your only reference. And good luck keeping your job, acting like this."

Despite the warm water, Bella shivered, chilled to her core. "Are you telling me you'd fire me if I moved out?"

"I'm far too savvy a lawyer to admit something like that. However, being it's still shy of noon on a workday and you're luxuriating in your tub, I'm well within my rights to terminate you. On the spot."

"Something you wouldn't know if you respected my privacy!"

"Who was on the phone?"

"None of your business."

He glared at her, and she fought against withering under his gaze. When he finally spoke, his voice was low, far more intimidating than the booming tone of their argument. "Get dressed and get down to my office. Now. Three minutes, or you are fired."

"I need at least five. I'm in the tub!"

He turned his back on her. "Clock's ticking." He strode out, pulling the door closed behind him.

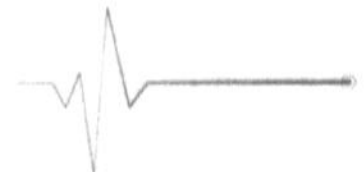

BELLA WASN'T SURE WHETHER THEY agreed on three minutes or five, so to play it safe, she shot for three. Which meant she would look positively frightful, her dad would be even angrier, and she'd have a hell of a time managing her hair later.

But she made it with seventeen seconds to spare, and an uncomfortable and growing wet splotch on her back from her hair soaking through her shirt.

She knocked on his office door and stepped across the threshold.

He glanced at his watch and frowned. "Sit."

Swallowing a sigh, she took a chair facing his desk. He paced for a moment, then finally sat in his seat, leaned back, steepled his fingers, and stared at her.

His scrutiny unnerved her. Then again, it always had. She fidgeted, and when he scowled at her, she sat motionless, waiting for his opening salvo.

But he didn't speak.

Unable to stand the silence any longer, she spoke first, breaking one of his immutable laws—the person who speaks first loses the argument. "So, why'd you burst into my room?"

"I thought we established every room in the house is mine?"

"What do you want, Dad?"

He leaned forward, resting his forearms on his desk. "What do I want? I want you to take your job seriously. I didn't spend decades on this firm and thousands on your education just for you to sit on your laurels and coast, expecting my name to make your life easier."

Ah. The 'you're-indebted-to-me' speech. An oldie and not-so-goody.

"Isabella, you're my daughter. People expect big things from you."

People? Who was he trying to fool? By people, he meant him.

"I can't have you blowing off work while the rest of the firm puts in sixty-plus-hours a week."

Sixty? Seriously? The only people working twelve-hour days were him—because he loved his job more than his family—and her, because she wanted to avoid his lectures and disappointment.

Didn't really work out for her at the moment.

"It's my name on the door. My reputation. If you hope to add your name someday, you have to up your game."

Was he that clueless? She didn't want her name on the door. She wanted to walk out the door and never look back.

Not that she'd ever tell him that.

"Relax, Dad. I got caught in the rain, so I took a bath. It's not like I was at the spa in the middle of the workday."

"I think the problem is I've been too relaxed."

She coughed to cover the snort bursting out.

"I don't appreciate that, Isabella."

"Oh, come on. Too relaxed? When have you ever let up on me? Ever?"

"You live here rent free."

"And have no freedom in your house."

"You set your own hours at work. When you bother working at all."

"Set my own hours? I do almost nothing but work from the moment I wake up until I go to sleep at night. I'm at your beck and call."

"You've been out of the house a lot lately, and I haven't said a word."

"I took two walks in as many days to clear my head, and both times I've heard about it."

He leaned back in his chair. "Here's what's going to happen. You're going to prepare your case, and you aren't leaving this house until I've approved everything you've done."

A chill swept through her, and she shivered. How she'd love to blame it on her dripping hair and sodden shirt, but those weren't the cause. It was her father—his lack of faith in her, his insistence that she run all her work by him. More time with him, less freedom, less fun.

Less Jensen.

She sighed. "Is that all?"

"One more thing. Do *not* wait until the last minute to give me your work. We need time to get it in shape. So, don't dawdle, and do not waste my time."

She pushed to her feet, looked out his window to avoid meeting his gaze. “And if I decide I don’t want to defend criminals?”

“Good luck finding a new job without my reference, and better luck finding a new place to live.” He grabbed a folder off his desk and started perusing it, effectively dismissing her.

Bella held her head high as she left the room, but her stomach clenched. She didn’t want to stay in her father’s house, but what choice did she have? If she left, he’d make sure she was blackballed at every firm in the tri-state area. She couldn’t support herself without a job. If she stayed, he all but promised to make her miserable until she conformed to his every wish and whim.

The bastard.

Given her alternatives, she seriously considered whether she could live under a bridge and eat out of trashcans. Frustrated and disgusted with herself, she headed for her room. She’d decide before she got there whether she’d get down to work or get out her suitcase.

She’d never walked so slowly in her life.

DESPITE BELIEVING SHE’D DONE A good job earlier when she prepared the defense, she spent hours combing over the file. She took notes, researched precedents, crafted arguments, studied the facts. At four o’clock, she was confident in presenting her case to her father.

He barely gave the file a cursory glance when he finally looked up at her. “I don’t see anything in here about what you learned from your talks with your client.”

“I haven’t spoken with him.”

Shaking his head, he tossed the file on his desk. “The work you did is all basic and rudimentary. How can you hope to create a personalized defense when you haven’t even spoken to your client?”

“Why do I need to meet him?” It was bad enough she had to defend the guy. Did she have to have a face-to-face with him first? "Everything I need to know is right here."

"I'm not even going to dignify that with a response. Go. Now. Attorney visiting hours end at nine-thirty. This isn't ready until you have his statement."

Don't talk back. Don't talk back. Don't talk back.

She bit her tongue. Hard. But at least she didn't argue.

Instead, she grabbed the file, spun around, and left his office without a backward glance. The prison was a forty-minute drive—without traffic. She had plenty of time to drive there, meet her client before visiting hours ended, and return home at a decent hour. That didn't mean she wanted to dawdle, though. She just wanted to get it over with and have enough time to add the information to the file and get her father's approval.

Like a child.

She sighed, gathered her keys, purse, and briefcase, and headed out. Lucky for her, traffic was light. It didn't hurt that she had a bit of a lead foot, either, averaging about twenty miles an hour over the speed limit on the parkway.

Probably because she was so damn angry.

In any event, she arrived at the jail in about thirty minutes and in a foul mood. She presented her identification to the gate personnel and was directed to the visitor parking area. After a mental inventory of what she couldn't bring inside, she decided to leave her purse in the car and only bring her briefcase and ID. No phone, no laptop, no money, not even her emergency bottle of aspirin… nothing on the forbidden list. She even took off her jewelry.

She stepped out of the car and started across the parking lot. Steve Forbes, ADA and mortal enemy of her father's, approached her.

"Steve. What's the prosecution's office doing at a jail?"

"Hi, Bella." He shook her hand. "Seems one of the inmates wanted to rat on someone in exchange for a reduced sentence. Ken sent me to check it out."

"How'd it go?"

He smirked. "Like I'd tell you. You and your dad would try to scoop him up and work us over."

Bella tried to smile, but it felt so fake, she stopped pretending. "We aren't that bad, Steve."

His tone softened. "No, not you. You get a bad rap, working with your old man."

She shook her head.

"Sorry. I know, he's your father. But you could do so much better than defending these scumbags. Ken would snatch you up in a heartbeat."

"The DA hates my dad more than you do." She looked down, fidgeted with her briefcase. "He'd never hire a Perish."

"Don't count on that."

Bella looked up at him, tipped her head to the side. "What's that supposed to mean?"

He shrugged and glanced at his watch. "I've got to run. Think about it, Bella. We don't make the kind of dough you do, but we are on the right side. You could do a lot worse. You are doing a lot worse."

Stepping around her, he walked over to a generic American-made sedan and climbed in.

So, what if he wasn't rolling in money? She didn't need a lot to get by. She'd love to be on the right side of the courtroom.

But she was a Perish.

The gate guard cleared his throat, and she glanced at her watch or where it would be if she hadn't taken it off. Putting her never-going-to-happen career change plans aside, she headed for the door. Inside, she gave the name of the inmate she wanted to speak with, handed her briefcase over to be searched, and proceeded to the metal detector.

Beep, beep, beep.

What the hell? She started patting her pockets.

"Ma'am, are you wearing any jewelry? Have any body piercings?"

"No."

"Any braces or medical implants?"

"No."

"Any concealed items we need to be aware of?"

She shook her head, couldn't fathom what the issue was. "Nothing."

"Please step over here."

She followed the officer around the metal detector, past the table where her briefcase sat, and over to a clearing where two other officers stood, hands on the weapons holstered on their belts. The man she followed took a wand and waved it slowly over her head and around her body. It squawked by her chest. He repeated the wand search, and it went off again in the same space. Bella closed her eyes and sighed. She'd been in such a hurry to leave, she didn't think to change her bra.

Feeling the heat rise to her cheeks, she whispered, "It's my underwire."

Face void of expression, he put the wand down and gestured to a door. "This way."

No point in arguing. He opened the door and she stepped into a large, chilly room where two female guards stood. Then he walked out, closing the door behind him.

The guard closest to her held up a white linen bundle and a brown paper bag. "Here's a dressing gown. You may go behind this screen to change." She gestured to a three-panel screen in the corner barely tall enough to hide the important bits. "Take off your shirt and bra and put them in this bag for examination."

"That won't be necessary." Bella slipped her hands inside her shirt, even as the guard closest to her dropped the bundle and both guards drew their weapons.

"Freeze!" the bundle-free guard said. "Hands. Let me see your hands."

Bella felt the sweat bead on her forehead, her upper lip, under her arms. Who would want to touch her bra after that? "Easy. Just trying to help." She unhooked her bra and slipped it out through her sleeve. "Do you still want it in the bag?"

The guards glanced at each other and slowly returned their weapons to their holsters. The one farther from her looked like she was fighting back a smile. The other guard snatched the bra out of her hand. "Wand her," she said to her partner while she examined the garment.

The pseudo-smiling guard ran another wand all around her. No squawks or beeps. The first guard handed the bra back to Bella. "You'd be wise not to wear underwire here."

"I totally forgot before I left home. Usually, I wear something else."

"Make sure you do next time, and if you do forget, follow procedure and change into the gown. Save us all the hassle."

Bella managed to put the bra back on while not removing her shirt. A feat she hadn't tried to do in quite a few years, and it took some effort to manage. "I was trying to save you the hassle. Who wants to wait for someone to change and examine the changing area? This was faster."

"And more dangerous. You could have had a concealed weapon. We could have shot you."

She sighed. "Can I leave now?"

Grumpy Guard nodded toward the exit. "Go."

Bella didn't miss the smirk on the other guard's face before she opened the door.

She retrieved her briefcase from the male guard who'd searched it and glanced inside. He'd left the papers messy, all disarrayed and out of order.

Her dad, the long drive, the guards, the hassle… Forget foul mood. She was downright pissed off.

Hadn't even met the creep yet, and she already needed a drink. A glance at her watch and she knew if she rushed the interview, she could be back in town in time for dinner—which would definitely not be at home and would definitely include alcohol. Maybe pizza and beer at the pub…

Scowling, she followed the guard through a series of checkpoints and presented her ID more times than she could count. Finally, she was directed into an attorney's meeting room, so designated because there were no recording devices inside. Her client already waited for her, and his guard stepped out a different door when she stepped inside.

She sat down and assessed her client. He didn't look any worse for wear. No cuts, no bruises. Not too gaunt, so he must have eaten well and made use of the exercise facilities in the yard. Nothing about him to indicate he'd been a problem inmate or didn't get along with the other men at the facility. If there had been any problems, it would have been in his file. Hell, he probably wouldn't be up for parole at all.

"I'm here because you requested counsel represent you at your parole hearing," she said. "I need to take your statement, and you can ask me any questions you might have."

He smiled at her. "Where do we start?"

CHAPTER 5

JUST A FEW DAYS EARLIER, Jensen had been living a stable, if somewhat boring, life. Had he realized the mess he'd find himself in when his father summoned him home, he wouldn't have taken the call, let alone made the trip. At the moment, he didn't want to see his father, didn't want to think about what had happened when he'd called Bella earlier and didn't want to even consider the possibility of Wade's parole.

His dad pissed him off. Bella having another guy at her house after leading him on pissed him off more. And the possibility of Wade getting out really pissed him off.

He couldn't settle his thoughts, couldn't get his mind on anything else.

So, he headed to the gym to burn off some of the rage.

An hour of kickboxing, a strenuous arm workout, and a three-mile jog on the treadmill didn't eliminate a single ounce of anger. It just made him tired and sore. So instead of confronting his father or Bella, instead of facing his feelings about Wade head-on, he showered off the sweat and crashed until dinner.

He would have slept longer, but his mother insisted he join them.

When he walked down the stairs, he heard the clatter of flatware on china.

Late. He'd hear about it from his father. He slid into his seat, and Sylvia carried over a platter of fried chicken.

"Right out of the pan, Jensen. I made this batch with extra hot sauce in the batter, just for you."

"Thanks, Syl. Smells great."

"By all means," Royce said, "let's make special food for Jensen, who didn't even want to join us."

"Dad." Faith waved a forkful of something undoubtedly tofu that resembled a fried chicken patty. "I've been eating special food for years. That never bothered you. Just tonight, Sylvia made seitan for me. That took more time for her than making a batch of chicken with extra hot sauce."

"But Jensen doesn't have a moral objection to what we eat or any dietary restrictions we need to address."

"Maybe you'd be happier if I put vanilla ice cream on it," Jensen muttered.

Sylvia put two pieces of chicken on his plate and 'tsk-tsked' him under her breath so his dad wouldn't hear. But he got the message. He cleared his throat and looked down at his plate.

His dad stood up and strode to the refrigerator into the kitchen. Jensen kept his head bowed. Eye contact with anyone would only result in more discomfort or an angry outburst. His money was on angry outburst.

Royce returned, standing behind Jensen. "Far be it from me to deny my son anything."

He looked up at his dad, but it was too late. Royce plopped a huge scoop of ice cream right on top of the special chicken Sylvia had prepared.

"And I didn't even have to throw money at this problem."

It took Jensen every fiber of self-control to not pick up the plate and shove it in his father's face or slam his dad's head down to the table and rub his damn nose in it.

Instead, he slid his seat back. Slow. Deliberate. Pushed to his feet, ignored the burning in his muscles.

"Thanks for the chicken, Syl. It looked great."

Rather than waiting for her response, for his mother and sister to protest, or for his father to erupt, he turned and strode down the hall. Time to get some distance from his family and put Bella out of his mind. He knew just what he needed. His friends.

JENSEN'S FRIENDS WERE UNLIKELY TO be at any of the local bars so early in the evening. Hell, they probably weren't even home from work yet. So, he'd have to eat alone and call them later. Not a problem. He was used to eating alone.

Besides, it might be too early for a bar crawl, but it was certainly late enough to have a drink.

Or a bottle.

He drove into town and pulled into the parking lot at Sean's Pub and Grille. A large painted sign, faded and peeling, crowned the dark brick building. The logo portrayed Sean as a burly, leprechaun-like man holding a sandwich in one mitt and a pint of ale in the other. Jensen didn't know if anyone named Sean ever owned the place, but ever since he could remember, it was owned by a bigger-than-life Greek woman named Eleni. Not only could she spin a better yarn than the best bartenders he'd seen in Philly, she made a mean gyro. Easily the best in the city, probably the state.

Climbing out of the truck, the smell of stale beer, fried food, and grilled meat wafted to him. His stomach growled. He needed to drown his sorrows but feeding them first sounded like a great idea. Headed for the door, he pulled his phone out of his pocket and scanned it for missed messages or calls. Nothing from Bella, but he didn't think he wanted to hear what she had to say, anyway.

Before putting the phone away, he sent a text to his friends. Time, he let them know he was back in town. He could use a night of booze with his buddies. No thinking about Wade. No family drama. No frustrating women. No worries about his future. Just a night out with the boys. He was starting early, but they could catch up when they got there.

The inside of Sean's looked pretty much as he remembered. A long, worn bar stretched along the back of the room, black swivel-stools lined up against it just as neatly as the bottles on the wall behind it. The dining room sat off to his left, laminate tables and padded wooden chairs dotting the rough sawn pine floor. To his right was the entrance to another room, a stage covered with a drum kit, amps, and mics lining the far wall. The dance floor in front of it, currently empty, waited for the entertainment and crowds that would show up later that night. A fleeting thought about who might be playing later danced through his brain… and right back out again. He just didn't care.

He turned left, took a seat in the dining room, and waited for the server. The smells he'd noticed in the parking lot intensified in the little room, as if the alcohol, grease, and smoke of several decades' past, had seeped into the very walls of the place.

Many people wouldn't like it, but to him? Heavenly. Like sliding into old slippers and listening to a favorite song. The smell welcomed him home. Far more than his father ever had.

He sighed and shook his head to force the thought from his mind. He'd come for a distraction, not for wallowing.

Where was that damn server, anyway?

"Hi." A perky voice came from behind him. He started to turn, but a girl in skimpy, cut off jean shorts scooted past the chairs at the table next to him, then she turned to face him and leaned over, affording him a clear view down her low-cut crop top. "Know what you want to drink?" She whipped a menu from under her arm and slid it onto the table, then cracked her gum and gave him a huge smile.

No one could be that happy working there. Obviously, she thought a flirty disposition, a glimpse at her cleavage, and a wiggle to her hips would earn her a bigger tip. Probably worked on most guys, too. Might even have worked on him a different night.

He picked up the menu and handed it back to her, not bothering to smile back. "Three gyros. Side of onion rings and a Manhattan."

The briefest frown crossed her face before she sighed and headed for the bar… with only a natural sway to her hips.

"Keep my glass full," he called after her, "and there's a big tip in it for you."

She turned back to him and winked. "You got it, sweetie."

He noticed her smile as she turned away, and the strut returned.

He couldn't be much older than her, but for some reason she made him feel ancient. He didn't recognize her, and she had a face to remember, definitely a body to remember, too. But he didn't know her from school or around town.

Then he stopped giving her any further thought. He just wasn't interested.

He didn't look up when she returned with his drink. "Here you go. You're food's almost ready."

When she turned away, he raised the glass to his lips, smelled the orange around the rim, the spice of the whiskey and bitters. He closed his eyes, breathed deeply of the aromas, and sipped the drink. Relished the burn in his throat and gut. "Hey!" When she stopped and looked at him, he raised his glass. "Bring me another."

Her raised eyebrows didn't escape his notice before she turned her back to him, but he saw her head to the bar. Satisfied she was bringing his re-fill, he downed the first glass in three swallows. Then he fished the cherry out of the bottom of the glass.

The waitress returned with his second drink, then she headed for the kitchen. He downed the second one as fast as the first, felt the burn in his gut less even as the fog started creeping through his mind. He dug out the second cherry and popped it in his mouth just as she brought his food to the table. Leaning back so she could put his food in front of him, he nodded his head toward his glass.

"You sure you don't want something else? Coffee? Water?"

He stared at her.

"Beer?" Her voice was substantially weaker.

He raised his eyebrows.

"Another Manhattan, coming up." She left the dining room for the bar.

"Make it two," he called after her.

A family drifted in as he tucked into his first gyro. Two boys in baseball uniforms, shoving each other, a bored-looking teenage girl who regarded her family with eye-rolls and sighs, and a harried mother holding in one hand what was undoubtedly the sticky palm of a tiny girl in pigtails, and in the other the back of the highchair she pushed from behind the hostess stand. She had a phone tucked between her shoulder and her ear, and none of the children seemed to pay her any attention.

"Damn it, Donald. You said you'd meet us here." She kicked a chair away from the table, slid the highchair into place, and settled the little moppet in the seat. "We're already seated. We can't leave." She snapped her fingers at the boys, who'd started wrestling instead of sitting. She waved at the girl to get her attention, pointed at the boys, tipped her head toward them.

The teen merely rolled her eyes again and turned away, scooting her chair farther from the boys.

The woman lunged over the table at the boys to break them up and gestured toward their seats. Then she tipped her head up, closed her eyes, and took a deep breath. "Donald, their game starts in less than an hour." She slumped into her chair and dropped her chin to her chest. "Well, thank you very much." She ended the call without a goodbye, stuffed her phone in her pocket, and muttered something Jensen couldn't quite make out.

Something like juiceless, commemorative cactus.

Jensen snickered and popped an onion ring in his mouth.

That didn't make sense. He thought about it for a while. Had to focus hard before he figured it out. Most likely said *useless, insensitive jackass.*

His version was funnier, a lot funnier. His snicker turned into a chuckle, then morphed into a full-blown belly laugh. The woman glared at him. Before he could respond, the waitress brought his refills and grabbed his empties. "Be right with you," she said to the woman. Then she turned and headed toward the kitchen.

This time, when she walked away, he appreciated the sway in her hips.

It reminded him of his view of Bella as they climbed the hill.

That wasn't funny. Not at all. He quit laughing, tossed both his drinks back, barely feeling the burn, and scowled at his plate. Heard the harried woman mutter, "Men. They're all the same." He glared at her, leaned back in his seat to see into the bar. His chair almost tipped over, and he righted it with a *thud.*

The two boys laughed and pointed. The woman frowned and shook her head.

He leaned back again, although not as far, and yelled into the next room. "Hey, sweetheart. Bring me another." When the woman sighed, he yelled again. "Make it easy on yourself and bring two again." He brought his chair back to all four legs and marveled at how unsteady it seemed. Tried to rock in his seat to see if it wobbled and almost fell out of the chair.

Maybe he was the juiceless, commemorative cactus and that started him laughing again.

Gales of laughter continued to consume him, to the point that he didn't even notice his friends arrive until Austin clapped him on the back, nearly knocking him to the floor.

"Hey, man." Jensen fought for balance while the guys sat down. "Brett, Miles. Damn good to see you guys again."

Austin's eyes narrowed, "You're drunk."

Jensen shrugged, "Just a little buzzed."

The harried mother snorted.

He squinted in her direction, tried to focus on her. Failed. But he answered her anyway. "Something you want to say?"

She threw cash on the table and started herding her kids. "Not to you." She lifted the little one out of the highchair and began weaving through the maze of tables.

Jensen pushed his chair back, blocking her way. Now that she stood close to him, he could see her better. It pleased him when her eyes widened and started scanning the room.

"What? You can say whatever you want about me under your breath, but where's your bravery when you're face-to-face with me?"

She looked over his head and said to her sullen daughter, "Go get help."

Jensen pushed to his feet, wondered when the floor started rocking. "Help? From whom? The husband who stranded you here?"

Her face blanched, and she blinked as tears filled her eyes.

He leaned over toward her. "You know what they say about people in glass houses."

And then he was being dragged—backward—out of the room by two sets of strong hands. He arched back to see Austin and Miles dragging him away from the table. Struggling proved futile, they overpowered him easily. A glance back at the dining room showed Brett talking to the mother—Jensen snickered when he thought about the alternate meaning of the term 'mother'—walking her to the door where most of her kids waited. The teen stood alone at the bar, leaning over it and trying to see into the kitchen. The mother beckoned her… and that was all Jensen saw before his friends muscled him into the club area. They shoved him into a seat. He tried to focus on the stage, where a scrawny kid conducted a sound check.

Brett joined them, sat down beside Jensen, and slapped him in the face.

It should have stung, but no pain registered. He squinted at his so-called friends, his blurry gaze landing on Brett. "What the hell was that for?"

"You're joking, right?"

Jensen shook his head.

"Hey, Ashley." Austin leaned back in his chair and called out the doorway. "Can you bring some coffee in here?"

"Coming right up," came the muffled reply from the next room.

"And another drink," Jensen called.

"Just the coffee," Austin and Miles said together.

"What's with you guys?" He looked his three friends over. "I haven't seen you in ages, and this is how you greet me?" He pushed to his feet, adjusted for the spinning room, and plopped back down.

The waitress—guess her name was Ashley—came in with four mugs and a whole carafe of coffee. She looked at Jensen. "Do you want me to bring your food in here, or can I clear your plates?"

"I'd really just like another of my Manhattans."

"He'll take his food," Brett said, "and probably another pot of coffee. Maybe some ice water."

"Be right back."

"Seriously, man," Miles said. "You're drunk off your ass. Slurring your words. Picking fights with housewives. What the hell's going on?"

Jensen looked his friends over. Or tried to. He couldn't quite make them out, despite squinting at them. Besides, the room kept lurching, and this time, his stomach went with it.

Ashley returned with a tray filled with another coffee carafe and his meal—cold gyros and greasy onion rings. The mere sight of the food kicked in his gag reflex.

The smell made his eyes water, his stomach flop.

He lunged to his feet and stumbled across the room. His mouth filled with saliva, his abdominal muscles contracted, and he barely made it to the men's room and into a stall.

The acid stung his throat as he expelled the contents of his stomach into the bowl, the water splashing up toward his face. Repulsed, he retched again, the circuit continuing until his stomach had emptied, his cramps ceased, and his dry heaves subsided. The smell threatened to choke him, and he quickly flushed the contents. He wiped his mouth with the back of his hand, and, feeling the sweat on his upper lip and the droplets of splatter on his face, he gagged once more.

Not wanting to continue the vicious cycle, he pushed out of the stall and headed to the sink to rinse his mouth and clean up.

Brett leaned against the sink, arms crossed over his chest. "Did you spew all the jackass out of your system?"

Jensen's mouth filled with saliva again, and he prayed his stomach wouldn't rebel. “Please don’t say,” he paused, swallowed, and continued with a tight throat, “spew.” He nearly ran back to the stall but pushed the nausea down and continued to the sink. It took him a second to open the tap, then he bent down and stuck his face right under the spray. The cool water soothed his flushed skin, and he scrubbed at his face, remembering with a sour churn of his stomach, the toilet water and vomit splattered there. Without even coming up for air, he filled his mouth a few times from the running stream, rinsing and spitting and repeating. Then he stood and gargled, bent and spit again.

“Better?” Brett asked.

Jensen turned off the faucet. “You called me a jackass.”

“Technically, I didn’t. And you were acting like one. Worse, actually.”

Did he act like a jackass? He had a vague recollection of exchanging words with that lady. Couldn’t fathom why. He should have sympathized with her. Looked like her kids had been stuck with a shitty father, too.

He pushed past Brett and opened the door. Back at the table, he glanced at his food and pushed it away before even taking his seat again.

Brett followed him out and sat across from him. “So, spill. What’s up?”

That’s what best friends were for. They put up with your shit, called you on it. Helped you deal with it. Offered support without even knowing what was going on.

Miles poured coffee and passed the mug to Jensen.

The hot brew burned his tongue, scalded his throat. But it worked wonders for getting the taste out of his mouth and bringing a small bit of clarity to his muddled thoughts.

“My father summoned me home.”

“You weren’t doing anything, anyway, were you?” Brett asked. “Your graduation was last week, right?”

Jensen sighed. “Don’t remind me. I can’t think about all that right now.”

“Then what?” Miles asked.

“It’s not that my father insisted I come home, although that’s bad enough. It’s why he wanted me here.”

When he didn't continue, Miles prompted him. "Okay. Why?"

"It's Wade." He sighed. Struggled to find the strength to continue. "He's up for parole. Dad wants me to speak at the hearing."

Brett expelled a long breath. "Wow. That really sucks, man. Are you going to do it?"

"You've met my dad, right?" He stared into his mug, thinking of all the times one or more of his friends had witnessed his dad go off on him for no reason. It rarely occurred when he was young but happened more and more frequently when he grew older. Actually, it happened most when the subject of school came up during breaks, which was why he'd gone home less and less over the years, until his visits had become brief annual obligations.

"Sorry," Miles said. "What are you supposed to talk about?"

Jensen shrugged. "I don't know. My parents met with an attorney today for some advice, but I left before I heard what happened."

"Why?" Brett asked.

"Again, you've met my dad, right?"

"Maybe you need to talk to him," Miles said. "Tell him about school."

"I'm not doing that. He needs to make the effort to fix our relationship before I confide in him. Besides, I started talking to someone else about it."

"And?" Miles asked.

"And I guess it just wasn't the right time. Or the right person. She…"

"She?" Brett asked.

"Yeah." He thought about Bella. Her eyes, her smile. Her easy disposition. Her other man.

Clearly, he'd misread her signals, or she sent those signals to too many guys.

"Want to talk about it?" Miles asked.

He shook his head.

"About your dad—" Austin started.

"Don't want to talk about him, either."

Austin sighed. "Your call. It's the wrong call, but it's yours to make."

He poured himself another mug and looked at Brett. "You've been quiet."

"I have something on my mind. Sorry. This clearly takes precedent."

"No, man. What's—?" Jensen desperately wanted a change of subject, wanted to be there for Brett as he'd always been there for him. Neither mattered, though. His mouth flooded with saliva again, even as his stomach cramped and roiled. Shoving his chair back, he rushed to the bathroom again and threw up a stomach full of bitter liquid and bile. Spent more time with his head under a stream of cold water.

He returned to his friends, wet, but a bit more lucid. Unfortunately, not much more lucid. He knew he'd been in the middle of something important before he left. Wanted to return to the conversation. He just couldn't remember what it was.

Before he could give it much thought, Simone walked in and made a beeline straight for his table.

There had been a time when, for him, the sun rose and set with her. She had been his everything. They'd dated throughout high school, and he thought she was his forever. Before graduation, he'd envisioned their lives together... their wedding, their home, their kids and grandkids.

But college had a way of proving high school notions frivolous and fleeting.

He hadn't been through the first semester of his freshman year at university when he'd already moved beyond her. When he broke it off, it was with every intention of remaining friends. But she wouldn't take no for an answer. She kept visiting his campus on weekends, showing up at his house on his holiday breaks. Before his junior year started, he'd given up on a cordial relationship with her. She must have gotten the message, because he finally disappeared from her radar. Or maybe he just stopped noticing her, like a persistent fly you eventually stop swatting at and just ignore.

But now, he was all too aware of her. Seeing her zeroing in on him at the bar was simply too much for him to handle. He looked and felt like shit. His soaking wet head, his roiling stomach, his muddled thoughts and heated emotions... No, he didn't need a confrontation with Simone at the moment.

"I can't deal with this right now." He pushed to his feet.

"Wait," Brett grabbed his arm.

He shook out of his friend's grip and made his way to the door.

"Jensen!"

He heard Brett calling his name, but he had no interest in going back, so he kept on toward the door.

The air outside enveloped him, cloaking him in a shroud of heat and humidity. Choking on the thick moisture, he bent at the waist and panted. Swallowed the saliva again pooling in his mouth. He closed his eyes, rested his hands on his knees. Sounds started reaching him again. A male sigh. A woman's 'ahem' as she cleared her throat.

When he looked up, Austin stood there, staring at him. He wasn't alone.

Bella stood beside his friend, biting her lip and staring at him with wide eyes.

Fuck. He so didn't need this.

"Jensen. What's wrong? Are you okay?"

"Fine." He turned to Austin. "I'll see you later, man." He turned back to the parking lot and started heading toward his car.

Austin grabbed his arm and spun him back around. Jensen looked at his hand and then looked up. "What are you doing?"

"You're drunk. I'm not letting you drive."

He looked at Bella, then back at his friend. "I think we both know it's clearly out of my system."

Austin shook his head. "You of all people should know it clearly isn't. If you weren't drunk, you'd know."

"Him of all people? Why?" Bella asked.

Oh, he was so not getting into his personal life with her. Gratitude flickered through him when Austin also ignored the question.

"I'll drive you. Miles can pick me up."

"You have friends inside?" Bella asked.

Jensen looked away, so Austin answered. "Yeah."

"I can take him home. Go ahead back inside."

Austin turned his attention to Jensen and raised an eyebrow.

How bad could one drive be? Besides, he had no reason to be upset. They'd never been on a date. Hell, they'd never even really discussed a date. Just some harmless flirting.

"Go, man," Jensen said. "Bella will get me home."

"You need a ride tomorrow to get your car?"

"I'll let you know. Faith can probably take me."

"Bella." Austin extended his hand to her. She shook it. "Thanks for looking after our boy."

Jensen didn't know what he meant by 'our boy.' Did he mean his and their friends'? Or did he mean his and Bella's?

"My pleasure." She grabbed Jensen's hand and led him toward her car.

Jensen looked back. Austin waggled his eyebrows, smiled, and headed back inside.

Damned if Austin hadn't meant his and Bella's.

JENSEN WALKED HAND-IN-HAND with Bella, noting that he bumped into her a lot. Highly unlikely that she bobbed and weaved on her way to the car. Man, he hated her seeing him vulnerable.

Then he remembered, again, that it didn't matter. She was nothing more than an acquaintance to him.

By the time he got settled into the passenger seat of her Mercedes, his head hurt as much as his stomach. God, what he wouldn't give to be home in bed. His home, not his father's. But technically, for the near future anyway, his only home was his father's.

The day just kept getting worse.

"So, where am I taking you?"

Tahiti. Florence. Barcelona.

Any place with a bed.

He sighed. "You know, I can just take a cab."

"Why on earth would you do that? I'm happy to give you a ride. I like spending time with you. Even if you're… not feeling well."

"That's really kind of you." Might as well just clear the air entirely. He'd already made an ass of himself. What was humiliation in front of one more person? "What would your boyfriend think of you hauling around a drunk guy who's been flirting with you? You're allowing yourself to be put in a compromising position."

She backed out of the parking space and drove slowly through the lot. "I would never date a man who had a problem with me doing a favor for someone."

Despite all his logical reasoning, jealousy reared up and kicked him in the gut. He had no interest in discussing her boyfriend. He reached for the door handle, fully intending to jump out, even if the car was moving. The doors locked. He didn't know if it was automatic after so many seconds or if she locked him in. Either way, he felt trapped, and he didn't like it. He searched for the 'unlock' mechanism.

"But," she continued, and stopped before entering the road, "to answer your question, I don't have a boyfriend. So, the point is moot. Now, right or left?"

"Don't lie, Bella. I heard him."

"I'm not lying."

"Please." He scoffed.

"I don't lie, Jensen. I was home. At my parents' house. You heard my father."

Doubt and hope warred throughout him. He sneaked a glance at her.

"Right? Or left?"

He hoped believing her didn't end up biting him in the ass, but he decided to trust her. "Right."

"Right it is." She turned onto the road.

He continued giving her directions as she drove. Maybe the day wasn't turning out to be the horrible one it had started as.

CHAPTER 6

BELLA DROVE IN SILENCE, WONDERING whether to take Jensen home or take him somewhere else. He'd clearly had a bad day, given she'd found him drunk at a bar around dinnertime. But she didn't know if she wanted to get involved with someone who looked for solutions at the bottom of a bottle.

She peeked at him through the wisps of hair framing her face. The belligerent man from the parking lot was gone. Jensen looked like a little boy who'd broken a window and had to face the consequences.

The consequences being his father.

Still not knowing the extent of Jensen's problems, she felt for him. His slumped shoulders, half-closed eyes, and greenish complexion told her more than any of his words could. He was both physically and emotionally sick.

Taking him home seemed like the worst course of action.

"Take a right at the stop sign." He sighed, seemed to slump lower in the seat.

When she got to the intersection, she waited for the road to clear, then made a U-turn.

"What are you doing?"

"It's early." She glanced at him. "I thought we'd get some coffee in your system, sober you up a bit before you head home."

"That's just a myth." He pushed up, leaned his head back against the headrest, and closed his eyes. "Not only does coffee not metabolize alcohol faster, it leads to impaired reasoning by voiding the sedative effects of the alcohol and stimulating cognitive function. Intoxicated people who would typically move slowly and reason they were too drunk to do certain things—like drive, for example—find themselves operating at a higher speed and consequently believe they are cognizant enough to perform tasks that ultimately prove dangerous."

"You sound like a medical text."

He sighed and muttered something she couldn't quite make out.

"Okay, well, I also heard you should drink water because alcohol dehydrates you."

"It would be better to have had water between drinks, but that's basically true. Especially for people who—"

"Who blew chunks after guzzling down half the contents of a public bar?"

"I was looking for a nicer way to say it, but sure."

She suppressed a smile. "What about bread? Does it absorb the liquor?"

"No." He took a couple deep breaths.

Maybe he felt sick again.

He cracked his window to let some air in. "Food might make it take longer for the alcohol to enter your bloodstream, but the amount of alcohol doesn't change."

"Did you learn this from your dad? Or years of drunken binges at college?"

He didn't answer.

She drove past the lake and jumped on the bypass. About fifteen minutes later, she pulled into the parking lot of one of her favorite little eateries and took a space near the door. The structure was natural tumbled stone with ivy creeping up its walls. A six-foot-tall fence surrounded what appeared to be a massive property behind the building, and a sign above the sturdy wooden door read "Eden" in green script. She smiled and stepped out of the car.

Jensen heaved himself to his feet, but instead of closing the door, he leaned against the open frame. "I thought we were going to a deli or something."

"Or something. This is one of my favorite places to grab a snack."

"I thought this was a lawn and garden center."

She laughed. "No. It's a health food restaurant."

"I was thinking something like fondue."

"You don't want something that heavy. Not while you're, well, let's say not up to par. Trust me."

He furrowed his brow, then winced and raised his hand to his head. "Whatever. Let's go." He closed the car door and headed for the restaurant.

She was surprised that he thought to hold the door for her, given he seemed to be struggling to move. Smiling her thanks, she led them inside. There were plenty of tables near the windows offering natural light and pleasant views, but she chose a table near the restrooms. Just in case.

A waitress appeared and slipped two menus onto the table. "Hi. I'm Janna. I'll be your server this evening. Do you know what you'd like to drink?"

Jensen scowled and flipped over his menu.

Again, Bella found herself suppressing a smile. "Two mineral waters, please."

"Coming right up."

"Cute," Jensen muttered.

"What?"

"The shirt." He nodded to the retreating waitress. "The embroidered fig leaf."

She chuckled. "I didn't figure you for having an eye for fashion."

"I don't. I just know my grandmother would have appreciated it. She's basically a religious zealot. You don't have to spend much time with her before you start noticing anything with a biblical motif."

"Are you two close?"

He shrugged. "We do the occasional holiday and phone calls maybe once a month or so. I mean, I love her. I just don't really have anything in common with her."

"Well, you know what they say. You can't pick your family."

He snorted, and Janna brought their drinks. "Ready to order?"

"I'm sorry. We haven't even opened the menu yet. Give us a few minutes?"

"No problem. Take your time." She walked away.

Bella reached across the table and grabbed Jensen's hand. "I'm sorry. I assume my last comment brought your father to mind. Do you want to talk about it?"

He took a sip of his drink and flipped open his menu.

She started to pull her hand away, but he squeezed it. Then she looked at him, but he wouldn't meet her gaze. Instead, he released her fingers and held the menu in front of his face.

Knowing she'd probably order the hummus platter—because she always ordered the hummus platter no matter how good everything else looked—she opened the menu and started scanning the selections.

Jensen dropped his menu to the table and looked at her. "Uh... this is a vegan restaurant."

"Yeah."

"I'm a carnivore, Bella."

"I eat meat, too, Jensen, but you need healthy food right now. Everything they serve here is grown right on the premises. They have a huge garden out back and a greenhouse. All the food is organic. No pesticides, no GMO. It's gluten and dairy free."

"So, flavorless soy crap. Or even worse, that pseudo-meat chemical taste."

"Have an open mind!"

"My sister's vegan. I've tried that stuff. It's nasty."

"Maybe she doesn't know how to prepare meals."

He scoffed. "My sister. Cook? That's hilarious. No, our housekeepers make her food when they prepare our meals. Usually they eliminate the good stuff in ours and make her a small dish of the remaining stuff that barely resembles food, along with a big salad. I hardly care for the salad. Definitely hate the faux-meat."

"You'll love almost anything you order here. Maybe avoid the soy stuff this time."

He closed his menu and sat back in his chair. "I'll just get a fruit plate."

"I'll order for you. Is there anything you really hate?"

"Beets. Other than that, I'll eat almost anything. Anything that's actually food, that is."

"Then what's with the attitude? You eat vegetables."

"They're a side dish, not a main course."

"Just trust me."

"Fine. But no soy." He sat back and closed his eyes.

When the waitress came, she ordered the hummus platter—surprise—as well as two bowls of tomato-basil bisque, porcini risotto, and a fruit plate. She also asked for refills.

"Did you order enough food?" he asked.

"You need your nourishment. Besides, I'm sure it won't go to waste."

"I have a feeling you'll be taking a lot home."

Janna returned with two new glasses, garnished with lime and mint sprigs, and cleared the empties. "New recruit?" she said to Bella.

"New, yes. Recruit? Unlikely. He's not very open-minded."

Janna patted him on the shoulder as she walked away. "You'll be pleasantly surprised."

"So, we have a few minutes," Bella said. "Do you want to talk about it?"

"About what?" He fidgeted with the edge of his napkin and didn't meet her gaze.

"Any of what's bothering you. Your dad. Your sister. Whatever had you drinking your dinner."

He shook his head. "Do you want to talk about your dad?"

She sighed. "No. I don't suppose I do."

They sat in uncomfortable silence for a while. Maybe she shouldn't have taken him to dinner. She didn't really know him. Yet she'd traveled miles from home with him—a strange man. She'd done smarter things.

But she didn't fear him. She knew she was safe, and she really wanted to help him. Not that she could blame him for not opening up to her. He barely knew her, too.

If nothing else, she could rectify that. She wanted to get to know him better, anyway.

"So, I propose this. Let's put our drama aside for the night and just have fun. No worrying about work. No thinking about family. No bitching about the food."

The corner of his mouth quirked up.

"Let's just enjoy the evening. Talk. Laugh. Whatever. What do you say?"

"Not one comment about the food?"

"Only if it's positive."

He met her gaze. Started to say something, then stopped. Finally, he said, "You know, that sounds great."

She smiled.

His phone rang, and he reached into his pocket and rejected the call without even looking at caller ID.

"Shouldn't you get that?"

"Nope. I'm out with a beautiful woman and trying to enjoy myself. I'm not waiting on any important news." His face darkened for a moment, then he shrugged. "If it's my family, that can only spoil my mood. They can wait."

Deciding against prodding him to explain his brief mood shift, she went with his new attitude and smiled at him. "You said I was beautiful."

"I meant the waitress."

Her mind blanked, her confidence plunged.

"You have a mirror. You must know you're hideous." He grinned at her.

She relaxed a little but remained uncertain how to proceed from there.

Jensen reached across the table and grabbed her hand. "You know I'm joking, right? Shit." He looked away but kept hold of her fingers. "My timing really sucks lately."

She squeezed his hand. "You're fine. It was funny." It wasn't really.

"It wasn't really."

Amused that he parroted her thoughts, she smiled at him.

He met her gaze. "You aren't beautiful, Bella."

Her smile faltered, but she determined to show no reaction.

"You're stunning."

Air refused to inflate her lungs. She sat, her fingers entwined in his, the ambient noise from the restaurant fading into oblivion. There was only Jensen, his blue-eyed gaze sincere, his voice husky, his hand warm and firm.

"I didn't mean those insults earlier, and I don't mean to scare you off now." He shrugged. "Hell, I probably wouldn't have said either of those things if I wasn't still a little drunk."

"A little?" she asked.

He continued like she hadn't commented. "But you should know, I've been thinking about you since I met you. You… captivate me."

To hell with that stupid phrase from Jerry McGuire. Drunk or not, Jensen had her at 'stunning.' 'Captivate' sent her over the edge. She felt the heat rise to her cheeks and took a sip of her drink.

Unable to meet his unwavering stare, she rearranged her flatware. "Thank you. No one's ever said anything so… so remarkable to me before."

"I meant every word. Well, the good words."

She smiled. "I've been thinking about you, too."

"Yeah?"

She looked up into that deep sapphire gaze. "Yeah."

A grin spread across his face. He pulled his fingers away from hers and began rubbing his thumb in small circles over her knuckles.

He was very good with his fingers. Her face flamed again as her thoughts took an errant turn.

Janna brought their food then, and she looked like she fought back a smile. After placing the plates on the table, she tucked the tray under her arm, winked at Bella, and walked out of the room.

Seriously, what kind of attorney had no poker face? If the waitress could tell where her thoughts had gone, surely Jensen could.

Or maybe not. He was drunk, after all.

She chanced a glance at him. He made no attempt to conceal a wolfish grin.

Man, she must really be transparent, or he wasn't as drunk as she thought. Or both.

She pulled her hand away from his, arranged her napkin on her lap, and picked up a piece of pita bread.

Jensen nodded at her. "I thought this place was gluten free."

"It is. There's no wheat in this."

"A wheat-free pita?"

"It's delicious. Try it." She scooped up a generous portion of hummus and passed the bread triangle to him.

He cocked his brow but took the wedge. Looked at it from one angle. Then another.

"Just taste it."

Shrugging, he popped the whole thing in his mouth. He chewed once slowly. Then again. Then he nodded his head and chewed in earnest. After swallowing, he said. "That's not half bad."

She snorted. "Ha. It's freaking amazing, and you know it. Try your soup and the rice."

He spooned up a sip of the bisque, tasted it, and closed his eyes. "Mmm. That's good. Sweet."

"I know. Right?"

"I never tasted it so good before. Even our housekeeper's soup isn't this good. What's the secret?"

"I don't know. It might be the tomatoes. Maybe it's coconut milk. The chef doesn't share his secrets. Well, usually, anyway."

"Usually?"

"I've persuaded David to give me a few recipes in the past. Never this one, though."

He raised his eyebrow. "David? You're on a first name basis with the cook?"

"Okay, one, he's a chef. Trained at the International Culinary Institute in Switzerland."

"I didn't realize Switzerland was famous for food. Is it all neutral flavors?"

"Don't be an ass. And two, his food is so good, if he gives the recipe away, people won't buy his if they can just make their own."

"So, why'd he give any of the recipes up to you?" He slurped another sip of the soup.

"I can be persuasive."

"I see." His tone had a frosty edge to it.

She ignored his mood and pushed the rice closer to him. "Taste the risotto."

He sighed and picked up his fork. She saw the pleasure on his face before he ever spoke. "It's not bad. Maybe a little bland. Kind of neutral."

She plucked a carrot off the hummus platter and threw it at him. He missed batting it away, and it hit him in the forehead.

"You get one free one, and that was it."

Choosing another carrot, she grinned and held it between her finger and thumb, ready to throw.

He lifted a spoon full of the tomato bisque. "I hear tomato stains are a bitch to get out."

"You wouldn't dare."

"Try me."

She considered for a moment, then put the carrot down. "It's not polite to throw food, particularly in public."

"Says the girl who threw a carrot." But he put the spoon back in the bowl.

"There's one more thing you should know about David."

He scowled and stirred his risotto. "What? You're dating him? He lives with you? You're engaged?"

"You know, you're hostile when you've been drinking."

"So, I've been told," he muttered.

"Chef David is fifty-three years old and happily married to a lovely woman who tends the gardens here. I met them when I was just a little girl. He and my father were boyhood friends, and Dad still does some legal work for him."

"Sorry." Jensen looked up at her. "I don't know what my problem is lately. I'm just on edge."

"Don't worry about it. Not tonight." She took a sip of her drink and chose an olive off the hummus platter. "Tonight is all about having fun."

"So, I can throw food?"

"No, you may not. But if you're looking for more activity than lifting a fork and spoon, I know what we can do when we leave here."

He lifted an eyebrow. "Activity? Something… strenuous?"

She smiled. "If you do it right."

He started scooping the risotto in heaping spoonfuls, barely chewing between bites.

"OKAY." HE GLARED AT HER. "When you said strenuous activity, I didn't think you meant this."

The attendant put a pair of women's size seven inline skates on the rental counter. Bella grabbed them along with the men's size twelves and headed for a bench just outside the concession stand.

"Maybe exercising will metabolize the liquor faster," she said.

"I'm not even drunk anymore. All this is going to do is make me more dehydrated. And likely embarrass me."

"You can't skate?"

"The last time I was on skates was junior high."

"They say it's like riding a bike." She slipped off her shoes and grinned. "You never forget."

"Yeah, they say that about something else, too."

She chuckled. "We've got plenty of time for that."

It embarrassed her that she was so excited to be at a skating rink, let alone with a date. Her father had never allowed her the freedom to socialize, particularly with members of the opposite sex. Friends would talk about bowling, skating, movies—all kinds of fun things. She'd lived vicariously through them and their exploits. Being there now, especially with Jensen, was like a dream come true. Even if they were at least fifteen years older than most of the clientele. It still looked like so much fun.

The lights dimmed and the DJ announced a couple's skate. The disco ball sent spinning sparkles around the room, and a love song blared from the speakers. Young teenagers swarmed the floor and started skating slow laps, holding hands or embracing like dancers.

"Are you ready?" she asked.

Jensen grabbed her hand and lifted it to his lips. "How about we sit this one out?"

"Come on. It's a slow one. I'll hold your hand."

He cocked his head to the side.

Maybe that was too much. "Just until you get used to it, or you can just skate beside me."

"I have a better idea." He leaned toward her, placed his hand on her cheek, and leaned in for a kiss.

Did she really think she needed to skate laps across a scarred wooden floor to enjoy herself? Clearly the most fun a person could have at a roller rink was kissing a gorgeous man, sitting hip to hip with him and swaying to the music.

She put her hands around his neck, twirled her fingers through the hair curling at his collar.

He pulled her closer, and she got lost in the moment.

Bright lights pulled her out of her reverie. Orchestral music blared from the speakers, and the DJ beckoned everyone to the center of the floor to skate the chicken dance. Staying and skating had lost all appeal to her.

"Let's get out of here." She hurried back into her shoes and stood, holding her hand out to him.

He took it and pushed to his feet.

She led him out the door, a more private destination in mind.

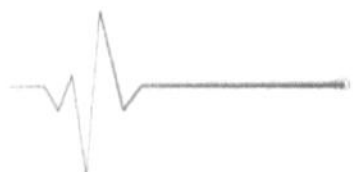

BELLA LAY THE WRONG DIRECTION on her bed, her feet on the headboard and her head on a pillow. After the evening she'd spent with Jensen, she needed advice.

Who better to ask about men than the one person on the planet who knew her better than anyone—her former college roommate and life-long best friend?

It also didn't hurt that Chloe was a serial dater. She probably knew the male mind better than anyone.

Who was she kidding? That, more than any other reason, was why she called her so close to midnight.

"I'm confused."

"It's not astrophysics, Bells. It's chemistry, plain and simple."

"I hated chemistry. All those moles...."

"God, I forget how literal you lawyers can be."

"It was a joke, Chloe."

"A feeble one."

"What do I do?"

"About what? I don't see a problem here."

Bella sighed and gritted her teeth. "What. Do. I. Do. About. Jensen?"

"Aw, sweetie. Don't do anything about him. Just do him."

"Damn it. I'm serious."

She'd just spent the most fabulous evening of her life. After the rocky start, they'd had an amazing time. They went to their spot at the lake, watched the stars, held each other. His kisses had promised so many more delights. His fingers began to roam. She'd never enjoyed herself more.

Until the panic set in. Her mind went on overdrive. Thoughts and worries collided inside her until she nearly screamed and ran away.

She froze. Completely unresponsive.

The unspoken question in his eyes told her he thought maybe he'd done something wrong, maybe he'd crossed a line. Maybe he just didn't do it for her. But he didn't complain, didn't push, didn't question her.

He'd been content to hold her, stare at the sky, and talk about absolutely nothing until she was ready to leave. A complete gentleman. Which only made her want him more.

But neither spoke of getting together again.

"Bells," Chloe said, snapping Bella back to reality. *"You've got three options. Tell him and hope it doesn't scare him off. Don't tell him and pray he doesn't notice. Or string him along until he gets fed up and leaves."*

Bella sniffed. She had a secret, not the plague. "What if I don't like any of those options?"

"I guess you have a fourth."

"Yeah?" Did she dare hope?

"End it now." And the line went dead.

Chloe could be such a bitch. Bella wished she'd never even called her.

Instead of dwelling on Jensen, she looked over her case file. At least she had some control over that.

CHAPTER 7

JENSEN HAD SUFFERED NEARLY CONSTANT headaches and stomachaches since his father tracked him down and summoned him home. Didn't matter if he ate or skipped meals, exercised or sat like a lump, got drunk or stayed sober… he felt like shit.

When dawn broke on the day of the parole hearing, he was awake to watch the sun creep past the horizon and climb into the sky. The view from the deck never failed to impress him, but this time, it failed to make him feel better. His head still pounded, stomach still churned.

Rage still coursed through his veins.

He had tried to prepare his statement the night before. His mother told him what the attorney had said—basically he didn't need to revisit evidence, he just needed to say what he felt about Wade's potential parole and why he felt that way. Easy enough… in theory, at least. But when he sat to organize his thoughts, they tangled and tumbled in complete disarray. After staring at blank note cards for hours, he gave up and decided to wing it, praying his emotions would guide his words.

With the morning light, however, he felt less than confident. If he couldn't give his words feelings when in the comfort of his home, what was the likelihood he'd voice them eloquently when in the emotionally charged venue of the hearing?

Jensen sipped his coffee and stared at the blank notes he'd brought out with him. Morning and a change of scenery did nothing to clear his thoughts. He'd have to improvise when he spoke. Hopefully he didn't make an ass of himself.

And hopefully it would satisfy his father.

BEFORE THEY WERE ALLOWED INSIDE the hearing room, Jensen paced in the hallway. His parents and Faith stood near the door talking to Tony Cooper, the arresting officer. Detective, actually. His father had been under investigation when Cooper first entered their lives. After the detective cleared his dad and then arrested Wade, he'd somehow become friends with the family. At least, friendly.

Oh, who was he kidding? His parents saw Cooper more than they saw him. Of course, they considered the cop a friend.

On any other occasion, Jensen might be jealous of Cooper's relationship with his dad. Maybe he was a little envious even on that day. But given the guy was going to give a statement against Wade's release, Jensen had nothing but gratitude for him at that moment.

He cracked his knuckles, a nervous habit he'd had since boyhood.

"Jensen," his father said, tone sharp, impatient.

No point in causing an argument then and there. His dad always hated it when he cracked his knuckles. Used to say it would damage his fingers and make surgery more difficult. When he'd finally told his father he didn't want to be a surgeon, the criticism had stopped. For a little while, anyway. It started up again the first time he'd visited from college.

Just another of the many, many reasons his visits had become fewer and further between.

Jensen sighed. Never in a million years did he envision this day. He was unprepared for how difficult it would be. The waiting? Torturous. He just wanted to get it over with.

What he really wanted was to not have to deal with it at all.

Before coming home, he'd say a perfect day would be a hike through the woods, a swim in the lake, and a bonfire with his friends. Roasting hot dogs and marshmallows. Drinking beer and telling stories.

Now, though, Bella fit in that picture. Hell, she was the picture. Didn't matter if they did any of those things or none at all. He just wanted to see more of her. Sure, he didn't know her that well. But he felt like he did, and he wanted to know more.

He wanted to be anywhere but there, and he wanted to be with anyone but Wade. But Bella? She kept creeping into his thoughts. He could even face the hearing better if she was there. He'd have asked her to go with him, but he didn't want any part of Wade's poison infecting what the two of them had. That's why he didn't mention it to her. That, and they weren't really at the share-the-worst-moment-of-your-life stage of their relationship yet.

Besides, he didn't want to appear needy when they were just starting out. She'd already held him while he fought back tears and nursed him back from a drunken binge. She didn't need to see him lose it in front of a panel of strangers, too.

"Jensen?"

Bella?

He looked up, saw her standing at the end of the hallway. How had she passed him without his noticing? Had he wished her there? Was she a figment of his imagination?

"Jensen?" his father asked. "Who is that?"

Nope. Not his imagination.

Bella approached him. She looked less like the natural beauty he'd been hanging out with and more like a woman who would grace the cover of *Fortune* magazine. Fancy black suit, those shoes with the red soles. Strand of pearls with earrings to match. And all that gorgeous brown hair swept up in some kind of twist. She looked like business—like a shark—cool, detached. Unaffected, unflappable. Unbeatable.

He'd wished for her, but not *this* version of her. This version he hardly recognized. And he wasn't sure he liked it.

"What are you doing here?" he asked. A tiny ember of hope flickered. Maybe it was to support him. But he quickly doused it. He'd never told her about any of this, so how would she know?

"My job." Her hand flicked to her necklace, the first sign he'd seen of her nerves.

"Are you a caseworker or something?" Seriously? No social worker he knew came from money like she did. She had to be—

"No. I'm an attorney." Her voice dropped lower, to barely a whisper. "A defense attorney."

That stomachache he'd been dealing with kicked up a notch.

A defense attorney.

God, no. Anything but that.

"What are you doing here?" she asked.

He could barely speak the words past the rage flowing through him. "My family is speaking at a parole hearing."

Her eyes widened, her hand stilled. The color drained from her face.

"Jensen." His mother touched his arm.

He'd never heard her approach. A quick glance behind him showed his father and sister had stayed by the door. Thank God for small favors.

"Why don't you introduce me to your friend?" his mom asked.

But he just stood there. Numb. Furious. Friend?

Ha. Hardly. He could call Bella many things—at the moment, some pretty colorful and vulgar things—but friend was not one of them.

"Mrs. Keller, I presume." Bella extended her hand, shook his mother's when she offered it. "I'm Bella Perish. It's a pleasure to meet you."

"How do you two know each other? School?"

"No, ma'am. We met just recently."

"Oh, how nice. Is that why you're here?"

"No, Mom." Jensen answered his mother, but his gaze never left Bella's face. "She's a defense attorney. She's here to set criminals free."

DID HE PUT OFF SOME sort of cosmic beacon that drew problems to him?

He'd wished for Bella to be there, but not in that capacity. He wanted her to be there for him, not for Wade and people like him. Why did she have to be there as a defense attorney?

His fault. He should have asked her what she did before he got so damn wrapped up in her. Served him right.

His mother cleared her throat. "Oh. I see. Well, then, if you'll excuse me." She retreated to the rest of the family.

No support there. Mom would say she just wanted to give him time and space, but what she really wanted was to avoid confrontation. She hated confrontation. Of course, she'd have to deal with Dad, so she was shit out of luck there.

He turned his attention back to Bella. He felt shit out of luck, too. Then Bella's words registered, and his blood ran cold. "Wait. Did you say 'Perish' was your last name?"

"Yes." She blinked at him.

"What's your father's name?"

"Victor."

"Perish. Do you have a sibling? Someone else who works with your dad?"

She paused. Looked away. Her answer sounded fake, forced. "No."

He struggled to make sense of what his sister had told him, what Bella was saying. He couldn't put it together. Finally, he moved on, leaving a question nagging the deep recesses of his mind. "Why didn't you tell me you were a defense attorney?"

"Why didn't you tell me your family was a victim of a crime?"

"Who walks around saying that?" His words, too loud for a private discussion, carried through the hallway and caused people to turn their gazes on him. He grabbed her arm, pulled her aside, away from the crowd, and lowered his voice. "Seriously. When people first meet, they discuss their careers. They don't mention the most horrible events in their histories. That's at least a third date discussion."

She scoffed. "That's not my understanding of what happens on a third date."

He gritted his teeth, clenched his fists. "Now's not the time, Bella. You should have said something."

"I told you I work for my father. That's he's difficult. If you were really interested, you could have looked us up. Then you would have known."

"How? You never even told me your last name."

That left her momentarily speechless. When she finally spoke, her tone sounded resigned. "You're right. I guess I didn't. I felt like I was really getting to know you. It didn't occur to me that I never gave you my full name or asked yours. Which, by the way, you never volunteered."

Jensen sighed. "Yeah, well, that part's not all your fault."

"So, are we good?"

His mouth popped open, and he had to make a determined effort to close it. "You're kidding, right?"

"What? It was just a little misunderstanding."

"A little—" He ran his hand through his hair. "Bella, I'm here to try to keep a man behind bars. A man who killed my sister and nearly destroyed my family. How can I possibly be involved with the woman working to set him free?"

She shook her head. "I don't understand what you're talking about. I'm not here representing a murderer."

"Then why are you here?"

"I'm representing a man convicted of theft. No one died. He wasn't even armed. And not that I owe you the details of the case, I felt the same way about him at first. Until I found out he was unemployed, and his little girl was sick.

He tried to take some medicine and rice from a drugstore. Hardly a hardened criminal. If anything, the system failed him, not the other way around."

He blinked. A tiny flicker of hope sparked inside. Maybe he could get past this. Maybe she was the Robin Hood of attorneys and only defended people she thought got a bum deal. Maybe it wasn't as bad as he thought.

Even as he searched her face for unvoiced answers, the doors at the far end of the hall burst open. A large man in a dark suit strode toward them, his countenance so much more than confident. Much like that of a king entering his court. The man scanned the hallway. His gaze didn't linger on Jensen, but rather focused with laser-like intensity on Bella.

"Isabella. You're here early."

She raised an eyebrow but didn't answer him.

He glanced at his watch. "Come with me. I'll review the case with you before we start. Then you can see how it really is done." Without acknowledging Jensen, or anyone else in the hall, he strode toward the hearing room and walked inside, not even bothering to clear his entry with the guards at the door.

Bella looked at Jensen, the apology in her eyes never leaving her lips. Not that he'd accept it from her if she gave voice to it. Then she stepped around him and followed her father wordlessly inside.

It was only then that Jensen realized he'd stepped back, away from Bella's father. He could hardly blame her from bowing to his will. The guy was a force of nature. He'd never even acknowledged Jensen's existence, yet Jensen had responded by giving the guy a wide berth.

Maybe Bella wasn't one hundred percent to blame. Her dad made his look tame, and she said she was only there for what he could only hope was a down-on-his-luck guy with a sick kid.

Not her fault her father swept her up in his wake.

Of course, now she would be sitting beside her father as he defended Wade.

Wait. Isabella?

Victor. Isabella. Perish. V. I. Per. Viper.

The hallway dimmed, tilted. His stomach lurched.

"Jensen."

His father snapping at him brought his focus back to the situation at hand.

"Obviously, we can go in now. Why are you just standing there?"

He didn't answer his father. He just headed for the door.

"Now, listen. When we go in there, just keep your mouth shut. It would—"

Jensen stopped listening. "Yeah, I got it. Give it a rest."

One overbearing man was enough for the hearing. Two, he couldn't tolerate. He ignored his lecturing father and entered the hearing venue.

CHAPTER 8

BELLA KNEW SHE WAS DIFFERENT from most attorneys. As a general rule, most young lawyers would kill for a chance to sit second chair to a legend like her father. Not her, though.

She detested it.

She never considered it an opportunity for her to learn from a master. In her case, it was an opportunity for her father to observe her and create a list of all her faults.

This time it was so much worse. She didn't just suffer under the critical eye of the Great Victor Perish. No. She also had to contend with the censure of Jensen and his entire family.

She chanced a glance across the room. Jensen and his father seemed to be arguing. Most likely about her. She couldn't hear them, but both had furrowed brows and red faces. His father gestured rather violently a few times. His mother and a girl who was probably his sister sat huddled together, staring at the members of the parole commission, staying out of the heated discussion.

"I said, what would your strategy be?"

Bella looked at her father. She fought not to cower under his stare, but he positively glowered at her.

"I expect you to not only focus, but to give one hundred percent of your attention to cases where I ask you to participate."

"You don't want me to participate. You're still angry with me for not preparing my case the way you wanted—"

"The way I taught you. The right way."

"—so, you're making me second chair this case without giving me time for any prep work before dragging me in here. This is just another one of your many punishments masquerading as lessons."

"Regardless of my motives, at present, you aren't giving any attention to the matter at hand." He tapped folders on the table. "Instead, you're staring at the enemy."

"The enemy? You act like we're going to battle. They're just a grieving family."

"That's where you're wrong, Isabella. And that's exactly why I'm concerned about your commitment to the job. Every trial, every hearing, every discussion in judge's chambers or at the bench—it's all a battle. You can only win if you're battle ready. That means having all your weapons primed and knowing when and how to use them. You're ineffective because you're soft and ill-prepared."

"Ineffective?" The loudness of her voice surprised her, and she dropped her tone to just above a whisper. "How can you say I'm ineffective when you haven't even learned the results of my hearing yet? Which, by the way, I won."

"You're ineffective because you aren't prepared for this case."

"Why would I be? It's not mine."

"You've been looking over the file. Presumably. But when I asked you about this case, not only could you not answer my questions, you didn't even realize I'd asked you anything. You're head's not in the game. Ineffective."

"Well, for starters, this isn't a game. It's a man's freedom on the line and the emotional well-being of the survivors of his victim. And second, this isn't my case. So, what if I glanced through the file? That's far different than preparing it for weeks, studying the facts and the nuances of the materials. You can't say I'm ill-prepared when I have no reason to be prepared for this hearing at all."

"You should be prepared for any contingency. I have no doubt that I could have taken your case today without having worked on it and still made certain he got released. I know you can't say the same for my client."

"And I shouldn't have to! You've studied the facts of his case, the reports from the jail. You've met the guy, interviewed him. I haven't done any of that."

"And I haven't done any of that for your client. But that wouldn't have stopped me from securing his release."

"You act like I lost. I won my client's release."

Victor merely continued staring at her.

"That's it. I'm out of here." She stood up, grabbed her briefcase, and started to scoot past her father toward the aisle.

He grabbed her arm. "Sit. Down."

She stared at him, torn between taking her stand—especially because of Jensen and his family—and fearing her father. It didn't amount to much of an internal struggle.

She sat back down.

Coward.

Only once she'd returned to his side did he let go of her arm. "Never embarrass me like that again, Isabella. Do you understand?"

She nodded but didn't meet his gaze.

"I asked you a question."

"Yes, sir." Shame stung her cheeks, burned her eyes. She swallowed past a lump in her throat but said nothing else. Instead, she sat, small in her seat, looking down at the table so as not to see the reactions of anyone in the room.

Her father gestured again to the folder in front of her.

"Review this. Quickly. They're about to start."

She knew her father would never allow her to so much as utter a peep during the hearing. But she studied the file. There would likely be a quiz later, and she hated to think what would happen if she failed it.

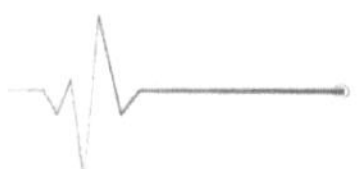

BELLA HUNCHED OVER THE TABLE, staring at the file her father had presented her with. She tried to learn the material. She really did. She rifled through the pages but found it impossible to focus on anything but Jensen. Words floated in front of her. Wade Unger. Doctor. Pharmaceutical theft. Motorcycle tampering. Involuntary manslaughter. But those words barely scratched the surface of the file. Meanwhile, Jensen's face turned scarlet, his jaw ticked. She could feel the anger emanating from him, waves of rage tangible to her even across the room. She lifted the file in front of her face, hoping to hide from his ire. Yet she could still feel it.

She slouched in her seat, tried to hide behind her father. So intent was she on at least looking absorbed, she jumped when her father not-so-subtly nudged her.

The prisoner had arrived.

A guard escorted Wade Unger to their table. She compared his appearance to that of his photo in the file. Prison had not been kind to him, nor should it have been. His hair had grayed. Hell, his complexion had grayed—no longer the healthy tan of a vibrant man, but rather the washed-out tone of an invalid. His wrinkled skin sagged on his skull, like even his skeleton had withered over the last eight years.

He looked like a corpse, but Bella found no sympathy for him. He might look like the walking dead, but Jensen's sister was dead.

And Unger was responsible.

Something didn't feel right. The proceedings seemed off. Five members of the Parole Commission sat behind a table—where a judge would be in a courtroom—facing everyone in attendance. More people attended this particular session than Bella had ever before seen at a parole hearing. Usually only the hearing examiner conducted the proceedings. Maybe two of them, certainly, never five. And since when did a potential parolee need two attorneys? Bella was accustomed to case managers attending. They sat with the prisoner. But Unger's case manager sat behind them, not with them. Several members of the prison staff, not just one or two, stood in the back, including the warden.

No, this wasn't like any hearing Bella had ever attended. She didn't know why things were different, but they were, and she definitely didn't like it.

Especially with Jensen having such a high stake in the outcome.

The hearing examiner brought the room to order, read off Unger's name and case number, glanced through his file.

"In the interest of moving these proceedings along, we'll waive the review of the charges for which Mr. Unger is currently incarcerated."

"So stipulated," her father said.

That violated both protocol and her father's code of conduct. In his view, rule number one—never to be broken—was to follow procedure.

She chanced a glance at Jensen. Neither he nor his family seemed surprised. Clearly, they didn't know how unusual it was to waive the reading. And why would they?

"I see this is your first offense," the examiner continued, addressing Unger.

"Yes, sir."

"And your supervisor is pleased with your work."

"I asked his immediate supervisor to attend today," the warden said. "If you'd like, he can elaborate on his written review of Mr. Unger's performance."

Bella flipped through the file. His job was with animal husbandry. A drug dealer should never be given that work duty at a prison. Not only would he have access to narcotics, he'd be taken away from the prison proper to work in a minimum-security area.

The examiner glanced down, flipped through some pages. "It says here that Mr. Unger is always prompt, is gentle with the animals, and has actually assisted with diagnosis and treatment of a few sick cattle."

"That's right," a man next to the warden said.

"Do you have anything to add to this report?"

"Nothing but more praise," the man said. "He's been an asset to the program."

"So noted," the examiner said. "There's no need for further reporting."

Diagnosis and treatment?

What was going on?

He looked at Unger. "I see here there's a plan in place should your parole be granted."

Bella's father stood. "There is, sir. A landlord of an apartment complex in downtown Cathedral Lake has promised him a room with reasonable rent, and a local business has agreed to hire him, guaranteeing he'll be able to make his way independently."

Seriously? A room? A job? Where were the details? Where were the questions? The concerns? Her instincts sounded warning bells and whistles. Something was up. Nothing about this hearing was normal.

"Very well. This panel sees no reason to deny parole—"

"Pardon me." A man sitting with Jensen's family stood. "It's customary for the victim's family to have a chance to speak at these hearings."

The examiner slid his glasses down and stared at the man over the tops of the frames. "Detective… Cooper, isn't it?"

"Yes, sir."

"Are you telling me how to do my job?"

"No, sir. But the family of Hope Keller is here to offer their perspectives on—"

"I've been doing this a long time, Detective. I know exactly what they feel, what they wish to say. They've been given the opportunity to voice their opinions. I've thoroughly reviewed a written statement from the victim's father." His gaze traveled over Jensen and his family before settling on Vanessa. His tone gentled. "I have no doubt this is difficult for you, ma'am. You lost your little girl. But nothing we do here will bring her back. So, what we must do now is move forward with the best interests of all living parties involved."

He glanced around the room, addressed the whole assembly. "It is this panel's opinion that Dr. Unger has paid his debt to society, has shown nothing other than remorse for his actions, and will be more use to the community as a working member rather than a burden on its resources."

He looked at Unger. "It is with all these factors in mind that we grant you your parole, effective immediately."

If Bella had even the slightest doubt about the proceedings being off, it was squelched with that last comment. No one—not for any reason—received an immediate release. There were procedures to follow, forms to fill out, preparations to be made. It took days, weeks. She'd seen it take months, certainly not mere seconds.

Unger stood and shook her father's hand, then he reached for hers. No way would she congratulate him, nor would she accept his thanks. She just looked at his hand and turned her back on him. She heard him being led away.

She looked at Jensen. The devastation on his face mirrored that of his mother and sister. His father's face seemed set in stone and he looked toward Unger, the hatred palpable even across the room. The detective—Cooper?—stepped in front of him, forcing his gaze off her father's client. Before any of them could say or do anything else, some of the men who had been standing in the back with the warden approached them and led Dr. Keller into the hallway, making the detective stay behind.

Jensen started to go after them, but Cooper held him back. Then Jensen looked across the aisle and met her gaze. He raised a brow as if asking her what had happened or what he could do.

She shrugged and shook her head. She hadn't a clue.

"And that," her father said to her, "is how a hearing is won."

"Won?" She all but sputtered her reply to him. "How is cheating winning?"

His face darkened and he bent down, almost nose-to-nose with her. "Watch your tone, young lady. There are elements at play here that you can't even begin to fathom. But you will never, and I mean never, challenge me like that again. Especially in public. Are we clear?"

She set her jaw.

"Isabella. I asked you a question."

"Clear."

"Good. Now let's go. We can get in about six billable hours if we skip lunch."

"I'm done."

He glared at her, his face turning a frightening shade of puce.

She swallowed and rushed on. "Done. For the day. I need a break."

When he spoke, his voice was soft. Deadly. "You're done when I say you're done."

Despite her fear, her anger surged, and she couldn't stop her outburst. "No. I'm done now. This was a fiasco. A sham. And you're shutting me out and dragging me down all at the same time. I need a god damned break!" She gathered her things and turned away.

"You leave now, young lady, and that break will be permanent."

She hesitated for the tiniest of seconds before storming out of the room without a backward glance. Hell, if she'd stand there and get lectured and threatened on top of getting lied to. She needed to clear her head.

Then she'd start digging into what really just happened.

CHAPTER 9

JENSEN LEFT COOPER—LEFT HIS family—behind and went to find his father. Dad had prepared a written statement? Then why were they all forced to go and sit through this? Why did his father summon him home at all? And what the hell had just happened in there?

He found his dad down the hall with the men who'd escorted him out. Not knowing what else to do, Jensen approached them, but they glowered at him and stopped speaking as he drew near. His father waved him away. He stood his ground, but his father glared his way and spoke one sharp, tense word. "Jensen."

What else could he do? He had no recourse but to leave.

He caught up with his mother and sister, who were being escorted outside by Cooper. The detective had one arm around each woman. Faith had tears rolling down her cheeks. "I thought Dad would at least do something. Say something. Anything." His sister moaned. His mother sobbed hysterically.

"Mom."

She cried too hard to hear him, or she felt too despondent to care. He wasn't sure. So, he looked at Cooper for answers.

The cop shook his head and kept walking. He whispered something to them in soft tones.

Jensen watched them until they rounded the corner at the end of the hall and walked out of sight. His dad didn't want his help. His mom and sister didn't need him. He had no one to turn to, no one to ask questions, no one to share his anguish.

The rage roiled inside him. The helplessness consumed him, threatened to swallow him whole, to consume him into a deep, black void.

He wanted to cry, to scream, but no sound escaped him. He needed to collapse to the ground, dissolve into the earth like his sister before him. But his legs stubbornly held him upright.

If he didn't do something, anything, to react, to make sense of what just happened, he'd… he'd… hell, he didn't know what he'd do.

Explode. Implode. Boil, evaporate. Dissipate.

He sucked in a deep breath, readied himself for a desperate howl.

Then she entered the hallway.

Bella.

Viper.

She set Unger free. She lied about who she was, what she did. She bore the responsibility for all of it.

And she would pay.

Dearly.

He exhaled his breath. Slow. Deliberate. Controlled.

Then he stalked her as she avoided the elevator and headed for the stairs. He waited until she was part way down, then he took the stairs two at a time and caught her on the landing.

Jensen grabbed her arm and swung her around. Her eyes widened, but she didn't try to pull away. Didn't even flinch.

Her mistake. She should be frightened. The mood he was in? She didn't know him well enough to know how angry he was.

Fuck, they didn't know each other at all.

That cooled him off. A fraction. Not enough to get him to back off, though.

She glanced at his hand and then up into his face. "I'm sure you're quite upset about what just happened, but that doesn't give you the right to manhandle me. Let go of my arm."

He squeezed it tighter, partly because he needed to do something, partly to see what she'd do. When she didn't give him any reaction at all, his frustration grew, and he flung her arm aside.

She brushed off her sleeve and straightened her jacket. "Now that you've calmed yourself, we can discuss this rationally."

"Calm? You think I'm calm?"

"Calmer than you were. Calm enough to listen to me."

"Listen to you?" He scoffed. "And why would I do that? So, you could tell me more lies?"

"Lies? I never lied to you."

"So, you told me you were a defense attorney? You told me you and your dad were some power team that no one wins against? You happened to mention you were representing my sister's murderer and getting him released early?"

She sighed and shook her head. "A, we've already established that I didn't discuss my career. Why would I? You didn't ask, and I don't enjoy my work. But I didn't lie about it. I don't lie. B, my father and I aren't some legendary duo that—"

"Viper."

She closed her eyes, took a deep breath. "I hate that moniker. It's ridiculous. But I know I told you I have issues with my father. I may not have elaborated, but it certainly wasn't a lie. And C, I wasn't representing Dr. Unger. My father was. I wasn't even aware of his case until he saw me in the hall and called me in. And, not that you'd know or care, he didn't ask me because we're some unstoppable force together. He insisted because he wanted to teach me something."

"Oh, yeah." Jensen sneered at her. "And what was this valuable lesson from the great Victor Perish? How to hurt innocent people and endanger society?"

She tipped her head to the side. Her eyes sparked with something dark—anger, frustration. But she spoke with a calm tone that almost conveyed pity.

Almost.

"Jensen, I understand how you must feel. But I didn't set out to hurt you. I never lied to you. And I'm very sorry about what happened, particularly the part my father and the firm played. But—"

"There's always a but."

She continued like he hadn't interrupted. "—you have to understand something. This was not a normal, run-of-the-mill parole hearing, and not just because of my father being there, either."

That stopped him. Cold. Finally, someone willing to give him information. Biased as that source was, he'd take what he could get. "What do you mean?"

"I mean typical parole hearings are beneath my father. Nothing about this procedure—nothing—went by the book."

"What was different?"

"Where do I even start?" She dropped her bag to the floor and leaned against the railing. "There were too many people on the panel. Too many people in attendance. They didn't review the file. They didn't let the victim's family speak. No one with anything negative to say was given the opportunity, and the people with positive things to say practically fell over themselves to do so."

"You mean, it was like they were following a script?"

"I don't know about that, and I'm not about to make an allegation I can't substantiate. But too many things didn't follow procedure, and parolees are never released immediately."

"So, the panel is crooked? Maybe Wade paid someone off?"

"I can't say that, either. All I can definitively say is this was unusual. Off-the-charts unusual."

He sighed. He couldn't say that he felt any better, but at least he felt better informed.

She bent and picked up her bag. "I'm sorry. For all of it. But I'm not sorry for the time we spent together before today. But mostly? Mostly, I'm sorry for what might have been." She looked like she tried to smile, but it never quite materialized. "Goodbye, Jensen."

He watched her walk down the stairs and out of his life.

And all the pain he felt earlier rushed back.

Maybe more pain than before.

But he refused to dwell on it. He headed home. His family needed to hear what he'd learned.

"**WHAT DO YOU MEAN YOU** can't tell me what's going on?" Jensen fought not to scream at his father. Instead, he stood and started pacing around the kitchen. "I just told you what Bella said. Everything about that hearing was wrong. Something's going on, and clearly you know about it. Or at least some of it."

"Some things are better kept on a need-to-know basis." His father stayed seated and sipped from his coffee cup. "And you don't need to know."

Jensen glanced at his mother and then his sister. Both stayed silent and avoided his gaze. He spoke to his father. "Need to know? You insisted I come home because I needed to be a part of this hearing. Clearly, I didn't need to be here. Apparently, I could have sent in a written statement. But I was here because of you. I sat through that entire ridiculous farce of a hearing. So now, after everything went horribly wrong and we know something more is going on, you try to shut me out?"

"I didn't insist you come home. I just thought you'd want to be here. Didn't you want to support your sister? Voice your opinion?"

"You didn't tell me what I was coming home for! You just issued your mandate and expected me to obey you. If you thought I'd want to be here, you should have told me about the hearing, let me make my own choice. Given me the option to write a letter and avoid all of this. I certainly wasn't needed there. None of us was."

"Maybe you didn't need to speak, but don't think for a second your mother and Faith didn't need you there. They needed the support."

"But not you, Dad. Right? Not you."

"Look, I—" Royce ran his hand through his hair and sighed, but never finished speaking.

Jensen thought for a moment. His dad knew more than he was saying. He was prepared for what went down. Hell, he had actually told Jensen in the hall outside the hearing not to bother talking.

"You know, Dad, we didn't get to say a word today which is against procedure. And you knew we weren't going to speak. You know a lot more than you've told us. I want to know what's going on. I want to know why, and it seems you're the only one who has answers."

"Things change, Jensen. I knew you'd want to be here for your sister. I thought things would go differently. Apparently, I was wrong."

"Right." What a liar. "Well, there's a first time for everything. Write the date down. Dad admitted he was wrong."

"Jensen." His mother's voice was a soft censure in the growing cacophony of their heated debate. "Your sarcasm isn't helping anything."

"Did he tell you?" Jensen searched his mother's face for any indication that she knew more than he did. "Do you know why the hearing was handled that way? Why we couldn't talk? What those men wanted?"

Faith shoved her chair back and leapt to her feet. "Stop it! Just stop it! You've always picked and picked until you found out every little detail. Been so angry and obstinate if you felt left out of something. But guess what? Not everything is about you. People are allowed to keep secrets from you, Jensen. You aren't entitled to know everything about other people's lives."

"This isn't about other people, Faith. It's about us."

"You're such a hypocrite. You want to know every little detail of dad's conversation with those men, all the while you're keeping secrets of your own. So, put up or shut up, Jensen. Because I'm sick of being in the middle of all this."

Secrets? He only had one secret, and he hadn't shared it with Faith. So how did she know? What did she know?

"Secrets?" his father said. "What secrets? Faith?"

Faith looked at Jensen, then her father, then Jensen again. Without another word, she ran out of the room. Jensen heard the front door slam.

"Well, Jensen?" his father asked.

He thought about telling his father. He knew he was almost out of time and had to tell him soon, anyway. That, or give up on any kind of fulfilling future. This was as good a time as any to fess up. But without his dad opening up, he couldn't make himself share his secret. Instead, he stormed out of the kitchen and out the front door.

Faith was nowhere to be found, but he wasn't in the mood to talk with her, either. He had another person in mind.

JENSEN SAT ON A BENCH in the park, hoping to blend into the background. He didn't want people staring at him, didn't want to interact with the world. The only thing he wanted was answers. So, he'd called Tony about twenty minutes earlier and spent the time waiting for him people watching.

Mothers with bags under their eyes pushed strollers down the path, stifling yawns and offering their children snacks of crackers, fruit, or dry cereal. Older children skateboarded or rode bicycles, laughing and chasing each other. Office workers hurried through the park, often talking or tapping on their phones as they headed to or from the corner coffee shop or some chic nearby eatery.

People looked tired, happy, busy… but none looked as worried or anxious as he felt. He wished to God he hadn't come home. But, home or not, this would be happening. At least with him back in Cathedral Lake, he could try to figure out what was going on, try to manage the situation. He owed it to Hope to try.

Detective Cooper strode down the path. Like Jensen, he'd changed out of the suit he'd worn to the hearing and wore the attire Jensen was used to seeing him in—jeans, V-neck t-shirt, boots. When he reached the bench, he sat and tucked his aviator shades on his neckline, letting them hang from the point of the V.

Neither spoke for a few minutes. Cooper stretched his long legs out in front of him and pulled a pack of gum from his pocket. He took a piece and offered the pack to Jensen, who declined.

Cooper stuffed the gum back in his pocket and popped a piece in his mouth. He cracked it a few times, then turned to Jensen. "Glad as I am to spend my lunch break with a friend, I'd like it to include words. Or food. Or both."

"Sorry. Want to go grab a slice or something?"

"Nah." He patted his stomach and sighed. "Too many pizzas and burgers lately. Gotta start watching again."

Jensen looked at the man sitting next to him and glanced down at his abs, obviously flat from good genes or hard work—or a combination of both—and smothered a snort of derision. The guy didn't have to watch anything. Where Jensen, on the other hand, had to work out six days a week to even approach that level of fitness. Other than the day he overdid it to burn off some steam, it had been days since he'd hit the gym.

Soon he'd be a gangly wire-framed weakling or a big blob of goo.

He stared across the park, bemoaning yet another way he didn't measure up to people in the world around him. Mental note—hit the gym. Regularly.

"So, I'm guessing we aren't here to discuss my diet. What's up?"

"This morning. The hearing." Jensen had so many questions, but he didn't know where to begin. He sighed and rubbed his hands over his face.

"Figured that's what you wanted. Look, kid—"

"I'm not a kid, Tony. Haven't been since I met you." The guy couldn't be that much older than Jensen, anyway.

Cooper turned and looked at Jensen. "Too true. So, I'll be frank. What happened today? I've never seen anything like it."

"That's why I called. I spoke to one of the attorneys for Unger. She said the same thing. And my dad and those guys? What was that all about? He won't tell me anything, but he sure didn't seem surprised by the results of the hearing. I just want some answers."

"I've told you all I know. The hearing didn't go like a regular hearing. But I don't know what those guys said to your dad. You'll have to ask him."

Frustration surged through Jensen, overwhelming the tenuous hold he had on reason. "You're a law official in the thick of this thing, but you don't know anything? Bullshit. You're shutting me out, too, just like my dad. If you aren't going to share what you know, then what the hell good are you?"

Cooper rested his elbows on his knees and turned to look straight into Jensen's eyes. "You can be a real dick sometimes, you know that? I didn't have to come here, didn't have to talk to you at all. You want to be treated like an adult? Act like one."

Jensen sighed. "Look, I'm sorry. It's infuriating. I'm summoned home for this damn thing, only to be shut out of it. Either I'm involved or I'm not. It can't be halfway. I don't know what to do about it."

A woman pushing a stroller down the path while trying to shepherd two energetic boys looked at Jensen and stopped in her tracks. She yelled to the boys, grabbed them both by the shoulders, and turned them in the opposite direction. Then, shooting him one last dirty look, she spun the stroller around and hurried after the boys.

"What the hell was that all about?" Cooper asked.

Jensen recognized her from a foggy memory of his drunken binge at Sean's Pub and Grille. God, he was such an ass. "Like you said, Tony. Sometimes I can be a dick."

The detective stood and put his sunglasses back on. "Yeah, well, don't feel too bad about that. Given everything going on, I'd say you're entitled to a bad mood or two. Just don't make a habit of it."

"Easier said than done."

Cooper took a few steps down the path, then stopped and turned around. He walked back to Jensen. "Listen. I wasn't lying when I said I don't know anything. But I have my suspicions."

Jensen looked up at him. "I'll take it."

He looked around and lowered his voice. "Those guys with your dad? I know they weren't local PD. Not even local state patrol. I don't think they were the warden's men, either."

"What makes you say that?"

The detective shrugged. "Partly the way they handled themselves. Partly because of how they were dressed. Mostly intuition."

"So, if they aren't from your force, the state police, or the prison, who are they?"

"Who's left, Jensen?"

He ran all the key players through his mind. No one from the hospital. Certainly, none of the drug dealers. No respected men from the Cathedral Lake community. If they weren't cops or prison guards, he had no idea who they were. He shrugged and looked at Cooper.

"Feds, Jensen."

"The Feds? What the hell do they have to do with Unger? Or my dad?"

"Like I said, I only have a hunch. Talk to your dad again. If you figure anything out, let me know." He turned and strode down the path.

Jensen watched him walk out of the park. There was no point talking to his dad again that left him with only one option.

CHAPTER 10

BELLA STOOD ON THE STOOP of the gorgeous brownstone, looking at the identifying placard on the wall—*Tod Jeffers, Therapist.*

Why did she listen to Chloe anyway?

Therapy is all the rage, she'd said. Anyone who's anyone spends time on the couch, she'd said. Why get advice from me when you can get advice from a professional, she'd said.

If you find a hot one and fuck him, you won't even have to pay, she'd said.

Really, why did Bella listen to her? Chloe's advice had gotten her into plenty of scrapes over the years, so Bella was torn. On one hand, professional help had to be better than Chloe's advice. But, given that Chloe's advice was to seek professional help, it was likely bad advice. Bella agonized over the decision and finally decided her best recourse was a pro. Chloe used her connections to get her an appointment with an exclusive and highly regarded therapist that afternoon. Apparently, the guy was seeing her after his regular hours ended which would surely cost her. Damn it, anyway. She'd sat in her car, staring at her cell phone, cursing every person, place, and thing that had conspired to get her to that point. Then she'd driven across town for her first ever therapy session.

But standing at the door, on the threshold of facing her fears and failures, she seriously considered continuing to live in misery and denial. In fact, she began to embrace that lifestyle and turned to walk back to her car.

Then she heard the door swing open. "Isabella Perish?"

The deep baritone voice washed over her like hot fudge over ice cream, melting her resolve, and she hungered to see if the voice matched the man. Very slowly, deliberately, she turned around.

It matched. And then some. How inappropriate would it be to salivate upon meeting one's therapist, anyway? Maybe she'd reconsider Chloe's last piece of advice. The guy was smoking hot. Way too good looking to be a shrink. A body she could bounce a quarter off. A face male models would covet. Hazel eyes to get lost in. Thick, dark hair that screamed, 'run your fingers through me' as the waves kissed the collar of his shirt.

Oh, yeah. She could see herself on his couch.

And in his bed.

Her cheeks flamed as she reigned in her apparently long-neglected libido. A mental mantra—He's your therapist, and he's too old for you, anyway. He's your therapist, and he's too old for you, anyway—ran through her head, and she cursed Chloe. Every damn time she listened to her, it bit her in the ass. Perpetual headaches and drama.

"Dr. Jeffers. I'm Bella Perish." She extended her hand. "Nice to meet you."

He shook her hand. "Were you going somewhere?"

She chewed on her lower lip and met his gaze. It would be so easy to get lost in the hypnotic flecks of green and blue. Instead, she cleared her throat and turned toward the street. "Um, well. Yeah. I… I reconsidered this. Therapy isn't for me."

"And you've talked to so many therapists that you know this from experience?"

"What?" She turned back and looked at him. "No! I'm not crazy. I've never even seen a—" Well, clearly the word 'shrink' was inappropriate. "—therapist before."

He smiled. "'Crazy' isn't a clinical term, Ms. Perish, and no one said you were."

Okay, she'd never been to therapy, but a therapist's job was to help, right? The description was in the title of the position, for pity's sake. So why did he immediately have her off-kilter and on-edge?

She sighed. Paranoia much?

Maybe she needed his help more than she thought. She chewed on her lip again and pondered her options.

Dr. Jeffers didn't wait for her to make up her mind. He pushed his door open wide and gestured for her to enter.

Kind of hard to avoid going in when to do so would insult him or so she rationalized. Stooping down, she ducked under his arm and walked inside.

And tried hard not to notice how amazing he smelled. Bold citrus, warm spice. Damn near edible.

She took a deep, shuddering breath and waited for him to direct her out of the foyer.

He led her to a spacious yet cozy office, expertly decorated, with bookshelves along the wall and a comfy-looking furniture grouping around a refreshment-laden coffee table. After gesturing to the leather sofa, he walked to a chair on the other side of the table and sat.

Leaving her to face the ubiquitous therapist's couch.

Without another option, she took a seat on the very edge of a cushion, keeping her feet firmly planted on the ground. No way would she become a cliché and lie down for her session.

"So," Dr. Jeffers said, "you mentioned you were having some man trouble." He glanced at a file. "Care to be more specific?"

"Men," she said.

"Pardon?"

"Men. Not one man. Two men."

"Are you conflicted about dating two men at once?"

The laugh burst out of her before she could contain it. She wiped her eyes and sighed. "I'm sorry. If you understood my dating history, you'd realize how ridiculous that is."

He put the file down and sat back, crossed one leg over the other knee. "I'm afraid I don't understand what your problem is, then."

"Two very distinct problems, two very distinct men."

He waited for her to continue.

She really considered getting up and running out, but that would be the final humiliating straw on her already enormous haystack of shame. Completely unbearable. It would break her.

"My father and my… well, I don't really know what he is."

"All right. Let's tackle things one at a time. Tell me about your father."

What could she say about Victor Perish? He was opinionated. Driven. Obsessive. Domineering. Overbearing. Controlling. Manipulative.

How to say any of that and not come off like a spoiled brat?

"Isabella?"

"Bella. Please. My father calls me Isabella. I hate it."

"Okay. Have you ever told your father you prefer to be called Bella?"

This time she didn't try to stifle her reaction—a very un-lady-like snort of derision. "Tell him my preference? No one tells Victor Perish to do things a different way. If he told the sun to rise in the west, it would."

"He seems to have quite a hold on you. Why do you think that is?"

Why, indeed? Why did she bend to his every wish and whim? She knew damn well and didn't want to give the reason voice. She took a sudden interest in the rug on the floor, the pattern swirling and dancing in what looked like an ordered, yet carefree, manner. If only her life could be as simple and easy as that beautiful textile.

All she had in common with it was that they both got stepped on and the rug fared better than she did.

"My father is…" Complicated? Difficult? Arrogant? "… an imperial man. He believes the things he creates need to stay perpetually under his control. And he always gets his way."

"And you feel like one of the things he created?"

"I am one of the things he created. Not only am I a physical manifestation of his relationship with my mother," and, ew, never think about that again, "he sculpted me from day one, cultivated my opinions and interests to align with what he believed was best for him."

"And why should you do what's best for him?"

"What?"

"Why should you do what's best for him? It's your life, you deserve to live it how you choose."

"I don't do what's best for him. I do what he believes is best for me."

"That's not what you said."

"Yes." Wasn't it? It was what she said. Or what she meant. Damn it, he was confusing her. "Yes, it is."

"Bella." He uncrossed his leg, put both feet on the floor, and leaned over, staring at her and preventing her from missing his point. "That is a classic Freudian slip. You clearly said what you felt is the truth, not what the perception has become."

She shook her head. "I'm… I'm just… muddled."

"You need to start distancing yourself from your father's control."

Her heart rate sped up, her pulse pounded in her ears. She wiped her damp palms on her pants. "He'll never allow it."

"How can he stop it? It's your life. You're an adult. What's the worst that can happen?"

She kept rubbing her hands over her thighs. "He can fire me. Blackball me in my field so I can't get another job. Throw me out of the house so I'm homeless and can't afford my own place. Cut off my trust fund and credit cards so I can't begin to get by on my own. He cannot only ruin me. He can destroy me. For all I know, he may have done so already."

She thought of how she left the parole hearing that day and shuddered.

Oh, God. What had she done?

"Do you really think he'll do all that? To his flesh and blood? His creation?"

"If I disobeyed him, yes. I don't just think it. I know it." Think about it like it hadn't happened. Like it was a future what-if scenario.

Surely, she hadn't walked out on her father that day. She'd never be that reckless. Right?

"I don't know that I believe that, Bella. After all, even if we discount all his love for you, for him to do all that would be to admit imperfection. There may be no love lost between you two, but he still has his reputation to protect."

Oh, if only Dr. Jeffers knew how wrong he was. She blinked back tears even as she pushed back the painful, unspeakable memories. A name she hadn't spoken in years. A face she hadn't seen in longer. Sniffling, she reached for a tissue and dabbed at her eyes.

"Why don't we table this topic for a moment? What is the problem with the other man in your life?"

Bella stood, paced around the room, finally settled for standing at the window and looking out over the neighborhood. A young boy and girl rode bicycles down the street. They giggled, swerved, then held hands with each other as they continued their ride. She sighed. That afternoon would become a sweet memory for each of them, something they could recall when they were adults and smile at how innocent young love was.

She had no such memories.

And she feared she'd never create any. Save for that one special night she'd had with Jensen.

Before her nerves scared him away.

Before her career erected insurmountable barriers between them.

"Bella?" Dr. Jeffers prompted.

She closed her eyes and rested her forehead on the glass pane of the window. She expected it to be cool, refreshing, but instead found it warm from the late afternoon sun. Almost hot. Definitely uncomfortable.

Was it too much to ask for one soothing moment in her day?

Backing away from the window, she avoided meeting his gaze. She wandered to the bookcase and started running her fingers over the spines of the books. More than one bore his name as author or co-author. Clearly, he had the expertise to help, if she was brave enough to tell him.

"I can't really call him 'the other man in my life' because I'm pretty sure I chased him away."

"Can you tell me what happened?"

"My job. My father. Me." She hung her head and closed her eyes. "My father forced me into one of his cases, and it just happened that this guy was on the other side of the aisle."

"You said you're a defense attorney, right? So, he was the plaintiff in a trial?"

"Close enough. In any event, we were already on shaky ground, and this pushed him over the edge. There's no going back from there."

"And what made your relationship tenuous before that?"

She snickered. "Relationship? That's generous. We had a few chance meetings and one night out."

"But you thought it was a relationship-in-the-making."

"I did. At least, I hoped it was. But I messed it up."

"Because of your job?"

"No." She shook her head. "Before that. The night we went out. Well, we didn't really go out so much as we just ended up out." She flung her hands in the air. "Oh, what does it matter? I ruined it."

"Bella. Tell me what happened."

Her cheeks burned. She couldn't face him, knowing her face reddened with humiliation. Instead, she pulled a book off the shelf and mindlessly leafed through it.

"You can talk to me, Bella. That's why you're here."

"We met at the lake." She spoke into the pages. "It seemed we had a lot in common. At least, one big item in common. Our domineering fathers. He was easy to talk to, and we bonded pretty quickly."

"That all sounds promising."

"The night we ended up out together? He kissed me."

"And you didn't feel a spark? That's not uncommon on a date with a relative stranger. Sometimes attractions need time before they grow into something more. "

"A spark?" She let out a sad bark of a laugh and looked at him. "I'm surprised I didn't burst into flames."

He smiled. "I see. Then what was the problem?"

She turned away again. "Things advanced past the kissing stage. It scared me, so I put on the brakes."

"Bella, there's nothing wrong with taking things slowly. I'm sure he didn't mind. Any man—any worthy man—would understand."

"No." She shook her head again. "No. You don't understand. We had an unspoken agreement that things weren't moving too fast. We were on the same page, escalating things like we did."

"People change their minds all the time. Caution is fine. Your virtue is in question, and men should hold that in high regard."

She ran her hands through her hair. "That's the thing. It is about my virtue."

"I don't follow."

"My virtue. My vir-tue. I still have it, and I panicked. I think my mixed signals scared him off."

Dr. Jeffers sat silently for a moment, so Bella turned to face him. "Guys don't like that, right?" She searched his face for a reaction—anything. Compassion. Repulsion. Anything at all. But his expression remained unreadable. She sighed. "I'm a freak of nature. A leper. A pariah. Doomed to die alone."

Finally, he spoke, like a father to his frightened child, his tone a balm for her wounded psyche. "If I understand you correctly, Bella, there's nothing for you to be ashamed of. In fact, I think it's refreshing to find a young woman of your obvious intelligence and beauty to have been so discriminating over the years."

"Discriminating? You're joking, right?"

He cocked his head to the side. "I'm afraid you've lost me again."

"I'm not virtuous because I've been picky. I'm a virgin because my father is a control-freak! All-girl boarding school. Course overloads in college. Working for his firm and living under his roof. Constant scrutiny." She paced around the room again. "I've never even been on a real date!"

"Never?" His voice—quiet, sympathetic—nearly broke her.

She choked back a sob. "When I managed to go out with my best friend, I ended up being the DUFF a few times. Other than that, nothing."

"The duff?"

"The Designated Ugly Fat Friend a guy gets stuck with when his buddy hooks up with a girl. In this case, Chloe, who has probably hooked up with every guy in the tri-state area."

"Ugly and fat? You? I don't think so."

"It's just a term."

"Well, if you got paired off with someone because your friend went off with his friend, I don't believe the man in question would consider it a hardship."

"And yet none of those pairings ended up leading anywhere."

"Have you considered that it's because you weren't interested in the men you got stuck with? Not because they rejected you, but because you sent off subconscious signals rejecting them?"

Huh. No. She'd never considered that. She looked at him, tried to gauge if he was trying to placate her, but he seemed sincere. Maybe there was something to that theory.

"Think on that for a while," he said. "In the meantime, I also want you to think about the signals you sent to this man you're interested in."

"Jensen? I already told you. I froze. He had to perceive it as a rejection, but it was just my fear."

"I'm sorry. Did you say *Jensen?*"

"Yes." She lifted her eyebrows, an unspoken question. What did his name matter?

"Jensen Keller?"

Dread formed a cold pool in the pit of her stomach. "Yes. Why? Do you know him? God, you aren't going to say anything to him, are you?"

He shook his head. Too quickly for her comfort. "Bella, I'm afraid I can't see you any longer. I have a few therapists in mind who you would—"

"I just bared my soul to you, and now you want to pawn me off on someone else? Are you kidding me?"

"I've been involved with Jensen and his family since his sister was killed. I'm assuming that's the hearing you referred to earlier?"

She nodded.

"It's a conflict of interest for me to see both of you, and he and his family were my clients first. I'm really sorry. I should have pressed you for names sooner. This is all my fault."

She collapsed onto the sofa, covered her head with her hands, and wallowed that she had become the cliché patient breaking down on her therapist's couch. "This is too embarrassing. Humiliating! I told you all this personal stuff, and now you're repulsed by my inexperience. And you're going to tell him—"

"No. Bella, no." He crossed to her, helped her to a seated position, and stooped down to meet her gaze. "It's not like that. I would never intentionally reveal your secrets to another client. But because the two of you have so many intersecting issues, I need to protect both of you from my knowledge of both situations. I could inadvertently give something away or guide you in a manner I wouldn't otherwise."

Bella looked up and stared at him through tear-blurred vision. "But you already have my information, and you can slip and reveal something to him."

He shook his head.

"Don't deny it! You just said that's a possibility. That's why you're cutting me loose."

"It's highly unlikely that one session will lead to a slip. It's when I get to know you over time that we would have to worry."

"You've known Jensen over time. You didn't let anything about him slip." She knew she sounded like a belligerent child, but she couldn't help herself. She lashed out to avoid feeling the rejection that already seeped into her soul.

"Actually, I did. I revealed our relationship to you, which was unprofessional and wrong. Now you know he sees me, which violates my doctor-patient confidentiality clause. One session with you and I already have compromised Jensen. Do you see now why I can't treat you? Not because you repulse me. Not because I want to protect one of you over the other. Just because I can't. It isn't fair to either of you."

She sniffled.

He looked deep into her eyes. "Think about your job. You couldn't represent two opposing parties. It's a conflict of interest and unfair to both as well as you. It's the same for me with respect to you and Jensen."

She knew he spoke the truth, but she needed the validation, so she pressed. "It's really not because of me and my… condition?"

"Condition?" He smiled. "Bella, virginity isn't a *condition.* It's a gift. Treasure it. Value it and only give it away when the time, place, and person is right."

Blinking away the tears, she dabbed at her eyes again and gave him a wavering smile.

He patted her on the shoulder and stood. "Now, let me give you a few referral names." He crossed to his desk, grabbed a piece of paper and a pen, and started writing names and numbers from memory.

"Do you think you can brief my new therapist, so I don't have to say all this again?"

He paused in his writing and looked at her. "I can, but I think it would be best if you talked it out again. It will do you good to revisit these thoughts, events, emotions. Saying the words aloud will let you process everything better."

"I'll think about it." She'd have to think about *everything.* After this fiasco, she didn't even want to go to another session with him, let alone a new therapist.

He handed her the paper with the names on them. She noticed they were all women and bit back a sigh. Clearly, he thought men would be repulsed by her inexperience. Pocketing the paper, she headed for the door.

"One last bit of advice, Bella, before you go."

"Yes?" She turned to face him.

"Any well-mannered man will understand why you slowed things down, if you trust him enough to confide in him. And if you're attracted to someone, have faith in your feelings. You wouldn't be interested in him if he didn't appeal to you on a moral level as well as a physical one."

"Are you telling me this because you know Jensen so well?" It didn't sit well with her that he'd reveal so much about Jensen's personality to her. What would he reveal about her to Jensen, then?

"No. I'm talking to you as a man. Not a therapist. Not Jensen's therapist. Just a member of the male population. Yes, there are plenty of guys who would look at you as a conquest. There are others who would buckle under the pressure of making things easy for you. But a gentleman—a man truly worthy of you and your love—will respect you and treat you right. It doesn't matter if you choose Jensen or someone else. It will happen for you when the person is right."

"Thanks, Dr. Jeffers." She turned and left.

It didn't matter any longer. Maybe Jensen would have been patient with her if she had explained her situation. But after what happened in the courtroom, she'd blown her chance with him.

She walked to her car and looked down the street. The bicyclists were long gone, but children's carefree laughter carried to her on a soft summer breeze. Oh, to be young again. To be that innocent again. Now she was jaded. Cynical.

She sat in the car and blasted the AC, hoping to cool her flaming face. Hoping to God she didn't burst into tears as she sat there, because she didn't know if she'd be able to compose herself and drive home.

Home? She didn't even know if she had a home to go to.

Her cell phone rang, distracting her from her morose thoughts, and when she looked at the caller ID, a tiny glimmer of hope flickered deep inside.

Before she answered, she prayed to avoid any further conflict.

Then she took a deep breath and swiped her finger across the screen.

CHAPTER 11

JENSEN WAITED FOR BELLA AT their spot by the lake. He'd had better ideas. Meeting someone he felt such rage toward in a spot where he'd felt such… well, he didn't know what he'd felt when they met at the lake. But it definitely hadn't been rage, and the conflicting emotions certainly wouldn't make for an easy meeting.

Damn dumb idea.

Still, he needed a place where they wouldn't be interrupted or overheard. A place they both could get to easily. A place where neither felt a home-turf advantage. All he could think of was the lake.

Their spot. At the lake.

He leaned against the rock—their rock—and looked out over the water. The sun reflected off the surface, white flashes on dark water, and he squinted against the glare. People splashed and played, their frivolity sending irregular ripples across the lake, the waves they made lapping against the craggy hill on which he sat upon. A beautiful day. One he hated to mar with anger, resentment, hostility.

Yet there he sat, waiting for Bella, a woman he rued meeting, whose very existence infuriated him at the moment.

"Coming over." Bella's voice carried to him, and he glanced up just in time for skittering rock dust to land in his eyes. Give her credit for warning him so he didn't get kicked in the head, but the grit scratching his retinas hardly made a better alternative. His eyes watered, but they continued to burn. He blinked and rubbed at them.

"Oh, Jensen! What happened? Are you all right?" She clutched at his hands.

He pulled away from her. "I've been better."

When she finally answered him, she spoke with a quiet tremor. "How can I help?"

"For the moment, you've done enough." He swiped at his eyes again, then covered his face with his shirt to try and blot the wetness away. Her sigh caught his attention, and he poked his head out to face her.

"I'm sorry. There. I said it again. Is that what you want? Fifty apologies? Sixty? I'm sorry." She inhaled sharply. "I'm sorry. I'm sorry. I'm sorry. I'm—"

"Bella!"

She recoiled like she'd been slapped, but she stopped yammering.

"Bella, I didn't ask you to meet me because I want to hear you grovel."

"I'm not groveling," she muttered.

He sighed. Ran a hand through his hair. Wiped his eyes again.

"I knew I hurt you," she said, "but I didn't realize I'd hurt you this badly. How can I make it up to you?"

"What are you talking about?"

"Why did you call me here?" Her voice sounded soft, defeated. She leaned back against the rock and started playing with the grass. He studied her slender fingers, realized his eyes had gone from agonizing scraping to minimal stinging. Another quick wipe with his shirt, and he saw clearly again.

Bella looked awful. She had dark circles under her red-rimmed eyes, her hair looked like she'd been attacking it, and her fingers had a slight tremble. He could do nothing but stare at her.

She looked up at him. "Are you done crying? Do you want to talk now?"

"Crying?"

She tilted her head to the side and raised her eyebrows. "Yes, crying. Water leaking from one's eyes down one's cheeks. I'm assuming you're familiar with the concept, as you were just doing it."

He blinked a few times, dumbfounded. Then he understood. By the time she'd scrambled down from the rock, his eyes had been irritated from the debris she'd knocked loose. Of course, she thought he'd been crying. The absurdity of it all hit him. Hard.

A snort escaped him. Followed by a chuckle. Then a quick bark of mirth. He collapsed onto his back and held his stomach while gales and gales of laughter consumed him.

It took a while to settle down, and he had to wipe tears from his eyes again. Looking back, it wasn't that funny, but so much had been bottled up inside, it had to burst out somewhere, somehow.

When he'd settled, he looked at her. The scowl on her face said more to him than any words could.

"I'm sorry," he said. "Really. I wasn't laughing at your expense."

"Maybe I'd better just go." She started to stand.

He grabbed her hand. "Bella. Please. Stay. Let me explain."

She bit her lip and looked up the hill, but she didn't leave.

"When you said you were climbing over the rock, I know you were telling me, so you didn't kick me, which I appreciate. But I wasn't expecting you to say anything, so I looked up and a bunch of rock dust fell in my eyes. I wasn't crying. My eyes were just tearing. When I figured out what you were thinking, it just hit me kind of hard."

"It wasn't that funny."

He sighed. "No. It wasn't. I guess I just have a lot stuck inside. It needed to come out somewhere."

She looked at him for a moment, then she sat beside him. "I am sorry about, well, about everything."

"I know." He looked at her, felt a stirring deep inside. Felt his body betrayed him. "I don't want to talk about all that right now. I'm not ready."

"Well, why did you call me here, then?"

"I need to understand what happened at the hearing."

She leaned against the rock again, lifted her head, and closed her eyes. "In general, I'd say ask me anything. But in this case, I don't know how much help I can be. I already told you what I know."

"But something's going on. Behind the scenes."

"That's the problem." She rubbed her temples. "It's all behind the scenes. I'm not privy to the secrets. All I know is, nothing about that hearing happened the way hearings typically work. The entire procedure was off, and there were way too many people there."

"Some of those people took my dad aside afterward."

She turned and looked at him. "Then why are you here with me? Ask your dad."

He sighed, shook his head. "I did. All we did was fight. He won't tell me anything. What did your dad tell you?"

Bella looked out over the water. "Absolutely nothing. Other than all the things I'd done wrong, anyway."

"We're quite a pair, aren't we?"

She smirked, then a serious look crossed her face.

"I guess it's my turn to apologize," he said. "I didn't mean to give you mixed signals."

"I thought that was me who did that to you."

"What?" He spun to better face her. "What are you talking about?"

"What are you talking about?"

"Referring to us as a pair. When… well…" He let her fill in the blanks.

"I didn't take it that way."

"Then what were you talking about?" he asked.

A soft blush tinged her pale cheeks. "About the other night."

Her words, barely audible, caught him off guard. "I had a good time the other night. Didn't you?"

"You mean, you weren't angry that I slowed us down?"

"Bella, it was our first date, and a spontaneous one, at that. Why on earth would I be angry?"

"I thought you thought—well, I didn't want to lead you on. Then when I stopped, you seemed to, I don't know, withdraw a bit. And—"

"I was trying to get my libido under control. My mood had nothing to do with you. I'm not the kind of guy who only wants one thing, and then bails when he doesn't get it." The more he thought about it, the angrier he grew. What did she think of him, anyway? He spat out his last remark. "Or does get it."

"Jensen, I'm sorry. I wasn't implying that of you. There are just some things you don't know. I brought a lot of baggage to that night. The issue was all mine, not yours."

"Baggage? Such as?"

He noticed her blinking back tears. "I don't tell my secrets to just anyone, Jensen. If we were going to try again, that would be one thing. But I'm not just going to air my dirty laundry in front of the masses."

"Everyone has former lovers, Bella," he said. When she turned away, he reached for her chin and turned her to face him. "The difference is, not everyone compares their new lover to their old ones. It's not fair."

"Compare my—God, if you only knew how ridiculous that is."

This woman confused and infuriated him like no girl had since Hope. A pain stabbed him in the heart just thinking about his sister, and he pushed her out of his mind.

"Well, I guess that's that, then." He stood and stretched.

"Jensen," Bella began, but didn't finish. Tears fell freely down her face, and she turned away from him.

Why did women always use tears as a weapon? No man knew what to do with a sobbing woman. The men who left were assholes. The ones who continued the arguments were bigger assholes. The men who tried to offer advice only make things worse. Proven fact. There was simply no rationalizing with distraught women. The men who offered comfort and consolation lost the argument and most arguments thereafter. One instance of kindness, and they were forever labeled a pussy. It was a no-win situation.

He scowled at her, sat back down, and felt like an asshole, anyway.

Probably better than the alternative, though.

He patted her awkwardly on the back until she calmed from unrestrained, gut-wrenching sobs to soft hiccups. "Sorry. I don't have a tissue or anything."

She sniffled and wiped her eyes with the heels of her hands. "I'm okay."

"I wasn't trying to pick a fight."

"I know." She sighed. "I just wish we weren't in this place."

"The lake?"

"God, men can be so dense sometimes." She leaned against the rock. "No. I mean this place in our relationship. Or what there is or was of it. If it ever was an 'it' at all."

He scowled. "I knew what you meant. I was trying to lighten the mood with a joke."

She shook her head. "Sarcasm isn't funny."

"It's a defense mechanism. You need a thick skin in my family."

"My father has a sharp tongue. Most of the time, cutting remarks—made in jest or not—just hurt."

What the hell was wrong with him? Why did he constantly shove his foot in his mouth? Why did he care so much that he did? Did he or did he not want to patch things up with her?

Something about her appealed to him. Shit, that was the understatement of the year. He was like a planet to her sun, stuck in her gravitational pull. Baggage, misunderstandings… none of that mattered. It killed him to admit it, but he couldn't give up, couldn't walk away.

He still wanted her.

So, he chose his words carefully and left it all to the fates. "I guess it's safe to say we've both said and done things we want to take back. That doesn't mean we have to keep making those same mistakes, right?"

She looked at him, her gaze raking over him, lingering on his eyes, searching their depths. He couldn't read her thoughts, couldn't fathom what she'd say, or if she'd say anything at all. The silence lingered on.

Until finally she spoke. "No pressures? No strings? No commitments?"

"No. No pressure. But you need to know, I don't share. If there's someone else—"

"No. No one else now."

"Leaving your options open?" The thought hurt more than he wanted to admit.

"Oh, no. Nothing like that. I just meant, no expectations. We take things slow."

Relief washed over him. She had no one else in her life. He smiled. "I'm in no rush. But at some point, there needs to be transparency, or this won't go anywhere."

"Transparency? I thought we just laid all our cards on the table."

"The baggage, Bella. I don't need to know every detail from each of your relationships, but if there's something holding you back, when we get to a certain point, I'll expect to learn what that is."

"So stipulated."

He chuckled. "Always the attorney."

She looked away again. "In the interest of transparency and full disclosure, I have something to share with you."

"About the hearing?" Warning bells clanged through his mind, echoed through his brain.

"No. About the attorney-thing. I may have lost my job today."

"You work for your father. How could you possibly have lost your job? If my dad ever got his claws on me, I'd never get out from under him."

She lay on the ground and looked up at the clouds, again avoiding his gaze. "I know it seems that way, particularly with my father. But absolute control is paramount to him. If he can't have it, he simply eliminates the perceived threat."

"I don't understand."

"You said your dad and mine sound a lot alike. When you told your dad you didn't want to follow the career path he laid out for you, he didn't like it, but he supported you."

"Well, support is a strong word, but—never mind. You never actually told your dad you didn't want to be a lawyer, right?"

She shook her head. "There's more. It's a totally different situation. When you asked your dad about the men in suits, he didn't tell you anything, but he didn't fire you and throw you out of the house."

He felt the color drain from his face, couldn't fathom what she said was true. "I'm sure you're mistaken."

"Well, I can't be certain. At least, not until I try to go home. But I think, given the way we parted ways, he's not inclined to welcome me home with open arms."

He took her hand. "What happened?"

"He basically said if I left, that was it."

"Have you tried to go home yet?"

"No. Not yet. I guess I don't really want to know if it's the truth. Particularly given I think it is."

"Bella." But no other words came.

She shook her head. "Don't worry about it. I'll be fine." But tears filled her eyes again.

He didn't know what to say or do. Helpless. Totally useless. He didn't have his own place, so he couldn't invite her over, and there was no way he could bring Victor Perish's daughter home to his family. They weren't at a place in the relationship to be living together, anyway, even if it was only for one night.

Surely, she was wrong. Her father wouldn't have cast her aside so recklessly. Right?

"Bella, why don't you go home? Try to set things right?"

"Is that what you're going to do with your father?"

He sighed. "No. Not yet. I have another idea to figure out what's going on."

"Such as?"

Should he tell her? A thousand reasons not to rushed through his brain. Followed by one word—transparency.

Resigned, he let her in on his plan. "I'm going to start tailing Wade Unger."

"Oh, Jensen, I don't know. That could be dangerous."

"What choice do I have? No one will tell me anything. This whole thing reeks of some cover up or conspiracy. Cooper thinks those guys with my dad were feds."

"You definitely don't want to get on the wrong side of them, or of whomever they're plotting against."

"Unless you have a better idea, I'm doing it. I need answers, and I don't know how else to get them."

"Promise you'll be careful?"

"Of course." He smiled, hoped more confidence came through on his face than he heard in his voice. Or felt in his heart, for that matter.

"Well, I can probably get you started then."

"How so?"

"My father gave me Unger's file to review. I only got to glance through it, but I saw the addresses of the proposed work location and his potential housing options."

"God, I could just kiss you right now." He didn't mean it the way it sounded, but it was out there.

She gasped, and her mouth opened in a perfect *O*. A perfect, desirable, kissable *O*.

Hell, maybe he did mean it. He grabbed her and pulled her close. Then, before either of them could change their minds, he dipped his head and took her mouth with his.

His intention? A quick, thank-you type kiss, the kind reserved for grandmothers who doled out treats. But don't they say the road to hell is paved with good intentions? He didn't feel damned, though. She took him straight to heaven.

The kiss lasted far longer than he meant it to, went far deeper than he planned. When they pulled away, he couldn't think straight.

"Now, that's a thank you." Her face flushed. She smiled a sweet smile, then turned away.

"If you like my grateful kisses, you're going to love my—" What the hell was he doing? "Never mind." He turned in the other direction. What was it about this woman that threw him off his game so badly?

She giggled. "I look forward to it."

He turned and looked at her. She wasn't laughing at him. She just genuinely seemed happy with their progress. He grabbed her hand and squeezed it.

A quick squeeze back, and she stood. "Well, I guess we have our plans. I'll text you the addresses, so you don't have to memorize them."

He got to his feet, too. "Thanks." Awkward silence, anyone? He was about to hug her when she reached into her pocket and grabbed her phone. After a minute, she put her phone back in her pocket and his phone beeped. Addresses received.

"Well, it'll be dark soon. Time to go. I guess I'll see you around, or something." She started up the hill.

Jensen followed her. At the road, he saw her head for a sporty little Mercedes convertible right behind his truck. "I'll call you, and not just about what I find out."

She smiled and climbed into her car. After turning it on, she rolled her window down. "Be careful." She waved and took off.

Okay, so no kiss goodbye. The one earlier would have to tide him over. He had no doubt it would, even as it led him to cravings for more.

Putting her out of his mind, he swiped his finger across the screen of his phone and checked out the addresses she'd sent him. Then she was the furthest thing from his mind.

Uttering a string of curses, he got in his truck and headed toward the one address he'd recognized.

CHAPTER 12

WHEN BELLA ARRIVED HOME, NO signs of life greeted her. The house stood dark and silent, not a light in the window, not a sound from inside. She hit the button on her garage door remote, but nothing happened. Power outage? Hmm. It hadn't even rained, let alone stormed.

Wondering what happened, she got out of her car and headed for the front door. After fishing her keys out of the bottom of her bag, she slipped it in the lock.

It didn't turn.

In an instant, all her fears rushed back to her. If her father was anything, he was a man of his word. He cut her off. Deactivated her garage opener. Changed the locks.

Fighting down panic, she pounded on her front door. Surely someone inside would answer. Marta or William… any of the servants. Or her mother.

Who was she kidding? They could be standing right on the other side of the door and they wouldn't open it to her if Victor forbade it. Which clearly, he had.

Breath escaped in fast, shallow gasps. Vision, spotty.

Hands, sweaty. Phone slipping. Snatch it.

Squint at the display. Fumble past start screen.

No. Fucking. Service.

Fists in the air, she screamed. All she had, all she could muster, expelled in one curse to the heavens.

He'd cut her off. Cut her out. She'd been lucky her phone lasted as long as it had. What else had he taken from her? And how much more would he take?

Even through her disbelief, she realized she shouldn't be surprised. He'd threatened her with this consequence, and he always did as he said.

And, damn him, he'd done it before.

She climbed back into her car and sat, tried to collect her thoughts. She only had about three hundred dollars on her. By this time, her cards and bank account would be frozen. Taking a card out of her wallet, she grabbed her phone to call the credit card company and try to talk her way back into an active account.

Except she'd already forgotten he'd shut her cell phone down. She threw it down, watched it ricochet off the floorboards on the passenger side and bounce under the seat.

Surprised he hadn't had her car repo'ed.

A quarter tank of gas and lack of funds left her with few options. Sighing, she put the car in gear and headed to Chloe's.

By the time she arrived, the tears had slowed to a trickle. Squaring her shoulders, she approached the grand double doors of the building Chloe lived in and headed for the elevator and immediately stepped out of it. She couldn't reach the penthouse without a pass code. Her thoughts swirled inside her head, a vortex of anger, panic, confusion, regret.

If she didn't start thinking clearly, she'd be done for.

The guy behind the desk was her least favorite of all the employees at Chloe's building. Dressed in the trademark charcoal suit required of all employees, the arrogant man assessed her tear-streaked face, her disheveled clothing, her likely wrecked hair, and he turned his nose up. She knew he had to recognize her. She'd been there a million times. But he determined to drag the process out. So, what if he looked better put together than she did? A perfect appearance didn't make a perfect person. Her father was proof positive of that. She choked back a sob. A sloppy appearance didn't make her less of a person, either.

After a laborious delay, the desk attendant finally called upstairs. Then promptly informed her, "The party to whom you wish to speak is apparently unavailable to you."

In other words, Chloe didn't answer the damn call.

"Do you have a phone I can borrow?"

This time he looked down his nose at her. "We are not in the habit of lending our services to those who… do not reside here." Could a person sneer through tone? She swore she could hear him sneering.

"Very well. Is there a pay phone nearby?"

He gestured down the hall and turned his back on her. What. A. Jerk. She'd tell Chloe about it, but being faced with unemployment herself, she hardly wanted to subject anyone else to the prospect. Even that asshole.

At the pay phone, she fished for a quarter—were phone calls still only a quarter?—but had no change, save a dusty penny stuck in the corner of her bag. After taking a dollar out of her wallet, she looked at the phone. It didn't accept bills. She glanced around for a change machine, but no joy. Hanging her head, feeling so close to breaking, she slunk back to the desk. The pompous dick had left his station. Probably expected her to come back and wanted to make her sweat it.

In a few minutes, a bubbly young girl dressed in a charcoal skirt and crisp white blouse came out of the back office. Her picture had to be in the dictionary next to helpful. Instead of making change or even giving her a free quarter, she gave Bella a desk phone and stepped a discrete distance away.

And… Bella couldn't remember Chloe's number. Did it end with 3-7-5-2? Or 7-5-2-3? Was there a 7 in it at all?

Thank God in heaven, she had a business card of hers tucked into her card folio. She flipped through it until she came to her friend's card. Ah, 3-4-5-2. She'd been close. Ish.

She dialed, waited for one ring, two. Panic set in at three rings. Maybe Chloe didn't answer calls from numbers she didn't recognize. But, surely, she'd answer from her building? Her only recourse was to leave a message and hope she didn't delete it, unread. And pray she came home that night.

After the beep, Bella spoke into the receiver. "Chloe, it's me. Bella. I'm in a jam and sitting in the lobby at your place. Don't try me on my cell. Either call the desk for me or come home as soon as you get this, please? Thanks." And she hung up.

Miss Bubbly approached her, a sympathetic smile on her face. What if Mr. Arrogant told his minion to kick her out if she didn't hear from Chloe? Where would she go? How would Chloe find her?

"Miss?" the girl said. "You're welcome to wait in the lobby until we hear from Ms. Thompson. Could I get you anything while you wait? Coffee? A danish?"

Relief, however brief, flowed through her system. Coffee sounded heavenly, but she didn't think her nerves could take it. "Maybe just a glass of water?"

"We have San Pellegrino and Voss."

Voss was delicious, but the bubbles sounded wonderful. "I'll have a San Pellegrino, please. Thank you."

"Go ahead and sit. I'll bring it right out."

Bella made her way over to the furniture grouping in the lobby and sank into the cushions. She closed her eyes and rested her head against the back of the chair. Exhaustion threatened to claim her, and she startled when a voice spoke softly in her ear.

"Ms. Perish? Ms. Thompson rang. She wants you to wait for her in her apartment. The code is 7-8-6-2."

"I don't think I'll remember that. I often mix numbers up." No way was she admitting how frazzled she felt.

"I'll get you a pass key." She waited for Bella to rise, then she walked with her to the desk. A quick duck behind the counter, some rapid clacking of keys, and presto—she handed Bella a keycard. "Do you need help with anything?"

Bella smothered a small chuckle. She had no bags. No outfits, no shoes.

No makeup or jewelry. Nothing but her business folio and the clothes on her back. "No, I'll be fine, thanks." She shifted her bag on her shoulder and gripped the pass key firmly in her fist.

"Well, I had planned to pour this for you and garnish it with lime, but you'll probably find it easier to carry in the unopened bottle." The girl passed a green bottle over the counter. "If you need anything before Ms. Thompson returns, don't hesitate to call down."

"Thanks." Bella feared she would collapse right there at the desk if she didn't leave right then. Before exhaustion claimed her, she got on the elevator for the second time. This time, however, she was prepared, and she slid the pass key into the slot. Access to the penthouse, granted. The light behind the P button turned green, and she rose higher and higher. When the doors slid open, she stepped directly into Chloe's foyer.

Home sweet home. Just not her home. She had no home.

She burst into tears.

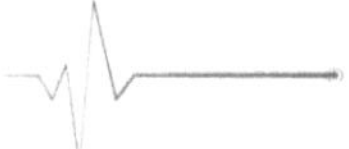

BELLA DIDN'T REMEMBER WALKING TO the sofa, kicking off her shoes, or covering herself with a blanket. But when she opened her eyes, she was lying on the sofa. Her feet were bare, and a blanket covered her, keeping her warm and toasty in the chill from Chloe's air conditioner.

She was at Chloe's?

Oh, shit.

The events of the last—well, she had no idea what time or day it was, so she couldn't be certain—but all the horrors came rushing back. The hearing and Jensen. The argument with her father. The talk at the lake. The freezing of her assets.

She'd give anything to not be awake at her friend's place. If only that was the dream—or nightmare—life, and nothing that happened earlier was true.

A quick rub of her eyes and she blinked against the soft light of the side table lamp.

No. Not a dream.

Chloe peered down at her. "Now what in the hell have you gotten yourself into?"

Bella scrambled to a seated position and fought to untangle herself from the cashmere throw covering her. "I didn't get myself into anything. It's what I got out of that's the problem."

Her friend sat beside her and reached for a cocktail glass on the coffee table. "Do tell." She took a sip.

"My dad threw me out."

Chloe fought against a spit take and ended up coughing until her face turned red. When the sputtering subsided, Chloe took a deep breath. "Victor tossed you out?"

Bella nodded, too tired to even cry any longer. "We've been fighting. More than usual. I disobeyed him at a hearing today, and he said if I walked away, I'd regret it. When I went home, no garage access, the locks were changed. Then my cell stopped working, and I'm assuming my credit cards have all been canceled. I never got around to checking."

"You walked out? On *Victor?* After… after what he did to Troy?"

Troy.

Even hearing his name sliced another deep gash into Bella's heart. She closed her eyes against the onslaught of pain. Managed to nod an answer to Chloe's question.

"Talk to me, Bells."

But Bella couldn't. Chloe knew Troy was gone. Just didn't know the why. No one but Bella knew the real reason. She had so much to atone for, and despite everything she had done to be the perfect daughter in his absence, she'd fallen far short.

How could she possibly find the words? Troy was a constant aching echo in her heart. A gaping, self-inflicted wound she could never mend. And because of it, she never—well, hardly ever—allowed herself to consciously think about him. Let alone what had happened.

"Bella. I'm your best friend. We've known each other since practically the womb. Our families go back way before that. I know we were young when it happened, but I knew even then that Troy leaving damn near destroyed all of you. But you never gave me the full story. Now it looks like you're in a similar situation. I can't help you if I don't know what needs to be fixed. Why did you walk out on your dad? What was so special about that hearing? And what happened to Troy?"

No.

Bella wouldn't talk about Troy. Couldn't. Not now. Probably not ever. But she could talk about her latest debacle.

Close eyes.

Deep breaths. In. Out. In. Out.

Open eyes. Focus.

Clarity.

Control.

Diversion.

"What time is it, anyway?" she managed.

Chloe glanced at the chunky gold watch on her wrist. "Three-fifteen."

"It's the middle of the night? How long did I sleep?"

"You were asleep when we got here."

"We?"

"I have company."

Chloe never brought 'company' home with her. She must really have been worried about Bella to have opened her sanctuary to a one-night stand.

Bella threw the blanket aside and climbed to her feet. "I'll get out of your hair."

"Sit your bony butt down and talk to me."

Bella wavered for a moment, glanced at the sofa and then down the hall.

Chloe pushed her back down to the sofa. She landed with a soft plop and bounced a bit on the firm cushion.

"My butt's not bony."

"Agree to disagree."

Bella hadn't noticed before, but her friend stood there clad in a barely-there teddy with an untied robe covering it. Clearly, Chloe had better things to do than listen to her problems. She looked at the door again.

"Don't even bother. It's the middle of the night. You aren't going anywhere. Now spill." She took another sip of her drink and perched a hip on the arm of the sofa.

"Dad always gets a little testy this time of year."

"Because of Troy?" Chloe asked.

Block the memory. Block the thought.

"One can only assume," Bella said, "and I would imagine the case he was dealing with didn't help matters."

"What case?"

"I'm getting to it. Like I said, we've been fighting. A lot. He's unsatisfied with my work. Micromanaging my time, my social life."

"Or lack thereof."

"Or lack thereof," Bella agreed. "He's being Victor. Just—" What was the word? "Just more of himself. More of the parts of him I don't like, anyway. He gave me a particularly rough time about a parole hearing I was handling, which went perfectly, by the way. Then I bumped into him when I was leaving."

"Quite a coincidence, don't you think?"

Hmm. Was it? "Eh, it's not really that unusual. I've run into him at the courthouse before."

"The courthouse. Not a penitentiary. I can't even imagine your dad attending a parole hearing right out of law school. He surely doesn't bother with them now."

"That was only one of the weird things that happened."

"What else?" Chloe asked.

"The whole process was off. And Dad knows why but didn't tell me and that made Jensen so angry."

"Jensen? The hot guy you told me about?"

"Yeah."

"Why would he care if your dad is up to something?"

"I guess I forgot to mention the most important part." Bella looked away, not wanting her friend to analyze her face as well as her words. "The case my dad took? It's defending the guy that killed Jensen's sister."

"What?" Chloe's shrill cry echoed through the penthouse.

"Jenna?" a male voice called from the hallway.

"It's okay, babe," Chloe called back. "Just girl talk."

The guy mumbled something, and Bella heard the bedroom door click.

"Jenna? Still not using your real name?"

"Of course not. This is a one-night thing. No real name. No numbers exchanged. No strings."

"He knows where you live."

"Eh. I planned on staying the night at Channingswood, but then the desk called."

Channingswood. Only Chloe would stay at a five-star hotel for a quickie. Bella didn't approve of her friend's extracurricular activities, but she certainly didn't want to make things worse for her. "And I screwed it up for you."

"Oh, no. I still got what I wanted and will again before he leaves." She waggled her eyebrows and grinned.

Bella shook her head. Chloe didn't bring men to her apartment. Ever, as far as she knew. Distance and deception were part of her MO. And, despite disagreeing with her friend's lifestyle, she'd ruined Chloe's track record with one phone call. "And because of me, you've made a string. He'll be able to come here to find you."

"And good luck to him getting in here. The desk has known you as long as they've known me, and they still stopped you from coming up. I'll be fine."

Thinking about Mr. Arrogant, the desk attendant from hell, helped Bella to relax a bit.

"Besides," Chloe said, "I don't think he's looking for any strings, either. Now, back to Jensen."

Bella sighed. “It’s just awful. He’s so angry, and he has every right to be.”

“So, talk to him. Patch things up.”

“Patch things up? That’s funny.”

“If he’s worth it, make the effort.”

Bella sighed. “I tried. Kind of. We’ve come to an understanding. But I’m not optimistic. I mean, really. Who could get over losing a sibling and then dating the person who got the killer paroled?”

“But you didn’t get the guy paroled. Your dad did.”

“Oh, what does it even matter?” She’d been over it and over it, again and again. No point in rehashing it. “Long story short, Jensen’s angry, but he’s talking to me again. We’re supposed to try dating again, but I just don’t see him ever getting over this, no matter how hard he tries.” No point in mentioning their investigation plans. “And my dad told me not to walk away from him, but I did. Now I’m jobless, homeless, and feeling pretty damn useless.”

Chloe slipped down to the sofa and put her arm around Bella’s shoulders. “We’ll figure it all out, honey.”

Bella rested her head against her friend’s shoulder and fought back tears.

“Listen,” Chloe said. “It’s late, you’re worn out, and nothing is going to get settled now. Why don’t you get off this sofa and go sleep in the guest room? I’ve already put some clothes and pajamas in there for you.”

Bella looked at her friend’s teddy and flushed.

“Don’t worry.” Chloe smiled. “I own more than just lingerie. You’ll be comfortable. In the morning, we’ll deal with it.”

Bella stood and stretched. A bed would probably feel really good, but she doubted she’d be able to sleep with her thoughts whirlpooling through her head.

“Unless you’re ready to talk about Troy?”

Not on her life. “Goodnight, Chloe. And thanks.”

She headed down the hall, her friend right behind her.

“Do you want a sleeping pill?” Chloe asked. “I can’t guarantee it’s going to stay quiet.”

Bella flushed again and stepped into the guest room, listening to Chloe's throaty laughter until she closed the door.

CHAPTER 13

AFTER JENSEN SAID GOODBYE TO Bella, he drove around for a while. If he went straight home, he'd likely get into it with his dad.

Not that he didn't have a good reason to.

He couldn't take his mind off the addresses Bella had sent him. Despite the adamant mantra running through his head—*Do not go there. Do not go there.*—he succumbed and drove to the one he recognized.

He parked his car across the street from his father's clinic and gazed at the building. The windows gave nothing away but the darkness beyond, and the sign on the door read *CLOSED.*

Well, what did he expect? To see Wade sitting in the lobby, bright lights spotlighting him and his sure-to-be nefarious actions?

What an ass!

The street remained quiet. Few cars drove past, fewer pedestrians walked by. Still, Jensen sat there, staring at the dark building, wondering what the hell was going on.

Seconds passed. Minutes. Almost an hour. No breeze blew in his windows. The air was still, a bit stifling. Crickets chirruped somewhere, their songs floating to him from whatever weed clump they hid in. The clinic sat right in the center of the business district. No grass to be found. Maybe the crickets made their home in the plantings in front of clinic.

His mom and dad had done the best landscaping they could in the urban space, enhancing the curb appeal. People admiring the plants would ask who was responsible, which resulted in great word-of-mouth advertising for their nursery. Plenty of people asked. The place looked better than any other building on the street. One of their work crews built planter boxes on all the windows, and his parents had filled them as well as two giant urns flanking the doorway with colorful plants and flowers. Many he recognized as the same kinds from his own yard, but despite his father's constant tutelage on the subject, he never remembered the names of most of them.

Jensen sighed. What the hell was he doing here? What could possibly happen in a dark, empty building? He'd just about given up and reached for the key in the ignition when someone walked around the corner and stopped in front of the clinic.

Slipping down in his seat so not to be observed, he trained his gaze on the man at the door. Wasn't his dad. Wasn't Wade, either, although that's who he expected. No, this guy was tall and stocky, had dark hair. Wore dark clothes. He looked around and then turned his attention to the door.

Shit! The guy was breaking in!

Jensen shifted in his seat and reached in his pocket for his phone. He'd just tapped 9-1-1 on the screen and was about to send when the light turned on in the clinic.

What the—? *Ben?*

The man skulking on the walk and slinking into the clinic well after hours was none other than Ben Lyndon. Jensen hadn't seen him since he'd found out Ben had really fathered his sister, Hope. He'd driven to Ben's house and punched him right in the face. Didn't help, though. All he did was hurt his hand. Guy had a head like stone.

Ben, Wade, and Jensen's dad had been the best of friends. When Hope died—when Wade killed her—all the secrets came to light. Jensen's dad had been crushed. It almost ruined his parents' marriage, his dad's career. But Wade went to jail, and his dad cut Ben out of their lives. Jensen didn't think they'd ever have to see Ben or Wade again.

But Wade got paroled, and, apparently, now Ben worked with his dad at the clinic.

Surely not. Right? His dad would never have consented to working with Ben again. Wouldn't even consider speaking to him or being in the same room.

Or would he?

Jensen watched Ben rifle through papers on the desk, then head into the back rooms. Lights soon shone from the hallway where he had disappeared. No, Ben belonged there. He hadn't broken in. He had a key, and he wasn't sneaking around.

What the fuck was going on? His family was no healthier, no saner, than before Hope died.

He sat up, turned the key in the ignition, and put the car in drive. It took all his will power not to floor it and peel out down the road. God, how he wanted to. But he didn't need the attention.

His thoughts whirled, and he couldn't grab any of them long enough to make sense of anything. What he most needed was clarity, but no one would provide him the answers he sought, and it was getting late. Even if he kept snooping around, he probably wouldn't learn anything.

Soon he found himself sitting in the parking lot of Sean's Pub and Grille. He salivated and his stomach lurched. Definitely wasn't ready for another drunken binge. But a sandwich wouldn't suck. When had he last eaten? His stomach growled its answer—too long ago. So, he went inside.

He'd been sitting in the dark so long, the dim lighting seemed almost bright. He blinked, tried to focus, and heard his name. Turning toward the dining area, he saw Austin, Brett, and Miles sitting at a table along the wall. Miles lifted his beer bottle and pointed to an empty chair beside Brett. Jensen made his way over and took a seat. Could be just what he needed—forget about everything and just hang with the guys.

"Hey."

"Man, what the hell happened to you?" Austin asked. "You look like shit."

"Thanks." Jensen lifted his hand to flag down a waitress. This one was older than the one he'd seen last time. He wondered if they were mother and daughter. They had similar features, only this poor woman looked haggard. He probably would, too, if he had to work there. Who was he kidding? Austin just told him he looked awful. This lady probably seemed dewy fresh compared to him.

He ordered a dozen wings—extra seasoning—and a hot sausage sandwich.

"And what'll you have to drink, hon? Got a nice microbrew from a place up in the mountains. Been a big hit."

Jensen swallowed down a gag reflex. "Thanks, but I think I'll just have Pepsi. Lots of ice. Maybe bring two, I'm pretty thirsty."

"Got it. Be about forty minutes on the wings. Got a few big orders in front of you, and only so much room in the fryer. Want the sandwich first, or do you want both together?"

"Whenever it's ready. I'm starving."

"Be right back with your drink."

As she walked away, his friends all started yammering at him.

"No beer? Still hung over?"

"Sandwich and wings? Thanks, but we already ate. You didn't need to get us anything."

"So, what gives? Why you look so worn out?"

Jensen sighed. Maybe a night out with the guys wasn't such a good idea. He didn't feel like answering questions. He went out to forget, not to over-analyze. Still, his friends wouldn't back down, and a few sets of fresh ears might not hurt. Or it might. He felt like he'd been shoved sideways through a meat grinder, and he didn't feel like revisiting the process.

The waitress came back with both a glass and a pitcher of soda. "Your sandwich will only be a few more minutes."

Before he could thank her, she scurried off again. He took a sip of his drink, trying to avoid the penetrating stares of his buddies. Unsuccessful, he tipped the glass up. Still they stared, so he drank more. After he drained the glass, he poured another and took a sip.

"Fine, you don't want to talk," Miles said, "don't. We will."

"Okay, talk."

"We were just discussing the summer lineup for concerts at the Amp."

Jensen nodded. What did he care about summer concerts?

"Austin scored a coup. Sergio's coming."

Jensen almost dropped his glass. "Sergio? You signed *the* Sergio to play a summer set at the Amp?"

Austin shrugged and looked away.

"Shut the fuck up," Jensen said.

"It's no biggie," his friend said.

But it was. Sergio Lodico was the Elvis of the era. Didn't matter what kind of music a person liked. Everyone liked Sergio. All the girls loved him. All the guys wanted to be him or even in his orbit. Parents, grandparents, little kids… didn't matter. Sergio's music sat at the top of a bunch of charts. Almost every song he released hit platinum. He packed stadiums at ticket prices of over one hundred bucks.

And he was playing a free concert at the Amp?

No. Fucking. Way.

"How the hell did you manage that?" Jensen asked.

"Pulled a few strings, cashed in a favor or two. It really wasn't hard. He likes to do things for people. He's a nice guy. The big deal is that, with his name on the docket, I've been able to score some other big names, and he's promised to consider us for the PAC next winter. The town's going to make a fortune off this deal. Restaurants, hotels, merchandise. It's good."

"I'm sure your dad is more concerned about the money your company will make off the ticket sales," Miles said.

"That's still a year and a half away. The bigger deal is what the town gets now. That's why I'm glad it worked out."

Austin's dad was about as easy to please as Royce. He owned several properties in the city, including three restaurants, the convention center, and the Performing Arts Center. Austin worked for him but at great personal cost. In the few years since he'd sold his soul to his father, he had managed to get the Amp built in Cathedral Lake and had organized a few fundraisers for local charities. Jensen's mom—Cathedral Lake's former fund-raising queen—had helped him get the ball rolling. Even though she had become busy with the nursery, she probably recognized the same father-son dynamic in Austin's life as in her own son's and had worked hard to make Austin's work-life less burdensome.

"Planning to avoid talking to us all night?" Miles asked.

"Huh?" He'd been lost in thoughts, wondering why he'd let his father ruin so much of his life, that he'd timed out for a bit. "Sorry. Just thinking."

"Well, clearly Austin's big news can't keep your attention, so why don't you just tell us what's eating at you and get it off your chest?"

Jensen leaned back in his chair. "I really don't know what to say."

"How 'bout you answer our questions, then?"

"Fine." He sighed and thought back to what they had asked him when he sat down. "I'm not still hungover—" That wasn't a total lie. It was more like he was repulsed by liquor, not sick from it. "—and I didn't order you food. I haven't eaten today, and I'm starving."

"What kept you so busy?" Miles asked.

"And why do you look barely fresher than road-kill?"

Jensen glanced around the table. These were his best friends, guys he knew all his life. He knew they'd understand. Might even be of help.

But saying everything aloud seemed about as appealing as lighting his hair on fire.

The waitress set a giant sandwich down in front of him. "Still probably another fifteen on the wings, hon."

"That's okay. This'll hold me over."

She laughed and walked away.

He dug into his sandwich, fully aware of the three sets of eyes trained on him.

"What the hell, man?" Austin said. "You leave for college, hardly ever visit, dump a huge secret on us then barely keep in touch, and now you're in town and don't even want to hang out. That big city education of yours make you think you're better than us or something?"

They were right. He'd been self-absorbed, and they couldn't possibly know, because he'd told them next to nothing.

He sighed, sat back, drained his glass. "The hearing was today. They let the asshole go."

"Oh, man," Miles said. "That sucks."

"Sorry about that," Brett said.

He knew they'd understand, even if they were mad. "That's not even the worst part."

"There's something worse?" Austin asked.

"Oh, yeah." He took another bite of sandwich and then continued. "There's something going on. The hearing proceedings were highly unusual. We didn't get to talk, which was the whole reason I was summoned home. Dad knows what's going on, because he provided a written statement. Not that I know what it said." Curse words tumbled through his head, and he took another bite of the giant sub. "They let the bastard go immediately. Immediately! Bella said that never happens."

"Bella?" Austin asked. "The girl from the parking lot?"

Jensen nodded, took another bite.

"What's she know about it?" Miles asked.

He snorted around the sausage, swallowed, and shook his head. "Get this. She's an attorney. Her firm represented Wade."

"Shut up." Austin pounded his fist on the table.

"Really. And to top it all off? Wade is working at my dad's clinic. Turns out, Ben is, too."

"What?" Brett asked. "How did you find all this out?"

"Doesn't matter." He took another bite. Didn't matter that the sub was huge. He'd almost finished it and still had room for the wings. Surprised he still had an appetite with everything going on. “Point is, my dad’s been lying. Keeping secrets. And the girl…” What to say about Bella? “It’s complicated.”

“Complicated?” Miles asked. “That’s putting it mildly. A clean break. That’s what you need.”

“It’s not always that simple,” Brett said. “When feelings are involved, things get complicated. You don’t want to intentionally hurt someone you care about.”

“We’re not talking about you,” Austin said. “And the situation is completely different.”

Jensen looked at Austin, then Brett. “What’s he talking about?”

Brett flushed and looked down. Then he cleared his throat. “I don’t think this is the right time to get into it.”

“It’s not,” Austin said. His voice cut. A sharp, final tone closing the topic. Then he looked at Jensen. “So, what can we do?”

Jensen shrugged. If Brett had problems, they couldn’t be as bad as his own. No point in taking on another burden and pressing for details. Probably couldn’t concentrate on what they told him, anyway.

The waitress brought a steaming plate of wings over and set them down in front of Jensen. “Well, look at that. I didn’t think you’d get through the sandwich, and here you are waiting on the wings.” She leaned over, grabbed the nearly empty pitcher, and straightened. “I’ll fill you up again.”

When she walked away, Jensen’s gaze followed her. His jaw dropped when he saw Simone walking in the door and heading for their table. The room had filled up, and she had to do a series of shuffles and twists to make her way through the labyrinth of chairs and tables. “Seriously, can this day get any worse?”

“Listen, man,” Brett said.

“You know what? I think I am full.” He stood, opened his wallet, and threw a bundle of bills on the table. “That should cover it. If it doesn’t, let me know and I’ll pay you back. I gotta go.” He began threading his way through the maze of patrons, purposely going out of his way to avoid Simone.

When he got to the doorway, he looked back. Simone had taken his vacant seat. She, Miles, and Austin stared at him. Brett didn't even look his way.

Jensen didn't know what the deal was, and, at that moment, he didn't care. But he did have a niggling feeling in some tiny crevice of his brain that told him whatever Brett's situation was, it would be impacting him. And soon.

Biting back a curse and a sigh, Jensen headed home.

CHAPTER 14

WHEN BELLA FINALLY DECIDED TO crawl out of bed and face the horrors of her new reality, she couldn't even do so refreshed from a good night's sleep. The bed had been comfortable. Even the clothes had worked out—Chloe left her an over-sized t-shirt and cotton shorts to sleep in. But despite her exhaustion and comfort, she'd barely dozed twenty minutes since she lay down. She couldn't get her thoughts to stop churning in her head or the queasiness to settle in her stomach.

It didn't help that Chloe and her guest hadn't done much sleeping, either.

The guy left the penthouse just before dawn. Chloe had cracked open the door and peeked in at her then. Bella pretended to sleep, and Chloe left without disturbing her. Bella didn't want to deal with more discussion. She had already said everything she was willing to say. Wouldn't say more. Definitely didn't want to talk with her just-satisfied friend. It rather grossed her out thinking Chloe had come to see her so soon after being with that guy, anyway. Maybe after Chloe showered him away. Not enough degrees of separation there.

But dawn had given way to a bright, sunny morning, given the glare coming from behind the blinds. And despite the passing of hours, her problems didn't dissolve.

So, she'd climbed out of bed. Washed her face, brushed her teeth, combed her hair. Chloe's guest bath was always fully stocked with spare sundries. She pulled on the slightly-too-tight and way-too-short shorts her friend had left for her, as well as the might-as-well-not-bother tank. She stepped in front of the full-length mirror, just to see how bad it really was.

Then wished she hadn't looked.

Maybe Chloe could get away with that look, but she couldn't. Nor did she want to.

She poked around in the closet, rooted through some drawers. Chloe had stored her winter wardrobe in the guest bedroom. Bella didn't find anything promising until she stumbled upon a man's dress shirt. Who left shirts behind in a woman's apartment? For that matter, what man had ever been there to leave one behind? Chloe did her entertaining away from home.

Bella didn't want to dwell on it. She looked it over. It didn't look fresh-from-the-laundry-pressed, but it didn't look dirty, either. A quick sniff confirmed that. It had the softest hint of a cologne, so faint she couldn't make it out, but nothing that smelled rank or foul. Not thrilled with the option of wearing a previously worn shirt, particularly when she didn't know the owner or what he'd been doing when he took it off, she made one more sweep through the closet. Unless she wanted to walk around in Chloe's ski parka, the man's shirt was her only option. So, she slipped it on over the tiny tank, buttoned and tied it at the waist, rolled up the sleeves. Unable to do anything more with her appearance, she walked out to the common area in search of coffee and Chloe.

Chloe sat at a barstool by her kitchen island, sipping a cup of coffee and reading something on her iPad. She wore the robe from the night before, but one side had slipped off her shoulder, and Bella couldn't see any straps. Determined not to dwell on her friend's state of undress—or her state of anything else—Bella walked over to the coffeepot near the sink and helped herself to a cup.

"Morning," Bella said.

"Hmm?" Chloe's voice was slow, distant. She hadn't looked up from her reading. "Oh, yeah. Good morning. How'd you sleep?"

Okay. Bella could make small talk. She didn't want to get into her troubles before the caffeine kicked in, anyway.

After a few minutes of half-hearted, one-word answers from Chloe, Bella stopped talking altogether and started making plans. She had to check on her accounts. That was first. Then, depending on her monetary situation, she needed to make living arrangements. Probably update her resume.

She looked up to see Chloe staring at her. "What? What's wrong?"

Chloe's mouth, usually turned up in a smirk, had fallen slack. She blinked and stood straighter, fixed her robe. "Nothing. Nothing. I was just surprised to see you in—long sleeves."

Bella smoothed her hands over the shirt. "The sleeves are rolled. The tails are tied. I just wanted to cover…" Her voice trailed off. It wasn't the sleeves that bothered Chloe.

It was the shirt.

"I'm sorry." She started untying the tails and rolling down the sleeves. "I didn't realize. I shouldn't have just taken this without asking first."

Chloe stepped over to her and put her hand over Bella's restless fingers, stilling them. "You didn't do anything wrong. I was just surprised. Relax. No big deal."

Bella tried to study her friend's face, to see what she really meant, but Chloe had already turned away.

"I have some errands this morning. Make yourself at home. I've left a spare key for you on the table in the foyer, and the front desk knows you'll be staying here." She walked down the hall toward her bedroom before she'd even finished speaking.

So, Bella stood there, alone in the kitchen, wearing a man's shirt and wondering who he was that he'd affected her friend so deeply.

It was so much easier to dwell on that than on her own problems.

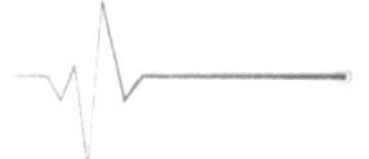

BELLA SPENT HOURS AT CHLOE'S desk calling every bank she had an account in, every credit card company she had a card with, every credit union she'd ever done business with.

Every asset, frozen.

Despite her desperate pleas to convince every customer service rep she spoke with that she didn't authorize the suspensions of the accounts, no one listened to her. The best she got was a suggestion telling her what legal options she could pursue to reverse the situation. The worst was the rep who told her she should be more responsible before hanging up on her. Wouldn't surprise her if her father had paid the guy to rub it in.

Why, oh, why, had she not taken her father off the accounts once she'd graduated?

Because her father hadn't wanted her to. Told her it was easier for him to make deposits if she needed him to. Which she never did. And that wasn't the case, anyway. But she didn't insist on autonomy, and now she was paying for it.

The best she could come up with for funds was to clean out her safe deposit box. And she certainly didn't have enough in there to live off. She barely had enough in there for a weekend getaway to Vegas. Not that she'd ever taken a trip to Vegas for the firsthand knowledge.

She opened Chloe's computer, but didn't know her password, so she was cut off from the Internet. It killed her, not knowing if she'd been fired, although deep down she knew the answer.

With no other option, she called the office. Instead of identifying herself, though, she took a different tactic.

"Hello. May I speak with Isabella Perish, please?"

"What is the matter regarding?"

"She's my attorney. I need to discuss a legal matter."

The receptionist sighed. *"Miss Perish is no longer a member of the firm. Her accounts have been distributed among other associates. If you just tell me—"*

Bella hung up the phone. Blinked back tears. Damn, her father worked fast.

So that was it. She was homeless. Jobless. Penniless. Phoneless.

Less of everything.

Panic knocked the wind out of her lungs and then sapped the strength out of her body. She slumped to the floor, stunned. Scared.

Alone.

She'd wanted autonomy, and it looked like she finally got it.

She just hadn't realized it would cost so much.

Damn it, anyway. Her father might be on her accounts, but the money in them was money she'd earned. Well, most of it, anyway. He had no right to take it from her.

She scrambled to her knees, picked up the phone again. Punched in a code to block the number from showing up on caller ID. Dialed a number from memory.

Waited.

One ring. Two. Three.

Waited.

Voicemail.

No point in leaving a message. Her mother was screening her calls which meant she wouldn't call Bella back.

Desperation and despair clawed at her, choked her. She looked around, frantic, her head whipping side to side, jerking like she was having a seizure.

No help. No escape.

She dug through her bag, tossed the contents on the floor, and knocked everything aside. Cosmetics and Kleenex scattered over the rug, and her wallet slid under the desk. Finally, she found that crumpled piece of paper, smoothed it out so she could read it.

Dr. Jeffers had written the names of other therapists for her. But she ignored his recommendations and focused on the number in the letterhead. He'd know what to do.

She lunged for the phone, had to dial three times before her fingers hit the right keys.

More ringing.

More waiting.

More voicemail.

Devastation avalanched on her, crushed her under its weight. She collapsed back down to the floor, lay sprawled on a rug that cost more money than she had access to.

And she cried.

She cried for her loss, for her stupidity.

She cried from frustration and fear.

She cried for her brother, and all she'd done to cause him pain.

And then she cried some more. Soul-crushing, gut-wrenching weeping, sobs so deep and long-buried, they welled from depths she didn't know she possessed and lasted longer than she thought humanly possible.

How long she lay there, she didn't know. But eventually the tears slowed to soft hiccups, then to quiet burbles, and then—

Silence.

Each breath came soft and silent. Her pulse slowed from the thundering in her ears to a whisper through her veins.

No phone rang, no music played.

She heard her life. Her future.

Emptiness.

Only the stillness didn't frighten her. She thought on it, waited. But she'd calmed.

It was okay with her, she realized. Everything was.

For the first time since leaving her father—no, for the first time ever—she didn't have her day planned for her. She didn't have anywhere to be, anything to do. There was only time.

Time and herself.

That thought should have paralyzed her, but it didn't. The tears had cleansed her.

She felt free. Free to take a walk. To sit in the park. To sing, to dance. To do whatever she wanted.

She scrabbled to her feet, wiggled her hips. Spun in circles with her arms to the side.

The world was at her disposal, and she knew just what to do.

BELLA LEANED AGAINST THE WARM rock and looked across the lake. Funny how life could change so much in just twenty-four hours.

A day earlier, she was defending a criminal and defending her actions to her father. Last evening, she had no money, no job, no prospects. This morning, she hit rock bottom.

And then it happened.

Everything could be changed if she stopped following her father's orders and just followed her dreams.

So, she did. She placed the call to the DA's office.

Steve was right. Ken was more than happy to hire her. Not only did he not care that Victor had spread the word far and wide to blackball her, he considered it the best recommendation she could have offered. Offered her the job on the spot. She would start a week from Monday.

Her father would probably never speak to her again, but that was probably inevitable, anyway.

She stood and stretched, looked up when her hand brushed something hanging over the rock. Recognized it as Jensen's foot.

He jumped down beside her. "Hey. Glad you're here."

"Thanks."

"I tried calling you. Sent you a couple of texts, too."

"Sorry. My dad shut off my phone service."

"What?"

"I told you I left things in a bad place. He cut me off everything. Changed the locks, froze my accounts. I got to the house last night only to discover I had no place to live, no money to fall back on, and no job to see me through."

"He cut you off, and he fired you?"

She smiled and rested her hand on his arm. "Best thing that could ever have happened to me. Really."

"But… but what are you going to do? Where did you even go last night?"

"I stayed at a friend's place. This morning, when the enormity and completeness of what Victor had done finally sunk in, I hit rock bottom. I don't think a forklift could have pried me off the floor. And then I had a moment of clarity. Complete peace. And I knew what I had to do."

"What did you do?"

"I got a job and an apartment. The only thing I need to figure out now is whether I want to try to get my existing wardrobe or just start over."

"I'm guessing it's a fairly extensive wardrobe."

She sighed. "Yes. Large and lovely. I hate to give it up. But I'm moving forward. I don't want anything from my past—anything he could claim he gave me—weighing me down as I start over."

"What about mementos? Collections?"

"The only mementos I have are awards I won trying to please him. I don't need those. Nor do I need the chachkies he's given me over the years. I guess I would like the photos…" Her voice trailed off as she thought about what she left behind. She could buy new clothes and shoes. Her cosmetics probably needed to be replenished, anyway. None of her jewelry held sentimental value. She didn't need academic awards or music boxes. But there was one box, shoved way in the back corner of her closet, she needed. It was all she had left of Troy, and she'd be damned if she'd give that up.

"Hey? You okay?" Jensen asked.

She shook her head, cleared her thoughts. "Sorry. My mind wandered. Anyway, what are you doing here?"

"Same as you, I imagine. I needed to think."

"We should buy a bench and put it here."

"No way. That will just attract people."

"Wouldn't want that."

"No, we wouldn't. Well, I know I wouldn't. I've had it with people. I can't even manage to be civil around them these days."

"You're being civil now."

He tilted his head and stared at her.

"What happened, Jensen?"

She sat and listened while he explained who Ben was and how he had seen him at the clinic. He filled her in on everything he'd learned, everything he thought. Almost broke down when he discussed his father. Her heart ached at his anguish. She knew all too well what it was like to be shut out by a father. No one should have to endure that kind of pain, especially not someone like Jensen. And definitely not on top of Unger's release. Where was the justice for Jensen's sister?

Why were fathers so callous? Why did the children always suffer?

Why were the two of them still playing the victim?

"Jensen." She grabbed his hand, squeezed it. "It's time we stop letting our fathers dictate our lives. From here forward, we do things our way."

"Easier said than done," he said. "I can't make my father tell me what I want to know."

"No, you can't. But that doesn't mean we can't find out in other ways. I'm going to look into Unger's case myself, see if I can't dig up some dirt for you."

"I appreciate the sentiment, but you aren't an attorney anymore."

"No, I'm not an attorney at my father's firm anymore. But I'm still an attorney, and honestly, I think I might have even more resources at my disposal now."

"What resources?"

"I told you. I got a new job."

"Which is?"

"I now work for the District Attorney's Office."

His hand dropped out from under hers, and she looked down at it. When she looked up, he had a smile on his face.

"You can access criminal files. Parole files."

"I'll have access to things I didn't have before, that's for sure, and that's where I'm going to start."

"When do you start your new job?"

"A week from Monday. But I bet I can get Ken or Steve to give me access codes today so I can—" she used air quotes, "—start familiarizing myself with the system and the cases."

Okay, really, who uses air quotes anymore? She dropped her hands and looked out over the lake. Oh, if only a breeze would blow and cool the shame burning her face. Maybe he'd think it was just sunburn.

He threw his arms around her. "I'm so glad we met. Thank you." He kissed her on the cheek, lowered his voice. "I mean it, Bella. I'm really glad and really grateful."

She turned and looked into his eyes. Decided this was another area of her life where she needed to take control.

Before she could talk herself out of it, she slipped her arms around his neck, pulled his head down, and kissed him.

CHAPTER 15

JENSEN HADN'T FELT OPTIMISTIC SINCE he'd first crossed the town line and entered Cathedral Lake. Summoned under false pretenses to a place he didn't want to be by a man he resented, he'd been lied to and manipulated. He'd had his world ripped out from under him. Again.

He should be in one of the worst moods of his life.

But there he was, driving down the road, humming. He was humming, for God's sake.

Because of a girl.

When they'd had their not-a-date, he thought he'd somehow blown it. She'd gone from full speed ahead to a dead stop, and he was okay with that. Well, as okay as his zipper had allowed him to be. But he'd wondered what he'd done wrong. He'd liked her and had been wondering where it would go. Thought it ended before it began.

He wasn't okay with that.

But when he found out who she was and what she did for a living, he'd been relieved it had ended.

And when he found out what she was really like? He'd been glad to start it back up again.

Watching a tennis match wouldn't have had his head going back and forth as much as his relationship with Bella did.

She worked for the DA now. She was on the right side of things. She wanted to help him.

Hell, she wanted him. The feeling was mutual.

He couldn't get her out of his mind. He kept thinking about that kiss she'd laid on him. Didn't expect it. In fact, if he had, he might have tried to avoid it. She clouded his judgment.

But calling it a welcome distraction didn't do the kiss justice.

No way did he want to go home while he felt so good. Just the thought sobered him enough that he stopped humming and turned off the radio. Still, he could feel a goofy grin on his face. He waved at a few passersby, hoped they thought he was glad to see them and wasn't just some idiot behind the wheel.

Killing time, he stopped at the park, sat at the same bench he'd met Cooper on before. His stomach growled when he caught the scent of the food trucks. Must be nearly ready to open.

When he was young, a few food trucks set up shop in the square to catch the lunch crowd. By the time he got his driver's license, several trucks made a living there, lunchtime through bar closing, and some even hit Sunday breakfast. Often, before or after school, he'd take a detour just to sample the goods. And if anything, since he'd gone away to college, even more trucks had joined the queue.

The Korean BBQ place had an amazing bulgogi platter, complete with noodles and the crispiest spring rolls he'd ever eaten. The pizza place served slices as big as his head, with sausage so spicy it justified stopping at the frozen limeade truck. The Indian truck made better butter chicken than any restaurant he'd ever been to. The Mediterranean truck made great lamb kebabs and falafel—piled so high on a pita, the bread wouldn't fold closed. He always loved the fig, Brie, and caramelized onion sandwich at the grilled cheese truck. There were at least three dessert places he couldn't get enough of. All that was on top of the new places he'd never tried.

His stomach growled again. This place was heaven on wheels. He shouldn't have had that omelet and toast for breakfast. It would cut into his ability to eat a big lunch. But which to choose...

While he walked the perimeter of the food trucks, he took in the smells. Damn, he should learn how to cook. He couldn't say if he smelled rosemary or rosewater, but his mouth watered. Savory, spicy, sweet. Fresh bread—must be the pizza dough—cinnamon. In addition to his tried and true favorites, it looked like one of the new places was a cinnamon roll truck.

Where to eat? And what a problem to have.

"Jensen."

He turned to see Cooper striding toward him. Shoulders back. Slow, confident stride. Looked just like a panther stalking its prey. Jensen knew the detective's eyes, hidden behind his ever-present sunglasses, scanned the crowds without turning his head. The consummate cop—alert, aware, ready to pounce.

Jensen wondered if he ever turned off that cop instinct. He doubted it. Everyone probably became their profession at some point. Stuck with it until retirement let them go back to who they used to be. Hopefully, not too late to enjoy themselves.

Jensen offered a handshake. "Detective. I was just about to grab lunch. Want to join me? I'm torn between Indian and Korean."

"Yeah, I'll join." He turned and started walking toward the west end of the square. "But we're going to Southern Comfort."

"What do they have?" Jensen hurried to catch up to him.

"Southern food."

Oh, so helpful.

When they got to the truck, Jensen scanned the menu. Their special was fried chicken with dumplings, greens, and a side of corn bread. Sandwich for the day was pulled pork, side of slaw. Jensen went for the sandwich, added two bags of chips to the order. Cooper got the special, extra greens, no dumplings or bread.

They sat at one of the many picnic tables set up in the tree line. Jensen dug into his sandwich, and the detective started pulling skin off the chicken.

"That's the best part," Jensen said.

"You eat like a child." He nodded at Jensen's plate. "That sauce is all sugar. So is the bun. Don't get me started on the chips or the slaw dressing."

"I don't know if I'm eating the slaw."

Cooper laughed and ate a bite of greens. "Yeah, wouldn't want to get any cabbage or carrots in your diet."

"I eat healthy. Sometimes." Jensen tried to remember the last time he had eaten healthy. Not since coming back. Then he smiled. Well, there was one vegan meal that was pretty good.

"You're getting soft, kid."

He hated it when Cooper called him 'kid' but didn't complain. He just took a bite of his sandwich. Man, it was delicious. He could snarf down three of them without batting an eye.

Some of the juice squirted out, fell onto the cardboard boat he ate over. He glanced at the mess, then looked further down. He hadn't been back long, but unless he was mistaken, he was starting to get soft in the middle. His shirt clung in the wrong places, and his shorts felt tighter than he cared to admit. He put the sandwich down, wiped his hands on his napkin, and took a sip of his iced tea. Both his good mood and his appetite seemed to have disappeared.

Cooper smiled, took a bite of chicken, and wiped his own hands. Then he leaned forward. "Listen, I'm glad I ran into you. I need to tell you, I tried to push for information. Talked to the chief about it. I don't know if he didn't know or just doesn't want me to know, but he told me to drop it. I don't think I'm going to be able to dig anything else up on Unger. Not without cause or without causing me a shit load of problems."

"I don't want you getting in trouble because of this. Let it go. I have a few angles I'm working on, anyway."

"Such as?"

"You sure you want to know?"

The detective sighed and stretched. "Probably not. Stay out of trouble, kid."

"Yes, sir, Detective, sir."

Cooper took out his wallet, removed a card, and handed it to Jensen. "Stop being a wise ass. This is my cell. I'll answer anytime, day or night. If you get into trouble, call me."

"Thanks, Tony."

Cooper grabbed his trash and Jensen's meal, turned, and tossed it all in the trash. "Go buy yourself something healthy. Better yet, hit the gym."

Jensen laughed as the cop made his way out of the park. He looked around, decided he didn't really need more food, and walked in the opposite direction, back toward where he parked. Cooper was right about one thing, at least. There were better ways of spending his time than by stuffing his face.

He headed toward the clinic.

THE STREET BUSTLED WITH ACTIVITY. He couldn't get a spot anywhere on the block, so he parked three blocks away and walked to the corner. Would have been faster to just walk over from the park. Without being able to sit in his vehicle, he had no way to hide. Wade or Ben—or, God forbid, his father—would be able to pick his stationary form out of the bustling crowd.

With no other recourse, he stepped into the pharmacy across the street from the clinic. He pretended to browse the magazines on the rack near the windows, but he really kept his attention focused on his dad's place.

With two windows, two lanes of traffic, and too many people walking up and down the street, he might as well have stayed in his car or at the park. He couldn't see anything.

"May I help you with something?"

Jensen turned and looked at a young clerk. She had a pink tinge to her cheeks and kept looking everywhere but directly at him.

"No, thanks. I'm fine."

She cleared her throat and looked down. "Well, uh… my boss told me to tell you that he stopped selling the kind of magazine you're looking for. He said two blocks over, there's a graphic novel place who keeps that kind of thing in stock."

Jensen stared at her, took a second or two to process what she meant. Then his face flamed. "That's not what—"

She turned and hurried back to the counter.

He shook his head and chuckled to himself. That poor girl, having to talk to the guy she thought was a perv and give him directions to where he could find porn.

On second thought, it really wasn't funny. What was the owner thinking, sending her over to him? People these days.

Before he found the owner and said or did something he'd probably regret, he walked to the door. Tried one last time to peer across the street, but he still couldn't see anything. Might as well head home.

Fuck it.

That was his father's clinic. He had every right to drop in if he wanted.

So, he strode out of the pharmacy and walked right across the street. Horns blared as he dodged traffic—probably should have waited until the way was clear—and one particularly upset driver yelled out his window and offered an obscene gesture. None of that fazed him, though. He stepped onto the side-walk, walked right up to the door, and let himself in.

He started to head to the back, ignoring the receptionist's frantic calls to him to stop, but when he got to the door, it was locked. He turned toward her, ducked his head to talk to her through the window. She had shut and secured the window and had rolled her chair far back from the glass.

He nodded to the door. "Open up."

She shook her head, eyes wide, face pale.

What was her name? Kelly? Katie? Kath? Kath.

"Kath, come on. Open the door."

Her brow furrowed, and she studied him. A nurse stepped into the office area and looked at her. "What are you doing, Meg?"

Meg. Huh. Wasn't even close.

Meg gestured toward the window where Jensen stood. "He's trying to break in."

The nurse turned around.

"Jensen!"

"Carley? Hey."

"What are you doing, standing out there? Get in here." She pressed a buzzer, unlocking the door, and Jensen stepped inside. Carley rushed over and greeted him.

"Haven't seen you in ages. How have you been?"

"No sense in complaining."

"Isn't that the truth?" She linked her arm through his and brought him around to introduce him to Meg. Clearly neither of them knew who the other was, and wasn't that more than a little sad?

Carley Markum had worked with his father for years. Jensen only met her after Hope had died, but they'd had an easy camaraderie since day one. Hell, she was a lot easier to talk to than his dad and a lot more fun. He used to wonder if something was going on between her and Royce, but after the way his dad had reacted when he learned about his wife's infidelity, Jensen doubted it. Carley was just chummy with everyone.

While Meg busied herself in her paperwork, Carley continued babbling at him and he made small talk for a while. He hadn't had a plan when he barged in, so standing there talking with her until he decided his next move was not only not a hardship, it was a blessing in disguise.

Then Carley's demeanor shifted, as did her attention. And Jensen knew. He knew without turning his head, without anyone speaking.

Wade had walked into the reception area.

"Jensen."

Wade's voice, somewhere between shock and resignation, grated on Jensen's nerves. Far more than he'd been prepared for. Rage burned through him, a wildfire unchecked, consuming his reason and sanity in combustible fury. He clenched his jaw, fought for control of his temper, for control of his fists. His vision tinged red on the edges, the only thing he could see—Wade's face. On that, he laser focused.

Good God, he couldn't control himself. He would kill the man. Choke the life out of him with his bare hands.

Already on the balls of his feet, ready to lunge, Carley stepped in front of him. Put her hands on his chest. Pushed softly. Gently. But with firm purpose.

"Jensen," she whispered. "This isn't the time or the place. Come with me."

She grabbed his wrist. Her fingers felt cool over his heated skin, started sinking in. She pulled, but he didn't budge. Couldn't move. When she gave a second, violent tug, he finally stepped forward and stumbled after her as she dragged him to an exam room.

She closed the door behind them. Hard. The click echoed in the room.

"Is that why you're here?" she asked. "For him?"

Words, emotions, and some things he couldn't even define tumbled through him. What to say? What to do?

He raised his hand, raked his fingers through his hair. Kicked the rolling doctor's stool across the room. It bounced off the light blue wall, leaving a charcoal-colored smudge on the paint before it ricocheted back toward him.

Carley stopped it with her knee, slid it under the counter. Grabbed Jensen and muscled him to a chair and forced him down on it.

"Listen to me." She snapped her fingers in front of his eyes, but he couldn't acknowledge her, his gaze trained on a fixed spot in front of him. Wade Unger. He could still see his face, hear his voice. Carley merely registered as a tinny echo in the recesses of his mind.

"Jensen." Her voice grew louder, began to penetrate his awareness.

"Jensen." That time, a sharp report.

He blinked a few times.

"Don't make me get the smelling salts."

He blinked again, tried to focus on her face.

"Or slap you."

"You wouldn't." His voice didn't sound at all like his. It was hollow, vacant. Pained.

"I think we both know I would. Now, take a few deep breaths for me. In."

He just sat there.

"I said deep breaths. In." She shook him a little.

He took a long draw of air.

"Good. Now, out. Slowly. Purse your lips."

He would not. But he did breathe out.

"Again." She walked him through a few calming breaths until he had settled. But he didn't want to know what his blood pressure was at that moment.

"You coming here was a bad idea, Jensen. A colossally bad idea. Monumentally huge."

"I get it."

"I don't think you do. There's a lot more at stake here than just your feelings."

He finally focused on her. "I wouldn't know. No one will tell me anything. What is at stake, Carley?"

"What do you know?"

"Nothing. Absolutely nothing. My father," he spat the word, "won't tell me a single fucking thing. So, tell me. What the hell's going on?"

"Has it occurred to you that Royce hasn't said anything to you because you can't control your temper?"

"Maybe I wouldn't be so damn angry all the time if I knew what the hell was going on!"

Carley crossed her arms and leaned against the door. "Yell at me again, and I'll remove you from the premises."

"I'm not—" He jumped to his feet and clenched his fists at his side. Then he unclenched his fingers and lowered his tone. "I'm not yelling. Not at you. I'm just talking loud."

"Well, this is a place of business. We have kids here. The elderly. Use some common sense, Jensen. You aren't the only person with problems. Don't bring all your baggage in here and dump it on everyone else."

Okay, she was right. A brawl in a doctor's clinic probably wasn't the best idea ever. He expected to see Wade there. He just hadn't expected the visceral response he'd experienced.

"I'm sorry. I just—" What? Words couldn't express the blind fury he'd felt, the primal urge to destroy the man who'd killed his sister and devastated his family. He bit back another oath and raked his fingers through his hair again.

Carley pushed off the door and walked over to him. She held her arms out to him.

He only hesitated a moment before stepping into her embrace.

This is what he'd needed. From his father. His mother. His sister. Someone. Anyone close to him to understand him. To hold him. To just let him grieve, let him vent. Let him rail at the universe and curse the situation.

Jensen clung to her, squeezed her. She rubbed his back, stroked his hair.

Finally, drained and calmed, he stepped back. That was exactly what he'd needed. That, and answers.

"Carley, please. I can't stand this. What's going on?"

She sighed and pulled the rolling stool out, then she sat and faced him. "Jensen, you've known me for a pretty long while now. I think you know I tell it like it is, and I don't pull any punches."

"That's why I'm asking you. I know you'll tell me the truth."

She shook her head. "That's the other thing you should know about me. I don't betray confidences."

Jensen started to object, but Carley stood her ground and held up her hand to stop him.

"Uh-uh. No. Listen. When I give my word to keep a secret, I keep it. And you know this. I never betrayed Ben's trust. Didn't betray your father's, and I've kept a hell of a lot more secrets over the years. The reason people tell me things is because they know I'm a vault, and their information is safe with me."

"But—"

"That said," she continued, ignoring his interruption, "I do tell the truth. So, I'm going to give you more than apparently anyone else has."

He backed up, leaned against the counter, gripped it so hard his fingers hurt.

"It's no accident that Wade is here. He was *placed* here. Do you understand what I'm telling you?"

He shrugged. "I know he was placed here. I'm trying to figure out why."

She shook her head. "No. That's not what I'm telling you. His parole officer didn't arrange this for him, nor did his attorney. But they're both involved in this situation. Wade was specifically selected to work here. He has a unique skill set and background that made him the only person who could fill the spot."

What the hell did that mean?

"And that's why Ben's here. Only he and your father are fully aware of Wade's history and able to realize when he's not being honest."

"Bullshit. Unger lied to them both for God knows how long, and neither suspected anything."

"Actually, that isn't true. Ben knew, or at least suspected, something long before Hope died."

"Before Unger *killed* her, you mean."

"Jensen." She sighed. "Now isn't the time for semantics. Listen to me. You need to stop poking around this. You're digging, and you aren't prepared for what you might find."

"I don't care. I want the truth, even if no one thinks I'm ready for it."

"It's about more than the truth."

"It's not some dire, life-and-death situation. Give me a—"

She tipped her head to the side. Stared at him, eyes wide.

"Oh, come on. How can Unger being here be dangerous?"

She shook her head. "You're just going to have to trust that it is. Now, stay out of it. I mean it. The last thing your father needs is to have to worry about you, too."

He snorted. "Well, there's a first time for everything, isn't there?"

"Jensen. Don't—"

"Unless you have something else to say, I'm going to go."

She shook her head. Slowly. Censure in the frown on her face.

"Thanks, Carley." He squeezed her arm, opened the door, and headed for the lobby.

"Jensen." His father's voice slowed his stride. Damn it, he'd almost made it to the reception desk when he heard his name. He picked up his pace and kept walking.

When he grasped the doorknob, his father's hand covered his.

"What are you doing here?"

"Can't a kid visit his father at work?"

"Sure." Royce moved around him and leaned against the door, blocking Jensen's departure. "But you didn't actually visit me, so I have to wonder, why are you here?"

"If you'd get out of the way, I wouldn't be."

"Jensen, we need to talk."

"About? Your constant disappointment in me? My embarrassing you at the hearing? My inability to do anything right? What?"

Royce sighed. "Why don't you come to my office?"

"Are you going to tell me what's going on, or are you just going to lecture me again?"

"Are you coming?" Royce held out a folder, gesturing down the hallway toward where the offices were.

He looked toward where his father pointed. Ben stood at a filing cabinet, pretending to look through folders. His gaze was trained on Jensen, though. Just when it looked like he might smile or wave, Jensen looked away.

"It was a mistake coming here. I have to go."

"Jensen."

He reached for the doorknob and stared at his father. Royce stood there for a moment, but then stepped aside.

Jensen forced himself to walk with steady, slow strides. He might be close to a meltdown, but he'd be damned if he'd let anyone know it.

CHAPTER 16

IT TOOK ALMOST TWO HOURS, three customer service reps, a supervisor, a manager, and every ounce of willpower she had not to strangle someone, but finally, finally, she convinced the cell phone company to issue her a new phone and transfer her old number to it.

Why not just reinstate the old phone? Because, that would be the simplest solution. And no mobile phone company she'd ever dealt with believed in simple. So, despite digging the phone out from under the passenger seat, taking it inside, and using her most effective argument techniques, she had to admit partial defeat. This meant she had to confirm cancellation of her first account, buy a new phone, create a new account without her father's name on it, get the old number activated on the new phone, and get her contacts transferred over. And by 'get the new number activated,' the company really meant she had to buy the rights to it for an exorbitant fee.

Served her right for having so many joint accounts with her father. It was one thing when she was in boarding school. Quite another since she'd become an adult.

But she'd been lazy. Or complacent. Or afraid her father would be angry with her and overreact.

Victor Perish? Overreact?

A fit of laughter overcame her. The whole situation was ludicrous.

She wiped her eyes, sobering quickly when she realized what she had to do next.

She called her mother.

As expected, no answer.

Bella didn't leave a message, however. Instead, she ended the call and redialed immediately.

Again, it went to voicemail.

So, Bella call-bombed her. She just kept hitting 'end' and redialing.

A sane person would have answered or turned off the phone. Not Bella's mother, though.

Bella could picture her sitting in the library, clutching the phone in her lap, agonizing over what to do, praying her daughter would stop calling and take the decision out of her hands.

Most days, Bella would play along. There was no point in harassing her mother. She always listened to Victor.

But Olivia Perish also had a soft spot for her child, for both her children. But especially for Bella, now that Troy was gone.

Thinking about her brother almost made her stop. Almost. After all—despite the social status and the material comforts Victor had provided Olivia—her mother had suffered greatly under her husband's tyrannical rule of the Perish family.

But Bella kept calling. Because seriously, if she and her brother could be forced out, who was to say her mother couldn't? Or wouldn't be better off for it?

After about five minutes of dialing, ending, and redialing, Bella got in her car. She continued the cycle until she reached the Perish residence.

Instead of going to the front door—pointless, really, because she knew no one would answer and her key wouldn't work—she headed toward the back of the house. The kitchen door was usually unlocked during the day so their staff could come and go easily. Without disturbing the Perish family, of course. Bella sighed and shook her head and continued dialing and redialing.

When she walked through the side yard, she glanced in the large bay window and stopped in her tracks. Just as she'd pictured, her mother sat on a chaise lounge clutching her phone. She perched on the edge of the cushion, feet crossed at the ankles, shoes still on her feet. She wore a pewter sheath that hadn't a wrinkle in it, and she'd applied a light dusting of makeup, tied her hair in a side chignon, and donned her trademark pearls.

To the casual observer, she looked like the consummate socialite. To Bella, however, she looked ready to snap. Her hands trembled slightly, the shadows under her eyes still showed beneath her cosmetics, and she shook one of her feet. Olivia Perish never fidgeted. Never.

Bella almost pitied her, but not quite. Her mother didn't have to be torn between daughter and husband—she chose to be. And that made all the difference to Bella.

Seriously, all she had to do was answer the damn phone. Her father would never know.

Well, he was Victor Perish. Maybe he would know.

It didn't matter. Parents should always answer their children's calls. Clearly Victor wouldn't win any father-of-the-year awards. But Olivia wasn't Victor, and she was a mother. Mothers should answer when their children call. They should always be there for their kids.

She hadn't been there for Troy. But Bella wasn't giving her the chance to freeze her out.

Resuming her clandestine trek around the house, she hunched over and darted through the yard and around the mansion. When she reached the back door, she tried the knob. As expected, it was unlocked. She slipped inside and listened for the staff. Not hearing any of the usual bustle and busyness, she thought about checking out her father's office, just in case he was still at home. Instead, she decided the better option was to confront her mother, whether Victor was home or not. So, she headed down the hall for the library.

She swung the door open a few feet, hurried inside, and closed the door again. Her mother never looked up, the hinges so silent she never noticed Bella enter.

She might not have noticed even if the hinges squeaked like the ones in a Wes Craven film. Her hands covered her face, and she sobbed—deep, gut-wrenching sobs—which had to distract her from anything going on around her.

Bella crossed the room and sat down beside her mother. When Olivia didn't even look up, Bella wrapped her arm around her shoulder.

Olivia jumped back and gasped. She raised her hand to her lips, widened her eyes and stared at her daughter.

"Mom," Bella said.

Olivia shook her head and whispered, her tone frantic, her words clipped. "No. No. You can't be here. You have to go."

"I'm not leaving until you talk to me. And until I get what I came for."

"What you came f—?" Olivia broke off her sentence and glanced at the door. Then she looked at her wristwatch. Finally, she met Bella's gaze. "Your father hasn't left for the office yet. He's given specific orders for you not to remove anything from this house. He said nothing here is yours. Not your clothes. Not your books. Nothing. He said he paid for it all, so it's his. He's having everything boxed. For charity. Or disposal. " She stole a peek at the door again. "You really can't be here."

"Well, I am here, and I have a few things to say to you. Then I'm going up to my room and getting what's mine."

"He says nothing here is yours. Not anymore."

"He can have all the material shit he wants. But there's something irreplaceable here, and I'm not leaving without it."

"At least let me get it, then. Some of the staff are up there right now. You'll never get in."

"So, go run them off. I'm not giving anyone the chance to go through my stuff and toss something I want."

"Isabella, please." Olivia twisted her pearls around her finger. "He'll *see* you."

"So now I'm not even allowed to visit my own mother? Has it really come to that? Because I argued with him over a work matter?"

"You don't understand how important—"

"Oh, I understand plenty, Mother. Far more than you. His job, his reputation? That's all that matters to him. I was only a means to an end, a legacy for him to shape and train and leave behind for posterity. And probably my children after me, too. He doesn't love me. Never did. He didn't love Troy, either. That's why we're so dispensable."

"Oh, honey, no! That's not it at all. He loves you. He loves you both. More than anything."

"That's why he's sent us both away."

"It's tough love."

"That's tough shit. I don't know if he believes that or if it's the lie you tell yourself to keep going, but it's ridiculous. Tough love is grounding a child when she breaks curfew. It's not disowning her for disagreeing with you and walking away."

"But that's just it, Bella. You're the one who walked away."

"And he's the one who wouldn't allow me to come back! Of course, I walked away. How was I supposed to stay in the same room with him? How was I supposed to sit there and let him tear me down? Especially when he was wrong? That's not a father-daughter relationship. That's not even a healthy boss-subordinate relationship. He's a dictator. A tyrant, pure and simple. And I won't stay under his thumb a moment longer." She stood. "Frankly, if I were you, I wouldn't stay, either."

Her mother also jumped to her feet. "And where would you like me to go? What would you have me do? I haven't had a job since college. All of my family are thousands of miles away. All my friends are his friends. If I go, I'll have nothing."

"If you stay, you have even less."

"I love him."

"I thought I did, too. But it wasn't reciprocated, and now I'm better off for moving on."

Olivia flung herself down to the chaise, threw her body back, and covered her eyes with her arm. "You're young and educated, Bella. You can still make your own life. Mine is over."

"And that's your call. But I'm going up to my room, and I'm getting what's mine."

Her mother let her arm fall to the side and met her daughter's gaze. "I don't suppose there's anything I can do to stop you?"

"No."

Olivia sighed. "You're putting me in an impossible situation."

"No, Mother. You've put yourself there. You could stand up to him. You choose not to."

"And how well did that work for you?"

"Goodbye, Mother." Bella headed for the library door. She didn't expect better than what she got, but it irritated the ever-loving crap out of her that her mother was so afraid. Getting out from under her father had been frightening at first, but now it was the most liberating and wonderful feeling. It could only help her mother to make a clean break, but as expected, she chose security over family.

What a sad commentary on their lives.

She reached for the doorknob, and her mother's hand covered hers.

"Let me go first. I'll clear the way."

Surprised, Bella stepped aside and let her mother open the door.

Olivia walked out into the hall, looked both ways, then gestured Bella to follow her. When they went the long way around to the staircase, Bella assumed the detour was to avoid passing Victor's office. Then Olivia hurried up the stairs, beckoning her daughter to follow.

Once upstairs, her mother stopped outside Bella's bedroom and put her ear to the door. A frown marred her delicate features. She put her finger to her lips and grabbed Bella's hand, tiptoeing down the hall toward Troy's old room. She opened the door, nudged Bella inside, and whispered, "Don't make a sound. I'll get you when the coast is clear."

Then she backed out of the room, closing Bella in behind her.

Bella hadn't been in that room since her brother left. She hadn't planned on ever seeing it again and being forced inside on a whim gave her no time to prepare for the onslaught of emotions that hit like a tsunami.

Nothing had changed. A used towel hung over his bathroom doorknob. Sports equipment lay in a pile in the corner. A dirty sock and a mismatched shoe peeked out of the bottom of his bed skirt. Photos of family and friends stuck out of his mirror frame. Trophies and books lined his shelves, and a model car—only partially assembled—sat on his desk.

It was like he was still there. The room had become a museum, frozen in time, a tribute to the young man who used to dwell there.

Bella ran her finger over the surface of the dresser. Not a speck of dust. Yet the room still smelled like her brother.

Did it? Was it her imagination?

Or did the staff continually spray his cologne in the room after cleaning it?

And how sick was it if they did?

Who preserved a room like that? What was her father thinking? Because only he could make such a demand and have it obeyed without fault, without question.

Her legs buckled, and she gripped the bedpost before falling. She wanted nothing more than to lie on his bed, breathe him in, and cry for all that had happened. But, given the state of the room, she was certain someone would notice the mussed covers when she rose again.

She stood there, clutching the furniture, breathing in her brother.

And missing him. Deep in the pit of her soul, she missed him. Mourned for him. Yearned for him.

Tears ran down her face, but she didn't wipe them. She barely noticed them.

A photo on the mirror caught her attention. A little girl, four years old, perched on her big brother's shoulders. They stood outside their lake house, the sun setting behind them. She remembered the day they'd taken the photo. They'd swum all afternoon, and that evening, they'd grilled hot dogs and toasted marshmallows over the fire.

It was the last time they'd spent a weekend there. The last trip.

The last one before the incident.

God, how she'd loved him. And given the smile on his face, he'd loved her.

She knew he did. Look at what he'd lost. All for her.

The door swung open, and Bella turned to talk to her mother. It was time she came clean.

But Olivia wasn't there. Victor stood in the doorway.

"**DO YOU WANT TO EXPLAIN** what you're doing in my house? In this room?" His voice, normally low and confident, trembled.

Did her mother sell out, or was she just that unlucky to be caught the first time she'd violated not one of his commands, but two?

Better to err on the side of caution and not reveal that she'd seen her mother.

"How'd you even know I was here? The door was closed."

"I owe you no explanation, but if you must know, I saw movement under the door. Careless."

She sighed. "I came to get something."

"From Troy's room?"

"No. But while I was here, I thought that I'd take one last look around before leaving."

"There's nothing in this house that belongs to you."

"Actually, that's not true." She stepped around him and headed down the hall toward her old room. "I've come to get something important to me. Something you didn't buy, so I have every right to it."

"If it's under my roof, I own it. Get out. Now."

She stopped outside her old door and looked at him. "Or what? You're going to fire me? Kick me out? Shut down all my accounts? Oh, wait. You can't. You already did all that."

"I'll have you forcibly removed."

"Yeah, wouldn't want you to get your hands dirty." She opened the door and stepped inside her room. "Make sure you get the help to do it."

"Don't think I won't. In fact," he took his phone out of his pocket, "I think I'll just call the police and let them deal with it."

Would he? Surely, he wouldn't want the publicity. But he didn't make idle threats. She bit her lip as she considered her options. Then, squaring her shoulders, she finally stood up to him. "Do what you want. By the time they get here, I'll be long gone."

"I'll have them arrest you for stealing."

She walked around boxes in different stages of packing. Some hadn't been assembled, some were empty. Others were half-filled, and still others were already sealed. Weaving her way to the closet, she stepped inside, wound to the back corner, and retrieved a box. Then she made her way back out. Victor stood in the doorway, blocking her.

"This is all I want. I'm going."

"You trespassed for that box."

"If you want to call what I did 'trespassing,' then yes, I did."

"You could have just asked for that."

"Asked for it? You said nothing here belongs to me."

He took a deep breath. "A simple phone call would have saved both of us this aggravation."

She tilted her head to the side. "Like anyone here will even answer my calls."

"I would have, but instead of reaching out to me, you tried the house line, you tried your mother."

So, the SOB *did* know she'd been calling her mom. Figured.

"You made your point perfectly clear when you threw me out, fired me, and closed all my accounts. I didn't think there was anything more to say."

"You could say you're sorry."

She forgot her fear and snorted in derision. “Sorry? For what? Having my own opinions and ideas? That’s what parents are supposed to want for their kids. But we’ve never really had a traditional relationship, have we? Certainly, never a healthy one.”

“And what’s that supposed to mean?”

She sighed. Was he really that obtuse, or was he leading her down a path just to trip her up with her own words? Didn’t really matter anymore. They were through. Her visit there today had proved as much.

“Let me answer your question with one of my own. When you kicked Troy out, you preserved his room like a shrine. It’s been years, and it still looks like he lives here. It still smells like him in there. That’s a lot of work to save the memory of someone you tossed aside. But me? You just banished me and already my life is in boxes ready to be tossed. So, how do you consider our relationship traditional or healthy?”

Victor stood and stared at her for the longest time. So long, she wondered if he’d even been listening to her. She was just about to step around him, when he turned and stepped into the hall.

Without turning around, he said, “If you have nothing more to say, I guess we’re through here. When all your things are packed, I’ll have them sent to you. Provided you leave your forwarding address. I’m sure the staff can get it from your mother. Your accounts will be unfrozen by the end of the day.”

He strode down the hall, flung open Troy’s bedroom, and slammed the door behind him.

Stunned, she stood there. What the hell had just happened?

She glanced down the hallway and saw her mother poking her head out of her bedroom door. Bella closed her door and approached her mother.

“What did you say to him?”

Olivia shook her head. “Nothing. I didn’t even know he had come upstairs until I heard him talking to you in Troy’s room.”

Did she even ask about Troy’s room? Or about her father backing off? She shook her head.

Instead, she said, "I'm leaving. I'd leave my forwarding address, but I don't think there's anything here that I want. Other than this." She lifted the box in her hands.

"Oh, Bella, darling. Please don't turn your things away. Most of them are quite lovely and would take a fortune to replace."

"I'm not worried about the clothes, Mother."

"Then worry about our feelings. Your father is reaching out to you, making a concession. Don't rebuff him."

"Because he's been so concerned about my feelings to this point?"

"Bella." She grabbed free hand. "Please. That's the biggest olive branch I've ever seen your father extend."

Bella didn't answer her. As far as olive branches went, it was rather anemic in her opinion.

She left without a glance back, and she walked boldly out the front door. Gunning the engine, she took off down the driveway and away from the toxic environment she'd been liberated from.

Only this time, she didn't feel free so much as on a leash.

Or a noose.

Sighing, she pulled over and took out her phone to send a text. She'd text both parents her forwarding address and let the chips fall.

When she put her phone back in her purse, she saw the paper Dr. Jeffers had given her. On a whim, she randomly chose a number—Dr. Hannah Morgan—and placed a call.

Was it good fortune, bad luck, or Dr. Jeffers' influence? She didn't know. What she did know was she had ten minutes to get to Dr. Morgan's office for a brief consultation.

DR. JEFFERS KEPT HIS OFFICE in the ground floor of his traditional brownstone. Dr. Morgan's office couldn't have a more different feel. She had a space in a sleek, upscale medical center on the outskirts of Cathedral Lake's commercial district. The whole way there, the entire time Bella walked from her car to the lobby, the duration of her chat with the receptionist… she second-guessed herself to the point that she had her hand on the handle of the door when the receptionist returned.

"Please don't leave. Dr. Morgan is ready. She'll see you now."

God, her timing was as bad as her decision-making.

Squaring her shoulders and holding her head high, she walked past the receptionist without making eye-contact. Her cheeks burned enough without seeing the pity on her face.

She entered the therapist's room and looked around. No wood floors. No cushy wingchairs. No stuffed bookshelves.

No, Dr. Morgan's office looked nothing like a gentleman's club. Shelves of toys and art supplies lined one wall, with beanbag chairs scattered on the floor in front of them. In a corner hung a swing suspended from beams in the ceiling. A low, trim sofa on the opposite side of the room faced one of those stability ball chairs. Rough brick walls and exposed pipes lent the whole place an urban feel. Urban loft meets upscale daycare.

Definitely not like Dr. Jeffers' office.

Definitely didn't give Bella a sense of security and trust, either.

For the second time, she turned to walk out.

"Please, don't rush off." A woman stepped out of a doorway Bella hadn't noticed before. Her brown hair was pulled back into a messy braid. She wore ripped jeans, a paint-splattered shirt, and absolutely no makeup.

Bella hesitated by the door.

The woman crossed to her and extended her hand. "I'm Dr. Morgan. You can call me Hannah."

Bella shook her hand but didn't leave the doorway.

"I know what you must be thinking," Hannah said. "I look more like an artist than a therapist."

Shrugging, Bella glanced around the room.

"Today I had a group session with several of my younger clients. Art therapy. I assure you, despite my appearance, I'm a qualified therapist."

"Children's therapy? You're a child psychologist?"

"A family therapist. From what Tod told me, you have some family issues to work through."

Bella bit her lip.

Hannah led her gently into the office. "Please, have a seat." She walked her to the sofa before sitting opposite her in the stability-ball chair. "It's good for the core." She patted her stomach.

After a short period of silence, Hannah leaned forward. "Look, Bella, Tod gave me a brief rundown of your situation, but he wanted you to fill in the details. Today is crazy busy for me, but I squeezed you in because of him."

"God, I must come off like a total basket case if you guys are dropping everything to see me."

"We don't use that term."

Bella sighed.

"I have five more minutes before my next session. Why don't you tell me what's bothering you most right now, and then you can fill out paperwork on your way out. I'll have Stephanie call you to schedule your next appointment, and we can really get to work. Sound good?"

Her life was in shambles, her first therapist cut her loose and recommended her to a child psychologist, and she had five minutes to pour her heart out, less if she wanted feedback before she left. What could possibly be wrong with that?

"My father threw me out, cut me off, basically disowned me. My things are already being packed. Dad ran off my brother years ago, but his room has been preserved like a shrine. We just had a massive confrontation… "

"You and your brother?"

"Me and my dad. He extended his version of an olive branch which wasn't much. I don't know what to make of any of it."

Hannah rocked side to side. "We're definitely going to need a long appointment."

AFTER FILLING OUT A REAM of forms—and she thought lawyers had a lot of paperwork—Bella went for a drive to clear her head. She finally pulled over at the beach and looked out over the water.

Before she had time to delve deeper into her thoughts, though, her phone rang. Unknown caller.

She hated to answer when she didn't recognize the number, but with everything going on, she decided she'd better.

"Hello?"

And, damn it all to hell, shouldn't she just have let it go to voicemail?

"Miss Parish, this is Wade Unger. I haven't been able to reach your father, and he had given me your number in case—"

"What do you want, Mr. Unger?"

"Doctor."

"You need a doctor? Hang up and call 9-1-1."

"No. My title. Doctor. Not mister."

"Dr. Unger." Pretentious ass. "I'm going to hang up now. If you need anything, call my father."

"Well, like I said, I've been trying. I can't reach him. But I think you're better suited for this job, anyway."

"I don't work for you, Dr. Unger. I don't even work for my father any longer." Hmm. Wonder if she should have told him that. Maybe she could have learned something if she'd kept quiet. She could be in trouble if the DA's office found out they'd been talking, and she hadn't informed him she worked for them.

Before she could decide how to proceed, Unger continued.

"Look. This isn't a legal matter, per se. But I've noticed Jensen Keller poking around. I need someone to get him off my back."

"It's not up to me to intervene on your behalf."

"It's dangerous, Ms. Perish. And I know the two of you are friendly. You could get him to leave things alone."

How in the hell do people find these things out? Was she the only person without a spy network and hacking capabilities? Surely a guy fresh out of prison couldn't possibly know more about her life than she did about his, and yet there they were—her knowing next to nothing and him knowing some of her personal business.

"Ms. Perish?"

"I'm here." She closed her eyes and squeezed the bridge of her nose.

"Please. I wouldn't ask if it wasn't important. Get him to stay away."

"Mr.—Dr. Unger. I don't believe anything I say to Mr. Keller will make a difference one way or another. If you really want him out of your business, I'd suggest you contact him directly, explain your feelings on the matter, and answer any questions he might have. Otherwise, you probably aren't going to shake him."

"One of the conditions of my parole is to leave the family alone."

"And yet you're working at Dr. Keller's clinic." Maybe she did know a thing or two that wasn't public knowledge.

He sighed. *"A necessary evil, I assure you. One the parole board understands and approves of."*

"They're the only ones," she said.

"Please just get him to stay away. I've probably already overstepped my bounds by contacting you."

He ended the call before she could respond.

Just as well. What the hell would she say to that, anyway?

CHAPTER 17

JENSEN HUNG UP THE PHONE and considered throwing it against the wall or stomping it into little pieces.

However, neither would do him any good..

When Bella called, he'd been happy to hear from her, even if the call was unexpected. Then she told him her *reason* for calling.

Like he'd ever give Wade the satisfaction of backing off? Especially when he asked him to? Fat. Fucking. Chance.

He drove back to the clinic, found a parking spot up the street, and he sat. Rolled down the window and turned off the engine. Waited.

And waited.

And waited some more.

Didn't matter to him how long he sat there. When Wade came out of the clinic, he would approach him, and he wasn't backing off. Not until he got answers.

Good answers.

A knock on his door made him turn.

Ben. Fucking. Lyndon.

"What the hell do you want?"

"Look, Jensen, I know we aren't on the best of terms, but—"

"Best of terms? Are you kidding me? That's how you want to characterize our relationship?"

Lyndon ran his hands over his face. "I know what you must think of me, and it's nothing I haven't thought myself."

"Doubt that."

"Regardless of your feelings, I still care about your well-being. I need to warn you, what—"

"Well, don't. Don't care. Don't warn. I don't want your concern. I don't want your opinions or advice. I sure as hell don't want your apology, not that you ever offered me one. Leave me the hell alone."

"Jensen, please. Just listen to what I have to say. Then I'll leave you alone."

"Listen to you? Why? For what reason would I ever even consider that?"

"Because of our history together."

"That's something I want to forget."

"Then do it for Hope."

The pain was swift, soul deep. "Don't. You don't get to bring her up. Don't even say her name."

"I get it. I do. But regardless of your feelings for me, you need to go. Now. And don't come back."

"Of course, you're warding me off. Why doesn't that surprise me?"

"I'm doing this for you."

"Ben, what are you doing here? Not here with me, but here, at the clinic. You annihilated any relationship with my family years ago. So, why?"

Ben looked down at his feet, then over toward the clinic. "What can I say? A lot of history. A lot of water under the bridge."

"Yeah, well the reason we study history is to avoid repeating it, so spare us all and just go away."

"Listen to what I said, Jensen." Ben patted the truck and walked away, disappearing around the corner.

Jensen punched the steering wheel. Once. Again. A third time. The horn sounded, drawing unwanted attention to him. He massaged his knuckles and slunk down in his seat.

He thought it had been hot before. Now rage heated his blood. The truck went from just hot to positively stifling. He sat there, hour after hour, sweating and raging and cursing every twist of fate that brought him to that moment. Ignoring Ben on principle and unwilling to risk missing Wade, he refused to leave even for a short while to buy a drink. His only concession to the heat was to occasionally turn on the a/c, but once he cooled down, he switched it off again, unwilling to pollute the air.

And still he seethed.

Finally, someone came to the clinic door and flipped the sign from OPEN to *CLOSED*. A short while later, the receptionist stepped out, followed by Carley.

Jensen slid lower in his seat. He doubted anyone would even look up the street at his vehicle, let alone recognize him through the tinted windows and the late-day glare on the windshield, but he didn't want to risk it. He kept staring at the door, waiting. Waiting.

Waiting.

Soon his father stepped out. He stood staring at the plant bed for a bit, then walked down the street, away from where Jensen sat. Ben came out about five minutes later. He looked around, then bent over one of the planters and moved a few of the plants aside. Then he stood and rubbed the back of his neck. Spinning around quickly, he glanced up and down the street. His gaze didn't linger on Jensen's truck, but it looked as though he frowned when he noticed it. He turned away quickly and hurried off in the direction Royce had gone.

Finally Wade stepped out. He carried a jacket bunched in his hands and tucked the bundle under his arm while he locked the door behind him. Then he bent down, adjusted the jacket, and rooted around in the plant bed. When he stood, he held a sprig of one of the plants in his hand. Despite the heat, he put the jacket on and tucked the sprig into his lapel. Then he walked off in the direction Ben and Royce had gone.

What the hell was going on?

Jensen jumped out of his truck and hurried after him. He followed Wade around the corner to a local diner, then inside. Spotting his target at a booth near the back, he took a breath and marched that way.

Wade's eyebrows shot up when Jensen slid into the seat across from him, then immediately his features smoothed into a dull expression. He leaned over the table and spoke with clenched teeth through a fake smile.

"What are you doing here? I told you to stay away. You must leave. Now."

"I'm not going anywhere until you tell me what the hell is going on."

Wade glanced around, but the smile remained plastered on his face. "Not here. Not now. You're jeopardizing everything."

"Jeopardizing what?"

"Would you lower your voice?" The smile had slipped away, he'd stopped clenching his teeth and spoke outright. Spat at Jensen was more apt. "You're in danger, and you're endangering me. You must leave. Now."

Jensen didn't move.

"Now, damn it."

"Not without—"

"I know. You want answers. You want to know something? Ask your dad."

"I did. For some fool reason, he's protecting you."

Wade snorted. "Hardly. He's protecting you. Now get the hell out of here."

Jensen failed to see how anyone, particularly his father, had his best interests at heart. So, he sat there, staring at Wade.

"Fine. You want answers? I'll give them to you. But only if you go. Now."

"Why?"

"I'll tell you everything. Later. But you have to get out of here."

"When? Where?"

Wade's hands trembled, and he bounced his knee so fast his whole body shook. "The ballfield. One hour. Now get the hell out of here!"

Jensen stood. "One hour. Not a moment more. Don't make me come and find you."

"Fine."

He walked out into the muggy evening, torn. He was so close to getting the answers he needed, but would Wade really show up? What if he was just biding his time, trying to get rid of Jensen?

But what choice did he really have, though? Wade clearly didn't want him at the diner. He'd never get answers if he didn't leave.

So, he walked down the street and loitered at the corner. He'd pretend to window shop, at least until he figured out what Wade was up to.

Fifteen minutes later, he realized how futile his efforts were. People walked in and out of the diner like it had a revolving door. But without being able to watch Wade, he had no idea if the people he saw had anything to do with him or not.

Sighing, he gave up and walked to his truck. Then he drove the two short blocks to the ballfield and parked, resigned to waiting. He rolled down his window and looked around.

The games had all wrapped up for the evening, and only a few people lagged behind. One was Old Red, the affable town drunk. Looked like he'd be sleeping off a binge right on the bleachers. At least, until someone shooed him away or the cops came by. A couple of kids tossed a ball back and forth on their way out of the park. One man stood outside the concession stand, locking up behind him. Soon, the only sounds Jensen heard were crickets chirping, the occasional car driving by, and the soft snores snuffling out of Old Red.

Jensen got out and walked over to the dugout. He watched the sky blaze with the burgeoning dusk, then the twilight haze descended. Soon, the sky turned a deep indigo, and it continued to darken, the stars and moon brightening against the deepening hue.

But still no Wade.

Jensen was too angry—at himself, at Wade, at the world in general—to do anything but sit there and stew. How could he have been so stupid? Why did he fall for it?

A whistle caught his attention. Far too sharp and clear to be Old Red. He sat straighter, peered out into the night through the dividing rail.

Another sharp whistle, coming from the direction of the bleachers. A shadow skulked there, but Jensen recognized the form.

Wade had come.

He whistled an answering tone and waved his hand over the rail. Then he watched Wade take the long way around, sticking to the shadows as much as possible. Soon there was a rustling noise, and then Wade sat beside him in the darkness.

"Where the hell have you been? It's been over two hours."

"It took longer than expected. I had to explain why I wasn't alone."

"You were alone."

"Not when you were with me. I told you it was a problem. You could have gotten me killed. Or yourself. Still might. I don't know if they believed me. I think they did, but I'm not sure."

"Who? *Who* believed you? And believed what?"

Wade sighed. "Are you really sure you want to know all this? Because once I tell you, you aren't going to be able to file it away in some dark corner of your mind and never drag it out again."

"Well, I can't very well go on the way I have been. Knowing whatever it is has to be better than the wondering and the waiting."

"I wouldn't be too sure."

"Just tell me what the fuck's going on."

Wade leaned back against the dugout wall. "You know, I'm still your elder, Jensen. I watched you grow up. I'd thank you to show me a little respect."

Jensen had to fight with himself not to ball up his fist and smash Wade in the face with it. "Respect? You're joking, right? You killed my sister. I think the respect ship has sailed and dropped off the face of the earth."

"I didn't kill Hope."

Jensen ran his hand through his hair. "You're playing the semantics card? Seriously? You cut the brake line of the motorcycle she was on. She died from the accident. That's all on you."

"I had no idea she'd be on that bike, and I never dreamed the asshole kid would panic and not hit the kill switch. Not to mention your dad giving her the transfusion without typing her. And your mother lying about Hope's parentage. Lots of people had a hand in her death, Jensen. Of all of them, I'm hardly the most culpable."

Rage roiled through Jensen, a hot lava flow ready to erupt. This time, he did clench his fist. Before he could stop himself, he slammed it into the side of Wade's face. His knuckles stung at the impact, and he shook his hand out before balling it back up and raising it for a second blow.

Wade grabbed his hand before he struck and forced it down.

"I gave you one free one, Jensen. I know it's been building in you for a while, and I probably deserved it. But all you get is one. You take another swing, and I tell you nothing."

God, it was tempting. He could beat the shit out of the guy—hell, he could kill him with his bare hands—and no one would know. No one would care. Eventually the answers would all come to light, and he wouldn't have to spare Wade to get them.

But he wasn't a killer. Hell, he hadn't even been in a bar fight in five years. Maybe more. And that one hadn't been his fault, anyway.

Wade may have paid his debt to society, but he hadn't paid the Keller family yet. Instead of taking it out of his hide, though, Jensen chose to take payment in the form of knowledge.

So, he clenched his fists in his lap. Counted to ten.

Twice.

Took a deep breath and another.

"Start talking," he said. "But if you stall, or I don't like what I hear, all bets are off."

Wade laughed. "*Like* what you hear? You might as well ball your fists back up, boy, because you aren't going to like any of it."

"They came to me about six months ago," Wade said.

"Who?"

"Who's telling this story? Me or you?"

Jensen didn't answer, but he vowed to keep the interruptions to a minimum.

"Anyway, they pulled me out of my cell on some bullshit accusation and made a big stink about taking me to solitary. But they didn't. Instead, they took me to a private room near the warden's office. It was two guys in suits, the warden, and two guards I'd never seen before."

"What'd they want?"

Wade shook his head. "Don't you get it? They wanted time alone with me, and they wanted gen pop to think I was in trouble. Explain my disappearance for a while."

"Why?"

He sighed. "The drug ring that dissolved when I got pinched? It didn't really dissolve. In fact, it's back and bigger than ever. Vice made a bust, shut down the supply, but they're worried the next supply will be from one of the big cities. A lot of that shit is tainted. They're worried about kids dying."

"So, what's that have to do with you?"

Wade looked around, dropped his voice even lower. "The Feds are using me. They made me a deal. They'd guarantee immediate parole, place me in a job where I have access to drugs, and give me immunity."

"Immunity?"

"For selling. They want me to start up the business here, so the drugs are clean. Fewer casualties."

Jensen shook his head. "No. No way. Cops—Feds or local—don't ask people to sell."

"Don't be naive."

"It's—it's ridiculous." Jensen balled up his fist again, ready to let Wade have it.

"It's not long-term. If I can get in with the guys moving this shit, then they won't have to bring it in from out of state. These drugs will be clean and easier to monitor. It's just until they build a case against the guy running the show here."

"Then what?"

"What do you mean? They take him down, and his network, so drug trafficking in Cathedral Lake and the surrounding towns dries up. No network, no way to move even an out of town supply. Then I go free for real. No drugs, safe town, I'm in the wind. Win-win-win."

"Too many wins, dickhead." Jensen shook his head. "When do you make up for what you did to Hope?"

Wade sighed again. "How many times do I have to say it? I never meant for it to happen. It wasn't my fault."

"A lot of people may have been complicit in her dying," he tamped down his own guilt for not being more protective of her, "but if it wasn't for you, she never would have been hurt in the first place." Jensen shoved him. Cocked his fist back and raised it over his head.

Wade jumped to his feet and tackled Jensen to the ground. He sat on his chest, pinning his hands over his head.

"I'm not doing this with you. I paid my debt, and I'm still not out of trouble. Don't you think maybe I've had it rough, too? Don't you think maybe I'd love to just wash my hands of it and walk away? But I can't!"

Jensen struggled, but the guy had gotten strong in jail. He briefly wondered what he'd had to endure, but then pushed it out of his mind. It didn't matter. Hope was gone. Unger deserved every shitty thing that happened and more.

He stopped fighting and stared up at Wade. "All I hear from you is about all your problems, all the ways you were wronged. All the reasons other people are culpable for what you began. You call me 'boy' like I'm a naive child. But who's acting like a spoiled brat? You. Always all about you. What about Hope? What about what we lost? What about sucking up, admitting your faults, and saying a God damned apology instead of thirty-three excuses?"

Wade let him go and scrambled to his feet. "I'm sorry? You want me to say I'm sorry? Like that matters?"

"It does matter." He jumped up and squared off against Wade, waiting for an opening to strike.

"It won't bring her back."

"I know! But it would help to know you gave a fuck!"

"Gave a—? Christ on a cracker, Jensen. You think I don't care? Do you have any idea how it tore me up inside when I saw her lying on that damned table? When your father cracked a vein open for her, and there was nothing I could do? When I was the one trying to bring her back, but she was already gone? It haunts me! It kills me! I knew the second I heard the EMT on the radio that the lesson I'd tried to teach that little SOB had gone horribly wrong. But I didn't know the full extent until I saw Hope's body on that table. Tension pneumothorax. Head injury. Internal bleeding. Abrasions. Do you have any idea what that was like for me, knowing what I'd caused?"

He sighed and raked his hands through his hair. "I carry that. Me! So yeah, I'm sorry. I'm so fucking sorry. But there's nothing I can do! That one mistake cost me everything, and you know what? I wouldn't care about any of it if I could just bring her back. But I can't! So, I cling to the delusion that it wasn't only me responsible, and I pray for salvation every damn day. And it's all pointless. Because here I am, no friends, no money. Ostracized in my hometown. Back involved with crazy-ass criminals who will just as soon shoot me as they will work with me. Facing your father and Ben every damned day, and not having a single thing I can say or do to make any of this right. Not only that but getting them dragged down with me. So, fuck you, Jensen. You don't know sorry. And my saying it to you—or anyone else—won't make a damned bit of difference."

Jensen dropped his fists, slapped at his shorts to get the dirt off—more to avoid looking at the guy than to clean up. "You're wrong, Wade. It makes a big difference. All we really wanted to know was that you carry it, too. It's too big a burden to bear on our own."

Wade sighed. "I do carry it. Every day. Every moment. If I could make it right, I would. So, I'm doing what I can to stop other people from dying. That's the best I can do."

Jensen nodded. "At least now I know. I don't know why my dad wouldn't tell me, though."

"You've been through enough. He didn't want you showing up at the clinic and getting involved. He doesn't want to put you in danger."

"Why would I be in danger? He and Ben are there."

"They're there to watch me. That, and because people won't think it's too weird for them to keep an eye on me. They have a vested interest in making sure I comply with the rules of my parole."

"But aren't the rules to stay away from us?"

"Yes, but Royce and Ben are the exceptions. For obvious and not-publicly-obvious reasons."

"Okay, then. But where's the danger factor?"

"The drug dealers."

Jensen heard the 'duh' in his tone, but Wade didn't say more.

"But surely the dealers don't come to the clinic?"

"That's the drop zone. In the plants out front. I put the stash there, they leave money behind."

"And no one questions the drug thefts coinciding with your working there?"

"Why would they? The drugs are off book. No record of them ever being received, so no record of them being missing."

"Why the hell isn't my dad recording the shipments? He can get in trouble all over again and for real this time."

Wade shook his head. "In a real situation, it would probably blow back on your dad. In the public eye, it still might. But your dad isn't the one doing the books."

"Who then? Ben?"

Wade scoffed. "No. The receptionist. She's working with the dealers."

Well, fuck.

CHAPTER 18

BELLA SAT IN HER CAR in the parking garage at Chloe's apartment building. She'd been parked there for a while, but for the life of her, she couldn't manage to get out of the car.

Numb. From the crown of her head to the tips of her toes. Numb.

What a day.

She replayed the scene with her father over and over and still couldn't make heads or tails out of it. He'd cut Troy from his life yet preserved his room like a museum exhibit. On the other hand, he couldn't have boxed her life away fast enough. But he backed off a little. Well, a little for normal people. For him, his concession was monumental. Of course, for most people, the situation wouldn't have devolved as far as it had—as fast as it had—in the first place.

Completely. Numb.

She turned her head and looked at the seat beside her, caressed the box sitting there. Unable to open it thus far, her heart constricted. Troy had been on her mind more in the last day than he had been in the last decade. Memories bubbled to the surface that made no sense to her. Some things she'd forgotten, some she would have sworn were complete fabrications.

None made her happy.

In all fairness, she'd put him out of her mind—intentionally—for years. Thinking about him hurt. She felt equal parts guilt for his banishment and sorrow for his absence from her life. The contents of the box were all the mementos she had tucked away after… the incident. She hoarded any reminder of him.

But she never revisited them.

Better that she saves them for posterity.

She'd always sworn when she was on her own, she would find him. Apologize. Try to rebuild something with him.

Despite being an adult, though, she'd never been on her own. Not really. Not until her father threw her out.

Was it too late? Too little?

She grabbed the box and got out of the car. Everything else about her life was moving forward. It was time she dealt with that last loose—and vital—end.

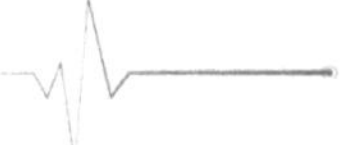

UPSTAIRS, LOCKED IN CHLOE'S GUEST room, Bella sat cross-legged on the bed, the keepsake box in her lap. She took a few deep breaths, traced again the letters she'd painstakingly printed on there in childlike-hand years before.

T. O. P.

Troy Osmond Perish. Her brother. Her protector. Her friend and hero.

The boy who gave everything for her and got nothing in return.

As she reached for the lid, her phone rang, cutting through the silence. Startled, she jumped, dropped the box and fumbled for the phone. She wasn't used to it ringing since her father had turned if off and hearing it as she sat there in silence startled her. She managed to right the box, pick up the phone, and swipe her thumb across the screen just before the call went to voice mail.

"What?" She didn't mean to, but she yelled it into the phone.

"Bella? It's Jensen. Are you okay?"

Good thing it was someone she liked. She hadn't had time to check caller ID before answering.

She lowered her voice to an acceptable register. "Hi."

"Is—is everything all right?"

She smiled. "Fine. What's up?"

He paused before he continued, and she could almost see him trying to decide if he should proceed with his reason for calling or press her about her feelings. She took the decision out of his hands.

"Really. I'm fine. The phone just startled me. It's the first I've heard it ring in a while. What can I do for you?"

"Oh, right. I forgot. Sorry."

"No reason to be."

Another pause, a shorter one. *"Can we meet and talk?"*

Bella glanced at the clock and then the box on the bed. It wasn't that late and getting out sounded like a great idea.

"Sure. Where are you?"

"Can we come over?"

"We? Who's with you?"

"Wade."

Bella's mouth dropped open. Jensen was with Unger? Surely not. Why?

"Bella? You there?"

"Yes. Um, listen. I'm staying at a friend's until I can move into my new place, and she's very private. I can't have him here. Can we meet somewhere else? A diner? A bar?"

"We really shouldn't be seen out with him."

"What's going on, Jensen?"

"It's complicated. Maybe my folk's place?"

She heard Wade arguing in the background.

"No, the nursery. Not the house."

There was more discussion on their end. Jensen sighed and mumbled something she couldn't quite make out.

Bella could hear the frustration in his tone. If he had to deal with Unger, he had to be seven-shades of irritated. She took the decision out of his hands. "Meet me at my dad's firm. Twenty minutes."

"I thought you were fired and locked out."

"I'll make it work."

There was more discussion in the background.

"Wade doesn't think it's a good idea."

"Well, Wade doesn't have much of a choice. I can't bring him here, and you don't have another option. So, it's this or nothing."

Jensen sighed.

"Just get there. I'll see you soon." She ended the call and looked at her contact list. No better time than the present to test Victor's word. With the touch of a button, she'd know whether he'd really answer when she called.

And if he did, she'd learn how far he was willing to go to reconcile with her.

Or how far she was willing to compromise herself to help Jensen.

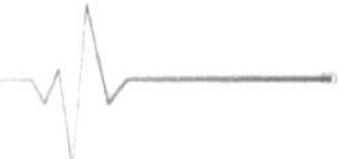

WHEN BELLA PULLED INTO THE parking lot of the law firm, her father's car was already there. He must have exceeded every speed limit by about twenty miles an hour in order to beat her there.

But in true Victor Perish fashion, he made sure he was in control. In this case, that meant he opened the doors and he ran the show.

Whatever. She didn't have any idea what she was getting into and having her father there could only be a benefit. He might be angry, but he was the best, and he wouldn't let her get into trouble.

At least, she didn't *think* he would. He'd never been that angry with her before.

But, no. He was a pro, and he did make his version of a compromise earlier.

No point in worrying over it now.

She made her way inside and looked around. It had been her second home for a long time. First when Troy was gone, and Victor started bringing her to the office, and then through summer internships and holiday jobs. Finally, the last few years, during her professional sojourn there. She'd always looked at it as an employee would or as a family member would.

This was the first time she'd stepped into the building as a prosecutor or whatever role she was playing in this new scenario.

To her, the office used to feel established, stately, reliable—the dark woods, the rich colors, the volumes of law books. But familiarity bred blindness. She didn't notice before the massive size of the desks and their accompanying chairs compared to the smaller, uncomfortable guest chairs. Hell, the welcome desk was up on a platform. A person standing in front of it would be eye-level with the receptionist while she sat. And the oxblood accents? They stood out, not because they'd been expertly chosen, but because they screamed power and dominance.

How had she not noticed these things before? Probably because she had been on the other side.

She'd looked down on clients. She'd sat on thrones while others perched on tiny seats. She'd worn the power suits and held court in vermilion rooms.

All that time, and she never even realized she'd been playing her father's game.

She felt dirty.

Standing there, in the dimly lit lobby, it occurred to her just what level her father would descend to in order to gain the upper hand. In anything.

Maybe she shouldn't have involved him at all in whatever was going on with Unger.

But it was too late. He was already there. He'd expect an explanation whether she canceled the meeting or not.

Resigned, she held her head high, pushed back her shoulders, and strode down the hall. She made her way to the glass-enclosed conference room directly across from the lobby doors. Victor had already taken a seat in there.

At the head of the table, of course.

He'd left the door open, and she walked right in without knocking. She stood just inside the doorway, met her father's gaze, and waited.

After all, Victor Perish had taught her that the person who speaks first loses.

He didn't address her. He didn't even get up to greet her.

They both held their ground—her standing, him sitting. Neither speaking.

She cracked. Couldn't take the silence another moment. "Father."

Didn't miss the slight twitch of the corner of his mouth.

"Isabella." He gestured toward the table. "Have a seat."

Where to sit? He had the power seat. Sitting to his right made her his number two, which she definitely wasn't. But sitting to his left was a seat of even less power. A decision he'd certainly deride later.

She glanced down the length of the table to the end directly opposite him. There was no chair there.

Did she dare?

Hell, yes, she dared. She walked to the other 'head' of the table, pulled a chair around, and sat facing her father. The black queen to his white king on the chessboard. She'd successfully countered his opening salvo.

Whether she could keep up with him, move for move, was anyone's guess, though.

"So, what is this all about?" he asked.

"Maybe we should wait for the others."

"The others?" He leaned back in his chair, steepled his fingers in front of him. "It seems you weren't entirely forthcoming when you called me."

She would not feel like a scolded child. Absolutely. Would. Not.

"I don't know much. But given one of the people coming is a client of yours, I thought meeting here was appropriate."

He frowned. "I thought you called because you needed my help. I thought you were reaching out."

"I did—I do—need your help. I needed a place for us to meet. I need you to be here because of who's involved. I need—"

"Who's involved, Isabella?"

She looked down at her lap. Her hands, clenched together, trembled slightly.

"Isabella. I asked you a question. Who are we meeting tonight?"

"Jensen Keller." Her voice, barely above a whisper, dropped even lower. "And Wade Unger."

Victor leaned forward, rested his elbows on the table. "What have you gotten yourself involved in?"

Anger washed through her. "What have I gotten *myself*—Are you *kidding* me? This all started because you forced me into that farce of a hearing and never gave me a second to prepare. No details about the agreement. I was totally blindsided! Now I'm in the middle of all this, and I still don't know what's going on."

"You need to leave. Now."

"I can't. Jensen asked me to meet him here. He said they have information for me."

"What do you need information for? You don't work here anymore. Unger isn't your client. Why do you need to be involved?"

"Because Jensen asked me to be. Because I help my friends. And because—" She ran her fingers through her hair. "—I deserve to know what's caused me so much trouble."

"Since when are your friendly with the opposition?"

"I don't work here anymore, remember? Jensen's hardly my opposition."

"I've reconsidered this whole thing. I don't want you anywhere near this case. Do you hear me?"

There was a first time for everything. Victor *never* had to reconsider. His first instinct was always absolute.

A noise in the lobby caught her attention. She looked over and saw Jensen and Unger walking toward the conference room. Pushing back her chair, she crossed to the door and waved to them.

Then she turned to her father. "At this point, it doesn't matter what you want. I am involved, and I'm not backing down."

"Isabella," her father warned in a low voice, barely indistinguishable from a growl.

But she ignored him and greeted Jensen.

She ignored Unger, too.

Gesturing toward the table, she said, "Come in. Have a seat."

"You didn't tell me anyone else would be here," Unger said to Jensen.

He shrugged. "I didn't know. And I really don't care at this point."

Unger looked around the room. "Well, it matters to me. The more people who are involved, the more dangerous this is."

"Your attorney is already involved," Jensen said. "Danger or not."

Bella sat down, pointed again toward the chairs. "Why do people keep saying this is dangerous? What's going on?"

Jensen sat down. He glared at Unger, who finally flung himself into a chair on the other side of the table.

"Isabella," Victor said, "I appreciate you gathering these men here for me. You may leave."

"I didn't gather them for you, and I'm not leaving. Jensen asked to meet me. We needed a secure location, and I couldn't think of a safer place, given Dr. Unger is a client of yours. No one should find his presence here strange."

"Oh, no," Unger said. "Not strange to visit my lawyer after I've been paroled. Especially this late at night. With a family member of the girl I killed. Nope. Not strange at all. Not suspicious in the least."

Bella looked at Jensen, saw him wince at the mention of his sister. She wanted to reach out to him, but it was neither the time nor the place.

"Well, you're here now," Victor said. "What's going on?"

"You know what's going on," Unger said.

Bella stood. "Clearly, I'm the only one in the dark here. Someone had better fill me in. Now."

She looked around the table. Her father had resumed his poker face, but his complexion had reddened. Anger was too mild a term, but she doubted anyone would be able to read him but her. Unger had crossed his arms over his chest, and he glared across the table at Jensen, who drummed his fingers on the arm of his chair. No one spoke.

"Well?" she said. "I'm waiting."

Finally, Jensen sighed. Looked up at her. Began talking.

She'd dropped into her chair before he got through his third sentence.

Unger and the Feds? A drug sting? No wonder everyone was so bent out of shape. It was dangerous. Incredibly so.

What the hell had she found herself in the middle of?

"Okay," she said when Jensen had finished the story. "Clearly, this was a bad idea. We need to get Mr. Unger out of this arrangement and placed into Witness Protection."

Victor leaned back in his chair. "No, Isabella. That's out of the question."

"You're joking, right?" God, her father was a royal pain in the ass sometimes.

"His arrangement was not a bad idea. It's actually a stroke of genius."

"I take that to mean it was your idea," she said.

Victor raised an eyebrow and looked away. When he looked back, he continued in a silky tone. "Actually, no. I was brought into the loop after the initial idea took root. Vice needed to keep a new player from moving in, and Unger allows them to do that."

"And that leaves the Keller family exposed and vulnerable. Haven't they lost enough?"

"It's not about what they've lost." Her father's tone grew harsher, his words more clipped. "It's about what other people have left to lose."

"I have a lot to lose," Unger said. "I don't want to do this anymore. I want out."

"You knew the risks going in," Victor said. "If you hadn't agreed, you'd still be rotting in that shithole. So, suck it up. You're a criminal. Your associates are criminals. Be grateful for the freedom you've been given and do your damn job."

"Well, I also have a lot to lose," Jensen said. "My whole family does, and my dad is right in the thick of this. It needs to stop."

"Your dad was briefed before any of this happened. He agreed. He knew the risks."

"I don't think anyone could possibly understand the risks until they're immersed in the situation." Jensen raked his fingers through his hair. "My father may have been briefed, but those were just words. Now he's working with two men he swore never to speak to again. His receptionist is in league with the drug dealers. It's all happening in his clinic, which can ultimately end up ruining his business. Or worse, get him killed. You need to pull the plug on this thing."

"Look," Victor said, "I see where you're coming from. I understand, I do. But now you need to see where the law is coming from. Even if I wanted to help, and, let me be clear—" he stared at Unger before looking back at Jensen "—I don't. But even if I wanted to, my hands are tied. There are more legal contracts stipulating the terms, and penalties for violating them, than I've seen in years. The red tape in this thing looks like rivers of blood. There's no going back now. Not until Unger gives Vice and the Feds what they want."

"I could just as easily end up dead before then," Unger said.

"Then we won't have to worry about safely extracting you," Victor answered.

"Dad!"

He turned to her. "Bella, I want you away from this. There's nothing you can do, and there's no reason for you to be involved. Stay clear of it. Stay away from Unger and from the Keller's."

Bella looked at Jensen, but he wouldn't meet her gaze. Then she stared at her father. "You can't tell me what to do anymore. I don't work for you, and I don't live under your roof. I can do whatever I want."

Victor stood. "If you won't obey me, then do me the courtesy of granting me a favor. I'm asking you. Please, stay away."

Asking? For a favor? Two indications of humanity in one night? Write down the date. Live long enough and you do witness everything.

Her father looked at Unger. "You, however, do have a working relationship with me. So, I'm telling you. Stay away from my daughter."

Then he turned toward Jensen. "I don't know what's going on between you and Isabella, but if you care for her, even in the slightest, you'll stay away, too."

He walked to the door. Before he walked out, he said, "You can see yourselves out. I'd suggest Unger go first and the two of you wait for at least fifteen minutes before following him. I'm locking up within half an hour, and I expect you all to be gone by then."

No goodbye, no further discussion. He walked toward his office.

Bella doubted she'd be welcome to follow him. She had nothing more to say to him, anyway. Order or favor, it didn't matter.

She wouldn't abandon Jensen to deal with this on his own.

Unger stood and left. He didn't say anything to them, either.

Jensen looked at her. "I'm sorry I got you stuck in the middle of this. But your father's right. You're free and clear. You shouldn't be involved."

She reached for his hand and squeezed it. "But I am, and I'm going to see it through."

He shook his head. "It's too dangerous, and we clearly aren't going to get Wade out of his deal."

"We haven't tried everything. Not yet."

"There's nothing more to be done. And definitely not by you." He released her hand and stood.

"Jensen," she began.

"No. Don't say it. You're out. I appreciate everything you've done, but I can't worry about your safety on top of everything else." He walked out of the room before she could say anything more.

Didn't matter, though. She hadn't given anyone her word that she would stay clear, and she had no intention of giving up.

CHAPTER 19

JENSON COULDN'T FALL ASLEEP. HE kept going over—and over again—everything he'd learned from Wade.

He also tossed and turned thinking about Bella. Just knowing him put her in danger. He wasn't ready to walk away from her, but he didn't want her in jeopardy. Especially because of him.

And his mind turned back to Wade again.

So went his night, ping-ponging thoughts keeping him up until dawn.

Sighing, he rose. Being in bed hadn't helped him sleep all night. There was no reason to spend the morning the same way. He showered, shaved, and headed downstairs for a cup of coffee.

The scent of cinnamon greeted him before he hit the bottom step.

Sylvia greeted him when he walked into the kitchen.

"Aren't you here early?" he asked.

"Your father's been going to work earlier than usual. So, I have, too. Making sure he has coffee and breakfast. Can I get you anything? I made cinnamon rolls."

"How could I possibly say no to that?"

So, his dad had been spending more time at the clinic. Was he watching

Wade or the receptionist? Did he let Ben in on everything he knew? How did he deal with all of that?

While he pondered his father's situation, Sylvia plated a giant gooey pastry pinwheel and placed it on the table. He poured his coffee and sat down. Digging in, he almost moaned. Still warm. He savored that first bite.

Cinnamon. Sugar. Butter. Frosting.

Pure. Freaking. Heaven.

After a pleasant conversation with Sylvia, two scalding cups of coffee, and three cinnamon masterpieces, he felt the sugar high kick in. Wouldn't be long before the crash hit. He also felt sick to his stomach. Looking down, he remembered his discussion with Cooper. He was getting soft.

He rinsed his dish, thanked Sylvia for breakfast, and headed back to his room. He lay down, stretched, and took out his phone. A few texts to his friends, and he had plans for the evening.

In the meantime, the sugar crash hit. He closed his eyes and thought about his father, Ben, and Wade. As he slipped into sleep, he wondered how he'd cope if his friends ever betrayed him like that.

JENSEN SLEPT LONGER THAN HE anticipated. The combination of carbs and a sleepless night worked to knock him out for several hours. He awoke feeling fresh and rested.

Time to leave.

His friends were right. He'd been acting like a tool and had totally cut them out for a long time. He planned on solving two of his problems with one activity—he was going to be with his friends, and he was going to get a workout in.

He placed his hands on his stomach and shook his head. Damn, he really had gotten out of shape.

Basketball was just what he needed. He stepped into a pair of gym shorts, slipped on a t-shirt, and donned gym socks and shoes. Then, throwing a towel and some water in a bag, he headed out.

One of the guys would have to bring a ball. He didn't have a clue where one would be at his house.

He drove past the ballfields as he headed for the courts. A glance at the dugouts brought memories of the night before, but he pushed them away. He was there to hang out with his friends and get some exercise. Nothing else. Glancing around the park, he smiled. It reminded him of when he was young. People were already showing up for the first of the games. Looked like the park would be crowded that night. Good thing he was getting there so early in the evening. Parking would be scarce later.

He parked down by the courts and waited for the guys to show. A few minutes later, he got a text from Miles. The night shift pharmacist called in sick. He had to cover for her and couldn't make it. That sucked. Jensen had been looking forward to them hanging out.

And so much for a two-on-two game.

Brett pulled in beside him and got out of his car. Jensen climbed down from his truck and walked over to him. "Hey. Just heard from Miles. He got stuck at work."

"Funny. I got a similar message from Austin. Trouble with his dad. He can't leave the office yet."

"Looks like it's just you and me, then," Jensen said. "Bring a ball?"

"I always have a football, a basketball, tennis stuff, and baseball equipment with me. Never know when you'll stumble on a chance at a game." He popped his trunk, pulled a basketball out of it and tossed it to Jensen.

Jensen caught it and frowned. He bounced it, and it hit on the ground with a thud, not bouncing back. "Clearly you play often."

Brett shrugged. "It's been a while."

"Don't suppose you have an air pump in there?"

His buddy rooted around in his car, then shut the trunk. "I've got an air compressor and a pump. No needle, though. Want to run to the store with me?"

"Not so much. Hurry back. I'll try to save your spot."

Brett took off, and Jensen glanced at his watch. It took at least fifteen minutes to get to the closest sporting goods store and fifteen back, plus shopping time. He had over half an hour to kill.

He checked his phone..He'd missed several calls and texts from Bella.

Missed might not be the right word. He intentionally ignored them. For her own good.

He put the phone back in his pocket without reading anything she'd sent or playing any of her messages.

The parking lot started filling up. Jensen stood where Brett had parked and pretended to be stretching. So far, the ploy worked. Eventually, that would be the only spot left, though, and he'd have to let someone take it.

A horn sounded and Jensen looked around. There were still plenty of spots left. He turned to the car, prepared to argue with the driver, when he saw it was Brett. Jensen stepped out of the way, and Brett parked the car.

"How in the hell did you get back so fast?" Jensen asked.

"I didn't feel like a forty-minute round trip trek for something I could accomplish in five."

Jensen looked at him, and Brett tossed a sealed package to him.

"I went to Axel's."

"Your brother's house? Why?"

"No, his shop."

Axel owned and operated Under the Gun, a tattoo and piercing studio. Jensen looked closely at the item in his hands—a five-inch long tattoo needle in a hermetically-sealed package.

Jensen busted out laughing. "Are you serious?"

"What?"

"This needle." He held it up. "It's five inches long."

"So?"

"What are you blowing up? The Goodyear Blimp? You need a short needle, so it doesn't bend or break off in the ball."

"It'll be fine." Brett snatched the needle out of Jensen's hand and looked at it through the plastic. "I think it'll work. Don't you think this looks like the same gauge as a regular needle?"

Jensen shook his head. "Let's just go and watch the Little League games. I'll buy you a hot dog."

Brett tossed the ball in his trunk and pocketed the needle.

Jensen raised his eyebrow.

"What? If I'm not using it, then I'll return it to him."

"Whatever."

They walked the short distance to the field. Jensen stopped at the concession stand and bought four hot dogs, two packages of red licorice, and two large sodas. So much for dieting and working out.

They sat on the bleachers and ate, commenting occasionally about the game and the people in the stands.

Brett elbowed him and nodded his head toward the other bleachers. "That lady's glaring at you."

Jensen followed his gaze. It was the lady from the bar… the one he'd insulted when he was drinking.

"Yeah. She's been doing that every time I bump into her."

"Who is she?"

"Don't you recognize her? She's the lady with all the kids from the bar. I think that's one of her sons on the pitcher's mound. The other—" He scanned the field. "Center field."

"Yeah, I recognize them now. You were kind of an ass that night."

"So, I've been told."

They watched the game in silence for a while, then Brett turned to him. "Listen, I've been meaning to talk—"

The crack of bat-on-ball interrupted him. The batter hit a line drive directly at the pitcher. It happened so fast, the kid didn't have time to react. The ball slammed into the boy's chest, and he immediately crumpled to the ground. He clutched at his chest but didn't make a move to sit up.

The coach leapt out of the dugout and ran to the mound. The boy's mother followed immediately and wrapped her son in her arms. Her other son ran in from the outfield, dropped to his knees, and grabbed his brother's hand.

Jensen grabbed his phone and dialed 9-1-1. Before the operator answered, he was on his way to the mound, Brett right at his side. The crowd started moving toward the mound, and the coach waved people off.

The boy's mother screamed for a doctor.

Someone yelled, "I'll get Doc Lyndon from the clinic."

"Go," she said. "Go!" She looked up then, and when she saw Jensen, she clutched her son tighter. "Get away! You get away from him!"

"This is 9-1-1. What is your emergency?"

"We're at the Little League field in Cathedral Lake. A boy's been hit in the chest with a ball. He's conscious, in pain. Breathing labored."

The boy's eyes rolled back in his head and he passed out.

"Scratch that. He's passed out." He studied the boy's face, his torso. Turned his head gently to the side and immediately back. "Left lung isn't rising properly. Trachea is deviated." He looked at Brett, glanced at his pocket. Wondered…

"Sir," the 9-1-1 dispatcher said. "Are you a doctor?"

Jensen closed his eyes and took a deep breath. "Med school grad."

The woman clutching her son looked at Jensen. "What's wrong with him? Why did he pass out? Why isn't he breathing correctly?"

"Sir, your name?" the dispatcher asked.

"Get the ambulance here. Now. He's got a tension pneumothorax and it needs to be decompressed. Immediately." He knew he shouldn't end the call, but the kid needed help. He tossed his phone to the coach and turned toward Brett. "Give me that needle."

Brett's eyes widened, but he passed it over.

The coach put the phone to his ear. "Hello?"

Jensen tuned everything out. The kid was dying. If they waited, he might not make it.

He pulled the boy away from his mother. She let him go but stayed right by his side. Her eyes were wide, her skin pale. But she didn't fight him.

Still no ambulance. Couldn't even hear the siren.

"Ma'am. I can help. Or we can wait. Your call."

"Doc Lyndon? Or the EMTs?"

"I don't know if either will be here in time. But I understand if you want to wait."

He didn't understand. The kid's chest barely rose. He was out of time.

Tears streamed down her face, but she nodded. "Do it."

"Are you—"

"Do it!"

He grabbed the hem of the kid's shirt and pulled, popping the buttons up the middle. Shoved the material out of his way.

Ripped open the seal of the package Brett had given him. Took the needle in hand.

Whispered a prayer. Recited the procedure.

"L2, second intercostal space," he murmured.

He placed the needle in the space between the first and second rib on the left.

"Midclavicular line."

Lined up the needle point with the middle of the clavicle.

Took a deep breath.

Inserted the needle.

Prayed again.

A whoosh of air sounded. The boy began breathing again.

Sirens sounded in the distance.

The mother clasped his hand and squeezed. "Thank you," she whispered. "Thank God for you."

He sat back and looked at the family. The boy would be okay. His brother and mother hugged each other then turned their attention back to the injured child.

He'd done it. He'd saved that boy. Saved a family.

The coach maintained a running commentary with the 9-1-1 operator. He waved at Jensen. "Hey, buddy. What's your name?"

Jensen had no interest in getting more involved than he already was. He held out his hand for his phone, and the coach passed it to him. Instead of talking, he ended the call.

"Brett," he whispered in his friend's ear. "Let's get out of here."

They both stood.

"Wait. Where're you going?" the coach said. "At least leave your name and contact information."

No point. The dispatcher had his number. They could trace him if they needed to.

God, he hoped they didn't need to.

Jensen led Brett past the first throng of onlookers. The sirens grew louder. He was almost out of time. Another minute, and he'd have to answer all kinds of questions. No way he could keep it from his father then.

He pushed past more people. They parted for him even as they whispered about him.

But two men stood in his way. He looked up, deciding whether to step around or through them.

And stopped dead in front of them.

They weren't going to let him pass. At least, not without an explanation.

Brett whistled under his breath.

Jensen took a deep breath. "Dad. Ben. Would you mind letting me pass? I'd like to get out of here before the ambulance and cops arrive."

CHAPTER 20

MORNING DIDN'T COME EARLY ENOUGH for Bella. She paced. Did a yoga routine. Showered and dressed. Drank coffee.

Drank two more cups.

Finally, it was late enough that Steve would be in the office. She called the number he'd given her, bypassing the secretary and ringing directly through to his desk.

"Forbes," he grumbled into the phone.

"Steve. Bella Perish."

"Oh, hey, Bella."

"Not a morning person?"

"Maybe in two more cups of coffee." He paused a moment.

She heard his swallow and muttered curse. "Too hot? I hear you can sue for that these days."

He chuckled. *"I need the jolt. Just not the burnt taste buds. So, what's up? Don't tell me you've changed your mind about working here. I haven't had enough coffee for that."*

"No, nothing like that. I'm calling about—" She'd had all morning to prepare, but now that he was on the phone, she didn't know what to say.

"Bella? What is it?"

"Is this line secure?"

"What are you involved in?" This time his voice sounded awake, alert, aware. Hyper-aware.

"What do you know about the Wade Unger case?"

He didn't answer for a while. *"What exactly are you looking for?"*

"You know what's going on, don't you?"

"Bella, I'm the ADA. I know what's going on with the scum we put away. The question is, what do you know? You don't work with your father anymore. You shouldn't be anywhere near this case."

"I'm so tired of hearing that. I'm smack in the middle of it, so telling me to keep my distance is useless."

"So, what do you want from me?"

"I want Unger in WitSec."

"Eventually, that's an option."

"No. I mean now. Call this off. Protect the guy. Get him out of here."

"Bella, you know we can't do that."

"The Keller family is in danger. He works at their clinic. He's arranged for criminals to work there. To pick up drugs there, drop off money."

"We know. That's part of his deal. He's going to shut the drug pipeline down."

"He's not high enough up to do that. All that's going to happen is someone's going to get hurt. Someone innocent."

"As long as it's not you. I'm okay with that. Everyone involved knows and accepts the risks, which are minimal. Vice has the clinic under surveillance 24/7. They tail Unger. They've installed wires. The Keller family is as protected as they can be."

"It's not enough." Terror gripped her heart in strong, icy fingers. "Nothing's foolproof. Someone can get hurt. Look at what happened to Hope Keller."

"That won't happen again."

"Please, Steve."

"I couldn't pull the plug if I wanted to. It's not my rodeo, and you aren't going to find anyone willing to stop it. Let it go, Bella. Please."

"Everyone keeps telling me that. But if you knew me as well as you thought, if any of you did, you would know I don't give up on my friends."

"And Unger is your friend now?"

She sighed. "I told you, I'm worried about the Kellers."

"Worry about yourself. Stay out of it."

"Goodbye, Steve."

"Bella? I'm not asking as a friend. I'm telling you as your boss."

She ended the call without further comment.

Her father, the DA's office. All her best resources were unwilling to help. She needed to approach things from a new direction.

But which one?

SHE POURED TWO GLASSES OF wine and handed one to Chloe. "How was your day?"

Chloe peered at her over the rim of the glass. "Is this some weird take on the 1950's wife's role? Because, one, while you're gorgeous, I don't swing that way. And two, no self-respecting woman serves her significant other like that anymore."

Bella sighed. "I'm not gay."

"Are you sure? That would explain a lot."

"Chloe, please."

"But still—greeting me at the door with wine? Where are my slippers and my pipe?"

"Are you through?"

"I still have a few sitcoms references I haven't gone through yet, but I can hold off. For now."

"I need your help."

"Clearly. Look at your hair. And don't get me started on your clothes. We really need to go shopping. I can lend you some mon—"

"I don't need your money, or your clothes. I'm moving out this weekend. I start my new job next Monday. My dad is sending me my things. I'm fine."

"You talked to your dad? That's great. I know—"

"Chloe. Shut up and listen. I need your help."

This time Chloe stayed quiet. She sipped her wine and stared at her friend.

Bella sighed. "I know you have contacts pretty much everywhere. What about the government?"

Chloe tapped a long, manicured nail on her glass. "I might know a few people. What do you need?"

"Jensen. The guy I've been talking to you about."

"Oh, God, no. Seriously? The first guy you think about screwing, and he's in trouble your legal mind can't get him out of?"

"No. No! He's not in trouble. Not that kind of trouble. He's in danger."

Chloe put her glass down. "What kind of danger?"

"His sister is that girl who was killed almost a decade ago… the one on the bike with the drug dealer."

"So, his sister was a druggie? What's that have to do with you?"

"She wasn't on drugs. She turned the drug dealer in. Her death was collateral damage."

"And what's this have to do with you?"

"The guy who cut the brake line on the bike? He's been paroled."

"And you think Jensen is his next target? I know just who to call."

"No! Will you listen? The guy is working with Vice and the Feds, trying to reestablish his role as a supplier so he can take the whole chain down."

Chloe stared at her.

"So, will you help?"

"Am I allowed to talk now?"

"Yes! Will you help me?"

"Help you with what? Bells, I don't know how you know this, or why, but it doesn't impact you. I don't even see how it impacts this Jensen guy, other than it sucks that his sister's killer is free."

"Because the guy is working at his dad's clinic. Stealing the drugs from there. The head drug guy has one of his people stationed there. Jensen, his family, his family's professional reputation—they're all at stake."

Chloe sat down, drained her glass, and looked at Bella. "And what do you want me to do?"

"Talk to some people. Pull some strings. Get him put in Witness Protection."

"Jensen?"

"No. Are you listening? Unger. The guy who killed his sister and is now undercover for the Feds."

Chloe shook her head. "You'd have an easier time getting your boyfriend and his family in WitSec than that guy. He's up to his neck in this thing. I could have access to the governor—actually, I do have access to the governor—and I still can't help you. Palms were greased, plans were made. Things are in motion. There's no stopping this thing. Your best bet is to stay out of it."

"Ugh!" Bella stood and ran her hands through her hair. "Why do people keep telling me that?"

"Because that's the best thing for you. And who have you told? Because if you're dicking around in a secret government operation, they aren't going to be really happy with you blabbing about it all over town. Not to mention, the more people you talk to, the more danger you put your man in."

"I'm just trying to help him."

"You can help him by keeping your mouth shut, staying out of the way, and letting the big boys handle it."

Bella sighed. "I can't stay away. I'm worried about him."

"If he cared about you as much as you seem to care for him, he'd tell you to stay out of it."

"He has. Repeatedly." Bella plopped down on the sofa beside her friend. "But I can't. I'm sick over it. I'm so scared for him."

"Aw, honey." Chloe wrapped her arm around Bella's shoulders. "You've got it bad."

"I don't know about that. I'm just worried for him."

"You have it bad. That's okay. And the fact that he's worried for you? That's good, too. It shows he's not just a good guy, he cares about you."

"Fat lot of good that does me if he won't see me."

"He'll see you."

"How do you know?"

"We're going to make you irresistible."

"That's not really playing to my strengths. Besides, he won't answer any of my calls or texts."

"Bells. Leave everything to me. Now we're playing to my strengths."

BELLA DIDN'T KNOW WHAT WAS more ridiculous. The fact that Chloe took Jensen's contact information from her phone and browbeat him into agreeing to dinner, or—and this was more likely at the moment—the fact that Chloe forced her into the dressing room of a ridiculously expensive lingerie store wearing something so skimpy and sheer, she didn't think Chloe would be caught dead in it.

And that was saying something.

"I'm not coming out." Bella cringed when she caught her reflection in the mirror. She didn't have enough hands to cover everything that was exposed.

"Then I'm coming in."

"Not while I'm locked in here."

"I will crawl under this door."

"Chloe. Seriously. This," she gestured at the wisps of material, not that Chloe could see her, "this isn't me. This isn't you." She whispered through the door. "I don't think I've ever seen anything this skimpy in porn."

"You don't watch porn."

"True. And lower your voice."

"Bells. Let me see it."

Bella recognized futility when it smacked her in the face. She unlocked the door, cracked it open, and stood behind it. Chloe barged in, smashing her between the door and the dressing room wall. When Chloe tipped her head to look around the door at her, Bella slammed the door closed.

"Drop your hands." Chloe flicked her hands toward Bella's.

Bella just bent down further. "There's something really weird about shopping for lingerie with another girl."

"Well, if you ever shopped for it on your own, I wouldn't have had to drag you here."

"This is too revealing."

Chloe squinted at her, wrinkling her brow. "Why are you still wearing your underwear?"

"Because I wasn't going commando in lingerie at the store."

"Then what are you covering up? I couldn't possibly see anything important with those granny-panties on. And where in the hell did you get a bra like that?"

"There's nothing wrong with my bra. It's supportive. And they aren't granny-panties."

"Doesn't matter. I've seen everything you've got before, anyway. Drop your damn hands."

Bella stood straighter and lowered her hands to her sides.

Chloe tapped her lips with her finger. "Normally, I'd say that shade of blush is too pale, but you're innocent, so I think it works."

"Would you lower your voice?"

"No one's listening."

Bella sighed. "I just don't think it's necessary to broadcast my—condition."

"Virginity isn't a condition. It's a malady, and I know just the medicine for you. Buy this. Never mind, I'll buy it for you. And that pair of silver stilettos."

"If I want this, I can afford to buy it myself."

Chloe raised her eyebrows.

Bella glanced at the price tag. Raised her own eyebrows even as her mouth dropped open. "Are you kidding me? I think there are too many zeroes on here."

"You pay for quality."

"I agree. And if there was more than a couple of ribbons and three tiny sheer triangles, it might be worth something."

"Maybe we should look at two-piece sets."

"I can't do this." Bella stripped off the flimsy scraps of cloth and put her own clothes on. "I'm done. I'll go to that dinner tonight, but that's it. We'll just have to be friends."

"Bella." Chloe pushed the discarded lingerie aside and sat on the bench in the dressing room. "You can't let fear keep you from pursuing this guy. You should have just slept with someone a long time ago and gotten it over with. Now it's become too big a thing in your head. And it's not."

"It is. I don't have casual sex. I don't have sex at all. If I am going to finally lose my virginity, after all this time, I want to be sure it means something to him as well as me. And I don't want to do it because I seduced him. I want him to want me, not the fancy wrappings I trapped him with."

"What's wrong with a little packaging? Guys like to know you made the effort for them."

"Well, this girl thinks maybe he needs to make the effort for her, or we should both make the effort for each other."

Chloe smiled. "That's not the way I usually do it, but you're right. He likes you just the way you are. Win him as you. That's who he wants, anyway."

"Thanks, Chloe." She stepped toward her, arms outstretched.

Chloe backed away. "Uh, no offense, but I'm not hugging you while you're wearing those."

Bella looked down at her shorts and oxford. "What? These are my clothes."

"I don't mean the college co-ed duds. I mean the old lady bra and granny panties. I have standards."

"They're not old lady underwear."

Chloe laughed and walked out of the dressing room.

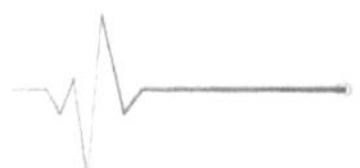

BELLA—ACTUALLY CHLOE—HAD ARRANGED for Jensen to pick her up in the lobby of Chloe's building for dinner that evening. She wasn't sure exactly how she'd convinced Jensen or what he was expecting, but she determined to persuade him not to cut her out of his life.

As a concession to Chloe's impossible standards, Bella did end up buying something special at the lingerie store. Nothing too risqué or tawdry, but she had found a sea foam push-up bra and matching lacy boy shorts. The color reminded her of their time at the lake, and she found the style both comfortable and appealing. Chloe approved, so it must not have been a total turn-off.

Besides, it wasn't as though Jensen would ever see it, anyway. It was more of a confidence boost for her than anything else.

Chloe did her hair for her, piling it in loose curls on top of her head. She insisted on doing her makeup, too, and went for dramatic rather than Bella's natural style. Despite the extra work, Bella had to admit the smoky eye was stunning.

She hadn't received her boxes from her father yet, so Chloe loaned her a sundress a shade darker than her intimates. Thankfully, she was shorter than her friend, so what was an impossibly short skirt on Chloe fell to an acceptably modest length on her. She looked in the mirror and twirled around. The material was so fine and soft, it floated around her and settled gently in place.

She looked as good as she could hope.

Her phone buzzed, and she glanced at the display.

"Jensen's downstairs. I have to go." She grabbed a clutch, slipped on heels she'd borrowed from Chloe that were just a tad too tight and way too high, and headed for the door.

"Why don't you invite him up?" Chloe asked.

"And suffer your inquisition? No way."

"If he's the one, I'll have to meet him, eventually."

"If he's the one, I'll introduce you. Someday. Just not now."

"Don't do anything I wouldn't do."

Bella sighed. "Goodnight." She closed the door on Chloe's laughter.

She rode down the elevator and compulsively fidgeted with her hair and clothes until the door opened. Stepping out, she spotted Jensen in the chair she'd sat in the night she first stayed with Chloe.

He stood, stepped toward her, and stopped.

She looked behind her, then down at her dress and shoes. Seeing nothing out of place, she looked back up at him. "What? Is something wrong?"

He shook his head. "You're beautiful."

She flushed and bit her lip. When she noticed his eyes flare, she smiled. "You look really good, too."

"Thanks." He smiled, offered her his arm. They walked outside.

"I'm glad you finally agreed to see me."

He sighed. "I still think it's an unnecessary risk for you. But I couldn't stay away anymore."

"Then why did it take Chloe nagging you to death to agree to see me?"

"She is tenacious." He chuckled a little. "Actually, I was just about to call you when she called me. She didn't have to nag to convince me. I wanted to see you."

She squeezed his arm. "I'm glad. I wanted to see you, too."

They got to his truck, and he helped her inside. After he got in, she asked, "I should have asked where we were going. Maybe I'm overdressed?"

He shook his head. "No. You look perfect."

"So where are we headed?"

"I need a favor," he said.

"Name it."

"I planned on taking you out. I really did. But something has happened, Bella, and—"

"That's okay." Face flaming, she clasped the handle and opened the door.

He grabbed her arm. "Where are you going?"

"Isn't this the point where you tell me it's not me, it's you, and then you offer an excuse to get out of dinner? Just save it." She turned again to the door.

He tugged on her arm. "No. God, no. If I didn't want to go out with you, I wouldn't have agreed to go. I want to take you out. It's just—"

She sighed. "Just what?"

"My dad. I… he… today, I was—" He sighed. "I have to have dinner at home. My father has some things to discuss with me."

"About Unger?"

"Unfortunately, no. About me."

She tipped her head to the side and looked at him. Furrowed brow, clenched jaw… she saw pain and dread in his expression. Fathers. She touched his face, left her hand on his cheek as she turned his head to face her. "It's no problem. We can do it another time."

"No." He shook his head, and she dropped her hand. "That's not it."

"Then what?"

"I want you to come with me. To dinner with my parents."

"You want me to meet your parents?"

"Well, technically, you already met my mom." He rested his head on the steering wheel. "I could use the support."

"Of course. I'm happy— Wait. Are they expecting me? I don't want to barge in on a private family moment."

Jensen took his phone out of his pocket and placed a call. "Syl? Hey, is there enough for a guest at dinner…? Just one. We're on our way now. Can you tell my mom, so she knows to expect company…? Thanks. See you soon."

He ended the call and looked at Bella. "All set on my end. Still up for it?"

What had she gotten herself into? She looked at Jensen, met his gaze.

Didn't matter. He needed her, so she'd deal with whatever happened that night. "Ready as I'll ever be. Let's go."

Jensen put the car in gear and pulled into traffic.

Bella forced herself not to fidget. Looked like the lingerie had been a waste of time. The evening had taken a one-eighty from flirting to fighting. She headed straight into a conflict—one she knew nothing about.

What was the social protocol for invading someone's home uninvited and interrupting an important conversation? She wished she knew.

CHAPTER 21

JENSEN MADE THE INTRODUCTIONS AS soon as he and Bella walked in the door. As he expected, his mother and sister greeted her with warmth and hospitality.

And, as expected, his father barely acknowledged she was there.

When Sylvia called them to dinner, his father stalked out of the room well ahead of the rest of them.

Bella stayed back, grabbed Jensen's hand, and waited for the room to clear. "I think I should go. Your father is less than pleased that I'm here."

"Yeah, but my mom and sister are thrilled, and Sylvia loves it when she can show off her cooking to other people."

"Be serious."

"I am. Besides, I'm happy you're here, and that should be all that matters."

"It's your dad's home, Jensen. And he clearly wants to talk to you."

"Well, I don't want to talk to him."

She sighed. "I'm not comfortable with this."

"If you wanted me as a buffer between you and your dad, I'd help you. And we know your dad is less than fond of me."

"My dad doesn't know you. And he's less than fond of everybody."

"If you really want to go, I'll take you home."

"No," she said. "You need to talk to your dad. I'll call a cab. Or ask Chloe to pick me up."

"And do what in the meantime? Stand on the porch?"

She looked toward the front door.

"Oh, come on. At this point, you'll just offend people if you leave."

His mother walked into the room. "Is everything all right? Dinner is getting cold."

"I'm sorry," Bella said. "I was just telling Jensen that I can tell I interrupted something, and I should go."

"Bella," Vanessa said, "I appreciate your concern, but you're fine. We're glad you're here. Royce will talk to Jensen whenever he's ready, whether you're here or not. But you're already here, so please stay."

Bella glanced at Jensen and then back to his mom. "It would be my pleasure to stay for dinner. Thank you."

His mom held out her arm, and Bella shot him a last look before following his mother to the dining room.

Thank God for his mom. Thank God Bella stayed.

Too bad it wouldn't make a difference. He recognized the look on his father's face. There would be no reprieve. Time to clear the air.

He followed Bella into the dining room and took his place at the table. She was on his left.

His dad sat on his right.

Damn it. He'd hoped he could maybe hide behind Bella, which she probably knew and chose her seat accordingly.

"Roll?" Vanessa asked and offered the basket to Bella.

"Thank you." She took the basket, made her selection, and passed it on to Jensen.

He grabbed for the bread blindly and threw it on his dish. Then he handed the basket to his dad.

"The thing about rolls rather than bread," Royce said, "is that bread is already cut." He selected a roll and picked up his knife. "But a roll, that's different. You have to analyze it, decide how you want to cut it. It takes thought, dexterity. Careful planning. Decisions."

"It takes careful planning to eat a roll?" Faith asked. She took the basket and passed it to her mother without taking anything.

"I don't think we're talking about rolls," Bella said quietly to Jensen.

"No," he whispered back, "we aren't."

"Royce," Vanessa said with an almost-imperceptible shake of her head.

He continued turning his knife in his hand and staring at it. "Funny thing about decisions. Make the wrong one, and it affects your life forever."

Faith looked at him. "That's why I don't eat wheat. It's terrible for you."

"Faith," Vanessa whispered. That time, when she shook her head, it was far more noticeable.

"Someone needs to try and change the subject," Faith muttered.

"I don't want to change the subject," Royce said. He continued staring at his knife. "I'm perfectly happy discussing choices. Decisions. Dexterity."

"Here we go," Jensen said.

His dad pointed his blade at Jensen. "You're quite handy with a knife."

Bella wiped her mouth on her napkin. "If you'll all excuse me, I should—"

"Please. Stay," Royce said. "Maybe Jensen will be more inclined to talk if you're here. Maybe he'll tell you why he's been lying to me. For eight god damned years!"

Jensen put his hand on Bella's leg, praying she wouldn't run. If he was in her place, he'd fucking bolt. Holding her down was all he could think to do to keep her there.

He looked at his father. "Do we have to do this now?"

"Well, I tried to do it at the park, but you ran off. I wanted to discuss this last night, but you got home after I'd gone to bed, and you left the house this morning while I was still in the shower. This is the first I've had a chance to talk to you, and I'm damn well going to take my opportunity to find out what's going on, because if I wait until we're alone, I might never have the chance again."

His mother put her fork down. "Jensen. What did you do?"

"What did he do? What did he *do?"* Royce rose and started pacing. He turned and faced Jensen. "He did a needle decompression on a tension pneumothorax! In the middle of the ballpark! That's not something you can just do, like applying an ice pack or a bandage. That's something doctors do. Something only a doctor would even know about. So, tell me, Jensen. My engineering major son. Just how are you so enlightened?"

Jensen threw his napkin on the table and stood. "How do you think? You already know. I didn't get my MBA. I went to med school. I start my residency next month."

"Finally," Faith said.

"He told you?" Royce yelled. *"You,* but not me?"

"No, Dad," she said. "He never said a word."

"How did you know?" Jensen asked.

"I opened mail addressed to you. Don't yell." She held up her hand. "It was by mistake. But I saw your classes. That, plus the amount of time your degrees took… Well, it wasn't rocket science to figure it out."

"And you've been too busy to bother telling me?" Royce said.

"Wasn't my place," Faith said.

"I *wanted* to tell you," Jensen said. "But first, I wanted you to accept me for who I was and not resent me for what I chose to study."

"Why would I resent you being a doctor? I always hoped you'd be one."

"Not medicine. Engineering! You resented me studying engineering. Nothing was the same between us once I told you I wanted to be an engineer. You barely spoke to me when I went to college. I waited and waited, but you never got over it. Why in God's name would I tell you I changed my mind and did what you wanted? If you couldn't love me unless I obeyed your every wish and whim, then I didn't want your love at all."

This time, Bella grabbed his hand and squeezed. Pulled him down to sit beside her.

How had she known he'd been ready to run?

Royce dropped into his chair, stared at Jensen. "Of course, I loved you. I've *always* loved you."

"Could have fooled me." He toyed with the napkin on the table. No way could he meet his dad's gaze. Or Bella's. Or anyone's there.

"Jensen, I—" His dad faltered, sighed. Took a deep breath before starting again. "I'm sorry. I kept my distance because I thought you wanted autonomy, not because I was angry."

He had to look at his dad then. Had to know if he told the truth.

Didn't believe him for a second.

"That's bullshit, Dad."

"Jensen!" his mother said.

He glanced at her. "Sorry, but it's true." He looked at his father. "You may love me now. Probably always did. But you withheld that love as punishment for my disobedience."

"No, you're wrong. Faith chose a different career path, and I didn't treat her any differently. Why do you think I faulted you and not her?"

"I don't know. Maybe because you didn't expect her to study medicine, but she did. Veterinary medicine, but still medicine. But me? I rejected it, which means I not only rejected your demands on me, I rejected you. Hard to forgive me for walking away from med school when that's your whole life. You probably thought I was walking out on you. The only difference is, I didn't mind us not having the same calling. You did. And you shut me out because of it."

"But we have the same calling!" Royce said. "I was right all along. You became a doctor."

"No thanks to you."

"No thanks to— Are you kidding me?" His father rose again. Looked down at him. On him. "I paid for that schooling you're so quick to dismiss. And your food. Your apartment. Your books and supplies. You didn't even have the courtesy to tell me what I was paying for!"

"How could I?" Jensen also jumped to his feet, stood toe-to-toe with his father. "You weren't talking to me!"

His dad raised his hand, and Jensen flinched. Royce looked at him, then his hand. Finally ran his fingers through his hair and turned around. He walked to the other side of the room before spinning back toward his son.

"Jensen, this is pointless. What's done is done. We're just going to have to agree to disagree on what happened before and move forward from here."

"What's done is done? Move forward? God!" He paced to the opposite side of the room from his father. "Nothing's done. I got stuck with Oakland Regional on Match Day. If I really want to be a doctor, I have to come back here for my residency."

"Stuck? Oakland Regional is one of the best hospitals in the tri-state area. They only take a handful of candidates a year."

"Doesn't change the fact that I'm back here. With you."

"Is that really so bad?"

"Yes!" Jensen walked around the room, finally leaned against the doorway. "I've actually considered not going, just to avoid this."

"Not going? Over my dead—"

Jensen snapped his head up and stared at his father.

Royce swallowed. Spoke in a much softer voice. "Jensen. Do you have any idea what I went through when I saw what you did yesterday?"

"I can guess."

"No. No, I don't think you can."

Jensen rubbed the back of his neck. "You were angry. Still are."

His dad shook his head. Then he pushed off the wall and walked over to his son. He placed his hands on Jensen's shoulders and moved his head around until Jensen met his gaze.

"That's the exact procedure Hope needed. All I could think of when I saw you save that boy was that you made a positive difference in that family's life. Where I—" He closed his eyes and took a deep breath. "I hadn't been enough of a doctor or a man to be a positive influence in mine. You saved that boy. But I… I lost Hope. I almost lost everything. Don't make me lose you now."

Jensen couldn't answer. He swallowed past the lump in his throat and stared at his father. Finally, Royce squeezed his shoulders and stepped away.

There was so much to say, so many feelings caroming through him. At a total loss, Jensen turned and ran out of the room.

JENSEN LEANED AGAINST HIS TRUCK and looked up at the sky. His keys, clutched in his fist, dug into his palm. But he couldn't get into the vehicle. Couldn't move. Couldn't breathe. He closed his eyes, tried to catch his breath. The evening's revelations suffocated him.

Poor Hope. And his dad? How had he not realized the burden his father had carried all those years? Sure, the guy had been a dick about his major, but he had relented. He'd given Jensen his support—or his version of support—about it.

Things would have been so much easier between them, so much less strained, if he'd just told his dad. But pride kept his mouth shut. He didn't want to repair their relationship by giving in to his father's wishes.

He finally came clean tonight, laid it all on the table. So did his dad. Should have been cathartic. But it wasn't.

Jensen didn't really play every card in his hand. He never gave voice to his deepest secret. Even when his dad revealed his.

"Jensen? Are you out here?"

Bella's voice pierced the silence, but it couldn't quite penetrate his maudlin thoughts. She must think so little of him after witnessing that display.

"Behind the truck."

He could hardly look at her when she approached him. But he owed her—something.

"I'm sorry. I can imagine what you must be thinking."

"I'm just glad you didn't leave me here."

"I almost did. But then I realized how unfair that would be to you." That wasn't entirely true. He hadn't run because he hadn't been able to function any further than getting out of the house. When he finally thought about her, it was more about her perception of him than it was consideration for her. In retrospect, he was glad he hadn't abandoned her.

God, he was a selfish prick.

"Do you want to go somewhere and talk?"

How about an undeserving, selfish prick?

"After everything that went down tonight, you want to spend more time with me?"

"You're being too hard on yourself. Let's take a ride." She held her hand out to him.

How emasculating. He couldn't move. He still wasn't sure he was breathing.

She pried the keys out of his hands, unlocked the door, and pushed him into the passenger seat. He would have sat there like a child and let her fasten his seatbelt, but she left him to his own devices and walked around to the driver's side. He pulled the belt slowly across his chest and strapped in, wondering if he would snap out of it or succumb to the suffocation and just slip away.

Bella drove them in silence. He had explanations and apologies swirling in his head, but he couldn't give voice to any of them. Soon she stopped by the ballfields.

The last place he needed to be at now.

"Let's go sit and talk."

He grabbed her hand when she reached to turn off the engine. "Uh, do you mind going somewhere else? This is where the boy—" Nope. Couldn't finish that sentence.

"He's okay, Jensen. You saved him."

He swallowed, nodded. "I know. But—I'm just not up for this right now."

She put the truck in gear and pulled out. "Anywhere in particular you want to go?"

"Our spot?"

She shook her head. "It'll be dark soon. I don't go there at night."

Despite his pain, he chuckled. "Don't tell me you're afraid of the ghost? It's just a rumor. Scary camp stories."

Cathedral Lake had gotten its name almost two hundred years earlier when the small community erected a cathedral on the hill overlooking the lake. Families came from all over the countryside to attend services there, and soon after, the small community developed into a thriving town.

Services continued there until about fifty years later, when rumor had it a demon-possessed monk lit every candle on the offering table before throwing Bibles into the flames. A fire tore through the cathedral, consuming everything inside, destroying the building and everything in it.

Jensen didn't know if that was how the fire had started, but the cathedral had never been rebuilt. The ruins sat, undisturbed, for decades and had spawned the legend that so frightened Bella.

The lake still attracted large crowds during the day. But people avoided that area at night. Claimed they heard Gregorian chanting coming from the ruins at sunset. Others said it was satanic curses in the middle of the night. More likely than not it was a combination of whistling wind and overactive imaginations. Regardless, the beaches cleared before dusk, the folklore or the fright keeping people away.

"Really, Bella?"

"I'm not discussing this."

Who would have thought this intelligent, rational woman would have been superstitious? What other little quirks and secrets had she hid from him.

Soon she parked in front of Chloe's apartment. Felt like a goodnight. Too soon.

Instead of getting out of the truck, she turned and faced him. The low sun shone through the windshield, bathing her in a warm glow. Breathtaking. He studied her—the piled hair, the glamour makeup, the dress. Clearly designer. She'd put a lot of work into her appearance for him. He'd noticed her beauty earlier, but not her effort. That meant so much to him. More than he could express. Then she smiled at him. It soothed him.

It probably didn't hurt that she held his hand while they sat there, rubbed her thumb over his knuckles.

Waited in non-judgmental, companionable silence. That was more than he'd ever given her.

She helped him breathe again.

He wouldn't suffocate. Didn't know if that was a good thing or a bad thing, but he knew he was okay. Well, physically, anyway.

"I inferred from your father's outburst that you performed some sort of medical procedure on a young boy. Yes?"

He nodded. "Yes. He got hit in the chest with a ball and his rib cracked. Lung collapsed. Couldn't breathe."

"But you saved him?"

"I really shouldn't have. I could have gotten in trouble for doing a medical procedure like that when I'm not a doctor."

"But you graduated med school, right? So, you are a doctor."

He thought about his degree. "Technically my title is 'doctor.' But I didn't even begin my residency yet. People get sued all the time for just performing CPR on strangers. I overstepped."

"Well, now you're in my wheelhouse."

"What?"

"You're talking law. Did you know our state has a Good Samaritan statute?"

"Which means what?"

"It means if you're able to assist someone in jeopardy, you're required to by law. That kid's mother couldn't sue you if your procedure had failed, but she had grounds to if you did nothing for her boy. Especially if he had lingering complications. Or died."

Huh. He didn't know that. Had never considered it from that point of view.

Didn't matter, though. That wasn't why he avoided the park. The real reason was because that's where his father learned of his deception. It be the spot that severed his relationship with his father. Permanently.

"So, Dr. Keller."

The title stunned him. That was his father.

But now, it was him, too.

Wow. Just… wow.

"I guess you're not an engineer."

He sighed. So much for no sanctions. He knew he'd have to come clean, eventually. Good a time as any.

"I never lied. I told you that's what I went to school for. And it was. Initially. Until I realized what I really wanted to do. Needed to do."

"It's okay. When you told me, we'd just met. You didn't owe me an explanation. Would have been nice to have had one after the fact, though. But I guess if you hadn't told your family, it was hardly fair to tell me."

"I wanted to. I just never found the right time."

"Maybe when you were upset about me following in my father's footsteps."

Ouch. He deserved it, though.

"I'm a hypocrite. I have no excuse. But I'm sorry."

"I know." She traced a random pattern on his wrist. "Honestly, though. It's okay. I—probably better than anyone—understand family drama and father issues."

"It all got out of hand. So fast."

"Well, you got it all out in the open now. You'll be able to work it out."

He shook his head. "No."

"Sure, you will. Even my dad and I have made progress. Slow progress, but even one step forward is better than the status quo."

"No, that's not what I mean." His face flamed, and he looked away, so she didn't see his shame.

"What, then?"

"Everything I said to my dad tonight? It's all true."

"That's what I'm talking about."

"No." He shook his head again. "No, you don't understand. Everything I said was true, but there's more. Something I didn't say that I should have."

She squeezed his hand and covered it with her free one. "What?"

"I've been clinging to the excuse that I didn't say anything after all these years because I knew he wasn't happy with my decision, and I wanted him to accept me for me. Which is true. But that's not the real reason. Not the only reason."

"Oh, my God, Jensen. Spit it out, already. Just tell me."

He leaned his head on the window. "When it was all said and done, I just didn't want him to be right. I didn't want to give him the satisfaction of winning. I've been clinging to all his faults as my reason for my distance and my silence, but in reality, it was me all along. I was petty. Immature. I made him miserable for years when he already had enough to deal with. And now he has so much more going on, and I'm just hiding behind my excuses."

If shame was an animal, it would have attacked and devoured him. But he wasn't that lucky. It was just an emotion that could consume from within. That's the way he was being eaten alive.

In some ways, it was far more painful than a quick animal maiming would be.

"Listen," she said. "Given my history with my father, I can tell you one thing. If you have the chance to repair things, then take it. You only have one dad, and he only has one you. Don't let pride stand in your way."

He played with her fingers, then looked out the window. "I've made a lot of mistakes."

"Who hasn't?"

"I'm not sure things can go back to the way they were."

"You don't want to go back to the way things were," she said. "If things had been right before, they wouldn't have gone wrong," she said. "So, stop worrying about going back and concentrate on moving forward."

"But—"

"No buts, Jensen. Get over your whining and do something productive to fix things."

She was right, but seriously, of all people to call him on his bullshit? She was the quintessential pot nagging the kettle. "Really? Is that what you're doing with your dad?"

Something looking like anger or exasperation flickered in her eyes, but just as quickly as he noticed it, it was gone. Then she sighed. "It's complicated."

"Yeah, because I wouldn't understand that." He let her hand go. "I know I've been acting like an ass. For years with my dad, and, to you, since—well, basically since we met. But you can't give me advice you aren't willing to take yourself."

She sighed. "Damn it, Jensen. I'm trying to help you. But I sure as hell don't need the attitude. Back off, or I'm leaving."

They both took a few deep breaths. She reached for the door handle, and he panicked. He was pushing her away, too.

"Wait. Please."

She looked at him, but still neither of them spoke. He didn't want her to leave but didn't have the words to convince her to stay.

Finally, she released the door handle and turned toward him. "Look, I'm not trying to be a hypocrite. I'm really not. But your situation is different than mine."

"How so?" Her father might be worse than Royce, but they'd both suffered in their relationships with their dads. And, unless he missed his guess, she was as complicit in her relationship troubles as he was in his.

"You have problems with your dad because you don't communicate. But you've opened the door. You're working on things."

"And you and your dad have begun repairing your relationship. I'm assuming you had to talk to do that."

"I'm still keeping a secret from my father. I don't know how to move forward while that looms over us."

"And I have a secret, too."

"Your secret is admitting you didn't want him to be right about your career path. I understand your shame in hiding the secret, but it's hardly life-shattering."

"And your distaste for following your father's plans for you is?"

"That's not my secret. Clearly. I am a lawyer, after all."

"But you didn't want to be a defense attorney."

"No, I wanted to work for the DA. But my father knew that, too. It's never exactly been a secret."

"So, what is?"

She looked at him and bit her lip. "My brother's gone. And I'm responsible."

CHAPTER 22

BELLA WAITED FOR A RESPONSE from Jensen, but he just blinked and looked at her. His silence concerned her more than any outburst could have.

"Well, aren't you going to say something?" Anything. Like what a horrible person she was. Or how she'd ruined numerous lives. What a cowardly thing she'd done. Anything.

"You didn't tell me you had a brother."

"I tell you I lied to my father and destroyed my brother, and all you can say is you didn't know I had a brother?"

"Well, counselor, the jury's still out on all of that."

"Trust me. It's an easy decision. I have no defense. I'm guilty." She sat back and stared out the window into the sky. Dusk loomed on the horizon, and the first stars began to peek out against the violet backdrop.

"Talk to me. Tell me about your brother."

Oh, if only the blackness would descend and hide her in the darkness. There was still enough daylight in the gloaming of the moment that he could see her face, witness her shame. Condemn her and leave her there with her demons.

And she deserved it.

She closed her eyes, pictured Troy's face.

It was time. Time. She confessed her sins. For her brother.

"Troy was a lot older than me. Already in college when I was little. But he was my hero. I worshiped the ground he walked on, the air he breathed. He was all the good parts of my parents rolled into one—with none of the bad. Smart and sophisticated, like my father. Easy to talk to, like my mom. And would you believe it? As much as I loved him, he loved me more."

"So where does the problem come into play?"

"We had a house at the lake. Not here. About two hours away. Up in the tourist section, where people spend summers. I loved to go there, and we spent many weekends there, as well as most of our summers. Sometimes even Thanksgiving or Christmas. That particular summer, I was just four. Troy was teaching me to swim, and I was learning all about the indigenous flora and fauna. Those were some of the best times of my childhood."

"So, what happened? I don't see the problem."

"Do you like S'mores?"

His eyebrows raised, but he didn't question her sudden change of subject. "Who doesn't?"

"I can't eat them now. Loved them as a kid, but…" She let her thoughts go unspoken while her memories consumed her.

"What do S'mores have to do with your brother?"

"We were at the lake house. Had just gotten there. My parents ran into town for groceries and left Troy to watch me. They wouldn't be gone more than two hours. It shouldn't have been a problem. Troy had watched me plenty of times for much longer."

She sighed just remembering.

"So, my parents left, and I asked for S'mores. That's what we ate at the lake house. S'mores, mountain pies, hot dogs. Sometimes potatoes or corn on the cob wrapped in foil and placed right on the flames. If it could be cooked over a fire, we made it and ate it there. Anyway, I wanted S'mores, and I think I found marshmallows, graham crackers, and chocolate after rooting around in the kitchen."

"You think?"

"The memories are kind of fuzzy. But where else would food be kept? Anyway, but Troy said the stuff was old and we should wait for our parents to get back from the store."

Jensen rubbed her shoulder. He must have been able to sense what was coming. She fought for the memories. They were fragmented, confusing. It had been too long since she thought through it all. The pain still clawed at her—did daily—but the details had grown fuzzy.

"Troy got on the phone. He was talking to his girlfriend, and I was jealous. I wanted his attention. But he shushed me and shooed me away, and I didn't want to wait. Not for his attention, and not for my treat. So, I went outside and tried to start a fire. I thought if I made him a snack, he'd pay attention to me and not her."

God, what had she done?

"I couldn't get a fire started. I didn't know anything about kindling or anything. So, I went to the shed, I guess, and I got out my dad's lighter fluid. Squirted it all over the wood. Lit a match."

She closed her eyes and saw the fire. These memories were vivid. She could smell the pungent fumes of the fluid, the acrid odor as the flames consumed the wood. And the smoke. God, all the suffocating smoke.

"I was too close to the house and must have used too much fluid. The whole thing went up in flames. Everything. It spread past the fire pit, took the house, a few nearby trees." Tears leaked from the sides of her eyes and fell into her hair. She choked out the last words in a whisper. "It all happened so fast."

"Troy? Did he… ?"

"He streaked outside. Seemed like he was there before I even dropped the match. He pulled me to safety." She rubbed her wrist, tracing over the faint discoloration where she'd scarred from the flames. "Then he tried to put the fire out."

"Oh, Bella."

"I stood there and watched while he battled. He didn't have a chance."

"I'm so sorry," Jensen said. "Was it… was it smoke inhalation? The flames? Did he suffer?"

"What?" She sat upturned and looked at him. "Oh. Oh, no. I'm sorry. You must have thought he— No. He's alive. He's okay."

He shook his head. "I'm confused, then. What happened?"

"The same thing that always happens. Victor. When he got back, the firefighters were just leaving. A neighbor had called 9-1-1. I had second degree burns on my wrist and Troy had third degree burns on—" she choked back sobs "—on his neck, arm, and side. We were both in the ambulance, ready to leave for the hospital. My father was furious."

"Because you were leaving?"

"Because of the house. Because he looked negligent. Because he looked bad."

"Are you sure that's why he was angry? Maybe he was just scared for the two of you."

She leaned back on her elbows again. "You'd think so. It was my mother who doted and fussed the whole time the doctors treated us. Victor said nothing."

"I still think he could have just been frightened for you."

"I was treated and released, and my mother took me up to see my brother. They admitted him, obviously, while they considered skin grafts and treatment options. My father came into the room with two police officers. They wanted to talk to Troy and me."

"But you were just a child."

"Didn't matter. They still wanted my story. But Troy spoke up first. I don't know why he said what he said. Maybe the painkillers confused him. Maybe he thought he'd get sympathy, having been so badly injured."

"What did he say?"

"He took the blame. For all of it. Said he was the one who wanted a snack and didn't want to wait for our parents to get back. Said he used the lighter fluid and lost control of the flames. Then he said, 'It's okay, Izzy. Tell them.' like he was begging me not to contradict him."

"Izzy? That's cute."

"That's what he called me. I hate that name, but it was okay for him to use it. Anyway, I didn't know what to do when he lied for me. I was four years old. I didn't know I should have spoken up. So, I followed his lead, mimicked his story. Laid all the blame on his shoulders."

"Then what happened?"

"I think there was discussion about pressing charges. I'm not sure. In the end, there was no legal reprisal. We didn't file an insurance claim, so there was no chance of fraud. And I don't know if there was any kind of fine, but Troy didn't do any jail time."

"Jail time? For what?"

"The fire. There are different penalties for starting fires, failing to control them. The charges depend on malicious intent, buildings or acreage impacted, monetary costs to the fire departments. He could have gone to jail. I don't know if my father had to defend him or if the DA just chose not to pursue charges. I should probably look up the details of the case."

"Why not just ask your dad or brother?"

"That's the part I've been hiding all these years." She lay back, played with a few blades of grass, and stared out the window at the darkening sky. "My father never got the truth from my brother or from me. As soon as Troy was released from the hospital, Victor threw him out of the house."

"What?"

"He cut him off, just like me. Only with Troy, it stuck. I haven't seen him since he lay in the hospital bed, lying to keep me out of trouble."

"Where did he go? What happened to him?"

"Wish I had the guts to find out. So far, I've barely spoken his name since that day. I haven't looked for him."

"So, get in touch with him now."

She sat up. "And say what? 'Sorry I scarred your skin and got you booted out of the family. No hard feelings, right?' What would you say to that if you were him?"

"I'd be so glad to see my sister again. I wouldn't care what she said to me."

Twist the knife, Jensen. Like she didn't feel bad enough already.

"Tell your dad or don't. I'm not sure it would matter. But reach out to your brother. He clearly loves you. Look what he did for you. Why deprive him of your love after all he suffered?"

"And what if he doesn't want to see me?"

"Well, I guess you won't know that until you reach out to him."

Did she dare try to contact her brother?

At this point, did she dare not?

THEY STAYED TOGETHER IN SILENCE for a long while. The sun disappeared behind the horizon line, leaving the sky to darken from indigo to black. Fireflies twinkled across the street. A cricket chirped somewhere close by.

They took a walk, held hands. She churned over what Jensen said to her, what she had to do, and she assumed he did the same.

They ended up on a bench in the atrium behind Chloe's building, sitting side-by-side and holding hands. At some point—and she didn't know when or how or who made the move—she ended up with her back snugged against his chest, his arms wrapped around her, her head resting on his shoulder.

She could stay like that forever.

The dress she'd borrowed from Chloe was sheer, and she felt the cool wood of the bench under her hip, directly contrasting the solid heat from Jensen's body. It didn't take long for her thoughts to drift from her family to something so much more wanton.

Must not have taken Jensen long, either. He trailed the tips of his fingers along her bare arm, up and down until she shivered under his touch. Then he shifted his arm, traced the neckline—not that it was anywhere near her neck—of the dress. Her skin pebbled with goosebumps, and she both feared and desired where his fingers would go next.

He moved her hair aside. Pressed his lips to her shoulder. Placed kisses on her back, her neck, her jaw.

She pushed back against him, her body craving more.

When his hand drifted lower, skimming under the flimsy material and along the swells of her breast, she jumped. Pushed off him. Jumped to her feet.

Scrambling to fix the position of her clothes, she turned to face him, grateful the darkness hid her flaming cheeks.

Wasn't sure if they burned from shame or desire, but it didn't matter. Either way, she didn't want Jensen to see.

"I'm sorry," he said, voice deep, husky. "I thought… well, I guess I didn't really think at all. Look at me, all over you in the courtyard of your friend's place."

She watched him push to his feet and adjust his pants over a prominent bulge. Couldn't miss that, even with the darkness.

Damn it all to hell, she'd done it again.

"You should get inside." He held a hand out to her. "And I should go."

She squinted at him, his face an unreadable, expressionless mask. Time for another confession.

"Jensen, before we go, can I have just a moment more of your time?"

He didn't answer.

"Please." She gestured at the bench.

He shrugged and sat, this time angled toward her instead of beside her or embracing her.

"It seems I'm sending you mixed signals, and I'm sorry for that. I'd like to explain."

"You don't owe me anything, Bella." His voice sounded cold, detached. He shifted forward.

"Please," she said. "Don't go. Just give me one minute."

He sat back again.

"I'm not trying to lead you on. I know you think I'm being a tease and that couldn't be further from the truth. I hate it when I see women use their sexuality to manipulate men."

He took a deep breath. It whooshed out of him in a long, hard sigh before he spoke. "Then what are you doing?"

Thank God for the darkness. Her face—her entire body—heated with the knowledge she prepared to share. "I'm, uh… responding to you. To what you *do* to me. To how great it feels."

"Maybe this wasn't the best time and place for this, but if it felt that good, you'd want me to continue. If you had any feelings for me, you wouldn't push away, you'd respond in kind."

"I don't know how."

"What? What do you mean you don't know how? The same way you do with any other guy you like."

"Jensen." She prayed he could hear her. Her voice was almost too soft for her own ears to pick it up. "There have never been any other guys. I'm a…."

Her lips formed the word, but no sound escaped her.

"I'm sorry. What?" he asked.

She didn't reply.

"What did you say?"

Well, she hadn't really said it, had she? She tried again, but, still, nothing came out.

"Did you say you're a virgin?"

Oh, God. Just what she feared. He said the word like it was a contagious disease. She'd always called it a condition, a situation. Chloe called it a malady. Clearly Jensen agreed.

Unable to do anything else, she nodded.

"Huh."

Did he say, 'huh' to that? *That* was his response?

"Um, can you say something? Please? I mean, more than 'huh' because I don't really know what that means."

He laughed and scooted beside her. She didn't find anything about the situation funny. Draping his arm over her shoulder, he pulled her close. "I just meant that I didn't expect that. I thought the problem was me."

She stiffened. "But instead, the problem is me, is that it?"

Jensen hugged her tighter. "No. No problem. No problem at all. Other than a slight miscommunication, which we just cleared up. So, no, no problem."

She shook her head. "I don't understand."

"Always at cross-purposes, you and I." He started trailing his fingers along her arm again.

Mmm, that felt good.

"Bella, I just thought you were rejecting me. Now I know it's not me."

"It's me." She pushed away from him.

"No. It's us. It's nothing. It's—" He sighed. "I'm saying it poorly. What I mean is, I'm glad you told me. I can handle things differently now. We'll go at your pace. You take the lead."

"Take the lead? I don't know what I'm doing. How am I supposed to direct things?"

She was going to die a virgin. And if this conversation continued, it would be right then and there. From embarrassment.

"We'll work it out. All I mean is, you set the limits. If kissing is all you're ready for, then I'll kiss you all night. When you're ready for more, let me know."

"What do you want me to do? Move your hands over me? Tell you where and when and how to touch me? That kind of overt display isn't really anything I know about."

He kissed her. A slow, sensual kiss, scattering her thoughts and fears like a gentle breeze blows dandelion tufts through a meadow. She broke apart and drifted in the sensation.

When he pulled away, he rested his forehead against hers. "I'm not saying I wouldn't love to hear you say those things to me. But let's take it slow. We'll work it out."

"You aren't repulsed by my… inexperience?"

"Repulsed?" He pulled back and looked at her. "Bella. That's the last thing I am. Being with you, in any way you let me, is an honor. I know you didn't save yourself for me, but I'm still flattered."

"I wish I knew what I was doing. Knew how to give you what you want."

He shook his head. "I want you. We'll figure out the rest. I just can't believe someone like you hasn't… Well. It doesn't matter."

"Someone like me?"

"Someone smart, funny, beautiful, talented, compassionate." He tipped his head to the side. "Are you fishing for compliments? Because I can go on."

She shook her head. "No. Just… just relieved that you understand."

"Of course, I understand…" But his voice trailed off.

"You don't understand, do you?" She bit her lip, fought to hold in tears.

"No, I do. Well, I understand why we've been having misunderstandings about this. I guess I just don't understand how you've gone so long without… I mean, didn't you ever date anyone? Or get carried away after a party? Experiment with your roommate in college?"

She snorted. "You watch too many movies. I think that happens far less than you fantasize about."

He laughed.

"I told you how controlling my father was. Through high school, there were simply no opportunities. In college, he made sure I was so busy I wouldn't have time for a social life."

"No one's that busy."

She sighed. "There was one guy. I thought we had a future."

"See, you did have time. So, what happened?"

"What always happens. Victor."

"Your dad stopped you from having sex?"

"Aaron was a sweet, understanding guy. He knew it would be my first time, and he wanted to make it special. No backseats or dorm rooms with socks on the door. So, he came to Cathedral Lake over winter break. He took me out for a gourmet dinner and rented us a beautiful hotel room. It would have been a magical night."

"So, what happened? How'd your dad get involved?"

"My best friend? She's Chloe Thompson of Thompson Development."

"The hotel people?"

"Among other things, yes. They own a gazillion hotels worldwide. Aaron reserved a suite at the Channingswood, which happens to be their flagship hotel here."

"I still don't see what Victor has to do with this."

"Mr. Thompson happened to be at the hotel that night. Probably happens once in a decade. And just my luck, we picked a night he was on site. He saw me get in the elevator, and he called my dad."

"Uh-oh."

"That doesn't begin to cover it. We were—let's just say indisposed—when Dad burst in without even knocking."

"Sounds like a lawsuit in the making. You were both over eighteen, right?"

"In retrospect, yes, Aaron could have sued Dad and Mr. Thompson. Instead, the fear of God—or worse—was put in him, and he ran from the room barely dressed. I never saw him again. Not even on campus. I have no idea what even happened to him. But that was the last time I even considered being with a man." She looked around. "Wouldn't surprise me to see my dad jump out of the bushes here and now."

He glanced around in melodramatic fashion and spoke in a bold tone. "I shall defend your honor, my lady. No one shall cast aspersions on your character when in my presence." Then he lowered his voice and waggled his eyebrows. "But what we do when we're alone is another matter."

She giggled and released a breath she didn't know she'd been holding. "Thank you, Jensen."

"For what?"

"For understanding. And not making me feel like a leper."

He kissed her on the nose. "A leper? Hardly. Now, you should get inside. I'm an understanding man, but I mean, look at you. I'm only human. My willpower does have its limits."

She blushed again and wrapped her arms around his neck. "Let's see how strong your willpower is."

"So that's the way you want to play this, huh?"

Giggling, she nodded. Now that she had the power, she grew excited. Bold.

Daring.

"All right, then. Let's see how long you hold out before you change your mind." He pulled her tight against him.

"I've held out this long." She bit her lip. She wasn't sure there was a way for her to lose this game.

"I may not be a lawyer, but I can be very persuasive."

"You don't say." Her body throbbed everywhere it touched his.

"Doctors know all kinds of things about the human body."

Her reply was lost when he captured her mouth in another kiss.

CHAPTER 23

JENSEN GOT HOME TOO LATE to talk to his father. That was just a side benefit, though. The important part of the evening had been Bella. She consumed his thoughts until he fell asleep. And in the morning, her face was the first image that popped into his mind.

He grinned amd got out of bed.

It did him a world of good to talk everything over with her the night before. He thought he made a good sounding board for her, too. They meshed well. He thought back over their evening together.

Oh, yeah. They meshed well.

He showered and headed downstairs.

"Good morning, Jensen." Sylvia greeted him with a cup of coffee. "Are you hungry? What can I get you?"

He sipped the coffee and closed his eyes. How could he possibly go back to Starbucks after having this every morning?

"Mmm. You make a mean cup of Joe, Syl."

She smiled. "Thank you. So, what do you want with it?"

He thought for a moment. His stomach wasn't growling. Seemed he'd been hungry since his first meal in the house. But that morning, finally, he didn't care about eating. "You know, nothing for me. I think I'm going to change and take a run."

Sylvia's eyebrows shot up. "Really? You're turning down my pancakes for pounding the pavement?"

He tossed back the rest of the coffee, absorbed the caffeine jolt even as the liquid scalded his tongue and throat. "I guess I am. I've been getting fat and sloppy. Time to get back into a schedule and back into shape."

"How about I have something ready for you to eat when you get back?"

"I'll probably just want a protein shake."

"That's not food."

"Bye, Syl. Thanks for the coffee."

He jogged upstairs, changed into running clothes, and headed outside. He could go around his house… hit the neighboring streets and subdivisions, but he was in the mood for nature. So, he got in his truck and drove to the park.

No way could he have gone back to the park so soon if Bella hadn't talked things over with him.

Soon he jogged through one of the trails that wound around the lake before going back to town square.

The fresh air felt wonderful as it expanded his lungs. Smelled like sunshine, rainbows, joy. He smiled and ran on, ignoring the beginnings of protests from his neglected muscles.

So, he smiled a little less as his calves cramped and lungs burned. He pushed on.

When he got to the lake, he forgot all about the lactic acid in his muscles and his constricting diaphragm. The side stitch and leg fatigue didn't register. All he could think about was Bella.

He ran across the smooth sand of the beach and looked across the water. Their rock looked impossible to climb to, the terrain there steep and craggy. But he knew better. There was an easy path to their special spot. But looking from the beach side, no one would know that. That's why he and Bella were never interrupted there.

Good information to have. Too bad he couldn't get her there at night. He laughed to himself about her silly fears. Then he glanced at their spot again. So secluded. Even in the daylight, they could have privacy there.

He jogged further down the beach and picked up the path again. Soon he wound back toward town. His thoughts alternated between Bella and his weary body.

How could he have gotten so out of shape in so few days?

By the time he reached the park, he thought his lungs might burst or his feet might fall off. He walked, kept track of his pulse as he cooled down, and sucked air. A chuckle surprised him, made his pulse spike again. He spun around.

"Finally realized how soft you were getting, kid?" Detective Cooper sat on the ground, legs spraddled, stretching his left arm over his head toward his right toe.

Jensen walked over to him, flopped down on the ground, and assumed a similar position. God, the stretch felt great… almost eliminated the stitch in his side. "Just coming or just going?"

"Finished my run. Five miles. Light day. How far'd you go?"

Five freaking miles? Guy didn't even look like he broke a sweat.

"About three. Took the short path past the lake."

"Better than nothing, I guess."

Jensen glared at him, then stretched to the other side. Only groaned a little.

Cooper smiled but said nothing.

"Hey, Tony. You still keeping your hands off the case?"

"That's what the captain said to do."

"That's not what I asked you."

Cooper put both feet in front of him and leaned forward, grabbing his toes and pulling his body down. "Why do you ask?"

"I've been digging around."

"Pretty sure you shouldn't be doing that."

"Pretty sure you're still digging, too, ace, or you would have answered my question."

The detective nodded, looked around, pulled his body lower—which brought his face even closer to Jensen's. "What have you learned?" His voice lost all humor, his tone low, barely audible.

Jensen looked around. Didn't see anything or anyone suspicious. But would he know if he did? "What have you learned?"

Cooper stood and started walking toward the ballfields, which would be empty at that time of day. "Let's walk this off."

A quick scrabble to his feet, and Jensen trotted over to the cop. They walked in silence until they got to the bleachers. Images of the boy collapsing on the mound pummeled Jensen. The look on the mother's face as she watched her son spiral toward death. Needle puncturing flesh. Audible release of air.

He calmed when he remembered what Bella had said. He'd done the right thing. The boy would be okay.

"Wouldn't happen to know anything about a guy saving a kid from a punctured lung here the other night, would you?"

He wouldn't meet Cooper's gaze. "Why? Something happen? Someone in trouble?"

"No. No trouble. Mother of the kid just wanted to offer a proper thanks to the hero who saved her son."

Hero? Him? "Oh. That's nice. I thought maybe the cops wanted to bust him for impersonating a doctor or something."

"Bystanders think he *is* a doctor. Said he performed the procedure like a pro."

Jensen nodded.

"Good Samaritan laws in this state say if you are qualified to perform a medical procedure, you are required to try."

So, he'd heard. "What's the cops' position if the Samaritan tried but failed?"

"In this case, that doesn't apply. But for future reference, people are safe if they try something like CPR. Not so much if they start cutting people open on a sidewalk. Then they better be qualified and know what the hell they're doing. Not necessarily the same thing."

Jensen nodded. "Good to know. For future reference."

They sat for a while, looking over the mound, out to the outfield, and around the rest of the park. Finally, Jensen couldn't stand the silence. "So, what do you know about Unger?"

"I believe I asked you first."

"No, you didn't. I asked you."

"Agree to disagree," Cooper said. "So, what do you know?"

Jensen sighed. Realized he wouldn't get any information unless he gave some first. Ended up telling him everything he knew.

"Quite the mess you've landed in the middle of."

"Yeah, I know. So, what do you know about it?"

"Officially, I know nothing. Captain said to back off."

"And unofficially?"

His eyes scanned the vista—left to right. Glanced over his shoulder and looked right to left. "Things are moving fast. There have already been a few drops. Unger's moving up the ladder fast. Should be meeting the leader soon, and then it'll be over."

"How soon? Wade didn't say anything to me about any of this. He acted like he's not gaining any ground at all and this could go on forever. I'm worried about my dad."

"Your dad's being watched. The clinic is under surveillance. That's how I know you've been there."

"I told you I went there."

"But I already knew."

"Did I tell you anything you didn't know?"

Cooper smiled.

"Fine. You know everything. How about enlightening me?"

"You already know too much. Back off, let the pros handle it."

"Why does everyone keep saying that to me?"

"Because we're already keeping tabs on enough doctors. We don't need to add a medical resident with a hero-complex to our list of things to keep track of."

The guy didn't miss anything.

Cooper stood and walked down the bleachers. Then he looked up at Jensen. "I mean it. Stay out of it. It'll all be over soon."

"Is there anything you can do to get them to call this off?"

"Jensen, I'm not even on this case. I'm homicide, not vice. I shouldn't be poking around in this shit as it is."

"But my dad. He's stuck there in the middle of all of it."

"He knew the risks. And he's being watched. Just stay out of it and trust the system, kid. It'll all work out."

Jensen didn't answer him. He wasn't a kid, damn it. And he wouldn't have to stick his nose in if anyone would just keep him in the loop. And help his dad.

Cooper headed off the way they had come, and Jensen stayed there, thinking. If no one was going to help his father, then he'd just have to do it himself. He'd tail Wade, find out who the players were and what was really going on. One way or another, he would get his answers and make sure his family was safe.

ABOUT THIRTY MINUTES BEFORE THE clinic closed, Jensen sat in his truck half a block up the street and assumed total stakeout-mode. He could see the front door—and the planter beds—from his vantage point but doubted anyone would look for him this far up the street. The long-range lens was already on his camera, and he'd filled up his gas tank, just in case he had to follow anyone.

He doubted the Feds were better prepared.

In fact, he knew they weren't, because he hadn't seen one of them. Surveillance, his ass.

On the other hand, maybe they were just so good that he was unaware of them. That made him feel better. Not great. Just better.

Rooting around through his provisions, he found his drink and a can of cashews. He popped a handful of nuts into his mouth and washed them down with the last sips in his second bottle of water. Maybe he hadn't prepared for every eventuality. After downing two bottles of water, he really needed a bathroom break.

When the passenger door swung open, he jumped.

Heart raced double-time. Bladder nearly failed.

He spun toward the passenger seat and scrabbled for his weapon, dropping the nuts. They scattered all over the truck even as he held his Swiss Army knife toward the person invading his space.

Bella burst out laughing. "What did you think you were going to do with that? Pop a cork? Trim a nail?"

He realized the absurdity of it before she finished speaking but refused to acknowledge it.

"What are you doing here?" he asked.

"I'm helping you."

"You being here isn't helping. I'll just be worried about protecting you and that will distract me from where I should be focused."

"Protecting me? From whom? And with what? The screwdriver?"

"I don't know from whom. Not yet. I'll have you know the blade on this knife is really sharp."

"You'd have to be on top of someone to use it."

"Well, I wouldn't be so concerned about the close proximity if I didn't have you here to worry about."

"Too late to address that detail. I'm here, and I'm not leaving."

The slew of expletives careening through his brain embarrassed him. Instead, he said, "Is there anything I can say or do to change your mind?"

She shook her head.

He sighed and bit back his frustrated retort.

"Besides, you need me."

"For what? You packing an army knife, too?"

She smiled. "If you don't need me…."

Jensen looked out the window, refusing to look at her. As the silence progressed, his willpower decreased. He didn't need to see the gloss on her oh-too-kissable lips. The shine of her luxurious hair.

How many—or few—buttons she'd fastened on her blouse.

No, he really didn't need the distraction now.

But he peeked, anyway.

She rooted through her bag and turned to him, a huge grin plastered on her face. In one hand she held something that looked like a miniature satellite dish. In the other, headphones. "Ta-da."

"Ta-da?"

"Yes, ta-da. As in, if I had a trumpet, I'd blow it and make the same damn sound. Ta-freaking-da."

He couldn't help but chuckle. Two little syllables from him and her smile morphed into a scowl. He glanced up the street again, noticed it was after closing time. That sobered him and he stopped laughing.

"Sorry. I don't know what that is."

"Don't know what—how can you not know what this is?" She lifted the thing as she referred to it.

"Bella, the clinic's closed. You need to go."

"We've covered that already. I'm not going. If for no other reason than you don't even know what this is. You really do need me. For more than what I implied." She adjusted the dish-thing, pointing it through the windshield toward the clinic. After turning a few dials, she put one ear pad up to her left ear, leaned toward him, and offered him the other. "We'll have to share."

He looked at the headphones. "Share what?"

A soft sigh escaped her. "The headphones." She shoved the free side toward him again.

"Is that one of those spy sound things?"

She turned toward him slowly and looked at him with wide eyes. "Spy sound things? Nice technical jargon. And yes, it's a bionic sound booster. It has a hundred-yard range, cuts background noise, and amplifies the sound. Even records it, if you want. Not that I can be party to that. Recording people when you aren't part of the conversation is against the law. Besides, I don't think we need a recording. Law enforcement already knows what's going on."

He scoffed, shook his head. "Bella. Those are gadgets on old spy movies and cartoons. They don't really work."

She shoved the earpiece against his ear. He heard sounds that could only be coming from up the street.

Did it really work? Was he really that naive that he didn't know it would?

What would he do without her?

"This way, you won't need your little knife. We'll be safe and sound in your truck, but we'll still know what's going on."

"I'm sorry. I didn't know these things were real. I—"

"Ssh. There's Unger."

Jensen grabbed his camera with the long-range lens and put the headphone back against his ear.

Looking through the viewfinder gave Jensen an advantage. Wade's lips moved like he mumbled something to himself, but Jensen never would have noticed how nervous he seemed without the magnified view. Or the enhanced sound.

Damn it, Wade was clearly not cut out for infiltrating a drug ring. The constant pacing gave him away, and if it didn't, the sweating and fidgeting with his collar would have. Finally, he leaned against a planter box and stopped murmuring. His face lost the tense frown and smoothed into a relaxed expression.

All. Business.

Maybe he would pull it off.

A woman walked up the street. She looked familiar, but Jensen couldn't place her. Then she spoke to Wade.

"Doctor."

"Hello, Meg. Forget something?"

Meg. The receptionist. The working-for-the-drug-dealers receptionist. God bless Bella and her spy tech.

Meg leaned against the planter, arm-to-arm with Wade.

"They're concerned." She whispered, looked up and down the street.

"About what?" Wade asked.

"You've been keeping some interesting company."

"I see you more than anyone."

"You've been spotted with Royce's boy."

Damn it, damn it, and damn it again. He thought he'd been careful, but probably not enough. He'd been downright careless when he didn't know what was at stake. What if his tenacity blew the whole thing?

"Yeah?" Wade said. *"So have you. What am I supposed to do? The kid's pissed off, looking for answers. He's either going to avoid me or confront me. Better to stay available for when he finally does blow. Keep the collateral to a minimum."*

"As long as they aren't the collateral."

"You can tell them I have everything under control."

She looked up and down the street again. Gave Jensen's truck a careful look.

Bella grabbed his hand. Other than that, neither of them moved.

"Anything else?" Wade asked.

Finally, Meg looked away. *"We can't*—you *can't—afford any mistakes."*

"The order's been placed. You're keeping the books straight. When it comes in, I'll be sure to take delivery myself."

"And—"

"And stay late to catalog it and stock it. I know what I need to do. You just handle your part, and I'll be sure to handle mine."

She pushed off the planter and turned to face him. *"You only have your own life on the line. I have others. Don't screw this up for me."*

"Don't you think I'm going to cover my own ass?"

"It's not your ass I'd be worried about. It's your life. These guys don't screw around, and I have more at stake than you do. So, I'll say it again. Don't screw this up for me." She looked again at Jensen's truck, then she walked the opposite way down the street.

Wade's face crumpled again into a mask of anxiety. He glanced up the street, shook his head almost imperceptibly, then walked away in the direction Meg had gone. Soon he climbed into a black car and drove away.

A minute later, Jensen's cell phone rang.

He looked at the display. Unknown number.

"You don't think that's—?"

Jensen shrugged and swiped his finger across the scree and put the call on speaker. "Hello?"

"What in the hell do you think you're doing? Don't you understand? You're putting us all in danger. You must stop spying on me. I spotted you the second I left the clinic. If I did, so could anyone else."

"Hi, Wade. Nice of you to call."

"Don't get cute with me."

Jensen looked at Bella and rolled his eyes. A giggle escaped her, and she covered her mouth with her hands.

"What's going on? Is someone with you?"

"If I really was spying on you, and you really did spot me, then you'd know."

"God, you're such an ass. Don't sit there telling me that wasn't you in the Avalanche up the street."

"Why do you know what kind of vehicle I drive?"

"Are you listening to me?" Wade's voice rose, and Jensen held the phone farther away. *"How could I not know? You're everywhere. And if I know, they know."*

"Who's they?"

"Damn it, Jensen. I'm in this up to my stethoscope. I don't need you mucking things up. It's not a game. Lives are involved. Just let me deal with this. Hopefully, we all get out in one piece."

"I'm not leaving you to your own devices. I don't trust you. My dad's stuck in this with you. Someone has to look out for him."

"That's what I'm doing. Not you. Stay out. Before they drag your family in deeper. Before they drag you in deeper."

"They? They *who?* And how deep? What will they do? How much danger is my dad in?"

Wade cursed and ended the call.

Jensen looked at Bella. "Just who exactly is *they?* Not just some random dealer. Not with the kind of heat he's talkng about"

"Doesn't sound like it." They sat in silence for a while. "You know, Jensen, if Unger noticed us, maybe he's right and the others have noticed us, too."

"Too late to do anything about that now."

"Maybe we should stop tailing him. At least for a while."

"No way. Now more than ever, I need to keep tabs on him. To keep my dad safe."

"You don't think your dad can do that himself?"

"If he could, he wouldn't have agreed to this deal to begin with."

She sighed. "We could hire a PI. There are a couple of really good ones my father uses."

He drummed his fingers on the gearshift, the tap-tap-tap-tap a nervous rhythm that did nothing to soothe him. "I don't know. I'd like to know first-hand what's going on."

"Well, I don't think you're going to spy on anyone if they suspect what you're doing."

"That's just the thing. We've been made, and we haven't even really learned anything."

"At this point, I'm not sure what more we can learn. Not when we're so exposed, anyway. We don't even know who these guys are. How are we supposed to keep tabs on them?"

He rested his head on the steering wheel. "What the hell did my dad get himself into?"

CHAPTER 24

AFTER JENSEN TOOK BELLA HOME, she paced.

She surfed the web.

She made warm milk.

Paced some more.

Finally went to bed. And tossed and turned.

In the end, she spent a sleepless night worrying about Jensen.

Before dawn, she gave up on decorum as well as relaxing and placed a call.

"This better be an emergency," Steve growled into the phone.

"Steve. It's Bella."

"Are you in imminent danger?"

"Uh…."

He sighed. Paused a long while. When he finally spoke, he sounded alert and angry. *"What have you done, Bella?"*

"Well, I don't know that I've done anything, exactly. But I kind of need your help."

"Perish, I told you to stay out of it."

"But you don't understand. Jensen, the son of—"

"I fucking know *who Jensen Keller is."*

"Well, see, he's been talking to Unger, and—"

"What part of 'stay out of it' was I unclear on?"

"But, Steve. There's so much you don't know. So much I don't know. If I can just get access to the files, the ones that specify the terms of Unger's deal, then I can—"

"No."

"Would you stop interrupting me? I'm trying to tell you—"

"I don't care. The answer is no. To anything you ask regarding this case. Was before, still is. Stay clear of it. Do you understand?"

"But—"

"Do. You. Understand?"

Bella didn't answer.

"Look, I'm not trying to be a hardass, but this isn't coming from me. It's straight from the top. It's not just your job at risk. They're threatening your license."

"I don't care."

"Well, I do."

"Let them do their worst to me. If I can just help Jensen, then—"

"It's not just you. My job is on the line, too. If I can't rein you in, I'm out. So, knock this shit off. Stay out of it. No poking, no prodding. No digging into anything. You aren't even Switzerland in this matter. You aren't neutral. You're Antarctica. Completely uninvolved. Get it?"

She sighed, gritted her teeth. Fought not to say something she'd regret.

"Bella. I want you to answer me. I need to hear you say that you're going to stay out of it."

Funny how before he didn't want to hear her talk, and, now, he wouldn't hang up without hearing her speak.

"I hear you."

"And you understand?"

"I understand."

"So, you'll stay out of it?"

"Goodbye, Steve."

She didn't know if she still had a job to start, but it didn't matter. Jensen needed help, and no one else seemed to be rising to the occasion. It sucked how everyone kept pushing them away, warding them off. They learned a lot on their own, so, clearly, they had skills.

And, damn it, they wouldn't have to push and dig so hard if people would just tell them what's going on.

Well, she'd go to her job come Monday. The worst that could happen would be that she got fired before she even started.

In the meantime, she had one more resource to try.

BELLA STOOD IN THE LOBBY of Jordan Reed's office. The receptionist's desk sat vacant, and the door to Jordan's office was ajar. She couldn't resist eavesdropping on the PI's phone conversation.

"Connie, it doesn't matter what you think of the wife. She asked us to find out if her husband was cheating. You found out. Give her the photos and your report… No, you can't pick and choose the photos and say the results were inconclusive… And you can't lie… Damn it, Con, I don't care if she's cheating with three men and her husband is only… Four? And the pool boy? How cliché. It doesn't matter. Maybe he should have kept his dick in his pants and hired us to surveil her. Give her your report. Today."

Jordan slammed the phone down on the receiver. "What a bitch." She continued muttering for a few minutes, then called out to the lobby, "You can come in now, Bella."

Bella smiled. She never could put one over on Jordan Reed. Didn't know a soul who had. Not even her father.

Bella poked her head into Jordan's office. "Hey. How'd you know it was me?"

"Please. A visitor in reception is child's play. Come in, have a seat."

Bella barely got comfortable before Jordan got to the point of the visit. "So, I'm guessing this isn't a social call."

"I wish."

"Tell me. All the details."

Bella relayed everything she knew about Wade, the parole deal, and the current situation at the clinic.

"So, what do you want from me?"

"Unger's getting deeper in this thing, and that's putting my friend's family at risk. We've tried to follow him a couple of times, but we must be conspicuous, because he knew. Maybe others, too."

"Who? Vice? The Feds? The dealer?"

"Probably all of the above."

Jordan sighed. "You aren't equipped for surveillance."

"That's why I'm here."

"You want me to tail the guy?"

"You are the best."

"Flattery will get you nowhere. You already owe me multiple favors."

"Three is hardly 'multiple.'"

"The very definition is more than one. And it's four."

"Three."

"McAllister."

Oh, yeah. That case was a bitch. "Fine, four. This will make an even five."

"I can't do it free this time. My receptionist is on maternity leave, and I've got to hire a temp until she's back. Might have to hire one or two more investigators, too."

"I don't care about the money. But I can't have you telling anyone you're working for me."

"Seriously, Bella? I'm insulted. I pride myself on discretion."

"I know, I know. That's not what I meant."

"Then what?"

"You can't tell my dad."

"This isn't for the firm?"

Huh. There's one thing Jordan didn't know. "I don't work for my dad anymore. I work for the DA." At least, she hoped she did. Maybe she'd soon need to apply for one of the positions opening at Jordan's firm.

"So, I can add the city prosecutor's office to my resume. I'm surprised they gave you the green light on this."

Bella didn't answer.

"They aren't hiring me. You are. Just how deep into this are you?"

"Deep enough." She held up her hand. "And spare me the lecture about the danger and me needing to stay out of it. I'm already in it. The question is, are you going to help me?"

"It's not safe."

Growling was not a viable response to frustration, but, boy, Bella seriously thought about it. Instead, she stood. "One way or another, I'm going to get the answers I want. You can make a few bucks in the process or not. What's it going to be?"

Jordan stared at her for a long moment. Bella assumed the visit had been a waste of time. She only hoped the PI didn't tell her father or boss about her involvement. Resigned, she shrugged and turned to leave.

"You're going to owe me double for this one. Especially if I can't tell your dad or your boss."

Bella stopped walking but didn't turn around. "I won't tell a soul you're working for me. Not even my friend Jensen."

"Text me Unger's work address, and you owe me triple."

Bella smiled and got out her phone as she walked out the door.

CHAPTER 25

JENSEN WORRIED FOR HIS PHYSICAL and mental well-being. Tailing Wade, avoiding his father, preparing for his residency—it all took a toll. Exhaustion didn't begin to cover it. Nor did anxiety.

Trying to get back into shape only made things worse. Nothing like tight clothes and no endurance to remind a guy how far he'd fallen.

And all that was before he added Bella to the mix.

If that wasn't a complicated relationship, he didn't know what was.

Not to mention she was another reason—a big reason—to get back into shape. Fast.

It wasn't long ago he was eating Philly cheese steaks and downing beers with his med school friends. That, then Sylvia's food—no wonder he'd gotten soft.

His phone rang, and he glanced at the caller ID. Bella.

He was in no frame of mind to talk to her. He could barely form a coherent thought. So, he let it go to voice mail. When he didn't hear a follow-up tone, he realized she didn't leave a message. Couldn't have been too important.

"Then why the hell did you even bother calling?" he yelled at his phone.

Forget the fact that he made calls all the time without leaving messages. She didn't owe him anything.

Didn't make sense to get so bent out of shape over her not leaving a message, especially when he ignored her call to begin with.

Why were things so complicated?

Life was so much simpler in Philly.

If only his father hadn't called him home.

Who was he kidding? His problem with Bella was a damn good one to have. He couldn't blame her. People kept telling him to stay out of it and he wouldn't. Why would he expect her to listen to him when he asked her to do the same? But she did think they should back off a little.

Which was just what he wanted her to do.

So why was he frustrated?

It was the whole thing. Her. His dad. Ben. Wade. That whole God-forsaken town.

Being home didn't really matter, though. It would all be going on regardless of where he lived. He would have had to return to Cathedral Lake soon, anyway. His residency would be starting in a few weeks. Regardless of his relationship with his father, deep down he knew he wouldn't toss his career in the trash just to spite him. So, he would really have been coming home.

"I should get an apartment." No one in his empty room answered him. "Great, now I'm not only talking to myself, I'm expecting answers. I really *am* losing it."

It would be nice if he could focus on one problem—any problem—at a time. This endless rotation of miserable thoughts just gave him a headache. Surely, he could come upon solutions for his troubles if he could just concentrate on each issue individually.

Except they all seemed to be tangled together.

He changed his clothes and drove to the park. There, after warming up, he went on a run. Maybe the fresh air and the cadence of his steps would bring some clarity to his thoughts.

The temperature rose to unseasonably high temperatures for early summer. The sun beat down on him. Sweat soaked his clothes, dripped from his hair.

He should have headed for the lake. If he had, he could cool off in the water. But he didn't take a nature trail from the park.

First, he had run a few laps around the ballfields. Then, without even thinking, he'd run into town.

Jogged right past the clinic.

Nothing looked out of the ordinary on the street or inside. Not that he had time to analyze any of it. So, he went around the block and slowed his pace, took in what details he could.

The leaves in the planters looked bruised. Some of the stems bent at sharp angles. Must be a lot of drops and pickups going on. More than he realized.

The clinic saw a moderate number of patients. No one looked suspicious. The same illnesses and injuries any clinic would have.

Foot traffic on the street picked up, as did the automotive congestion. Stores were opening. People stopped at cafes for morning coffee, or if they had the time and desire, breakfast. The workforce began their commute.

It all looked… normal.

His third time around, something struck him as odd. Or rather, someone.

A woman—average build, non-descript clothing—caught his attention. Most people wouldn't notice her. She would just blend in with the passersby. But not to him. He'd started to pay closer attention to things, especially things that were off. She didn't quite succeed in being unnoticeable, forgettable. She'd tied her hair back and wore large sunglasses, but he could tell she was striking, even though she tried to hide it. And why hide such an attractive appearance? No one would. Not unless she didn't want to attract notice. He could also tell she wasn't shopping, or eating, or on her way to work. No, she was looking for something, *watching* for something.

He'd seen her in front of three different storefronts on the street, and they all had one thing in common—they provided excellent vantage points for watching the clinic.

Unger.

The woman had to be watching Wade. Was she a Fed? Or Vice?

Or, God forbid, with the dealer?

What did he do? Did he pass her? Talk to her? Stop somewhere and spy on her?

He ran toward her, pretended to check his pulse rate by holding his neck and staring at his watch. So, when he smacked right into her—intentionally—she'd think it an accident.

But she stepped out of his way right before they collided. He couldn't do anything but glance and wave at her and keep running.

Maybe he wasn't good at the whole surveillance-thing. He shouldn't be drawing attention to himself. If he did, he should at least get something out of it. He didn't know if that woman found him memorable, but he knew for damn sure he hadn't learned anything.

Just had more questions.

Picking up his pace, he all but sprinted around the block, slowing down only when he rounded the corner and started down the main street again.

The woman was gone.

He stopped, bent over and rested his palms on his knees while he tried to catch his breath.

Good thing he went to med school. He obviously had no aptitude for investigation.

After his breathing regulated, he headed back toward his truck.

When he got within a hundred yards of it, he noticed the woman had made her way to the park. Actually, she seemed to be studying his truck.

What the hell?

She bent down, laid on the ground, and shimmied under it.

Jensen broke into a full-out sprint, but his progress was impeded by the traffic on the road. He had to keep slowing, stopping, and weaving around people on his way to the woman.

When he was about fifty yards from the truck, she crawled out and gently placed something on the ground.

"Hey!" he yelled. "Hey!"

She flung her arm wide. "Back! Get back! Go!"

But he kept running toward her.

She dashed toward the nature trails, looking over her shoulder and continuing to yell.

He gained on her, but he couldn't get around the people in his way before she was out of his sight. Instead of chasing her through the woods—when she could have chosen any one of a number of trails—he went back to his truck, stooped down, and looked at what she'd laid by his tire.

"What the—? A bomb?"

He didn't touch it. Could be evidence on it. Could still be live.

Grabbing his phone, he called Cooper. "Someone tampered with my truck. There's a bomb on the ground beside it. What should I do?" His eyes scanned the area. So many people.

"Where are you?"

"Ballfields."

"I'm coming. Call 9-1-1. Don't touch it. Get away and keep other people away from it." Cooper ended the call without a goodbye.

Jensen heard sirens before he even dialed 9-1-1. Cooper and two other units reached him before he began talking to the dispatcher. While he recounted the situation, the police set up a perimeter. The dispatcher talked to Jensen, but he couldn't focus on what she was saying. He held the phone out to Cooper, who pushed it away and spoke into a radio in his car. Jensen disconnected the call. The police were there, why did he need to stay on the line?

Cooper grabbed his arm and pulled him toward the established perimeter line even as another policeman took control of the bomb robot and sent it to the other side of his truck. "What the fuck, kid? I told you to stay out of it. How'd you even find the damn thing? Do you know how lucky you are? Yours wasn't—"

Words kept spewing from the detective, but Jensen tuned those out, too. He didn't need a lecture. He needed answers.

"Tony, enough. I get it. They aren't playing around. I don't need a lecture."

More emergency vehicles arrived. Police swarmed the area, directing people away from Jensen's truck. They had already been sent so far back, he couldn't even see what the bomb squad was doing. The crowd stood behind hastily erected Jersey barriers, craning their necks to get better views. Tony and he were still about twenty feet away from the line, and the cop continued dragging him along.

"I said I get it. They aren't playing around. Would you slow down?"

"The hell you get it." If anything, Cooper sped up. "Do you—"

The rest was drowned out by the explosion.

JENSEN WAS KNOCKED OFF HIS feet, thrown to the ground by an invisible force. He clapped his hands over his head. The ringing in his ears drowned out the shouting that the people around him seemed to be doing. Debris fell in chunks around him, little shrapnel missiles from the heavens.

Not Heaven. This blast came straight from Hell.

He hadn't believed he was in danger—not truly—not until that woman planted a bomb. She must not have been staking out the clinic. She had to have been waiting for him.

How'd she known where he'd parked his truck? Good thing he'd arrived in time. Scared her away before she'd been able to install the bomb.

He dropped his hands to the side and squinted at Cooper. His mouth moved, but all he heard was that tone.

Good Lord, he'd gone deaf.

"Jensen!" Cooper's mouth moved, looked like he screamed. It was softer than a whisper.

Jensen blinked a few times, shook his head. He looked around at the people running, some toward the disaster, some away. Noise crept its way back into his brain. A single high-pitched tone.

"Kid?" A bit louder than before. More sounds came through.

Sirens. Yelling. Crying.

Police radios squawked staticky responses to comments barked into them.

"Jensen! You okay?"

That time he heard Cooper clearly and winced at the sound.

"Is everyone all right?" Jensen said.

Cooper held his hand up. "Ssh. Don't yell. Your hearing should come back soon. Let's go get you checked out." He grabbed Jensen's arm and headed toward an ambulance.

When'd they show up?

He yanked his arm free of the detective's grip. Tried not to yell, even though he could barely hear himself think. "Are you okay? Is anyone hurt? Or—?"

Nope. Wasn't going to finish that sentence.

"We were closest. Let's get you checked out, then maybe you can go home."

"Go home? Are you crazy? I need to look at mug shots or maybe sit down with a sketch artist."

"For what?"

"The person who did this. I saw her! She was under my truck! She yelled for me to get back, and then she ran off."

"If this woman did set the bomb," Cooper said, "why did she warn you off?"

"I—I don't know. Maybe she had a change of heart?"

Okay, he knew that didn't make a lick of sense. Clearly Cooper knew it, too, because he just raised a brow.

"Did you hit your head?" He held Jensen's shoulder. Bent down and stared into his eyes.

Jensen shrugged him off. "No, I did not hit my head."

"You need to see the EMT."

"I need to find that woman."

"Damn it, kid. Haven't you learned anything about going off half-cocked?"

"Well, you won't even let me look at pictures to see if I can ID her. I need to do something."

"She's not the bad guy in this."

"What?" Why would Cooper defend her? Jensen looked around, took in all the destruction, all the injured being examined and bandaged. No way would he back off now. Especially when even the cops were trying to steer him in a different direction.

"I don't know what happened here today," Cooper said. "At least, not yet. But someone who sets a bomb doesn't warn her target away from the blast, and she certainly doesn't call in the threat."

"Call in…?" That didn't make sense. Why would that woman call 9-1-1 on herself?

"Someone called before you. A woman. Reported the bomb in your truck. Even said what kind of device it was. Let the squad prepare before they even got here."

"Well, thank God for that. Without her, the bomb might have gone off and hurt someone."

Cooper scowled and glowered at Jensen. "Look, kid—"

"Stop calling me kid! I'm an adult, damn it, same as you. I was just almost killed in an explosion. An explosion meant for me. So, stop treating me like a young nuisance. If anyone deserves respect in this whole thing, it's me. Because as far as I can tell, I'm the only person who's tried to do anything about this."

"About what? Wade's deal? Your dad's clinic? You want to be treated like an adult? Then grow the hell up. This isn't about you. None of it is. If you'd kept your nose out of it and let the pros do their jobs, this clusterfuck wouldn't have happened. The whole thing might be over by now. Do you know what's taking so long? The dealer is suspicious of Unger and his motives. Because of you. Because you're snooping around and hovering nearby. If this all turns to shit, and by the looks of things, it has, you have no one to blame but yourself."

"I just want answers! I want to know my family is safe!"

"Then stay out of the way and let us protect you and them."

"Us?" Rage rumbled through him, larger and louder than the explosion. "Us? So, you're working with them now? Is that it? Another cog in the system, and still I'm not privy to any information? Don't forget, Tony, it was my truck they blew to hell. My life they targeted. At what point in all of this are you going to stop telling me to stay out of it and actually start helping me?"

"Jensen! Jensen!"

He turned to see Bella picking her way over to him through the throng of injured and curious.

"Bella? What are you doing here?"

"Jordan called me."

"Jordan? Who—?" His words stuck in his throat. Behind Bella, keeping her distance even as she kept her gaze on him, was the woman who'd blown up his truck.

"Jordan Reed," Bella said. "Remember I told you—"

"Tony!" Jensen interrupted her and ran toward the woman. "It's her! Arrest her!"

Cooper grabbed him even as Bella stepped in front of the woman.

"Let me *go!*" He struggled against the viselike grip of the detective. "Arrest her! She's the one! Why are you holding me back?" He looked at Bella. "And why are you protecting her?"

He twisted some more, nearly broke free. Cooper put him in a half-Nelson and subdued him, pushing his head down while immobilizing one arm and restraining the other. He thrashed some more, but every move hurt and seemed to lock him down tighter. Finally, he stopped struggling and looked up at Bella. "Why?"

"I thought she could help." Bella's eyes were wide, and her gaze flitted from Jensen to the woman and back.

"Help? She nearly killed me."

The woman stepped forward. "No, Jensen. I saved you. I found the bomb in your truck and started to disable it. A failsafe kicked in, though. I warned you away. When I looked back, you were running toward me. Why'd you go back? You could have been killed."

Jensen tried to talk over his shoulder. "Are you listening to these lies? You can use this evidence in court. She said she triggered the failsafe."

"That's not what she said," Cooper said.

"Are you in league with her now?" Jensen yelled.

"Is this going to become a thing?" the woman said to Cooper.

Jensen couldn't see the detective, but he felt the resigned sigh that escaped him. "It's always something with you, Jordan."

"You know her?" Jensen asked.

"Oh, yeah," Jordan said to Jensen. "We're… acquainted."

"Fuck," Jensen muttered.

"I never kiss and tell," she said.

Cooper pulled Jensen away.

Didn't matter how much he fought. The cop had him at his mercy. "Where are we going?"

"Anywhere but here," Cooper muttered.

CHAPTER 26

"I HIRED YOU TO GET me information. Not to nearly get my… to get Jensen killed." Bella couldn't believe what had happened. It was only hours earlier that she finally felt like she was getting help. Now she stood in the aftermath of an explosion.

"Let's get something straight," Jordan said. "You hired me to find information, and I did. I found out the people involved in this know you and your boyfriend are snooping around. And they don't like it. You're lucky I found that device. Otherwise, it would be more than pieces of his truck splattered over these fields."

Bella took a deep breath, ran her hands through her hair. What had happened? She'd defended countless criminals since she began work—her father hundreds or thousands more—and they'd lost a few cases, causing some scary men to go to jail. They'd been threatened, followed, even harassed at work. But no one had ever gotten close to hurting her or her dad. And Jensen was a doctor! He didn't risk the ire of dangerous criminals. Well, maybe if one died on his table, but the criminal would have to be injured before even seeing Jensen, and Bella assumed that would put other people higher on the hit list than the doctor who tried, but failed, to save the guy's life.

She needed to focus. It wasn't about what might have happened in an alternate scenario. It was about what really happened. That very day. And what happened was Jensen had a bomb in his truck. He could have been killed.

The drug dealers were on to him. Maybe her, too. Maybe Unger, the Kellers, her dad. None of them were safe. Not until the bust was made, and that meant staying out of the way, not getting in the middle of it.

"I'm sorry, Jordan. I'm not mad. I'm just scared. I mean, I knew this was dangerous. At least, I thought I did. I just didn't realize what we'd gotten ourselves into. It's just all so…."

"I know."

"I'm sorry."

"Listen. I know this is difficult. But you need to reassess this situation. You felt left out before. I think that's a good thing. A great thing. It's time you step back. Maybe you should leave town for a while. Take Jensen with you. Or even better, get his whole family to go."

"I don't think his dad will go. I don't think he can go. Not while Unger is working there."

"Yeah, well, I don't think it's safe for him to stay, either."

"I'll talk to Jensen. See if we can't convince his family to take a vacation until this all clears up."

"Here." Jordan handed her a set of keys.

"What are these for?"

"You could be a target, too, and I can't be everywhere at once. Someone could have tampered with your car, and we wouldn't know until it was too late. Take mine. Don't go home. Don't go to your office. Go to a public place where you can watch the parking lot from a window. But don't sit obviously in a window seat. Sit more toward the interior of the restaurant. Or even better, a wall seat where you can see out the window, but people outside can't really see you."

"Don't you think maybe that's a bit extreme?"

"Do you want to risk it?"

Bella sighed. "No."

"I expect you to call me every two hours, and I want your password so I can track you with your phone-finder app."

Things had taken a turn. An unexpected turn. A frightening-as-all-fuck turn. Bella gave Jordan her information and her word that she'd check in regularly. Then she left—in Jordan's car.

She didn't think she had long to talk to Jensen and convince his family to leave. And given that he had to be forcibly removed from her presence just a short while ago, she was willing to bet the task wouldn't be nearly as easy as it could have been if he hadn't been so angry.

Happy thoughts. Think happy thoughts.

Right. Like she had any of those left to draw on.

BELLA SAT AT A TABLE against the wall, keeping her eye on Jordan's car in the parking lot. She vacillated between feeling silly and completely paranoid. At one point, she considered calling Hannah, but then she worried her phone was bugged. Paranoid. So, she didn't place the call.

Jensen pulled in about fifteen minutes after she arrived. It confused her at first when he got out of a vehicle that wasn't his truck. Then she remembered why.

Paranoia won again.

He looked around the lot, and she realized he was probably looking for her car, too. For a minute, she thought he would leave. But then he crossed the nearly empty expanse of asphalt and walked inside.

He went to sit across from her, but she shook her head and gestured beside her. He shrugged and sat. "I didn't see your car, and given there are only two in the lot, it should have been easy to spot."

"I have Jordan's car. She didn't think driving mine would be safe."

Jensen took a deep breath and let it out slowly. "Jordan Reed. The lady in the parking lot."

"Yes. Listen—"

"Can I get you two something to drink?" The waitress had walked up behind them, causing Bella to jump.

"Sorry. I'm a little skittish today."

"I guess you heard about the bomb up at the ballfields?"

Bella nodded.

"It has me a little jumpy, too. Can I recommend a nice, soothing herbal tea? Might calm the nerves."

"Just water with lemon for me."

"Two," Jensen said.

"Coming up." She walked away.

Bella lowered her voice. "Anyway, I'm so sorry about you and your truck. Are you all right? When I think what could have happened…"

"You hiring that PI probably saved my life. But why didn't you tell me?"

"I tried. I called you. You didn't pick up, and I didn't think that was something to leave on a message."

He stared out the window, unblinking and unmoving, and Bella wondered where his thoughts had gone. She said his name a few times and finally nudged him to get his attention.

"Hmm? Sorry. I was just thinking."

"About?"

He shook his head. "Doesn't matter. So, why did you call me here?"

"Here you go." Again, the waitress startled Bella. "Sorry. Maybe you should reconsider the tea."

"No." Bella clutched at her chest. Her heart threatened to pound its way right through her ribcage. "No, thanks. I'm fine."

"Okay. Do you know what you want to order?"

She doubted he'd eat the hummus. "Let's see... How about we start with the fruit platter?"

The waitress walked away.

"Fruit?" Jensen said. "I could use something a little heartier."

"I'll be happy if I manage to choke down any of it."

He shrugged.

"So, anyway," she said, "I just need to know you're okay."

"I am. Physically, anyway. My ears still ring a little, and I have a few cuts from the debris. Other than that, I'm fine."

A trickle of relief ran through her. If only they were on the other side of all this and she knew he and his family were all okay. For good.

"Next, I wanted to explain about Jordan."

"Cooper told me she's former military. The police force has tried to recruit her a few times."

"She doesn't talk about it, but, yeah, she was in the Army. Disarming bombs was one of her specialties."

"EOD?"

Bella nodded. "Something happened when she was in the Middle East. I don't know what. But now she's the best PI in the area. Says she'll never have another job where she takes orders from anyone. The police have tried to recruit her, but she's held firm. A vet with explosive ordinance disposal experience would be quite an asset to the force. Not that there are many bombs here. But it's good to have an expert on hand."

"One bomb was enough. But I guess someone with her experience would be great. Although, she didn't stop the bomb today."

"Actually, she did. At least, she gave the bomb squad time to stop it."

"Which they didn't."

"I asked her about that. She gave me a technical explanation, but a lot of it was over my head. The gist, I think, is that she only had seconds before the timer hit zero."

"But it didn't blow until well after she put it down and ran. Thirty or more seconds, easily."

"The timer wasn't for the bomb. How would they know when to blow it?"

"Then what was it for?"

"She said something about a tilt fuse and a mercury switch. I guess it was rigged to blow when it sensed movement. The bomber used a timer so he could install it and still have time to get away without his movements setting it off. He couldn't have been gone for very long when she got there. By the time she saw it, she only had time to remove it. There wasn't time to do anything else."

"Doesn't matter," he said. "I'm glad none of us is hurt, but the bomb still blew. You would think the bomb squad could have stopped it."

"Jordan said it's safer for EOD specialists to blow up a device with a controlled blast than it is to accidentally break a circuit and set the bomb off."

"That's probably true on a deserted road in Afghanistan, but this was in our hometown."

"The bomb squad moved everyone back a safe distance. It shouldn't have been an issue. Your truck notwithstanding."

He snorted in derision. "That damn bomb knocked me off my feet. I don't think we reached minimum safe distance."

"I don't know, Jensen. Maybe they goofed up, and the motion set it off. Doesn't matter. You're lucky she saw someone tampering with your truck. It could have been a lot worse."

"How well did she see the bomber? Can she describe him to the police?"

Bella shook her head. "She was too far away to get a good look."

"Damn it! Every time I think we catch a break."

"Just be grateful she knew there was a bomb at all. Otherwise… well, I don't want to think about what would have happened."

"It's hard for me to think about, too. I wish I didn't lose my truck, though. I guess I owe her a thanks. You, too, for getting her involved."

"Well, I'm not done yet."

"There's more?"

The waitress brought the fruit platter and two plates. Bella didn't jump that time, but her pulse still flickered.

She waited until the waitress left. "God, I don't feel like anywhere is safe. Jordan wouldn't let me near my car. She insisted on me going to only public places and keeping an eye on the parking lot. I can't live like this. Not for long."

"I'm sorry I got you involved. Maybe you should take a vacation, get out of here for a while."

"That's what I wanted to talk to you about. Do you think you could convince your family to leave town?"

"No. I doubt I could. Although I'd feel much better if Faith and my mom left. I know my dad won't go."

"Well, what about you?"

"What about me?"

She grabbed his hand. "Jensen. You're a target. There was a bomb in your vehicle. Yours. Not your mother's. Not your sister's. I really think you should get out of town for a while."

He yanked his hand out from her grip. "I'm not going anywhere. I can't believe you'd even ask, given how close we are."

"Close? All we've done was discover that we're in trouble and nearly get you killed! I think everyone has been right all along. We shouldn't have gotten involved."

"You're free to go if you want. In fact, I think you should." He stood, took out his wallet, and threw some cash down on the table. "But I'm not going anywhere."

"Jensen, wait."

But it was too late. He'd already headed for the door.

What should she do? Every fiber of her being screamed at her to run. Run far and run fast. But she couldn't go. Not without Jensen. Not without knowing if he'd be safe.

She followed him out to the parking lot. There she found him, leaning against the bumper of his borrowed car, staring at his phone.

"Jensen? What's the matter?"

"It's Faith," he said, voice hollow and flat. "She's been abducted."

CHAPTER 27

JENSEN DIDN'T KNOW HE'D INVITED Bella to his house. He'd walked out on her just before he got the call from Cooper. Probably had something to do with needing to know she was safe, even if he was angry with her.

Really, he had no reason to be mad. She was just worried about him.

Looked like she had reason to be, too.

He sat on the sofa and let his gaze wander around the room. His mother sat scarily still on her favorite chair, staring at nothing, tears rolling silently down her cheeks. The only sound she made was the occasional snuffle.

His father stood behind her, one hand on her shoulder. Jensen didn't know how comforting that could be. His mother didn't react to it and his father didn't pay attention to her. He was engaged in a hushed conversation with Cooper and Jordan Reed.

Bella stood looking out the window, arms wrapped around herself like she was hurt, or maybe like she was trying to hold herself together against the pain.

He wondered if it worked. He could use some pain prevention now.

Part of his brain completely refused to process the fact that Faith was gone. He might lose another sister for the same reason he lost the first one—a drug dealer. Like that spot in his psyche, the one that retained the memory or processed the data, simply shut down. Had gone cold, frozen, incapable of moving forward with what-ifs or what-might-have-beens.

The other part of his brain, though, the one that processed fear—it seemed to be working overtime. It sent surges of adrenaline through his bloodstream, priming him for fight or flight.

Which, though? Fight? Or flight?

He couldn't leave his family or Bella. But after the explosion, every cell in his body tensed to run. Screamed at him to avoid the danger. Convinced him that he couldn't be lucky twice.

Every time he thought about speaking up or even just running for the door, though, he thought of poor Faith. How scared she must be. How unfair it was that she'd been taken instead of him.

How he couldn't lose another sister.

So, he sat in silence. Stayed in the house. Stayed with his family.

Then some ridiculous impulse would surge through him, recommending a bold course of action, and he'd commit to fighting. White knight syndrome, equal parts courageous and ludicrous, sanctioning rash and reckless behavior in the name of bravery.

Which then panicked him all over again, made him consider running again.

For the love of all that was holy, why couldn't he make up his mind? The constant cycle of fear, denial, and foolhardy bravery disgusted him. A coward would have run by then. A hero would have acted.

What did that make him?

Rather than castigating himself over and over, he tuned out his unproductive thoughts and focused on eavesdropping on his father's conversation.

"—don't think that'll work," Cooper said. "We have no way of knowing how many people are there, where they're holding her, or what condition she's in."

Did they know where Faith was?

"We need to ask for proof of life before we do anything," Jordan said. "That will buy us some time."

His father moaned at the mention of proof of life, but he didn't argue.

"Listen," she said, "we only have a few minutes before the Feds get here. If we want to try to handle this on our own, it needs to be now."

"We aren't doing anything on our own," Cooper said. "We need to follow proper channels."

"And you wonder why I don't want to work on the force."

"You'd never last a day. It requires a level of commitment and dedication that you—"

"Don't you dare talk to me about commitment and dedication."

"Please," Royce said. "No fighting. Not now."

"Mr. Keller," Jordan said, "if you want me to work the backchannels, just say the word."

"What exactly do you propose?" he asked.

"No," Cooper said.

"This is my little girl we're talking about."

A noise outside distracted Jensen. Three large black SUVs whipped into their driveway. The cavalry had arrived, and they wore FBI windbreakers.

Jensen slipped out of the living room and made his way to the kitchen. Sylvia was there, putting pastries on a tray. The smell of coffee lingered in the air.

"This isn't really a social gathering, Syl," he said.

"I needed to keep busy."

He took a good look at her. Her eyes were red-rimmed, and her hands trembled slightly. She was family. Of course, she was upset.

Jensen walked to her and enveloped her in a hug. "It'll be okay. Cooper's the best there is, and he has plenty of help."

She squeezed him back, sniffled, and pulled away. "Go on back into the living room. I'll bring these snacks in as soon as I'm done plating."

He headed out of the room, but instead of going to the living room, he went to his father's office. He'd really love a good ten minutes or so to look through his dad's email, but he knew he didn't have time. Instead, he opened the desk drawer, pulled out a small notepad, pocketed it, and slipped his phone inside the desk.

No one could track him without his phone. Anyone searching for him would think he was somewhere in the house. He ran upstairs and stuffed pillows under his comforter. In a dark room, the lumps could pass for a sleeping man. Maybe he'd bought himself the time he needed

if he could get out of the house undetected.

He made it to his rental without anyone spotting him. Hopefully, no one would hear the car start or see him through the window.

At the end of the driveway, he looked back. No one followed him. He was in the clear.

If only he knew where to go.

Wasn't even on the road yet and he already missed his phone. The ability to connect to someone at the tap of a finger. The nearly instant access to the Internet. The functionality of GPS.

Funny how he felt naked without that one little device. Exposed. Vulnerable.

Hopefully, he didn't regret leaving the phone behind. Hopefully, it wasn't too little, too late.

Time to find Faith.

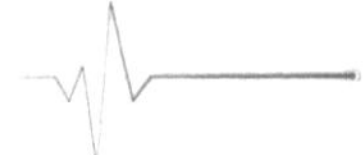

THE FIRST THING JENSEN DID when he got to the main road was head out of town. If anyone noticed his absence, they would likely start searching for him at the clinic and spiral out from there.

He missed his phone. It would have come in handy for cyber-snooping. Instead, he had to go to a public library for a computer workstation and Internet access. The closest one was downtown, but he'd be too easy to find there. So, he decided to drive thirty minutes to Clearbeach, where he doubted anyone would think to look for him.

Partway there, he became convinced he'd picked up a tail. A dark sedan, three car lengths back, changed lanes as often as he did. It was possible the car wove through traffic to pass the slow drivers—just like he did.

Or it could be that he was being followed.

He spent so much time analyzing the traffic in the rearview mirror that he forgot to pay attention to the traffic in front of him. A blaring horn startled him, and he looked forward just in time to cut back into his lane. He'd veered into oncoming traffic and barely avoided a collision.

Pounding heart. Sweating palms. Panting breaths.

Calm. Calm down. Deep breaths.

As if.

He focused on the road the rest of the way to Clearbeach, glancing back only occasionally and only for a second or two. He didn't notice the sedan again. Probably just a coincidence. He put it out of his mind.

Took him a while to find the library. After all, he didn't have his phone to look up the address. But a few wrong turns and some guidance from an overly chatty gentleman—no wonder men didn't like to ask for directions—and he finally found it.

Once inside, he stopped at the desk to ask the location of the public computers. While he suffered through another tedious bout of directions, a man hunched inside a black overcoat walked past him and headed for the staircase. Something struck Jensen as not quite right with the guy, but he quickly shrugged off the feeling. He had more important things to worry about than a stooped man in rain gear.

When the librarian finished her story, she looked at him with raised eyebrows. Guess she expected a reply. He had no idea what she had said—past taking the stairs and making two right turns around the circulations desk—so he smiled and thanked her.

The puzzled look on her face told him he got the response wrong, but he didn't care. He headed for the stairs and took them two at a time. When he reached the top, he made the two rights and stood in the doorway of the computer center.

Every single system was occupied.

He'd have to wait for an open computer. He was used to Penn's campus or even the library in his hometown, where every computer cluster had several systems for use. Four libraries the size of Clearbeach's could fit inside Cathedral Lake's, and there would probably still be room. A computer was almost always free there. In Clearbeach, there were three computers in the library. Total. It was a cute enough place, but come on. How could the library only have three?

To pass the time, he wagered who would vacate the room first. An old lady squinted at her screen. He didn't have much optimism there. Looked like she'd be a while.

A kid clacked rapidly on the keyboard. School had ended for the summer, so unless he was taking summer classes, a safe bet was that he was playing a video game. Definitely would be the last to leave.

At the remaining computer station sat the odd man who had passed him downstairs. What were the odds? If Jensen had just explored on his own, he might have beaten the guy to the last free seat.

He leaned against the doorframe and pounded his head against it. Damn it. He didn't have time to wait. Maybe if he just asked the elderly woman to cut in for a few minutes?

Probably not worth the hassle of getting her logged out and then logged in again. And the kid wouldn't give his space up.

Jensen looked at the odd man again. That was his only option. The only viable option. The man sat bent over the keyboard, but his monitor was dark, and he didn't appear to be typing anything. Maybe he was a slow starter. Or the system was broken. Or maybe he had followed Jensen to the library.

His pulse raced again, and he pushed off the doorframe, ready to bolt. The lady stood then and started making her way to the door.

Jensen didn't know what to do. He didn't want to be in a room with that man. But he had to find out what was going on.

Fight or flight. Or hurry through the task at hand and hope for the best.

The kid still tapped furiously at the keys. Jensen didn't want to use him as a buffer, but he had no alternative. Either the kid sat between him and the man, or Jensen left, giving up his chance to get online.

He vowed to rush, swore if anything looked suspicious—or more suspicious—he'd get out of there before getting the kid involved.

Sitting at the system the woman had just vacated, he made quick work of logging in and got online. In no time, he'd navigated to email and accessed his mother's account.

She really needed harder passwords.

He skimmed through her inbox, her folders, her sent mail.

Nothing.

Hopefully he'd have more luck in his dad's account.

His father had more cyber-savvy than his mom, and, consequently, had chosen a complex password. Jensen never would have been able to crack it, but his dad never remembered all his logins, so he kept them written in his desk. Jensen fished the little stolen notepad out of his pocket and leafed through the pages. Didn't take him long to find his dad's login and password.

Hope's birthday and the day she died. How original.

In no time, he accessed his father's email account and began scanning all the files. One from a MeggarsChoosers had no subject, so he clicked on it.

You were told not to meddle. To keep your family out of our way. You failed. Because of this, certain countermeasures have been put into effect.

We have your daughter. She will be returned to you, unharmed, if you comply with the following demands:

- Tell any and all law enforcement you've been in contact with to stand down.
- Assemble all the product into one package. We'll make arrangements for the drop-off.
- Send your son away until you've made the drop. His involvement in these matters will be met with swift and violent repercussions.

Failure to adhere to all these rules—in their entirety—will result in tragic consequences.

We will be in touch.

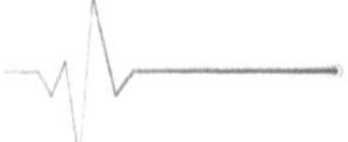

SO, THEY KNEW ABOUT THE cops. And probably the Feds, too.

They knew about Wade's deal.

And they knew about *him.*

Although, he knew that already.

Law enforcement wouldn't stand down. He didn't know how they'd proceed, but he knew they'd do something that could put Faith in grave danger.

Wade had been rendered useless. They were on to him. His life was worth less than Faith's, now that they knew he couldn't continue to supply them. Wouldn't surprise him if they already had him or had killed him.

Or if he had run.

Jensen saw no reason to back off at that point. In fact, he was probably the only person who could save his sister.

Faith.

Could it be that simple?

He went to the Cloud and began trying old passwords of his sister's. If he could guess what it was, he could use the phone-finding function to track her location.

He guessed it on his third try. *NEWKIRK#1.*

She'd used that one since she went vegan. No wonder so many people got their accounts hacked.

The phone-finding app pinged Faith's location.

She was somewhere near the lake. There was no place to hide there. It was completely bare.

Oh, God. What if they drowned her?

He sloughed that idea away with a shake of his head. If she'd been tossed in the lake, her phone wouldn't still work. Would it? Did she have a watertight case? He didn't know. More likely they had tossed her phone out the window on the way to wherever they held her.

But what if she really was out there somewhere? At least he had a place to start.

He logged off and headed downstairs. He'd made it all the way to his car when he noticed the creepy guy hurrying across the parking lot.

Jensen gunned it. Almost ran the guy down. He dove out of the way and rolled behind a car.

Instead of stopping to check on McCreepy, Jensen pulled out of the parking lot and headed away from Cathedral Lake. If the man was paying attention, Jensen wanted to point him in the wrong direction. In another block, he'd circle back around. A sizable head start was the only way he had a chance of getting to the lake unseen. He'd be well on his way before McCreepy knew he'd been misled.

And, hopefully, the guy didn't have backup waiting back in town.

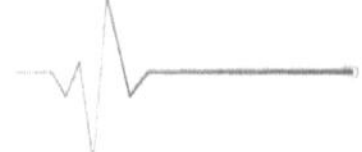

JENSEN DIDN'T NOTICE ANYONE BEHIND him as he sped toward the lake. He made great time, slicing a thirty-minute drive down to just over twenty. When he got close, he headed straight for the public area where beachgoers typically parked. This close to nightfall, the lot was next to empty. Only two vehicles remained, and it looked as though the few people lingering were packing up for the day. Guess they were afraid of the ghost, too.

Didn't matter. Soon he'd have uninterrupted access to the beach.

Even if he wasn't sure if being alone was good or bad.

"Wonder if I should ask them if they'd seen Faith." There he went, talking to himself again. Insane.

It didn't really matter. Without his phone, he couldn't show them a photo of her. But maybe they'd recovered her phone.

A long shot, sure, but he had to ask.

Jensen pulled into a spot close to the other two vehicles, got out of the car, and headed toward the families, who were now off the beach and walking across the lot. They looked at him as he approached. The two guys leaned in toward each other and had a hurried, whispered conversation.

He waved his greeting. "Excuse me. I don't suppose any of you found a phone on the beach today?"

Mothers began loading toddlers and toys into their respective vans while the men walked over to him.

"You lose yours?" one man asked.

"We were here all day," the other said. "Don't remember seeing you around."

"Actually, I wasn't here. My sister lost hers, and this is just one of the places she was today. Between the two of us, we're trying to track it down."

"Why not just use a phone-finding app?" he asked.

"She didn't have it activated. No way to track it. Besides, by now, the battery's probably drained."

"What's it look like?" the first man asked.

Seriously? His sister had been abducted by violent drug dealers, and these guys were harassing him like he was a thief? He swallowed a sigh and responded as calmly as he could. "A phone. No case, no scratches. Nothing to distinguish it from any other phone."

The guys looked him over. Neither said anything. Neither moved.

"Well, did you find a phone? We can call it if you did, prove it's hers."

"Why haven't you done that already?" the first guy asked. "Listened for the ring before talking to us."

"On this beach? Kind of unlikely I'd hear it over the wind and surf. Besides, I don't have my phone. I gave it to her so I could reach her if I had any luck."

"Thought you said the battery was probably drained."

"True. Just another reason why calling it would be pointless."

Jensen started worrying. Those guys were more than difficult. They were wasting an awful lot of time. The sun had set, and the stars had begun breaking through the gloom. The moon was barely a sliver, providing no noticeable light.

He didn't know anything about the people who held his sister. What if they had a network of henchmen? What if these guys were here, waiting for him?

A horn from one of the vans sounded two long beeps, causing Jensen to jump, his pulse to race.

The first guy clapped him on the arm and laughed. "We were just shining you on, man."

The other guy laughed and started walking toward the vans. "Sorry about the phone, man. Hope you find it."

Jensen took a deep breath and shook his head. His heart still hammered in his chest. "Why? Why would you waste my time like that?"

"Did you see all the crap our wives had to pack in those vans?"

"Your kids?" True, there were a bunch of them, but that was a shitty thing to say about family.

"No, not the kids. Well, not that they're crap. But they come with a lot of it. The towels and the toys and the bags and bottles. The food, the diapers."

"God, all the diapers. Full of actual crap," the other guy said.

"We haven't had any fun since the first kids were born. No guys' nights, no bar crawls. No sports nights or trips to Vegas."

"We don't even know what fun is anymore. I haven't busted anyone's balls in four years."

"We were due. Sorry, man." They reached their vehicles and climbed in. With a wave from one and a horn-honk from the other, they drove off into the darkness. Valuable time wasted.

Assholes. Made his dad look like a saint.

Saint....

Could it be that simple?

Jensen looked at the ruins of the cathedral up on the hill.

If his sister was being held inside, her fear would be real. Not of legend, but of tangible, terrible peril.

No way he could approach it in the car. If they were there, they'd hear him coming before he pulled out of the parking lot. Instead, he'd drive away from the lake, so they'd think he left. Then he'd hide the car off road and hike up to the cathedral.

If she was in there, he would get her. He'd get the drop on them.

A cracking branch echoed through the night, the loud report scaring Jensen more than the threat of demons.

The human threat was real, and it had the drop on him.

CHAPTER 28

"SSH. JENSEN. IT'S JUST ME." Bella whisper-yelled from the tree line and stepped onto the asphalt. She looked around, bent down, and dashed across the parking lot.

When she reached him, she noticed him panting, "What's wrong? Is it Faith? Did something happen?"

He shook his head. "Yeah. You scared me half to death."

"Sorry." He thought he was scared? He didn't believe in the legend. Being at the lake so late terrified her. She'd only do it for him.

And only in the direst of circumstances.

"How did you find me?"

"Honestly, I didn't know you'd be here. When you disappeared, everyone went into panic mode. Your mother was convinced you were abducted. Everyone else thought you ran off to find Faith on your own. The good news was that everyone forgot about me. I was able to sneak off and come here." She'd hoped to be there and gone again before darkness fell, but she hadn't quite made it. Only Jensen and his sister were keeping her there.

"I checked my parents' emails. I never found anything saying where Faith is."

"They don't know for sure. Not really. They're speculating a few different places. They think the lake is the least likely of their guesses, so they'll come here last."

"Faith isn't at the lake."

"Well, I can see that now. The FBI is insisting your parents stay at the house, in case the abductors call. The DEA and Vice are searching for her up at the vacation area of the lake. Where our house…" She would not think about Troy and break down. Not when Jensen and Faith needed her help so badly. "Anyway, some of them went there. Another group is checking out the old site where the dog fighting ring was."

"No, you don't understand. She's here. At least, I'm willing to bet she is."

Bella looked around. Without the moon, it was nearly impossible to see more than two feet past her nose. Even the lake looked like a puddle of ink surrounded by more blackness.

"Not here," he said. "Not at the beach. Up there." He nodded up the hill to the ruins of the cathedral.

"What? Why would they take her there? That has nothing to do with the drugs or anyone involved."

"Because no one would look there. No one will even stumble on her accidentally, since everyone thinks the place is haunted."

'Thinks' was a relative term. People believed Columbus was crazy when he thought the earth was round. Didn't mean it wasn't, though. As he proved.

The lake was the most tranquil and relaxing place she'd ever visited—during the day. But at night? That was a different story. She'd heard things coming from the top of the hill. Terrifying, soulless screams, deeper and more mournful than anything a human could possibly make. She wanted to help Jensen and Faith. She really did. But there had to be another way.

"There's just no evidence of that, Jensen. I heard what they said when you were off who-knows-where. Other than a hunch, why would you think she's here?"

"I pinged her phone. The signal came from here. At first, I thought maybe they drowned her or just tossed her phone here. But once I got here, it came to me."

"So, you don't know."

"No. Not for sure. But I have more information than anyone else does. My gut tells me she's there. I know it."

"We could be wasting a lot of time if she isn't. Why don't we call Tony and Jordan, tell them what you think? While they check on it, we can join the search somewhere else."

"You're scared."

"What? I am not."

He grinned at her false bravado. No way did he not pick up on it.

"Bella, it's okay. Just stay here. Call Cooper. I'm going to go check it out."

"Wait!" she cried, her voice a little too squeaky for her liking.

"I have to go. Faith needs me."

Bella wanted to go, too. She really did. But she simply couldn't get her feet to move. "Be careful. I'll wait for you here and call for help."

He kissed her on the cheek. "I'll be fine." Then he dashed into the darkness.

She looked around the parking lot. Jensen had disappeared from her sight in seconds. She couldn't even hear his footfalls. All she heard were the waves lapping at the shore and the music of the nocturnal animals in the woods.

Usually soothing, the sounds seemed more like a dirge now than a melody.

She hadn't thought through their plan. Now she stood alone in the darkness, criminals after her, a haunted building looming on the hill.

What the hell had she been thinking?

Maybe the monk's spirit would get the dealers and Faith and Jensen would be safe.

The wind picked up, rustling the leaves in the trees and whipping up the hillside. She heard a howl, or a moan, or something… inhuman.

Standing alone in the darkness at the foot of the hill holding haunted ruins, she grappled with the stupidity of her decision. No real choice left to her, she reached into her pocket for her phone.

The wind whipped around her, carrying with it a blood-curdling wail.

Bella stifled a scream.

THANK GOD FOR MUSCLE MEMORY. Bella crossed the parking lot and scaled the hill in record time, hardly aware of moving, the noises she heard great motivation for her feet.

If not the rest of her.

Of course, that took her toward the source of her fear, not away from it.

There's no such thing as ghosts. There's no such thing as ghosts. There's no such thing as ghosts.

The mantra running through her head did nothing to convince her that she was safe. She believed in God, and that meant the devil did exist. That meant demons existed. That meant the possessed, fire-starting monk could exist.

Where the hell was Jensen?

The stench of charred wood wafted to her on the wind. She closed her eyes and took a deep breath. Not possible. Absolutely. Not. Possible.

Her body trembled as her vision blurred. She saw the flames engulfing the building, climbing higher toward the roof, licking her arm. Overtaking her brother as he pushed her away.

Tears streamed down her face, and she crumpled to the ground.

All these years, all this time, and it hadn't been the cathedral haunting her. It had been her brother, her culpability in losing him.

Maybe the wails had been her heart and soul, tormented by guilt.

She gasped through the anguish, the pain all-consuming, stealing her breath, her sight, her hearing. Nothing in the moment reached her. She was transported back—back to her folly, back to her mistake. Back to the moment she ruined property and lives and relationships. She carried more than a small scar with her, she carried the burden of guilt, the weight of the misplaced blame, and the resultant banishment of her brother.

It suffocated her.

The memories of that fateful night slammed into her, one after another, assaulting her, smothering her. They morphed, confusing her, a cacophony of sights and sounds and smells. Crackling wood, leaping flames. Troy with lighter fluid and matches, her pulling at him. And the pain. Oh, God, the pain.

She clutched at her head, the images flying too fast to make sense of, like scenery out the window of a speeding train. Out of focus, gone before processed.

Sounds of approach broke through the deluge of memories. "Jensen?" she croaked, reached for him blindly in the darkness.

A warm hand gripped hers firmly, pulled her to her feet.

A man barked a short laugh, his breath hot in her ear. "No such luck."

Fear pooled in her stomach and threatened to explode in a shriek. Instead, a sharp pain radiated through her head, and she descended into darkness.

WHEN BELLA CAME TO, HER arms and legs had been bound, holding her in a spread-eagle position. Her wrists and ankles chaffed from the ropes. She blinked a few times, trying to clear the cobwebs from her brain.

Where was she? Why was she bound?

Reality came back to her with a rush, unwelcome and unsettling. She struggled to breathe.

She couldn't be there. Couldn't be in a burned husk of a building. Couldn't survive through another tragedy. Couldn't—

"Hey, it's okay," a female voice said. "Don't hyperventilate. Deep breaths, all right? In through your nose, out through your mouth. Again. And again."

Bella complied with the instructions. Her heart rate slowed, her breathing regulated. Soon, her mind cleared, and her thoughts came into focus.

"Faith? Is that you?"

"Yes. I'm sorry, I—"

"It's me. Bella Perish."

"Bella? What are you doing here?"

"Given our current situation, I guess 'mounting a rescue' isn't a great answer."

"Please tell me my brother isn't here."

Bella didn't know what to say. She didn't know who was listening, and she didn't know how much Faith had already endured. No way could she heap more onto her shoulders. "I don't know where Jensen is. I overheard—" Who could she have overheard? Not the authorities. "—your mother and father discussing where you might be. They mentioned the lake, so I came out here to check it out. On a hunch, I climbed the hill to check out the cathedral. Then—" Then what? Pain. The memory rushed back to her. "Then someone hit me on the head, and I woke up here."

"So, we're at the cathedral?"

"I think so. Unless they moved me after they knocked me out. You don't know for sure?"

"No," Faith said. "They blindfolded me as soon as they grabbed me. I know we're in a basement, because they dragged me downstairs, but I didn't realize where until you mentioned the cathedral."

"Are you all right?" Bella asked.

"Just some scrapes and bruises."

"Have they said what they want? Or what they plan to do with you?" She wasn't sure she wanted the answer, but information—any information—could be invaluable toward making an escape plan.

Although, realistically, what plan could she enact while bound in a basement? She felt lucky she hadn't been gagged, too.

"I don't know anything. Who took me, how many there are, what they want? Nothing at all. No one's said a word to me since grabbing me and knocking me out.

"Well," a man's voice sounded in the darkness, "let's change that, shall we?"

Bella couldn't see who spoke. The man was cloaked in darkness, hidden from her sight. She still struggled against the memories and fears from her childhood, but those fears amplified with her current predicament. His voice sounded harsh. Hoarse, scratchy. Like his diet consisted of only whiskey and Winstons.

A rough finger skimmed over her face, and she cringed away from it.

That barking laugh again sounded in her ear. It ricocheted off the walls, bouncing back to her. His anonymity frightened her more than had she been able to see him. He could do anything to her or Faith, and neither would see it coming until it was too late.

Not that seeing him would make it easier to react to him.

That finger again reached out to her, trailing over her collarbone, dropping lower, tracing the outline of her shirt.

She sucked in a lungful of air, strained against her bonds.

He cupped one of her breasts, squeezed hard. "Do that again. I like my women feisty."

It took all her strength, all her willpower, but she relaxed her muscles and stayed still.

He chuckled and dropped his hand.

Relief—however brief—flooded through her. She was at his mercy. Faith, too. They had to get free before the unthinkable happened. Jensen had to be nearby. If she could distract the guy long enough, maybe, just maybe, he'd keep his hands to himself until they could be rescued.

"What do you want with us?" she asked.

"What do I want with you? Interesting question." His footsteps echoed, and she couldn't quite tell where he stood. "The original plan was to hold Faith until her father sent his inventory to me. I didn't plan on you."

She'd been afraid of that. "So, now that you have me, what are your plans?"

"I have to tell you, I figured I'd just off you and be done with you. Throw you in the lake or leave you for the animals. If your body wasn't found, I couldn't be pegged with murder."

That wasn't technically true, but he didn't know that. How did someone so stupid succeed this long?

"But then I got to thinking. Your dad is that killer attorney, right?"

She wasn't sure what he meant by 'killer' attorney. Attorney who represented murderers, or attorney who killed it in court? Unsure, she chose to say nothing in response.

"He's got to be rolling in the dough. Like, Johnny Cochran loaded."

He planned on ransoming her. Whether she'd be delivered alive or dead remained to be seen.

"So, here's what's going to happen. I'm going to make my demands, and your fathers are going to fulfill them. Or suffer the consequences."

More footsteps. Where was he going? What was he doing?

His hands gripped her hips, his fingers dug into her flesh, and he pinned her against the wall, his body covering hers. He nuzzled her neck, fetid breath clogging her nostrils, making her gag.

"And the two of you are going to be grateful captives, or you'll suffer, too."

Bella struggled against him, but she couldn't move. She heard the jingle of metal, didn't recognize it at first. When she heard the rasping sound of a zipper, she knew it had been his belt buckle.

No. No no no no no!

After all these years, after all this time, to have her first experience be one of violence and violation would be too much to bear. She thrashed, bucked, but he just laughed.

A scream escaped her. A from-the-gut, no restraint, desperate shriek of torment and desperation.

He laughed again. "I told you I like it rough."

"Let her go." Jensen's voice came to her in the darkness. Protective illusion or reality?

The man pushed off her and turned away.

Relief coursed through her. Thank God. Her body wracked with tremors, her joints chafed against the ropes binding her. However temporary, she was saved. But Jensen was in danger.

"So, the prodigal son, and all that."

"I'm not here to argue with you or to hurt you. I came for Faith and Bella."

"Hurt me? Like you could."

"Let them go, and we'll get out of here. No harm, no foul."

"No harm? No foul? You've caused me nothing but, since I stepped foot in this town."

"Then maybe you should have left."

"You don't know who I am, do you? All your nosing around, all your snooping, and you still haven't figured it out."

Finally, the answers they were seeking. But curiosity killed the cat. She didn't want their relentless pursuit of details to result in their ultimate demise.

She wanted Jensen to run, to get help. But he stood there, engaging with the enemy. For Faith. For her.

"Enlighten me. Who are you? Why are you tormenting my family?"

"The name Sturgis ring a bell?"

Sturgis. Sturgis. It sounded familiar. But where had she heard it before?

"Willie Sturgis?" Faith said.

"Ding, ding, ding. And the little lady wins the prize."

"Willie Sturgis?" Jensen said. "You're in jail."

"Wrong again. Maybe you should let your sister do all the thinking in the family."

William Sturgis. Arrested for possession, drug trafficking, cruelty to animals. He'd been the one Wade had been supplying eight years earlier through the dirt bag on the bike. He should have been in jail for twenty years. At least.

"You made parole?"

"About three months before that asshole, Unger. Didn't you think the timing of his parole was a bit… suspicious?"

"I thought everything about Wade's parole was suspicious. I just didn't know it all came about because of you."

"I tried to get back in the game. No one local had filled my shoes, but people outside were starting to try and move product in. My network fell apart when I got pinched. When I got out, it was all too easy to reorganize. Force the foreigners out of my turf before they gained a strong foothold. Problem was the supply chain. I had trouble securing the merchandise. Then Unger got out. I figured I'd hit a run of good luck."

"Is that right?" Jensen asked.

"Till you. You started poking around. At first, I thought you were just trying to vindicate your sister, but then things didn't feel right. Didn't take much to realize I was being set up."

"So, you kidnap my sister and girlfriend? How's that going to help you?"

"I'm going to get the mother-lode from your dad, some relocation capital from Perish, and start over somewhere else."

"You still won't have a supplier. And you'll be the outsider that the locals want to get rid of."

"I'll be so flush, it won't matter."

Jensen sighed. Bella knew he was out of arguments, and that meant they were out of time.

"So, I've got all my plans worked out. The only loose end," Sturgis said, "is you. You're expendable."

Bella recognized the click of a gun's safety. She'd been worried before. Now she was downright terrified.

"Goodbye, Keller."

Bella screamed when the gun went off. Grit fell into her hair and onto her shoulders. Temporarily blinded by the flash of the firing, deafened by the report, she blinked and shook her head. She tried desperately to regain her senses and make out what had happened, what still went on.

Grunting and scuffling sounded to her right, and she strained to make out the shapes undulating beside her. It gave her hope that Jensen still fought. He probably hadn't been shot. Didn't mean he wouldn't be, though. Didn't mean the danger was over. He was fighting for her and Faith and for his very life.

"Everybody freeze!"

Detective Cooper. The scuffling increased. Flashlight beams skipped around the room. One landed on Bella's face, and she squinted against the glare.

"Bella?"

Jordan. Took her long enough. Bella had texted her… what felt like hours ago. Wonder how much time had really passed.

Her relief was short-lived.

The gun went off again.

CHAPTER 29

JENSEN FELT A SURGE OF relief when Tony burst in. It was over. His family was safe. Bella was safe.

But Sturgis didn't stop fighting. If anything, he fought harder.

Cooper joined in the struggle, and between the two of them, they were able to bend Sturgis's hand, point the gun away from them.

Then the gun went off.

No one screamed. No one slumped to the floor. He and Cooper overpowered Sturgis, took the gun from him, pinned him to the ground for Tony to cuff him.

Other agents flooded the room. He stood out of their way, against the wall, and fought to catch his breath. Beams of light danced around as more and more flashlights swept the room, their ambient light alone enough to illuminate their surroundings in a soft gray glow.

It was over. Finally.

Then Faith screamed.

He looked up, darted around the men and women filtering into the room, and fought his way to his sister. Someone had freed one of her hands, and she'd pulled her blindfold off. She stood, strapped to the wall, pointing.

Jensen grabbed her free hand while agents worked to release the rest of her bonds.

"Faith? What is it? What's wrong?"

She jabbed the air with her pointing finger. "Bella!"

His blood cooled to frigid, fled from his extremities to pool in the pit of his stomach. More light beams trained on Bella's form.

A dark splotch spread across her abdomen. Her head drooped, her hair hanging in front of her, curtaining her face.

He didn't want to know what expression it hid. Shock. Denial. Fear.

Pain.

Shoving people out of his way, he rushed to her side. Training took over, and he started barking orders.

"Someone get these ropes cut. Now! Anyone have a first aid kit?" No one said anything. "Anyone?"

"No," someone said.

Wasn't that standard issue in a cop car? But these weren't standard cops. Damn it. "Get the EMTs here. I need a blanket or jacket. Something to help staunch the bleeding."

Agents made quick work of her bindings, and she was laid gently on the floor at Jensen's feet. He dropped to his knees and grabbed at the jackets offered to him.

"I need a light. Train it on her face." Flashlight beams trained on her face.

A. B. C.

Airway clear. Breathing shallow. Circulation—

He felt her fingers. They were still warm. Good.

He had no way of checking most of her vitals. He put his fingers to her carotid. Pulse thready.

D. E.

Disability. She'd lost consciousness. He didn't know when. Had he heard her scream when the gun went off? Say anything after? He didn't know.

Exposure. "Move the lights here. To her abdomen."

They moved the lights, and he lifted her shirt, examined the wound.

She'd already lost a lot of blood. He pressed one of the jackets to her abdomen. "Help me roll her."

Hands descended and helped him tip her onto her side. The light bounced off the walls while people helped him. "Lights, damn it!" Immediately the beams trained on her back.

No blood. "Didn't pass through. It's still in her. ETA on the ambulance?"

"Five minutes."

"She doesn't have five minutes!" He rolled her back onto her back, bent her knees to take pressure of the abdominals, and reapplied pressure to the jackets over her wound.

What good was being a doctor when he was helpless to save the people he loved? His father couldn't save Hope, and he couldn't save Bella. Her life oozed out of her stomach, saturating the jackets he pressed on her, covering his fingers in sticky warmth.

How long until her blood cooled? Slowed? Stopped flowing altogether?

The voices and bustling around him faded away, and he focused solely on Bella. Had her breathing grown shallower? Pulse slowed? Bleeding worsened?

She wasn't breathing.

CPR. He needed paddles. An IV. He needed—

Someone yanked on his arm.

He blinked, refocused on Faith tugging at him. Jordan talking.

"Jensen. Jensen! You have to let her go."

Let her go? They'd just begun their relationship. How was he supposed to say goodbye?

JENSEN WAS TAKEN TO A private waiting area at the hospital. He paced the room, window to door, door to window. He needed someone to tell him something. Anything.

No wonder people attacked doctors when they came out of surgery. The waiting was agonizing. Pure torture.

People started trickling in. First Cooper and Jordan. Then Faith. Then his parents.

His mother embraced Faith when she walked in, then she held her at arm's length to examine her, only to embrace her again. Then she turned to Jensen.

"You saved my baby girl." She wrapped him in a hug, squeezed him tight.

It had been years since he sought comfort in her arms. Not since the day of Hope's death. But he stepped willingly into her embrace, needed the solace she offered. She rubbed his back and stroked his hair.

"Ssh. It's okay. It'll be okay."

He stepped away from her. How did she know? How could she know?

He looked at his father. It seemed he'd aged a decade in the last ten days. Jensen couldn't read the expression on his face, but he figured he was in for a lecture. How stupid he'd been. How reckless. How everything was his fault.

He squared his shoulders and stepped in front of his father. Bring on the lecture, bring on the yelling. He'd take that and more. He deserved it. No castigation was too much, no punishment too great.

His dad took a breath, and Jensen braced for the tirade. Instead, Royce pulled him into his arms.

"My boy. My sweet, stupid boy."

Jensen hadn't been a boy in years. Hadn't been 'my boy' in even longer. His dad had stopped calling him that around the time he first expressed interest in engineering, well before he'd told his father he wouldn't become a doctor.

Had his father perceived what he couldn't give voice to? Had it mattered anyway, when he'd changed his mind?

Did any of it really matter any longer?

Now, there they stood, locked in an embrace, childhood endearments mingling with insults.

"Thank you." His dad squeezed him harder, clapped him on the back, and released him.

"Dad, I'm sorry. I—"

"No. You have nothing to be sorry for. I should have told you what was going on. I thought I was protecting you, but in my determination to keep you isolated, I endangered you. All of us. It all could have turned out so differently, so wrong. You saved us. You saved Faith. Thank you. Thank you. You kept her safe when I didn't. It's me who's sorry, son. You have nothing to apologize for."

His boy.

He didn't feel exonerated, though. Not with Bella lying on a table, fighting for her life.

"Dad, Bella… I couldn't—"

The door burst open, and Victor Perish stormed into the room, followed by a wide-eyed woman Jensen could only assume was Bella's mother.

"Where's my daughter? What's going on?"

"Your daughter is in surgery," Royce began.

"You!" Victor spotted Jensen and stalked over to him.

"Don't you dare attack my son," Vanessa said.

"He's the only reason your daughter is alive right now," Royce said.

"Is he?" Victor said. "If she hadn't been playing Nancy Drew with him, she'd still be safe at home."

Something in Jensen snapped. "Really? That would be a fine trick, considering you threw her out."

"Jensen!" his mother said.

"What? It's true. Admit it." He stood nose-to-nose with Victor, not backing down. "You didn't like that she didn't want to represent your star client. Well, where's Unger now? You threw Bella under the bus in favor of that piece of shit, and when your whole deal fell apart, he disappeared. *That's* why Bella's fighting for her life right now. Not because of me. Because of your stupid arrangement with the DEA."

They continued standing, toe-to-toe, breaths heaving almost in sync. Then Victor sputtered, looking for words that never came.

Must be a first for him.

Finally, he turned and stormed to the other side of the room, his wife right on his heels.

Jensen stared after him for a moment, then looked away. Did Victor really believe that, or was he just lashing out? It didn't really matter what got Bella involved. She was only at the lake, only in the cathedral, because of him. Only shot… because of him.

He looked back at Victor. He'd expected an outburst, a scathing retort, a blistering dressing-down. Instead, the man had given up, retreated, and dropped into a seat, his wife bending over him and whispering to him.

Even the great Victor Perish had feelings. Who knew?

Jensen started walking over to him when Stanford Hammond burst through the door. "I'm sorry. I know you've been waiting a long time."

Stanford was his father's mentor. Jensen had known him his whole life. If his life was on the line, he'd want Stanford working on him. Bella couldn't have been in better hands.

"How is she?" Mrs. Perish asked.

"She's in recovery." He spoke to Bella's parents. "She lost a lot of blood, and the bullet did a fair amount of damage. We had to remove her spleen. But she's stable. She's still unconscious. We'll keep a close eye on her overnight. These next few hours are the most critical. We'll know more when she wakes, but I have every reason to believe she'll make a full recovery." He walked over to Jensen. "You saved her life, my boy."

Jensen shook his head. "No. She got shot because of me."

"And you slowed the blood flow and got her to us in time for us to treat her."

Jensen took a deep breath. "After tonight… I don't think I can do this."

"There's a reason we don't work on family and friends."

Royce clapped a hand on Jensen's shoulder. "Listen to him, Jensen. Listen to me. Treating the people we love is impossible for us to do effectively. We're too emotionally compromised. The clinical detachment we employ when we work on our patients flies out the window when we know and care for them. That you were able to stabilize Bella tonight, after the injuries she sustained, is a testament to you and the quality of your training. Don't let tonight define you. Or if you do, let it define you for the right reasons."

His dad, more than anyone in the room, would know about the difficulties of treating a loved one. He'd almost left medicine because of it. Yet he persevered.

Jensen could, too.

Stanford patted him on the arm. "I'm really looking forward to you doing your residency here. Don't disappoint me."

That was that. No one said no to Stanford Hammond.

Stanford walked over to Bella's parents. Jensen turned to his father.

"Dad, about med school, and lying. All the secrets."

"Stop," Royce said.

Jensen looked at him but remained silent.

"I didn't understand at first. I was angry and upset. I wanted to believe you just wanted to hurt me, to reject my opinions."

"No, Dad. Don't you see—"

Royce continued like Jensen hadn't interrupted him. "But I had time to think about things. I looked at them from your perspective. I can see why you'd feel like I turned away from you because I didn't get my way. I'm sorry, that was never my intention. I just believed that, if you had studied medicine, we'd have a lot to talk about. When you took a different path, I just didn't know what we'd discuss, so I stopped trying. But what you study doesn't define you or our relationship. I should have realized I could have talked to you about anything. I shouldn't have turned away."

"It didn't matter, anyway. You were right. I was interested in medicine."

"No, I was wrong. It didn't matter what you studied. You're my son. That's all that should matter. I cost us eight years." He hugged Jensen again.

Jensen hugged him back, clung to him. Finally had someone to support him, if just for the moment.

Royce stepped back and met his gaze. "I want to hear all about what I missed. How you changed your mind and decided to switch majors. Someday. Right now, though, it seems you have company."

Jensen looked up. Austin, Miles, and Brett filed into the room.

Miles walked over to him. “We came as soon as we heard. You okay?”

Jensen ignored the question. “What are you doing here?”

Brett tipped his head toward someone standing behind Jensen. “Faith called.”

“Faith?” He glanced at his sister, who was huddled in the corner with their mother. Then he looked back at Brett. “And you guys rushed over?”

Miles shook his head. “That’s what friends do, moron. That’s what we’ve been telling you since you got home. We’ve got your back.”

They walked past him into the waiting area and plopped down in vacant seats near Faith.

He was a moron.

He had to stop pushing people away, trying to do everything on his own.

That epiphany would mean so much more if Bella made it through the night.

JENSEN SAT BY BELLA’S BEDSIDE, holding her hand and murmuring to her occasionally. Her parents had been in the room with him for hours, and the three of them never spoke to each other. They’d just gone to get coffee, leaving him alone with her.

“I’m sorry.”

He’d said it probably two dozen times since her parents had left the room. Twenty dozen that he’d thought it without giving voice to the words.

“Oh, Bella.”

He could live with her leaving him. He didn’t deserve a woman he couldn’t protect, anyway. Especially one as wonderful as she was. But he couldn’t survive it if she never regained consciousness.

If she died.

He didn’t know which would be worse, but he knew either would be the end of him. There was no recovering from being responsible for the death of a loved one. That made him think about his father and Hope again.

Maybe redemption was possible.

But their situation was different. It had been a lie and a secret that caused Royce to endanger Hope.

No lie he told, no secret he kept, put Bella in harm's way.

Of course, the lie and secret that hurt his sister hadn't been his father's. But the actions that resulted in Bella's injuries had been Jensen's.

He winced at the sting of responsibility.

"I'm so, so, sorry."

"S'kay." Bella, hoarse and weak, answered him. Her fingers moved in his grasp. Her attempt at a reassuring squeeze?

"Let me get the doctor."

"No. Stay." Her eyes still hadn't opened. Her hand went limp in his. She'd fallen back to sleep.

She didn't rise again for another five hours. Jensen still sat by her side, and her parents had returned long before.

"Thirsty."

"Bella? Oh, Bella!" Her mother rained kisses on her hand and face. Her father had tears in his eyes. Jensen pressed the buzzer and stood aside. A nurse bustled into the room and burst into a smile. "I'll get the doctor." A quick trip out of the room and she was back, prepared to take a bunch of vitals. "How are you feeling?"

"Thirsty," she rasped again.

"Can't give you anything so soon after your injury, I'm afraid. I can get you ice chips, though."

Bella nodded.

The doctor stepped into her room. "So, you're awake. Let's see how you're doing."

Jensen stepped out of her room. Exhaustion overwhelmed him, and he swayed on his feet.

Before passing out, he had one more thing to do. He headed for the chapel. It was past time he started expressing his gratitude for his blessings.

CHAPTER 30

GOD BLESS MORPHINE. BELLA KNEW the pain would return as she weaned off the narcotics. In the meantime, though, she floated on a cloud of blissful comfort.

Made her nose itchy as hell, though.

Her mother hovered and doted and nearly smothered her with attention and affection. She'd finally let up when her father requested a snack and a coffee. "Not from the vending machine. Something from the cafeteria." Her mom looked puzzled but left without debate. When Victor asked for something, she made sure he got it.

Her dad sat on the edge of a chair and looked up into her face. She'd never really had that vantage point before. She was always looking up at him. From this angle, she noticed how tired he looked. How worn. He could still go toe-to-toe with anyone in his ring, but she wondered about the toll those battles took.

"Bella," he began.

Bella? He never called her Bella. Never.

"I'm so, so sorry. This was all my fault."

Was there a word stronger than never? Neverer? Neverest? Because he really never apologized. Neveristiest.

"When I think of what could have happened, I— Well, I won't share those thoughts with you. You should be spared that and so much more."

"Dad—"

"See, I wanted to protect you. Keep you safe. That's always been my goal. I thought working under my roof, with me standing guard, you'd be safe. I'd been afraid of you working with the DA because I didn't want you to be the target of any of the criminals you put away. I never expected a client of ours would turn out to be the danger."

Bella blinked back tears. She'd never heard him talk that way.

"After the fire, I vowed to keep you safe. At all costs. And maybe I went about it wrong. Maybe you shouldn't have been isolated. Maybe I should have shown you the world, readied you for it. I don't know. But I do know I never should have thrown you into it unprepared and alone. And for that, I'm forever sorry. I don't know how to make it up to you."

"Do you mean that?" She barely found the strength to voice the words.

"Of course, I do."

"I know how you can make things up to me."

"Anything. You name it."

"Forgive me."

"Forgive you? For what?"

"For the fire."

"The fire? At the cathedral? That was decades ago and hardly your fault. I think I should get the doctor." He reached for the buzzer on her nightstand.

She grabbed his hand, the effort Herculean, but managed to stop him.

"No. Not the cathedral. At the lake house."

"The lake house? What? Where is this coming from?"

"All these years, I let you think Troy was responsible. But it was me. I built the fire. I burned the place down. I'm responsible for Troy's injuries and all the damage." Tears fell down her cheeks, and she rubbed them away even as she swiped at the itch on her nose.

"No, honey. No. It wasn't you. It was your brother."

"No, Dad. That's what I'm trying to tell you. It was me."

He took her hand. "Honey, I had several long talks with your brother. It was him."

The memories that assaulted her at the cathedral rushed back to her. She'd thought they were fear-induced visions. But what if they weren't? Maybe that's why her memories of the fire had been hazy. She'd fabricated them. Troy had been responsible. She couldn't deal with losing him, so she blamed herself. It all made sense.

"He had a girl coming over. He wanted to set the mood. When you saw the flames overtake him, you tried to save him. Why did you think you had that scar?"

But her scar was small in comparison to the burns Troy had sustained.

"He was profoundly sorry. That's why he went away. For your safety."

"But he wasn't a danger to me. Not on purpose. And he never came home."

"He never wanted to. He didn't know how to face you."

All that time, lost. Gone forever. How she missed Troy. How she needed him now.

"Bella, I was wrong. I should have made him come home. I should have put him in therapy, helped him get past what he'd done. Probably should have gotten all of us help. Learned how to cope with everything. The fault is mine. Not yours, not his. It all stops with me."

Really? Was it true?

"Then make it up to me."

"How? I'll do anything."

"I want to see him."

BELLA COULDN'T BELIEVE HER EYES, her ears. She kept thinking it was the morphine.

But it was real.

Her whole family sat together in her hospital room. Her whole family.

She couldn't tear her gaze away from Troy.

He had confirmed everything her father had said. He'd started the fire. He'd gotten hurt when the flames got out of control. He'd been burned badly.

And he'd been devastated when his little sister got burned trying to save him.

She'd suppressed the truth for years, coming to terms with losing him by taking the blame.

"I just can't believe you're really here," she whispered.

He grabbed her hand, squeezed it.

"It's real. I'm here."

She rubbed her thumb over his knuckles, the skin there shiny and taut. The only indication of his burns the mottled appearance of the skin from his fingers up his forearm. No wrinkles or rough scars.

"You're wondering how it looks that good," he said.

Bella looked at him. "You were burned so badly. It shouldn't look this… this smooth."

"Dad paid for it all. Skin grafts and plastic surgery. It took years of procedures and therapy, but it's almost as good as new."

She looked at her father. "All this time, and you've been in touch with him."

"I've been waiting for him to come home."

Bella squeezed Troy's hand. "It's true. Your room is just as you left it. You just need to come back."

"Izzy." He sighed and covered her hand with his free one. "I have a life now. Away from Cathedral Lake and all the bad memories."

"But the bad memories weren't in Cathedral Lake. They were two hours away at a cabin we never rebuilt. You'll never have to see it."

"But I'll see you."

"Me? I'm a bad memory?" Despite the morphine, pain sliced through her, straight to her heart.

"No, that's not what I mean. It's been great seeing you again. But every time I look at you, every time I notice this," he lifted her arm and gestured to her burn scar, small in comparison to his, "I'll remember what I did. What I nearly lost."

"But, Troy, don't you see? If you stay away from me, you have lost me."

He shook his head, dropped her hand, and turned away.

"The fire?" she said. "That was an accident. But shutting me out now? That's intentional."

When he looked at her, tears were in his eyes.

"The way I see it, you've got two options. You can face what happened and move on from it, or you can keep running and hiding."

"It's not that simple, Izzy."

"Yes, it is. It's exactly that simple. Time to be the guy I idolized my whole life. You made a mistake. Deal with it. It could have been a lot worse." He started to speak, but she held up her hand. "A lot worse. That mistake has already been forgiven by the rest of us. Now you need to forgive yourself. And you need to stop compounding the problem with more mistakes."

"More mistakes?"

"Cutting us out. You've been doing that for far too long. Time to move forward. So, what's it going to be, Troy? Are we you going to try to put this behind you and mend our family, or are you going to run away? Again?"

BELLA SNIFFED THE GIANT BOUQUET Chloe brought her.

"Mrs. Keller helped me select them. I wanted to do an arrangement of yellow roses, but she said they wouldn't last very long. She recommended chrysanthemums, saying they could last a month if properly maintained. But I don't like them."

Bella glanced at the cheerful arrangement of chrysanthemums Vanessa and Royce had brought, and her face flushed. "Who has the time or patience for that? I'll just buy you new ones if you're still here when the blooms wilt. Anyway, we compromised on the freesia and alstroemeria. They're pretty, I think."

Bella had never seen Chloe so nervous. It couldn't be about the flowers. She decided to make small talk and wait for her to get to what was bothering her. "They're lovely, and the freesia smells divine."

"I'm glad you like them." She walked over to look at some of the other arrangements—a vase full of colorful carnations and gerberas, a fern, a bundle of lilacs. She scanned the cards. "Lots of names here I've never heard before."

"Those—" she gestured "—are from Austin and Miles. Jensen's friends. I've only just met them in passing. And that bouquet—" she pointed to another vase "—is from Brett and Simone, more friends of his. I can't wait for you to get to know him. All of them. Maybe we could go out as a group sometime."

"Me? With his friends?" Chloe scoffed. "I don't think that's a good idea."

Bella patted a space beside her on the bed. She waited until Chloe joined her and took her hand. "We've known each other a long time, and we've never kept secrets from each other."

"You never told me about Troy."

"I wasn't keeping a secret. I was in denial. Repressed memories and guilt. But I'm happy to tell you the whole story now."

"Spill it."

"Provided," Bella continued, "you tell me what's going on with you."

"Me?" She snorted. "Nothing."

"Beep beep beep beep beep."

Chloe raised a brow.

"That's my BS detector. You're in the red zone."

Chloe stood and paced.

"Does this have anything to do with that shirt I borrowed?"

When her friend turned around, she had tears in her eyes. "He was the one," she whispered.

"Oh, honey, come here." Bella patted the bed again.

Chloe crossed to her, threw her body down beside her.

Bella sucked air in as the jolt hurt her wound. But she didn't cry out. Her friend needed to vent, and she was about to spill her guts.

"Everyone has that one guy that got away."

"Not everyone," Bella murmured.

"Every normal person." Chloe turned, vibrating the bed.

Bella gritted her teeth and waited.

"I'm sorry, Bells. You know I lash out when I'm upset. The shirt guy? He was… special. When I brought him home, I really brought him home. To my parents' house. They were in Maui or Tahiti or somewhere. I don't know. But we had the place to ourselves. We had a great weekend. I thought we were at the beginning of something… of something. But when I got up Monday morning, he was gone. All that was left behind was his shirt. No note, no call or text. I waited for him to call me, but he never did." She sniffled, looked away.

Bella tried to roll to hug her friend, but the pain stole her breath. When she'd recovered, Chloe was already across the room.

"That's what I've been trying to tell you about Jensen. He seemed special to you, and I didn't want him to become your one that got away."

"I don't intend to let him go. You're right. He is special."

Chloe smiled at her.

"So, shirt guy. Have you tried looking him up? Maybe giving him a chance to explain?"

"Enough about me. You owe me the Troy story."

So, that was that. When Chloe changed a topic, that meant discussion over. No circling back. Trying would be futile, and, honestly, Bella didn't have the energy to try. So, she thought about Troy. "Where should I start? When I got the whole thing wrong and move forward, or when Victor brought him to visit me and work backward?"

"Troy was here?" Chloe's eyes grew wide, her voice turned shrill. "And Victor brought him?"

Bella smiled. "That's not even the best part."

"What, then?" Chloe asked.

"He's moving back to Cathedral Lake. We're going to be a family again."

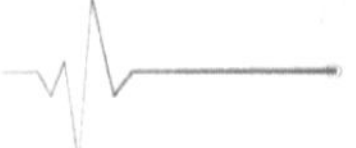

"SO THAT'S WHAT REALLY HAPPENED with my brother and the fire," Bella told Jensen. "I'd suppressed the memory, and over the years I just filled in the wrong details."

"The mind is a mysterious thing." He kissed her forehead. "I'm glad it all worked out."

"It's not over yet. I've scheduled us an appointment with a family therapist. We all still have a long way to go."

"So, you aren't taking that apartment?"

"No. I think it's best that we all stay under one roof for a while. Get to know each other again."

He sighed. "That's too bad."

She cocked her head to the side. "What? Why?"

"I was thinking one of us having our own place might be a good idea."

A blush flamed her cheeks, and she looked away. "I don't think I'll be cleared for any strenuous exercise for a while."

He turned her face toward him. "You're worth the wait, Bella." He leaned down and kissed her. If she weren't lying down, she might have swooned.

She cleared her throat. "So, is it all over?"

"As over as it can be. Sturgis is in jail. Cooper said he can expect another twenty years, probably with no chance of parole. The DEA and Vice aren't thrilled with the method, but they're okay with the results. Until out of town trade makes its way back here, things should die down."

"And Meg? Did they arrest her?"

"Oh, I forgot you didn't know. She wasn't really working for them. They threatened her family. Sent her all kinds of photos of her husband and kids at work and school and with friends. Told her they could get to her family anywhere, and would, if she didn't cooperate. She went to the cops, and that's when the plan started to take shape for Unger's parole."

"You keep saying 'they.' Did Sturgis have partners?"

"Meg says yes, but no one knows who, or even if she's right. She swears two different people called her, but she could have just been mistaken with fright."

"Guess we'll never know."

"Not unless Sturgis gives up a name."

"Your sister came to see me. She looks good."

"I owe you a huge thanks for that."

She shook her head. "No. I never should have been involved. I could have gotten you or Faith hurt or killed."

"And you almost died. Bella, I owe you an apology. I'm so—"

She put her hand over his mouth. "Ssh."

He stopped trying to talk.

Smiling, she traced her finger over his lips. "Isn't there something you'd rather do than talk?"

"I thought you weren't cleared for physical exertion." His eyes danced, and dimples flashed in his cheeks.

"Well, if that's the way you want it." She dropped her hand and faked a dramatic pout.

He leaned over and kissed her. "You know, I'm thinking maybe I'll move out of my parents' house. Get an apartment closer to the hospital. I understand one just opened up on Hawthorne."

She smiled. She didn't know he'd paid attention to her when she talked about her new place, but, clearly, he had. "Hawthorne? I know that building. I hear it's got a great view. Granite counters, stainless steel appliances, good closets."

"Know anything about the bedroom?" He nuzzled her neck.

"Spacious."

He kissed her collarbone. "You'll have to visit sometime. Give me your firsthand opinion."

She had a feeling she'd be spending a lot of time there in the coming weeks. They couldn't clear her for physical activity fast enough.

CHAPTER 31

IT HAD BEEN YEARS SINCE Jensen walked up the slope and stood at the foot of Hope's grave. Still, nothing had changed. Almost nothing, anyway. Grass had grown in thick and full where the dirt mound had once covered her coffin. His parents' plantings had matured from tiny sprouts to blooming flowers that anchored her headstone, and that fresh polished granite had dulled to a softer sheen.

But the mature trees still offered dappled sunlight, and the bench still tempted family and friends to stay and visit.

It looked like a comfortable place to sit, but he owed his sister better than that. So, he dropped to one knee and took a deep breath.

"Hey, sis. Been a while."

Like she didn't know that already.

"I bet you're wondering what took me so long." He looked down and toyed with a blade of grass. "I have no excuse. I suppose I should ask your forgiveness for that, too."

Forgiveness. It had been going around like the common cold.

Time to make his amends.

For good.

"I always knew, logically, that Wade was responsible for your death. He committed the pharmaceutical thefts and tried to scare that punk dealer by cutting the brake line. He was responsible. But I had guilt over it.

"I was your big brother. I should have protected you, should have paid closer attention to you. But I knew how hard you tried to be independent. You kept to yourself a lot, and I didn't push you to share. I kept an eye on you, but I didn't invade your space. I gave you your freedom. So that's on me."

He picked a clover and twirled it between his fingers. "Did you know I knew? I knew you were involved in something bad. I didn't know how bad, but I knew Salvo was trouble. Even then, though, I didn't step in. Didn't even approach you about it. I carry that guilt. Wade may have been the one who caused the bike crash, but if I had just..." He swallowed. Took a deep breath. "Maybe if I had been a better brother—more involved, more protective—this wouldn't have happened."

Jensen looked up at her headstone, squinted into the sunlight.

"So, like I said, I knew logically Wade was at fault, but I felt responsible, too. And that's why I've avoided visiting you for so long. Because I was guilty and ashamed."

He sat back on his heels. "I'm so, so sorry, Hope."

A breeze ruffled his hair, and he smiled. "I'll take that to mean you forgive me."

Jensen said a silent prayer for his sister, then he swung his legs around until he was seated, cross-legged, at the foot of her grave.

"So, have you been paying attention to what's been going on? Wade, that jackass, is out of jail. You won't believe how that happened." He proceeded to fill her in, from his deal and parole to him skipping town.

"Before he left, though, he did apologize to me for what happened to you. He carries the guilt with him every day. I guess that will have to be enough for us. Honestly, even though he deserves to rot in jail, I'll just be glad if I never see him again. I doubt he'd be dumb enough to come back to Cathedral Lake."

God, he hoped not, anyway.

"So, I met a girl. Bella. I think you'd really like her. She challenges me as much as you used to. And she helped me catch that asshat, Sturgis, who'd been working with Salvo. She was so brave. She almost died helping me. Stanford said I saved her life."

He stopped for a moment. "I guess I need to tell you about that, too. Faith and I stood up to Dad. Told him we didn't want the careers he'd planned for us. It was kind of ugly for a while. But guess what? Turns out, Dad was right about me. I switched majors. Now I'm a first-year resident at Oakland Regional. Bet you never saw that coming, huh? I'm going to specialize in emergency medicine, just like Dad. After engineering, I thought I wanted to go into research, help create better medical machines. But there was this accident, and now I know I want to help critically injured people. I know I won't be able to save them all, but I can make the difference for some of them.

"The accident. There was this kid who got hurt at the ball field. Same problem you presented with—tension pneumothorax. But I saved him, Hope. You don't know how good that felt. The mother—and man, wait until I tell you my history with her—anyway, she tracked me down a couple weeks later. Just to thank me. It was amazing to know I could make a difference like that."

He tossed the clover aside, picked another blade of grass. "Wish I could have helped you." He waited for the tightness in his throat, the pain in his heart, the churning in his gut—but this time, nothing. Instead of pain and guilt, he felt at peace.

A soft breeze blew by, and he smiled.

"So, anyway… Bella." He stretched his legs out in front of him. "I bet you thought I'd end up with Simone. Me, too. But get this… She and Brett hooked up. They'd been trying to tell me for years, but I'd been avoiding her. Just like I avoided you. Avoided any conflict. It was kind of awkward when I finally found out. But Simone and I had been over for years, and I have Bella now. The sting of betrayal was no worse than a mosquito bite. You'd think a friend stealing your ex would have hurt more, but it didn't. I mean, Brett didn't really steal her. He hadn't done it on purpose to hurt me. Neither had she. Most importantly, they're happy."

He wiggled his toes, tried to shake the pins and needles out of his feet. Finally, he stood and stomped the blood back into his extremities.

"We're all pretty happy, Hope. I think we're all going to be okay. It's not the same without you, but… yeah. We're going to be okay."

"Jensen," his dad called.

He turned. Royce was walking up the hill. "So, I guess you figured out Dad and I are getting along better now. It's nice, like when we were kids. Wish you were here to see him. He's changed."

Royce reached them and put a hand on Jensen's shoulder. "Have a nice visit?"

Jensen nodded. "Yeah. Yeah, I did."

They both stood there, staring at the headstone.

Royce sighed. "Well, rafts are loaded. Picnics are packed. Everyone's waiting for us."

"Bella?"

"Released this morning. After Dr. Harris gave the okay, Stanford looked her over, just to be sure. I checked her chart, too. She's fine. I wouldn't send her whitewater rafting, but she's recovered enough to float in calm waters."

"What a difference a few weeks makes, huh?"

"What a difference good emergency care made when she was shot."

Jensen looked down, feeling heat rise to his cheeks.

"Let's go," his dad said. "We've kept them waiting long enough."

His dad turned and walked back down the slope.

Jensen waved at the headstone. "I'll be back. I have so much more to tell you. And I've missed you. So… yeah, I'll be back."

A breeze tickled him as he followed his dad to the truck.

www.ingramcontent.com/pod-product-compliance
Lightning Source LLC
Chambersburg PA
CBHW030826310726
48980CB00006B/651/J